PAMELA MORSI

LETTING GO

MIRA®

ISBN 1-55166-656-1

LETTING GO

Copyright © 2003 by Pamela Morsi.

All rights reserved. Except for use in any review, the reproduction or utilization of this work in whole or in part in any form by any electronic, mechanical or other means, now known or hereafter invented, including xerography, photocopying and recording, or in any information storage or retrieval system, is forbidden without the written permission of the publisher, MIRA Books, 225 Duncan Mill Road, Don Mills, Ontario, Canada M3B 3K9.

All characters in this book have no existence outside the imagination of the author and have no relation whatsoever to anyone bearing the same name or names. They are not even distantly inspired by any individual known or unknown to the author, and all incidents are pure invention.

MIRA and the Star Colophon are trademarks used under license and registered in Australia, New Zealand, Philippines, United States Patent and Trademark Office and in other countries.

Visit us at www.mirabooks.com

Printed in U.S.A.

For my mother, Zoe Sylvester,
who has patiently read all my previous stories
where the moms are dead. Finally here's one
where Mom lives happily ever after.

1

—►◄—

"Face it, Mom," Amber Jameson said, gazing not at her mother but at the road in front of her. "Your life has been like macaroni salad, white, bland and ordinary. It's just that lately, your mayonnaise has begun to go bad."

Ellen Jameson glanced up from the newspaper section of the classified to eye her twenty-one-year-old daughter disapprovingly.

"There is nothing whatsoever wrong with my mayonnaise," she insisted. "We're simply moving closer to downtown because I'm hoping to get a job there."

Amber rolled her eyes. "Denial is more than a river in Egypt," she said.

"Denial is a river in e-jepp!" three-year-old Jet parroted from the back seat.

Ellen ignored Amber and turned her attention to the child. The sight of her little dark-complexioned, curly haired granddaughter never failed to lighten her heart.

"Are you learning geography?" she asked Jet. "You are so smart!"

"I'm smart," Jet agreed.

"Yeah baby-girl," Amber piped in. "You better hope you inherited your geography genes from me. Your grandma couldn't find her own ass."

The child giggled delightedly. "Gramma's ass," she repeated.

"Amber!" Ellen scolded her daughter and then directed her next comment to Jet.

"You mustn't say the words your mama says," Ellen told the little girl. "Mama has a smart mouth and a smart mouth is very ugly."

"Mama's not ugly," the little girl declared with the absolute conviction of one who loves.

Ellen smiled. She appreciated the child's loyalty. And she agreed. Amber *was* beautiful. One just had to look beyond her current fashion incarnation to see it. Her pretty chestnut hair was overgrown and bleached out to an unrealistic yellow blond color accented by one inch brown roots. Her hands were encircled on the wrists by tattoo "slave" bracelets, a permanent reminder of a difficult adolescence. And she'd never quite lost that last five pounds since childbirth. But she still had the long lean body that was too tall for gymnastics and too curvy for ballet.

"Mama is very pretty," Ellen explained to her granddaughter. "But ugly words are worse than ugly looks."

"Oh, right, Mom," Amber disagreed sarcastically. "Don't listen to Grandma, Jet. Grandma is full of it."

"Gramma's full of it," she repeated.

Ellen voice was a scolding whisper. "Stop talking that way in front of her, Amber."

"Then stop giving the kid platitudes that portray the world as unrealistically benign and fair," her daughter said. She gestured toward the expanse of downtown San Antonio in the distance. "It's hell out there and the sooner she knows that the less likely she'll get screwed over."

"What would you have me tell her?"

"The truth." Amber replied. She glanced at her daughter in the rearview mirror. "Jet, there's no such thing as a bad word, just ones that are hard to spell. And people will treat you a lot better for being thin and pretty than for being kind or smart."

"Amber!"

The younger woman didn't appear in the least contrite. "I'm just being straight with her, Mom," she said. "I wish you could have been as honest."

Ellen didn't argue with her daughter. She didn't have the strength. Besides Amber always won somehow. Instead she focused her attention on the road in front of her.

"The turn's coming up on your left," she said indicating the side street between the Purple Dragon Restaurant and Señora Oma, Psychic Advisor.

"I know where the turn is," Amber told her, irritated. "I don't need directions to get to Wilma's."

"Wil-ma! Wil-ma!" Jet began repeating her great-grandmother's name as if it were a yell-leader chant.

"Yes, we're going to see Wil-ma," Amber told her.

Wil-ma, with the accent on the last syllable, was Jet's name for Ellen's mother. It rhymed with all the other women in her life. There was Mama. There was Gramma. And there was Wil-ma.

"Slow down a little," Ellen cautioned. "The car handles differently pulling a trailer."

"I'm the one who's driving," Amber answered. To prove her point she turned left in front of oncoming traffic.

Brakes screeched. Horns honked. Ellen cursed, gritted her teeth, and waited for the inevitable crash.

When they were safely on the residential street, Amber spoke to her daughter in the rearview once more.

"Gramma said a bad word," she told the child.

"Gramma said a bad word," Jet parroted.

"I thought you said there *were* no bad words," Ellen complained.

The aging Chrysler, with attached orange trailer, bumped along the narrow shaded street filled with vintage bungalow homes. Mahncke Park was a working-class neighborhood. Hemmed in between the expressway interchange, Brackenridge Park and Fort Sam Houston, it was relatively clean and looked after, but far from the highly manicured suburbs where Ellen had lived the last twenty years.

Lush springtime growth disguised the deterioration of Wilma's neighborhood. It appeared sweet and quaint and nostalgic. But graffiti tags could be spotted upon the empty buildings. And the occupied homes, no matter how modest, had burglar bars on every window.

Her mother, Wilma Post, or probably more accurately, Wilma Pruitt Johnson Wilcox Abston Post, give or take a name or two, had finally, it seemed, settled into a stable life. She had been something of a serial bride. Widowed twice and divorced more than a couple of times as well, she had dragged her children, Ellen and her half brother, Bud, from one miserable Texas city to the next. Each new home came furnished with a new Daddy, and he was always called Daddy, as head of the house. Ellen could hardly keep the names straight, so she simply associated different towns with different stepfathers.

Wilma's last, a widower near eighty on his wedding day, had brought her into his little house just north of downtown. She'd taken care of him for about eighteen months before he died.

Mr. Post's children were still unhappy about that marriage. Whether their anger was derived from guilt about their father or simply a dislike of the chosen bride of his twilight years, Ellen didn't know. But one thing she was certain about. Her mother, who had always been unable to sit still anyplace very long, had been expected to move onto greener pastures long ago. Clearly she intended to stay put—just to irritate the in-laws.

That was a good thing. If Wilma hadn't had this place, Ellen and her family would have been homeless.

As soon as the thought crossed her mind, she pushed it back. Ellen no longer thought of the future. It was easier just to remember the past.

Wilma's home, not quite two blocks from busy Broadway, was badly in need of paint and repair. The grass was weedy and the shrubs overgrown. Amber pulled the car and its accompanying rental trailer onto the long narrow driveway at the side of the house. Wilma was standing on the front porch. At sixty-one she was still a tall, slim, attractive woman. And she was smoking a cigarette. She hurriedly flicked the butt into the nearby box-hedge when she saw the car, but not before Ellen saw her.

"She's smoking again."

Amber snorted. "Like she really ever quit."

"She told me she had," Ellen insisted.

Amber put the transmission into park and turned to her mother, explaining matter-of-factly.

"Wilma lies," she said.

"Wil-ma lies!" Jet repeated from the back seat.

Amber chuckled. Ellen sighed.

They climbed out of the car. Ellen ignored her mother, turning instead to open the rear passenger door and unhitch Jet from her car seat. The child was missing a sneaker. Ellen practically had to stand on her head to retrieve it from under the front seat. She straightened the little girl's sock before helping her get it on.

"Grandma loves Jet," she whispered closely, confidentially.

"Jet loves Gramma," the child replied just as quietly, and by rote. It was a pretend secret, as familiar as the alphabet.

Ellen took her hand as she got out of the car. Jet leapt the twelve inch distance from the door frame to the concrete as if it were a feat of athleticism and then applauded herself appropriately.

By the time they reached the front porch, Amber was seated with Wilma on folding lawnchairs. They were laughing and talking and smoking.

"Don't encourage her!" Ellen said to her daughter. "Mother, the doctor told you that you have to quit."

"He told me I can't smoke if I'm on oxygen," Wilma clarified. "You don't see that fancy tank out here, do you?"

"I won't allow any tobacco smoke in the house with Jet," Ellen declared firmly.

Wilma's eyes narrowed.

"I absolutely demand that my granddaughter not be exposed to secondhand smoke," Ellen insisted.

"Oh, puh-leeezz, Mom," Amber chimed in. "Don't start it. It's no big deal."

"It's a big deal to me," Ellen said. "And if you had any sense of being a mother, you'd feel exactly the same way."

Amber was rising to the bait, but Wilma waylaid her.

"I always smoked around my kids," she pointed out. "I don't see that it's hurt you none."

Ellen spoke slowly, distinctly as if to infer that her mother had difficulty understanding her. "Bud has asthma," she said. "He spent his entire childhood struggling to breathe. That's why he never comes to see you."

"He doesn't come to see me because of that hog-faced heifer he's married to!" Wilma said.

"I will not let you endanger this little girl's heath," Ellen insisted. "I *will* take us to a shelter before I let that happen."

It was an ultimatum and could not be mistaken for anything else. Wilma backed down.

"Don't get your bowels in an uproar," she told Ellen. "That's why I'm smoking out here. The little dickens is my grandbaby, too."

That was the end of it.

With Amber taking a break, Ellen didn't rush to unload the trailer. Instead, she got the sack of refrigerator transfers out of the back seat. The bag contained partial containers of milk, butter, ketchup and jelly that they'd had in the house for their breakfast. Ellen was too thrifty to throw them into the garbage.

As she passed her mother and daughter, she reminded them that she was stepping inside.

"Keep an eye on Jet," she cautioned.

They both waved and nodded, as if to assure Ellen that they were on the job. Truthfully, Ellen didn't trust either of them. She was personally aware of her own mother's parenting skills. And from what she'd observed so far, Amber was no better.

Jet was an amazing child. At least she certainly was in Ellen's estimation. Besides being well-behaved and good natured, she was also smart, funny and very, very pretty. Her big dark eyes, generous lips and *café au lait* skin set her apart as a natural beauty. It was as if God had taken all the physical traits of Africa and Europe, mixed them in a cosmic cocktail shaker and when the best rose to the top, He skimmed them off and made Jet Jameson.

That perfect little miracle was currently jumping an imaginary rope on the sidewalk in front of the house.

In the kitchen, Ellen set the grocery bag on the counter and opened the refrigerator.

"Damn it, Mother!" she said, angrily, knowing that Wilma couldn't possibly hear her.

The huge thirty-two cubic foot Frigidaire was packed to overflowing. There was no way to even see inside. Ellen's refrigerator wouldn't have had this much food on Christmas day!

She pulled out the first layer and found exactly what she expected—fresh produce. Bought yesterday or today, it was merely stashed in front of the less fresh stuff, some of it weeks old. Ellen pulled the trash can over beside her and began to dump the worst of it.

It was a good thing her life wasn't macaroni salad, she would have been the first one to simply throw it out.

It took her better than fifteen minutes to sort the fridge out to stow her things.

She returned to the car to unload her most fragile and important item. It was surrounded by packing material and secured with duct tape. It was not overly large or heavy, but she'd wrapped it so thickly that it was unwieldy.

Ellen carried it to the front step and then hesitated, resting it on her raised knee as she caught her breath.

"What the devil have you got there?" Wilma asked.

"It's Paul's urn," Ellen answered.

"Good Lord!" Wilma exclaimed. "What are you still doing with that?"

"I'm not doing anything with it," she answered.

"The widow is supposed to scatter the remains," Wilma pointed out. "Not lug them around in a jar for years on end."

"I haven't decided what to do with him yet," Ellen defended herself. "Until I do, I'll just keep him in the urn on my dresser."

Wilma and Amber exchanged a glance.

"Crematory Decorating Themes," Amber said, snidely. "It must be a program I've missed on *Home & Garden Television*."

She ignored them. There were no rules about when, or if, a widow had to dispose of her husband's ashes. Five years might seem like a long time to others, but to Ellen it was just yesterday.

She carried the urn to the back bedroom of her mother's house. Carefully she unwrapped it and placed it atop the chest of drawers. She had never believed that he was going to die. Even yet, it was hard for her to remember that he was gone. People thought she should be over it. Her own family said that she was supposed to move on. But she didn't want to. She shouldn't have to. Her life had crumbled all around her. Still, she had the memory of Paul and the ashes in this urn. It was something to hold on to.

Ellen walked back through the house. The place was furnished like a consignment store on steroids. Wilma's scraped, worn pieces from the WWII era had been dragged from house to house for forty years. Ugly reminders of Ellen's childhood alongside the legacy of Mr. Post's first wife—heavily upholstered Early American in an unpleasant orange.

It was hard to imagine finding a place among all this for the remnants of Ellen's peach and white ultramodern decor. Or for the piles of pink and primary-colored plastic that were the requisite possessions of a typical three-year-old.

On the porch Amber had finished her cigarette. Wilma had lit up another one.

"Come on, let's get this trailer unloaded," Ellen told her daughter.

"Don't know if you should bother to do that," Wilma said.

Ellen looked at her quizzically.

"What do you mean?"

"Lud came to see me this morning," she announced. "That man could drive Billy Graham to a pack of smokes."

Ludlow Post was Wilma's stepson and the late Mr. Post's eldest son and spokesman for the family.

Wilma didn't like any of them, but at least the rest of the children kept their distance.

"What did that old crankface want now?" Amber asked.

"He wants us out of here," she answered.

"Nothing new about that," Ellen pointed out. "He was ready to put your clothes on the curb the day of the funeral."

"He left an envelope—it's on my vanity table," she said.

"Okay, I'll get it," Ellen said.

She went inside and found the letter easily enough and carried it into the light of the kitchen.

It was from Pressman, Yaffe and Escudero, a prestigious local law firm. Ellen read it. A strange sound emerged from her throat and she leaned heavily against the counter. She began again and read it through a second time. Her heart was pounding, her chest felt tight. Her brow furrowed. She kept shaking her head.

With a sense of dread, she returned to Wilma and Amber, still sitting on the front porch.

"I don't understand this," she said, holding out the letter. "This can't be true. I don't think this can happen. What in the world could it mean?"

Wilma shrugged fatalistically. "I think that last line pretty much says it all, doesn't it?" She quoted from memory. "'You will vacate the premises immediately or be served with a court order.'"

It was later that same afternoon that Amber, already fifteen minutes late, got off the 9 bus at the stop nearest the downtown mall. She didn't mind the fact that the bus stop was on the other side of Houston Street. She was happy to walk the half-dozen blocks. Not just because she could walk through the heart of town, over the quaint bridges and past the Alamo, but truthfully, it was embarrassing to be seen without a car. Of course, everyone she knew was already aware that she had no personal wheels. That was bad enough. But she hated for strangers to see her, maybe judge her, maybe think that mass transportation was her only option.

It was her image thing again, she thought. She had a love/hate relationship with her own image. There was a part of her that just said, *Screw you! I'll be whoever I want.* That was the part that dropped out of high school three months before graduation. The part that gave birth to Jet instead of getting an abortion. And the part that partied hardy whenever the opportunity presented itself.

She had another side, however, a side she kept hidden. She was loathe to admit it, but she wanted people to admire her, to envy her. She wanted the whole world to see her as smart, sexy, successful. And she was pretty sure that they rarely did.

She'd also come to the very cynical conclusion that people are only what they appeared to be. She wanted to appear to be hip, in-the-know, and to-die-for hot. Pretty lofty ambitions for a bleached blonde with a GED and a three-year-old.

Arriving at the mall, she rounded the corner near the fountain and waved to Mildred in the cookie shop. A macadamia and white chocolate chip with a cup of coffee would have helped her day a lot. But she was already late and she had to be out on the floor as soon as she clocked in anyway. She was just glad it was Saturday and she was not opening the store. If she was five minutes past with the doors, the entire human race got their panties in a wad. And that kind of thing was always found out. Her boss, Carly, was best buddies with the witch who ran the Gap next door. She was convinced she was being spied upon almost constantly. Just because she was paranoid, didn't mean that they weren't out to get her.

Amber had been working at the mall since she was sixteen. Her very first job was at Salad Czar in the Food Court. She was exactly the kind of girl they wanted at their expensive lettuce boutique. She'd been a fresh-faced honor student; in the school symphony band and a member of the student council. She hadn't worked for the money. Back then there had still been plenty of money. Her dad was already sick, already dying. And her mother's endlessly upbeat reassurances were wearing. She'd gone to work to get away from her—to get away from them.

Now here she was, five years later, still living with her mother, and now they were all living in her grandmother's house. Mom had had to sell the place in Elm Creek to pay creditors. Amber might be of legal age and Jet's mother, but she felt no closer to being on her own than she had at sixteen. Amber had no illusions—her mother was the boss of everything.

She rounded the corner to the open gallery where sunlight spilled in from the pitched glass roof three floors up. Cesar was demonstrating his boomerang helicopters for a small crowd of wide-eyed children as their parents looked on uncomfortably, hoping not to be cornered into a purchase.

Kyle was at his cart, coaxing a smile out of a fat baby in a jogging stroller who was going to have his photo emblazoned upon a coffee mug or a T-shirt.

Amber heard her name called and she waved to Warren, the handicapped guy. With his broom and dustpan, he was a permanent fixture at the mall, endlessly sweeping.

Deliberately Amber slowed her pace as she approached the entrance to her current place of employment. If she didn't act late, there was always a chance that nobody would notice that she was.

Almost casually she walked into the pink-and-burgundy home of Frou-Frou Lingerie. The abundance of frothy decor and the scent of musky perfume was meant to lure as many males inside as females. The truth was, the company made very high quality bras and panties. But pointing that out was like insisting guys read *Playboy* for the articles. This store was in the business of selling sex.

Amber could sell that. In fact, Amber was pretty sure she could sell just about anything. And getting middle-aged businessmen to buy their flabby wives black lace teddies was not particularly difficult.

With a quick glance around, Amber assessed the place wasn't particularly busy, and both Metsy and Diedre were working. Amber nodded to the latter but before she had a chance to speak, Diedre gave her a warning look and gestured toward the register. Amber glanced over to see Carly occupied behind the counter. She was trying, unsuccessfully, to change the paper roll in the cash register. And she was looking particularly sour.

Deliberately Amber did not make eye contact. She

tried to walk right past her boss with the unconcern of the guiltless.

It didn't work.

"Good afternoon, Amber," Carly said, glancing pointedly at her watch. "You're running pretty late today."

"A little," Amber admitted. "Let me put my purse up and I'll help you get that paper in the roller."

"Hmm," Carly commented noncommittally. She didn't appear to be mollified. "Shall we step into the back for a little girl-to-girl?"

Carly was smiling broadly. Amber smiled right back. Underneath that smile Amber was moaning and cursing. Girl-to-girl was Carly's euphemism for a verbal butt-chewing.

Who needs this today? she mentally complained. But a smiling "Sure thing" was what she answered aloud.

Amber led the way to the stockroom and she stashed her purse in the locker, before turning to face Carly.

"The bus was late," she lied. "And the traffic around this place is terrible on Saturday."

Carly was still smiling. She shut the door and spoke only a little above a whisper.

"Let's keep this between us, shall we?" she said. "I don't want to embarrass you in front of Metsy and Diedre."

Amber wasn't fooled by that suggestion one bit. The other girls would know immediately why they went into the stockroom together. And they both undoubtedly realized she was late. Carly's motivation for keeping their little tête-à-tête private was personal insurance. The rules about what a manager could and could not say were very strict. There were guys in corporate HR that lived in constant fear of lawsuits. If Carly crossed over into catty and unprofessional, as she sometimes did, she wouldn't want anyone to overhear it. It was safer for it to be her word over the disgruntled employee.

"You just cannot let this happen," Carly began. "You can't just show up when it's convenient for you. We have a schedule to maintain."

Amber kept her face purposefully blank. She'd been through this with Carly half a dozen times over the last two years—and with other supervisors before her. They were all damn sticklers for their jobs and their schedules.

As far as Amber was concerned, if you were routinely where you were supposed to be, at exactly the time you were supposed to be there, then you obviously didn't have a very interesting life. Which, coincidentally, people like Carly—people over thirty—usually didn't have.

Maybe her life wasn't as interesting as it could be, but she wasn't about to advertise that fact to the world.

"This is the fourth time you've been late this month, Amber," Carly pointed out.

It probably would have been more accurate to say it was the fourth time she'd been *caught*.

"I have absolutely no problem with your performance when you're here," Carly continued. "But you've got to be here to work. Showing up, on time, is absolutely basic to being a good employee. It's the minimum we expect."

Amber tuned the woman out. She focused instead

upon her current Saturday night dilemma. Should she go out with some new guy who was a buddy of Diedre's live-in, or just go to the clubs and meet up with somebody there?

"As assistant manager you have to set the standard," Carly told her. It was all Amber could do not to roll her eyes.

In the world of mall retail, assistant manager was a job description in the twilight zone. It was a position that had no power, made no money and was the fast track to nowhere. It was a way to shoehorn dependable, hourly employees into a salaried position where they could be worked longer without incurring overtime.

Amber understood this. She had no illusions about the grandeur of management. She also knew she was extremely valuable to this store, and to Carly in particular. Except for interfacing with corporate muckymucks, Amber handled everything involved in the store's operation. She did the buying, kept the accounts, made the schedule, and put the payroll together for processing. The store's average $5,000 in daily sales was due in large part to Amber's efforts.

But Amber would never be the manager of this store or, for that matter, of any other. Managers were college graduates. Amber was not ever going to go to college.

But if I had gone, she assured herself confidently, *I'd be working in a much better job than managing this crappy little store.*

"You act as if the rules don't apply to you," Carly continued. "But they apply to you more than anyone else."

It was the usual speech. Carly didn't even seem particularly angry or interested. They had done this so often that they both found it pretty boring. Carly was never going to fire Amber. The woman was more likely to set her hair ablaze and run naked down to Spencer's Gifts and back. But she did have to come in and demonstrate her authority from time to time. This was merely one of those times.

As Carly began to wind down and turn her complaints elsewhere, Amber relaxed.

"That Metsy is too dumb to live," Carly told her with only a hint of confidentiality. "I asked her for a store improvement suggestion and she told me we should stop charging sales tax, because it's so hard for people to figure out if they have enough money to buy something."

Carly was looking to Amber for agreement and complicity. They'd have a good laugh together at their co-worker's expense and that would smooth over everything between them.

Amber wasn't willing to give it to her. She smiled, very slightly. Not enough to really commit herself to agreement, but enough that her boss would think she had.

Metsy was, to some degree at least, a friend. Of course she was a certifiable idiot, especially with numbers—Amber would never argue that. But she liked clothes and knew what looked good on people. Qualities that were always in demand in women's wear. Amber knew that. If Carly didn't, it wasn't Amber's responsibility to wise her up.

"We'd better get back to the floor," Carly suggested. "If we don't those two will spend the rest of the afternoon gossiping about what might have been said here."

They had actually been missed. A minirush had ensued and Diedre was holding up everything trying to fix the register tape which Carly had apparently screwed up. Customers were lined up. Amber and Carly had to immediately jump in and help.

It was more than an hour later before the next real lull ensued. Amber began to straighten and restock. Carly took the opportunity to leave.

There were smiles all around as she left.

"Have a great weekend!" Metsy told her cheerfully.

Carly was hardly around the corner when all three women were huddled for a confab.

"What's the deal with her?" Metsy asked.

"I was a couple of minutes late," Amber answered.

"Really? Who'd even notice?"

"Obviously Carly did," Diedre pointed out. "Is it serious?"

Amber shook her head. "She's just talking smack, as per."

"Why does she do that?" Metsy said.

"She's the boss," Diedre explained. "So she can."

"But Amber does everything for her," Metsy said. "It's like she doesn't even notice."

"I think it's some kind of unwritten rule in mall retail," Amber told her. "You're supposed to disrespect workers under twenty-five. You've got to marginalize their successes and exaggerate their failures. It's meant to get back at us for still being young enough to have options."

The three of them had a great laugh. It felt good

putting Carly down. It gave the three a sense of superiority about who they were and what they were doing with their lives.

Amber's cheerfulness was short-lived. One of the great disadvantages of being bright was the inability to fool yourself for very long.

2

$$\longrightarrow \!\! \longleftarrow$$

Bright and early Monday morning Ellen headed south in her aging Chrysler Concorde—the last vestige of a life she used to take for granted. Avoiding all expressways, she headed through downtown, past La Villita, the little village that was once San Antonio, and past the Tower of Americas, a vestige of the city's HemisFair in 1968.

She had gone to HemisFair. It seemed very long ago now. Much like her own past with Paul. Sometimes it seemed just like yesterday, all fresh and familiar. Other times it was like a lifetime ago, or maybe even another person's lifetime, or perhaps the faded relic of a dream. Whatever it was, it was not her life today.

Downsizing was the term that business people used. Ellen liked the sound of that. She had downsized her life. Or maybe she was just on the downside of life. Sometimes she thought that death was the next big thing for her. Her husband was dead. Her daughter was grown. Her career was gone. Retirement was impossible. Death was what she had to look forward to.

However, with that cheery thought aside, she realized that she was unlikely to die before the week was out or the year was out, or even before a decade or few were passed and gone. She was very likely to live, so she really needed to get a job.

Putting on her signal blinker a full block ahead of her street, she slowed down appreciably, giving every possible notice to drivers around her that she intended to turn. She had always tried to be fair, to be kind, to be good and to play by the rules. Driving, accounting, life, they all had their own sets of rules to go by. Unfortunately, following the rules didn't preclude catastrophe. But still, she did manage to make the turn without being slammed into by a three-ton SUV, or by a rusting pickup truck with three illegal laborers in the back. It wasn't as if everything was wrong.

She drove underneath the railroad overpass, a throwback to an earlier era and skirted some road repair. The area was rough and seedy. Second-rate businesses, pawnshops, furniture rental and tamale factories—a low-rent entrepreneurial district.

Horns honked at her as she slowed to try to see the address numbers. It was a hopeless cause, nothing seemed to be marked. Fortunately, in the middle of the next block she saw the sign she was looking for.

The background was the shape of Texas, and within it stood a neon trimmed cowboy with a lariat circling above his head. In medium-sized letters it read: *Roper's Accounting* and then beneath that, and quite a bit larger, *The Cowboys of Taxes.*

"Oh, brother," she groaned aloud.

There was an open spot right in front of the building, shaded and with time still on the meter. Ellen passed it right by. It made no sense to waste her luck taking a small gift when she was so much in need of a larger one. She drove around the corner by a little grocery store, the sales ads in its windows obscured by security bars. Stoically and with great sacrifice, Ellen pulled into a hot sunny spot and rummaged through the bottom of her purse for change.

"See, God," she said aloud. "I left that place in front for someone who might need it more than me. I'm a generous person. I'm not asking for a life of luxury, just a way to pay the bills."

It was evident, even to Ellen herself, that over time her prayers had become less of a reverent supplication and more of a continual harangue.

"Come on, God," she said. "I deserve a break today."

She turned off the car, flipped down the visor, and checked her hair and makeup. Smiling broadly she assured herself that there was nothing untoward stuck in her teeth.

"I deserve a break today," she repeated as she stepped out of the car. "Sheesh! I sound like a TV commercial."

The threat of Wilma losing her house had come as a tremendous blow. Ellen had made the move in with her mother only as a last resort. The next stop was the homeless shelter—a prospect that must be avoided at all cost.

The hot, south Texas sun was glaring down upon her as she walked along the sidewalk. It was ten o'clock in the morning and only May, but it was still too hot to be comfortable in her silk suit and hose. But she needed to be at her businesslike best. She'd been assuring herself all morning that she was up to the task.

A job interview was nothing compared to the challenges of the last five years—the last eight years really—if the truth were known. Since the day that the strained muscle in her husband's back had proved to be cancer, Ellen's whole world had turned upside down. And most of it had come to rest squarely upon her own shoulders.

She faced the door, nervous but determined. The building was old and smelly. She swallowed hard and reminded herself of the facts. There was no house, no business, no retirement nest egg, and nothing left in her checking account. Her mother was sick. Her daughter was irresponsible and, along with her little granddaughter, they were all counting on her. Gamely she pasted a confident smile on her face and went inside.

"I get it that there's no big miracle in my future," she whispered. "Just a little help is all I'm asking today."

The small dimly lit room was air-conditioned, but far from cool. Lime green paint was peeling off the stucco walls. The dark green linoleum tile was missing in several places.

Behind the low counter that served as a desk for the receptionist, a heavyset brunette woman of indeterminate age was talking on the phone. When the bell heralded Ellen's arrival, the woman looked up immediately and smiled.

"Can I help you?" she asked eagerly.

"I'm Ellen Jameson," she announced with a smile that hopefully looked genuine. "I have an appointment with Mr. Roper."

The woman nodded eagerly.

"Listen, Marlene, I gotta go," she said into the phone. "Somebody's here to see Max. You can call me later if you need to talk."

The receptionist paused as the person on the other end of the line responded. The woman took the respite opportunity to suck upon the straw of what must have been the largest carbonated beverage cup ever molded from plastic, emblazoned on the side with its name and explanation: Thirst Slaker.

"Believe me," she told the woman on the phone. "The worst thing about a colonoscopy is having nothing to eat the day before. The actual test is kind of entertaining really, seeing your own guts on a television screen is pretty interesting after all. And they take Polaroids of all your polyps. It'll be something to show at Bingo."

Another hesitation.

"Yeah sure, call me. Okay."

The brunette hung up the phone and immediately rose to her feet offering her hand to Ellen.

"Hi," she said. "I'm so sorry I was on the phone. I've got a friend going in for tests tomorrow. She's had diarrhea for a month. She's tried all the stuff over the counter and nothing works. I told her, hey, diarrhea is your friend, but then I'm speaking as a woman who's been constipated for thirty years. I'm Yolanda Ruiz by the way. And you're Ellen. You don't mind if I call you Ellen?"

"That's fine, I…"

"So I looked at your résumé," she said. "Pretty impressive. You're not divorced? A nice-looking woman like you, surely you're not divorced."

"Ah…no, I'm a widow."

"Oh, a widow, I'm *so* sorry. Car wreck?"

"What?"

"Did he die in a car wreck?"

"No."

"Oh, well that's good," she said. "Lots of younger widows have husbands who died in car wrecks. So what was it? Heart disease?"

"Cancer."

"Oh, cancer, I'm *so, so* sorry."

"Thank you."

"Lung? Brain? Where'd he have his cancer?"

"Bone cancer."

"Oh, yeah, I'm *so* sorry."

"Thank you."

"So now you're out looking for a job," she said.

"Yes."

"What happened to this CPA you worked for?"

"It was my husband's firm," Ellen explained. "And without a CPA, you don't have a CPA firm."

"Oh, right, sure," she said. "You got kids?"

"Yes."

"Girls? Boys?"

"A daughter."

"Teenager?"

"She's twenty-one."

"Good Lord! You must've been a child bride, huh?"

"Well, no, I…"

"Is she in college?"

"No, she works at the mall."

"She works at the mall," Yolanda repeated as if that was exceptional. "Does she have a boyfriend?"

"A boyfriend?" Ellen didn't quite know how to answer. "No. I mean, well, I don't think there's anybody special."

"Ahhhhh."

Yolanda drew out the sound through a half-dozen meaningful syllables.

"Don't worry," she said. "I got cousins, I got nephews. I've even got a kid brother who works at the post office. All the cute single men in the world work at the post office. We'll have her fixed up in no time."

"Well, I…ah…I don't know, she…"

"For crying out loud, Yolanda," a voice called out from the back. "Are you going to talk the woman to death or bring her back here for an interview?"

"I'm just getting acquainted," she yelled back. She turned to Ellen and said, "Don't pay any attention to Max. He's old and he's cranky. He's always been that way."

"Yolanda!"

"Go on back," she said. "He's been antsy all day. We really need some good help, he just can't imagine that you'd really come to work here."

"Yolan-da!"

"Second office on the left."

"Thank you."

The receptionist had no time to acknowledge her words—she was back to phone duty immediately.

Ellen walked the length of the office at a careful pace. Not so quick as to seem hurried, not so sedate as to seem slack. She was nervous. And that's the one thing she didn't want. A person couldn't help but *be* nervous, but it was dangerous to *appear* nervous.

She tried to imagine herself working here. It was all she could do to restrain a shudder. The office in the Bank One Tower had been professionally decorated, with beautiful views from three sides. This building had no views at all. The only windows were covered by dingy miniblinds.

She found Roper's office easily enough—there were only two and one was empty. The office was occupied by a large, lanky older man in a buff-colored sports jacket, a western shirt with pearl-colored snaps and a bolo tie. His white straw cowboy hat hung on the rack behind him. He waved her inside.

"Sorry about Yolanda," he said. "I tell her she's wasted here. She ought to work for the CIA. She can get information out of anyone."

"I heard that," Yolanda called out from the other room.

"Then stop eavesdropping," he answered back.

Ellen decided to ignore the entire unprofessional incident.

"Mr. Roper, I'm here about the accounts supervisor position," she said, offering her hand across the desk.

He took it in his own, his grip was strong, though his hand was marred with age. His smile was welcoming.

"Have a seat, have a seat," he offered. "And call me Max, everybody does."

The utilitarian plastic and chrome furniture was old, scarred and looked as if it had been picked up very cheaply at a university rummage sale. Max Roper was equally old school.

Ellen seated herself on the edge of the chair, back straight and chin up. Bravely, she put a determined smile upon her face.

"You're just a downright pretty thing," Max told her. "From this résumé I really expected an older girl."

Neither *older* nor *girl* were designations that Ellen particularly liked, but she chose not to take offense.

"I'm forty-two," she answered.

"Well, you look thirty-two," he said with certainty.

"And hell, I think I was still in knee britches at your age."

Ellen smiled politely at his attempt at humor.

He was still chuckling as he looked over her résumé.

"An associate degree in accounting," he said. "We don't see those much anymore."

Ellen flushed, embarrassed. She didn't look good on paper. That's what the woman at the state unemployment office had told her. For the kind of job she was seeking, interviewers saw men and women every day who were half her age and had twice her education.

It was a comedown in status, as bad as any other she'd suffered. She had been the top student in her class, a perfect four point grade average. But she'd settled for a two-year degree to get married and help pay for her husband's education. At the time it hadn't seemed to matter.

"I have over twenty years of experience," she pointed out.

The man continued to read through the pages in his hands. "Several different tax preparation companies, but that was a long time ago," he pointed out. "Then you were the manager for your husband's firm downtown," he said.

"Yes."

He gave her a long look. "Were you the real manager, or just on the payroll as such?"

He'd asked his question so frankly it would have been impossible not to give a truthful answer.

Ellen swallowed before tackling the man's directness.

"I worked for my husband when he was just getting started," she replied. "Then I went to part-time, while my daughter was a baby. Once my husband became ill, I began to work more and more. Ultimately, I ran everything. For the last two years of his life my husband was too sick to go to the office at all."

Max Roper nodded. He appeared sympathetic, but realistic as well.

"When your husband died you sold the business?"

"My husband's cancer treatment was not covered by our health insurance," she explained candidly. "I spent all our savings, cashed in our investments and retirement funds. I even borrowed against the business."

Just talking about that financial snake pit made Ellen's stomach tighten miserably. Vomiting during a job interview was never a good thing.

"I sold what I could and then filed Chapter Eleven," Ellen admitted.

Max leaned back in his chair and threaded his hands together on top of his chest.

"So you're broke," he said.

"Yes, I am." It was amazing how easily the admission came.

"Well, that's a damn shame for you," Max said. "But it's a stroke of luck for me. Can you start tomorrow?"

Ellen was shocked. She hadn't expected it to be so easy. She hadn't worked for anyone else in two decades, she'd come off a failed business and a bankruptcy. She hadn't even been able to get an interview among any of the firms run by her husband's former friends. Now, in a run-down neighborhood, and with peeling green stucco aside, this strange old cowboy accountant, who knew almost nothing about her, wanted her.

"Y-yes, I can start tomorrow," she assured him.

Wilma sat on the back step. She had been watching Jet race around the backyard, arms wide, flapping up and down, as she pretended to be a little bird. But she soon tired of that. Now she was seated beside her great-grandmother, expectantly. Wilma had no idea what to do.

From the pocket of her slacks she pulled out a pack of cigarettes. Menthols. She'd been smoking menthols since her throat got bad. About fifteen years, she guessed. Nobody believed anymore that menthols were better for your throat. But she'd grown used to them. Why change?

Wilma flicked the flint on her orange plastic disposable lighter and took a big draw.

She used to never ask herself about change. Change was a way of life. Clean slate. Start over. Get it right next time. Wilma'd lived an entire lifetime in the midst of change.

She snorted in a rather unladylike fashion and thought to herself. *Hey, maybe it's time to change that.*

Keeping a three-year-old was certainly a change for her. And not as easy as Wilma had hoped. All morning long she'd been run ragged. She'd played Button-Button, Drop the Handkerchief and Hot Potato a dozen times each. They'd straightened Jet's room, completed puzzles and read books. They'd even watched Barney on TV, a totally new experience for Wilma. The morning wasn't even half over and she was already wrung out like an old, thin dishrag.

"Why don't we go in and take a little nap," she suggested.

Jet looked at her with that serious expression so often used on clueless grown-ups. "I don't take naps in the morning, Wil-ma," she explained. "I only nap in the afternoon."

"Oh, right, okay," Wilma agreed.

What was she going to do until afternoon? What did this child usually do?

Wilma should have asked Amber or Ellen before they left. But she'd felt so sure of herself when she'd insisted that she could take care of a three-year-old. She had, after all, raised two kids of her own. Lots of grandmothers were taking care of little ones these days.

Of course, most of those women weren't great-grandmothers. And most had probably been maternal with their own children. Wilma had never been particularly competent or even interested in motherhood. She'd loved her kids, but she'd always been so distracted by the men in her life. She probably shouldn't have ever had children, she thought. But those were the days before the pill. If you didn't want children, you had to forgo men as well. She'd never been able to do without some kind of fellow hanging around her back door...and her bedroom.

She examined her cigarette closely for a moment and then expertly broke off the filter and dropped it in the dirt beside her. She ground it into the earth with her foot and then took a deep drag off her unfiltered tobacco. It tasted so good. But she couldn't help but feel guilty about it.

If she wasn't going to get any stronger, who would take care of Jet? So far, it was Ellen who'd done most of the childrearing. But she needed to get a job of her own. Not just for the money they needed so desperately, but also because she needed to get out and have a life of her own. She'd spent far too much time dwelling on all that she'd lost.

Lots of single women sent their kids to day care. But day care costs money. A lot more than Amber could afford to spend on it. Of course, Amber could quit her job, stay home with Jet and go on welfare. Somehow she was pretty sure that proud young woman would never do that. And even if they could find a nice place to keep her and could afford to send her there, there was still the problem of getting the child to the school and home again. That old Chrysler of Ellen's wasn't going to last forever. They aged in dog years. Every year on a Camry was worth seven on a Chrysler.

She'd hate to see Amber trying to drag that child across town on a city bus.

No, Wilma had to take care of the girl herself. She simply had to do her part, she decided. She felt as if for most of her life, she'd let her kids down. Right now, Ellen really needed her. She had to rise to the occasion, whatever that occasion might be.

"Let's go to the grocery store," Wilma suggested to Jet.

If she had no idea what the child normally did with her mornings, then why not do what Wilma normally did.

"Okay!" Jet agreed excitedly.

"Go find Wil-ma's pocketbook," she told the child as she stubbed out her cigarette. "I'll get my oxygen and we'll be ready to go."

The child scampered to the bedroom. Wilma followed her inside and dragged the cursed oxygen tank next to her chair in the front room. Once seated, she unwound the see-through plastic tubing draped around the handle and fitted the nose piece into her nostrils and hooked the lines behind her ears. She screwed the valve open. Immediately the gas began flowing and she felt significantly better.

"Emphysema's a disease you can live with," her doctor told her.

He was not, of course, the person who had to live with it. The stuffy M.D., thirty-five going on ninety, at Surety Health, Wilma's HMO, was younger than her children. What did he know about what she could stand and how well she could stand it.

With a stroke of his magic pen he had medicare provide her with a *mobile respiration unit*. She hadn't thanked him. Wilma hated the tank. She hated its clumsy omnipresence and she hated what it represented: old age, ill health, weakness and payback for a million cigarettes smoked. But without it, she'd be housebound at the very least.

"Here it is, Wil-ma," Jet said as she came running back into the room.

"Thank you, sugarplum," she answered.

Wilma hooked her purse on the handle of the oxygen tank.

"Now, I've got to take it real slow," she told the child. "So you've got to stay with me and hold my hand, because I can't chase you if you run off from me."

Jet's bright brown eyes were solemn and serious. "Don't worry, Wil-ma," she assured her great-grandma. "I won't let anything bad happen to you."

Wilma laughed at that and took the little girl's hand.

They locked the front door and headed up the street. There was a sidewalk for two blocks, then a large parking lot to cross before Broadway. Jet stayed right at Wilma's side the whole way. She chattered for a little bit and then began to sing. She had a sweet voice. She must have got that from Ellen. She'd always been something of a singer, too. Wilma remembered hearing her daughter rocking and singing lullabies to Bud when he was a baby.

Ellen hardly ever sang anymore. Another loss that remained unmeasured.

They reached the bus stop and Wilma seated herself upon the bench. Jet snuggled right up beside her and watched the street as they waited.

Wilma was thoughtful and sighed. Wilbur's family taking the house from her was a blow. Not because she particularly liked the house—she didn't. And she'd never really tried to stay anywhere for long. But she had been so glad to have it to offer when things went bad for Ellen. She knew that her daughter had been loathe to accept it. But finally the financial realities couldn't be ignored.

What the family needed was money. There was no way that Ellen was going to pull them out of her current tailspin without a thorough infusion of cold hard cash.

As far as Wilma knew there were only four ways to get money. You had to earn it, inherit it, marry it or steal it.

"I should rob a bank," she suggested to herself aloud.

"What did you say, Wil-ma?" Jet asked.

"Oh, nothing," she answered. "I was just thinking of something funny."

It was the truth. She had a pleasant chuckle at her own imagination, visualizing herself dressed in sleek black, cat-burglarizing among the casinos of Monte Carlo.

Stealing was definitely not an option.

Earning wasn't much of one either. Wilma wasn't averse to wages. At one time or another she'd done practically every kind of work a lady could do. And a couple of good paying jobs that no *lady* would have ever considered. But even the lowest tavern or the grimiest strip joint wouldn't be interested in an old woman pulling her oxygen canister. Besides, she didn't know how any income might affect the two hundred and ninety dollars a month she got from Social Security.

The number nine bus pulled up to their stop. Jet scampered up the steps and then held out her little hand to help Wilma board. Dragging the stupid tank behind her was the worst. While she got herself seated, Jet dropped the correct change into the meter, managing to charm the bus driver and the other riders as well. She hurried to Wilma's side and the bus headed up the street.

Wilma thought her prospects for employment were bad, but Ellen's and Amber's weren't much better. Eight bucks an hour was the best that Amber would do until she figured out some other direction for her life. Ellen might be able to make a living as an accounting clerk, but it would be very close to the bone. Without a saleable skill the three of them combined could barely make a decent living.

Inheritance wasn't much of a plan either. She herself was the only relative they had who was likely to die any time soon. And she didn't have much to leave anyone.

No, Wilma thought, if this family was ever going to get on firm financial footing again, somebody was going to have to tie a really lucrative knot.

Wilma was a great believer in Holy Wedlock. She'd loved each and every man she married, at least on the day she'd married him. It was a woman's only real chance. Two could not only live as cheaply as one, it was almost impossible to ever get ahead in the world if you were working at it all on your own.

Somebody had to get married. She would have been happy to volunteer. But she was washed up. Her life, or at least that part of it, was behind her now. Men, especially older men, did not find oxygen tanks attractive. That was understandable. Too much of a reminder of their own mortality. And how could a fellow tell if he was taking a woman's breath away. It might just be her emphysema.

There would be no more marriages for her. But maybe she could make something happen for Amber or Ellen, or both.

The few blocks' ride to the store was accomplished in a hurry. The walk across the street and through the parking lot took more time. Wilma was exhausted by the time they reached the front door of the store. One of the young bag boys recognized her and hurried out the door with one of their riding grocery carts.

"Morning, Mrs. Post," he said.

She nodded and seated herself gratefully while he loaded her tank in the basket for her.

"This is my granddaughter, Jet," she said.

"Hi, Jet," the young guy said.

The little girl shook his hand as if meeting a social acquaintance.

"Do I get to ride in the cart with Wil-ma?" she asked.

"Sure," the young man said. "You try to keep her from running into things, okay."

"Okay," Jet agreed. She scrambled up beside Wilma.

The electric grocery cart was Wilma's preferred method of transportation. She pressed the directional button to forward and then all acceleration was done through the handlebars. No brakes were needed. When you wanted to stop you just quit tilting the levers forward.

Wilma carefully drove the cart over to the produce section. She loved the bright colors and faint fecund smell of mother earth.

She pulled the cart in front of a tower of dark, rounded tubers nearly the size of grapefruit.

"Hand me one of those, Jet," she said.

The little girl complied.

"What is it?" Jet asked her.

"Why it's a beet, honey," Wilma told her. "Don't you know beets?"

Jet looked at the huge ball in her grandmother's hand.

"I know beets," she said. "They're little squares in yukky purple sauce."

"That's Harvard beets," Wilma said. "And out of a can as well, I'll bet. Of course they're yukky. But real beets, these beets, they're good. We'll take this one."

Jet put it in the basket.

"Do you like carrots?" Wilma asked her.

Jet nodded.

"Then get some of those," she said.

"Okay."

"They should be very orange and very straight," Wilma told her. "And firm," she added. "They shouldn't have any give in them at all."

Jet made her selection. Wilma checked it over and approved the choices, except for one that they both agreed looked like a witch's nose.

They bought salad greens and ripe tomatoes. Golden pears and fresh raspberries. Sweet corn on the cob and baby white asparagus.

Wilma was delighted. Jet seemed to enjoy shopping as much as she did.

They finally made their way to the front to pay, but not before they had more bags than they could easily carry.

"I wish I could simply drive this little cart home," Wilma joked with the clerk. "It's handier than a pocket on a shirt."

A voice spoke up from the next checkout line. "Wilma? Wilma, is that you?"

She turned to see Adele Wilson, a woman she knew rather casually. Adele had been dear friends with the late Mr. Post's first wife.

"Adele, how are you?" Wilma asked politely.

"Oh, I'm fine, just fine. Do you need a lift? I'm driving right by your house."

"Why, thank you," Wilma answered. "That would be so appreciated. We've just bought ourselves a load to carry. It would be wonderful to get a ride."

Adele's expression was momentarily puzzled and then it was as if she noticed Jet for the first time.

"Is that little colored girl with you?" she asked.

Wilma was momentarily taken aback, then gave a chuckle.

"You're showing your age, Adele," she said. "We don't say *colored* anymore, we say African-American. This is my great-granddaughter, Jet."

With no prompting at all, Jet smiled politely and offered her hand, just as she had been taught to do.

Adele took it rather limply and asked Wilma in a whisper, "Is she adopted? An orphan from one of those desperately poor countries?"

Wilma thought the woman must be losing it.

"No, this is my granddaughter, Amber's little girl," Wilma told her. "I think you knew that she had a baby."

"Well, yes, I knew she had a baby," Adele said. "But I didn't know…I didn't know she was…I'm so sorry, Wilma. I didn't know…" Her voiced lowered to a secretive whisper. "That Amber had been with a black man."

Wilma's back went straighter than it had been for a decade. Her mouth curved into a lovely smile that was all clenched teeth when she spoke.

"Oh, she wasn't," Wilma assured her. "It's me, Jet gets that dark complexion from my folks. Didn't you know that I'm black? From the Nat King Cole, Sammy Davis, Jr., side of the family. I'm an octoroon daughter of a mammy from the old plantation." Her voice was rising. Half the people in the building could undoubtedly hear. "We're some of those Thomas Jefferson relations. And you know what they say, no matter how many generations you can always get a dark throwback. But don't you worry your pretty white ass about it, Miss Adele. We done gonna walk on home in our barefeet carrying our watermelon on our heads and we ain't never gonna bother you no more."

Wilma gathered up the bags, slung them around her wrists, grabbed the oxygen tank handle in one hand and Jet in another and stormed out of the store.

"Of all the nerve in the whole world," Wilma whispered to herself. "I hope she gets strangled by her own hemorrhoids."

Jet looked puzzled, but Wilma didn't really know exactly what to explain. The stupid, pointless prejudice of narrow-minded people was hard for anyone to understand. How could an innocent child even begin to grasp it? But Wilma always faced the world straight up. And she wanted Jet to do exactly the same.

"Have you got any questions about what just happened between me and that woman in the store?" Wilma asked.

Jet nodded.

"Then ask me and I'll answer as best I can."

"What's a hemorrhoid?"

Wilma looked at her for a moment and then burst out laughing. "It's nothing that you have to worry about, my little sugarplum. And people like Adele, they aren't anything you have to worry about either. With any luck at all, by the time you get grown up, the ones like her will all be dead and buried. And I vow to go to that woman's funeral wearing only red high heels and my underslip."

3

Ellen's first week working for the Cowboy of Taxes was not as bad as she would have thought. The work was familiar, exacting and technical. It was the kind of thing she'd been doing all her life and there was a lot of comfort in confidence. Though any resemblance to her late husband's business ended there.

There was no plush waiting room with a cappuccino machine and Internet access. If someone had to wait, they'd do it on the green Naugahyde couch in front of the window. And the one computer in the building, an ancient prePentium with neither broadband nor DSL, shared the phone line with Yolanda's personal life.

The people were also a sharp contrast, their problems diverse and their money scarce. None of Max Roper's clients were trying to have their five-acre subdivision tract listed as a wildlife refuge in order to lower their property assessments. These were working-class people, cabdrivers, waitresses, tradesmen and hair stylists. Their tax problems were more direct. They owed money they couldn't pay, had spouses who couldn't be located, or earned income they had never declared.

"I just lost track of time and forgot to file," an elderly gentleman confided to Ellen one morning.

He was an amiable fellow in his mid-seventies, but he seemed to be a sharp old man. She was surprised that he'd made such an error.

"If you're only a few months late, Mr. Payne, there may be a penalty, but I'm sure we can catch you up."

The man eyed her for a long moment and then gave her an unexpected wink. "Well," he admitted. "I haven't filed in a good long while."

Ellen raised her eyebrows.

"When was the last tax year that you were in compliance?" she asked.

Mr. Payne consulted the papers he carried with him in an old, weathered Stetson hatbox. Ellen took the opportunity to take a sip from the cup at the edge of her desk.

"Looks like the last year I got around to filling out them forms was 1986."

Ellen inhaled her swallow of coffee, nearly choking.

This was *not* the sort of thing that had happened to Paul's clients. When she related the problem to Max, he took it in stride.

"Don't even look at any scrap of paper more than ten years old," he told her. "If the IRS doesn't collect in a decade they just write it off."

"That still leaves nine full years of nonpayment," Ellen pointed out. Max shrugged, unconcerned. "Send the IRS a check for a hundred dollars," he said. "And indicate a willingness to set up payments."

"But we don't have a clue as to how much he actually owes," Ellen pointed out.

"We'll figure it out," he said. "And probably quicker than they'll get around to responding to us."

"It's hard to believe that he simply forgot for a decade and a half," Ellen commented shaking her head.

Max chuckled. "I don't believe he forgot about it for five minutes," he said. "He had some scheme worked out where he thought he would never have to pay up. Now he's decided that it's in his interest to do so and he wants us to figure out a cheap and easy way to get back onto the tax rolls."

"Do you really think so?"

Max leaned back in his chair, propping one cowboy-booted foot upon the edge of his desk. "I've known Cleo Payne for forty years," he said. "When it comes to money, that man can squeeze the manure out of a buffalo nickel."

"If he has been deliberately evading taxes for fifteen years, maybe he needs a lawyer more than an accountant," Ellen pointed out.

Max nodded. "We'll get him a lawyer if it turns out that he needs one. Right now we should take our time and sort it out. You need to write IRS a letter," he said.

"Yes, of course," Ellen agreed. "But how can I ever explain failure to file for sixteen years?"

Max responded thoughtfully. "The truth is, Miss Ellen, life is long."

He hesitated there and she prompted him.

"Life is long," he repeated. "And that's exactly what your letter should be."

"I don't think I follow you," she admitted.

"Fifteen, eighteen pages minimum," Max told her. "Single spaced, long complex sentences. Use as much jargon as you can fit in. We've got to wear somebody down far enough that they're willing to wait rather than start wading through it."

Overwhelming officials with excuses was not exactly the kind of accounting to which Ellen was accustomed.

"The fine folks of our federal tax bureaucracy are overworked, overwhelmed and mostly over the hill," Max said. "Experience makes up for a lot, but it doesn't make a person all that eager to wade into sucking mud. We just have to make Payne's taxes look like a real pain to one of those people. I've got every confidence that a smart gal like you can do that."

Dutifully, Ellen agreed to pursue that direction and headed back to her office.

"Ellen, Ellen, come here," Yolanda called out to her.

The receptionist was at the counter, talking on the phone—apparently a personal call. As Ellen walked over she continued her conversation.

"You can't use bleach on running shoes," she said definitively into the receiver. "It makes the rubber come unstuck. Use whitewall tire cleaner."

Yolanda glanced up at Ellen, raising one finger as an indication to wait.

"Okay, okay," Yolanda said into the phone. "Hold on a sec."

She held the receiver next to her chest.

"These are clients that Max has been ducking," she said, handing Ellen a stack of folders. "Why don't you look them over."

Ellen eyed the pile warily. "Why has he been ducking them?"

Yolanda glanced back toward the older man's office and said loudly enough to be heard. "Max Roper is too lazy to live," she declared. Then added in a whisper just for Ellen's ears. "He hates to give these folks the really bad news. I hate to ask you, but it's either you or me."

Ellen looked down at the folders and then back at the open door to Max's office. With a shrug of acceptance, she went to her tiny, windowless cell and seated herself safely behind the desk. A quick perusal indicated that Yolanda was right. The half-dozen clients represented were in for some very bad news. And many of them should have been notified months ago.

The way Max handled that was to file an extension and slap a yellow sticky on the file that read "call immediately." Some of those yellow stickies were nearly gray with age.

Ellen adjusted her reading glasses on the bridge of her nose and began familiarizing herself with the files. Their problems were extreme, frightening, life changing.

She understood them completely.

Paul's illness, and subsequent death, had meant total financial collapse. They had been a prosperous, upper-middle-class family with a reputable business, a nice house with a reasonable mortgage, a bright daughter and money set aside for both her education and their retirement.

Now, if it weren't for Wilma, Ellen didn't know what they'd do.

It had been like watching a train wreck in slow motion. She had been acutely aware of everything that happened, but there had been nothing she could do to stop it.

She imagined these people felt much the same. She started making calls.

With matter-of-fact detail and brutal honesty, Ellen

clearly told the clients what they undoubtedly already knew. It was all bad news. Bad debt. Bad luck. Bad choices.

She didn't sugar the medicine. Any other accountant would have tried to soothe the fears with optimism, temper the despair with hope. Ellen didn't bother.

"Yes, of course, you'll eventually get out of debt," she assured a fifty-three-year-old businessman who'd been dipping his hand in his own company's till for a decade. "The IRS will most likely garnishee twenty percent of your salary for the rest of your life. And then claim the remainder of the obligation from your heirs upon your death."

It wasn't a cheery thought, but at least it was a fate one could get a handle on.

The second unlucky client on her list was a young mother with a crying toddler in the background. Her husband, a personal trainer, had apparently thought income reporting rules didn't apply to him. And his young bride, now a former wife, had trustingly signed every form.

"Bankruptcy isn't an option," Ellen told her. "It's an inevitability. The sooner you accept that fact and start living accordingly, the more chance you'll have of salvaging anything."

By the time noontime came around, Ellen had worked up an appetite. Grateful for the company of her own thoughts, Ellen stepped outside into the warmth of midday San Antonio sunshine. Even in winter, it was the kind of place where you made a point of walking on the shady side of the street. She took a deep breath and glanced in each direction thoughtfully. There were not many eating establishments in this part of downtown. Nearer the river and the tourist hotels there was a swanky taco joint on every corner. But Ellen couldn't afford swanky tacos anyway. Her choices were the sandwiches at the Empire Bar or the *menu del día* at Helgalita's. She chose the latter, less for any particular food preference than because she didn't want to eat with Max. Her boss had lunch at the Empire Bar every day at 12:30. He sat at the same table and had the same meal every day. Ellen admired the routine. Routine was a good thing for accountants. But the last thing she wanted was to spend one extra moment with him.

She knew Max spent a good deal of time eavesdropping on what she was doing. It was so easy to do in that office, and it was natural to do so with a new employee. Ellen didn't mind, but she sure didn't want to discuss it. After running Paul's business, it was very hard to fit herself back into the position of accounting clerk.

She was also embarrassed to be new on the job and forced to take care of personal business at work. But it was impossible to avoid. She'd tried numerous times to contact her lawyer. David Marmer had been their neighbor in Elm Creek and one of Paul's closest friends, and he'd handled the paperwork for her bankruptcy. Her first coherent thought after reading Wilma's letter from Pressman, Yaffe and Escudero was to get his help. Unfortunately, David never returned any of her calls.

"Neither one of us wants to see Jet raised out on the street," she warned God under her breath. "If you're going to take care of this, you need to get cracking!"

Heaven made no immediate response.

The sign in the window at Helgalita's announced

We Have Menudo. As Ellen made her way inside, she was hoping that they would also have something else.

The little restaurant had a sad collection of mismatched chairs and tables covered in orange vinyl covers. Ellen went to the high counter in the back of the room to place her order. A blackboard above the cash register listed the lunch choices of the day. She decided on the *divorciados,* an enchilada plate with one cheese with ranchero sauce and one chicken with salsa verde separated by a bed of rice. Ellen took her place in the line of those waiting for their food.

When she was called up to retrieve her small plastic tray of food and drink, Ellen made her way to a table tucked into the corner near the door.

She'd just picked up her fork when her attention was caught by a frail old woman, trying to open the door. She had a huge corona of blue/gray hair that dwarfed her tiny facial features. She was dressed very expensively in a chic designer knit suit. But her buttons were done up incorrectly. Her shoes and bag easily cost as much as Ellen's monthly income, but they were mismatched and too dark and heavy for summer.

The older woman struggled fruitlessly with the door. She kept trying to pull the door open rather than pushing it in. Ellen set her fork on her plate and went to help.

When Ellen opened the door, the woman tottered unsteadily, surprised that it gave way.

"Why on earth has Lyman changed this door?" she asked.

Ellen didn't know Lyman as it was her first visit to Helgalita's. So her answer was only a smile.

The woman eyed her curiously.

"What are you doing here at this time of day?" she asked. "Who is watching Sis and Willy?"

Ellen was momentarily taken aback at her question, then recognized it for what it was.

"I'm sorry, you've mistaken me for somebody else," Ellen told her.

"Don't try that nonsense again, Violet," she said. "I am sick to death of that silly game. You are Violet Mercer, Ralph's widow and I've known you since you were in diapers. Where is Lyman."

Before Ellen could respond, the woman looked around and gasped in horror. "What are all these people doing *eating* in the store? Get out! Get out!"

A few people glanced up, but mostly they ignored the old woman.

She raised her walkingstick as if it were the staff of Moses and struck the table where Ellen's *divorciados* were growing cold.

"Get these tables out of here!" she ordered. "Violet, where is the merchandise? Lyman? Lyman? Where are you?"

A dark-haired Hispanic woman of middle years and rotund build came striding out from the kitchen. The scowl of displeasure on her face was evident and she was waving her hands in angry dismissal.

"Hush up, hush up," she said. "Mrs. Stanhope, you're disturbing my customers again."

"Marjorie, where have they put the merchandise."

The Hispanic woman blew out a puff of exasperation.

"I am not Marjorie, I'm Helgalita," she said. "And this is not your husband's store—it's my restaurant. So sit down and shut up or get out."

The old woman looked back the way she came. The tone of her voice turned immediately contrite.

"Oh my goodness, I must have the wrong door," she said. "I'm so sorry to bother you, I must have mistaken this place for my husband's store."

"Your husband doesn't have a store," Helgalita said.

"What do you mean he doesn't have a store?" Mrs. Stanhope asked, her anger rising once more. "Lyman works fourteen hours a day, six days a week."

"Keep your voice down, Mrs. Stanhope, or I'll call the cops on you again," Helgalita threatened.

"Where is Lyman?" she demanded.

"Mrs. Stanhope, your husband is dead," Helgalita answered. "He's been dead for forty years."

"Dead?" the old woman whispered the word as if it were the first time she'd ever heard it. She looked as if she might crumple to the floor. Ellen grabbed her and helped her into the chair beside her table. The woman was obviously shaken and Helgalita apparently had little sympathy left for the old lady.

"I'll take care of her," Ellen told the woman. "Maybe if you bring her a cup of coffee."

Helgalita sighed, but nodded agreement. The rest of the room was beginning to return to their own concerns.

"Lyman is dead," the woman whispered quietly. "He's been dead a very long time."

"I'm sorry, Mrs. Stanhope," Ellen said. "Is there somebody I can call for you."

She thought about that for a long moment.

"Irma," she said. "You'll have to call my niece, Irma. I don't want to, though," she said. "She took away all my coats. I don't know what she wants with them, but she took every one of them out of the house."

"Maybe she put them somewhere for safekeeping," Ellen suggested.

Mrs. Stanhope shook her head. "I don't know," she said. "I don't understand anything she does."

"Do you have her number?" Ellen asked.

"No, no…" She hesitated. "I don't know. I'm sure they have it here at the store."

Ellen didn't want to remind her that this wasn't the store.

"Maybe the number is in your purse," Ellen suggested.

Mrs. Stanhope handed the bag to her. "You look for it, Violet," she said. "You can always find things that I can't."

Ellen opened the expensive bag. It was empty except for a mirrored compact and a lace hanky.

Helgalita brought the coffee and set it down on the table.

"Do you know how to get in touch with her niece?"

The woman shrugged. "You could call her, she keeps an office at home," she said. "She doesn't live far, just up on the edge of King William. That old lady got herself down here on her own two feet. I'm sure she can get herself home the same way."

In the end, Ellen walked with her. She told herself, and Mrs. Stanhope, that a little bit of exercise over lunch would do her a world of good.

It seemed to help the old woman as well. The stunned silence of Helgalita's revelation gave way to a quiet conversation and before they arrived at Mrs. Stanhope's home, Ellen found herself being enter-

tained with stories of her life with Lyman, their court-
ship, their home, his store.

"We were married at St. Mark's," she told Ellen.
"Do you remember that? You were just a baby. It was
so hot that day, so hot, I swear, I was afraid I would
simply melt away in that organdy gown. I wanted to
wear silk, of course. But Papa disapproved of the
match and Mama thought organdy would be better.
Lyman was so handsome, back then he still had hair."

When they reached the little house on the corner at
Chaffey Street. Mrs. Stanhope stopped at the gate of a
white picket fence, gray with age.

"Would you like to come in for some tea, Violet?"
she asked.

"No," Ellen answered. "I've really got to get back."

"Yes," Mrs. Stanhope agreed. "Sis and Willy will
be needing you, of course."

"Are you sure I shouldn't talk to your niece?"

"Irma? No, no, there is no need to bother her," she
said. "She gets so annoyed if you bother her when
she's working."

At that moment the front door opened and a neat,
buttoned-down, almost masculine-looking woman in
linen slacks and a polo shirt hurried out.

"Aunt Edith, shame on you," she scolded. "You are
not supposed to be outside. You've gone running off
to town again."

The older woman's eyes widened. She looked embarrassed, humiliated. At first Ellen attributed this to
the condescending tone of the woman on the porch.
Then she realized that Mrs. Stanhope was not so far
gone as Ellen might have thought.

"Oh, dear," she said, shaking her head apologetically. "I'm afraid I've had another one of my spells. I'm sorry, have I behaved terribly crazy?"

Mrs. Stanhope's expression was so forlorn, it tugged at Ellen's heart.

"Of course not," she assured her. "You've just gone to lunch with a friend. Nothing to worry about."

"Are you sure?"

"Absolutely."

"All right then," she said, obviously relieved. "I'd better go on in, Irma gets in such a huff about these things."

The woman of whom she spoke was still scolding. She had work to do and couldn't keep an eye on Mrs. Stanhope every minute. Irma had to be able to trust her aunt not to go running off every time she turned her back.

It was probably a reasonable complaint. But all of Ellen's sympathies were with the old lady. As if a little devil was upon her shoulder, Ellen looked up, momentarily wishing to be her mother. Rapier-tongued Wilma would never let anyone get away with being smug or superior. Uncharacteristically, the words just slipped out of Ellen's mouth.

"Irma, dear, you're looking very well today. It seems an age since we've talked. I hope you're well."

She had the woman's attention immediately. Irma scanned her from head to toe trying to find some familiarity she could recognize.

"Call me, I miss hearing from you," Ellen added, as fuel to the fire. She turned, heading down the street toward the office. She left the crabby, berating woman staring after her.

Let Irma see what it feels like to believe her mind is slipping.

* * *

The lights glittered on the dark waters of the river along the section of the Riverwalk most renowned for noisy bars and youthful drunkenness.

Amber, with friends Kayla and Gwen stood together on the edge of the walkway. They were laughing, joking, and hopefully, looking very hot. Kayla was the most stylishly decked out. Short and verging upon downright pudgy, it was difficult to tell if her midriff was showing by design or simply because she couldn't keep it stuffed inside her shirt.

Gwen was leaner, her long legs snugly encased in faux leather slacks. Her tight pink sweater hugged bra-free breasts that showed the impression of her nipples, one faced straight out, the other tilted slightly to the left somehow giving her chest a wall-eyed appearance. She was heavily made-up, almost garish. Her long dark hair, permed to extremes, hung around her shoulders like a cape. The hair, makeup and flashy clothes combined effectively to hide the delicate features that were her only claim to beauty.

Amber still had on her work clothes, having come directly from her job at the mall. Black slacks, sensible shoes and blended button-down were covered by a burgundy zip jacket. Work days were never her best days and, even on her best days, she could hardly afford to be a slave to style. Amber was actually grateful not to have to compete on that level. Long ago Wilma had given her wise advice.

"If you go out with girlfriends," her grandmother had said. "Make sure that you're always the best-looking one."

Tonight, like most nights, she was relatively sure that she was.

"He was like such a total loser," Kayla said, as she flexed her right ankle. The five-inch stilettos looked great, but they were hellish for standing on a stone path. "I just told him to kiss my ass goodbye."

Kayla's words were tough, but her lower lip trembled a little as she spoke them.

"That is too bad," Amber told her. "I thought he was sweet."

Gwen snorted. "He was just another loser looking for a booty call," she said. "He has a wife and kids somewhere for sure."

Kayla was stunned. "You don't know that," she said.

Gwen took a deep drag on her cigarette and nodded.

"When a guy that age doesn't spend half the evening putting down his ex-wife," she said. "It's got to be because he doesn't have one."

Amber hated to admit it, but there was some truth to that.

Kayla's bottom lip trembled. Amber felt so bad for her.

"He was good for a few laughs," Gwen said. "I hope you didn't start expecting some boring *till death do us part* crap."

"Of course not," Kayla said defensively.

Amber was pretty sure that to date, no one had ever offered Kayla any *till death do us part* crap. And if things didn't pick up pretty soon, it wasn't all that likely to happen.

Gwen, Amber thought, was like an older version of herself. She also had a kid. They both lived with their mothers, who did most of the child care. Gwen worked in hotel registration and went from one lousy, low-paying minimum wage job to the next.

Kayla's life was better. Her father had worked for the city water system for thirty years. He had managed to get Kayla a desk job in the office. She had her own car and a little apartment in a flashy singles complex. Kayla was somewhat naive and way too trusting. But she'd managed to do a good deal better than her sharper friends.

"He just wasn't the right one," Amber reassured her. "There's somebody out there who is going to be just perfect for you. You just have to hang out until he turns up."

"Yeah," Kayla agreed, a little too brightly.

"And if you're going to hang out," Gwen said. "You might as well be partying."

Gwen's voice had gradually gotten louder until the last word was like a celebratory cry.

"Hey, baby, I hear ya!" a guy on the other side of the river called out.

"Well what are you gonna do about it," Gwen called back.

"We're headed in your direction," he assured her. "Just got to find us a bridge."

"You'd better hurry," she told him.

"Baby, if I weren't so damn drunk, I'd swim."

The pack of young men disappeared around the bend.

"Do you think those are college guys?" Kayla asked eagerly.

"With those haircuts?" Amber replied. "They're flyboys if I don't miss my guess."

"Well, at least they'll have some cash," Gwen said. She was forever short of money and always counted on the men they met to do the drink buying. Amber had eight bucks in her purse. For any serious drinking she would have to rely upon the largesse of some likeable guy as well.

A gaggle of teenage girls, all in an identical costume of tight jeans and crop-Ts, came along the walkway. They made the mistake of hesitating in the area near where Amber and her friends were standing.

Gwen's eyes narrowed dangerously.

"Aren't you kids out a little late on a school night?" she asked.

A pretty brunette with the face of an angel and a peaches and cream complexion turned to give them a once-over and then blurted out a vile expletive.

Gwen responded in kind.

The expressive dislike went back and forth for a couple of minutes. Finally one of the young girls suggested nastily, "Let's move along. This is obviously a whore stand."

Her words so infuriated Gwen that the incident could have easily turned into a brawl. Amber laid a restraining hand on her arm.

"Hey, the flyboys are coming," she said, her voice both soft and soothing. "They'll buy us some drinks, we'll have some laughs. No need to let these infants ruin our evening."

Gwen backed down and let the teenagers pass on unmolested, but she was angry.

Amber understood it.

The younger girls were competition. And they were competition with all the advantage. Younger, fresher, less experienced with the world, they were just now making the choices that had already come to haunt Gwen and Amber.

Gwen had actually given birth twice. The first baby, when she was sixteen, she'd given up for adoption. Dwight, the child she'd kept, was eight now. The school said he was learning disabled. He mostly stayed with Gwen's mother or with her ex-boyfriend's parents. She and Amber had been hanging out together for a couple of years now and Amber had yet to see the little fellow. Gwen didn't even carry a photo of him in her purse. And she never mentioned him. Kids were a big liability with most guys. Once they found out a chick was somebody's mother, they lost interest real fast. That was even true of the ones who had kids of their own somewhere.

Gwen had kept Dwight because she'd thought that eventually his father would marry her. She hadn't completely given up on that until he'd married someone else. Gwen was in her late twenties now. Her only life plan had been to find a nice guy and get married. She hadn't managed to do either.

The flyboys arrived. They were obviously wasted. There were four of them and only three of the girls, but nobody commented on the math. The guys wanted to go to Howl at the Moon, but Gwen suggested they go to Swig's. Her argument was that the place could always be counted on for a young, partying crowd, but Amber knew she was deftly avoiding the crisis of who-pays-the-cover-charge.

There was a bit of a noisy hold up at the door, but eventually they were seated at a long table outside with a group of total strangers who were already well into the obnoxious phase of an evening of drunkenness.

Among the flyboys, the short, geeky guy just naturally took his place next to Kayla. The other three took turns talking to Amber and Gwen, keeping their options open.

The waiter came. The talkative blond guy, Derek, presumptuously ordered Cosmopolitans all around. The geek asked for beer instead and Kayla followed his lead. Gwen changed her order to a vodka and tonic.

Amber decided against Derek and directed her attention to Jeff. He was a bit too thin, but he was nice looking, tan, with brown hair and eyes. Preferring dark men, she focused most of her attention on him. He was quiet and easygoing, she thought. He wasn't a big talker, but his friend seemed to be taking care of that completely.

By the third martini, Gwen and Derek were definitely taken with each other. His conversation had become all sexual innuendo and they were sneaking feels of each other as if the people around them didn't notice.

Amber tried not to. She was feeling the early exuberance of alcohol and the conversation was not all that stimulating, so she suggested dancing. None of her comrades appeared overly eager for notching up the night, but everyone agreed.

It was Jeff who actually paid the tab at Swigs. They made their way back along the riverwalk as couples. Brian, the geek, and Kayla in the lead with Gwen and Derek, laughing loudly. It seemed that the more Derek drank the more he talked. He was drinking a lot. Kyle, the odd man out, was joking with them, finding nearly everything that was said to be absolutely hilarious. Jeff, his arm around Amber, brought up the rear. He snuggled up close and pressed a very sexy little kiss to the nape of her neck.

Amber liked the way it made her feel and kissed him back, on the lips.

"You sure you want to go dancing?" he asked her. "We could find someplace a lot more quiet and do some things a lot more fun. I promise, you'll still get plenty of exercise."

His grin was leering. Amber was put off by the suggestion.

"I don't have sex with a guy in the first hour," she said. Her tone was sarcastic.

He glanced down at his watch.

"It looks to me like it's already been almost two."

"Forget it," she said. "I'm here to have a good time. Not to get laid."

He shook his head. "Now, how am I suppose to have a good time if I *don't* get laid?" he asked.

Fortunately, they'd made it to the dance club and Amber was not obliged to answer.

Polly Esther's was wild, even in the middle of the week. For dancing, drinking and hanging out with the appropriate peer group, there was no better option. Music spilled invitingly out of the doorway as they made their way inside.

The guys took care of the cover as the girls took a moment to exchange quick pieces of information.

"The other guys are E4s, Brian's a staff sergeant," Kayla reported with a proud whisper. "He's twenty-six and says he doesn't have a regular girlfriend."

She said the words as if it were totally amazing. The fact that she was close to the same age and had yet to even keep any relationship going more than a couple of months was lost on her.

"What do you think?" Amber asked Gwen.

"I like your guy better than mine," she admitted. "I

picked too quick, now I'm stuck with Mr.
Chatterbox."

"Jeff is keen on getting laid tonight," Amber
told her.

Gwen laughed. "What a coincidence," she said.
"So am I."

The men came over and the secret sharing stopped
immediately.

Derek indicated the direction of the elevator. "They
told me Top Floor is where they rave."

Kayla, Gwen and Amber were all regulars, but they
pretended that Derek's announcement was news.

With three dance levels, and different decades of
music, Polly Esther's was exciting and noisy. It took
them a little time to find exactly the right table and to
get drinks ordered. Both Gwen and Kayla, with their
respective guys, took to the floor. Kyle quickly found
himself a partner as well and Amber and Jeff were left
watching purses, attempting to scream out a reasonable conversation over the din.

Jeff only seemed interested in drinking and even after the two other couples returned to the table, he
didn't ask her to dance. That seemed particularly unfair since it was she who had suggested the place,
specifically because she did want to dance.

The music continued, the drinks flowed. Amber
tapped her foot under the table.

After a while, she escaped to the rest room. Jeff had
turned out to be a dud. Okay, that sometimes happened, she reminded herself. It shouldn't keep her
from having a good time. Maybe he was pissed that
she didn't want to have sex the minute they met.
Maybe he wasn't a dancer. Lots of athletic-looking
guys just weren't dancers, she assured herself.

She was reapplying lipstick in the mirror when Kayla breezed in.

"Brian and I are cutting out," she said.

Amber watched her own brow furrow in the mirror. "Are you sure? You just met him."

"And I just like him," Kayla answered with a giggle.

"But you shouldn't just go off alone with this guy."

"Oh, puh-leeze," Kayla complained. "Brian and I are great together. It's like we've known each other forever."

"It may be *like* you've known each other forever, but you don't really know this guy at all," Amber pointed out.

"You are such a weeny," Kayla replied. "Lighten up, we're having a good time. You can get another ride home, can't you."

"Sure," Amber agreed. "Gwen and I will be fine." She gave her friend a quick hug. "Call me tomorrow, I want to hear every detail."

"Deal," Kayla told her and hurried out with a wave.

Amber took another glance in the mirror and forced a friendly smile. Kayla was right. Everybody was having a good time. If she just tried hard enough, she could have one, too. Jeff was undoubtedly pissed that she hadn't jumped at the opportunity to sleep with him. Playing hard to get wasn't necessarily the best way to get by in this town. Well, she was sure she could get a second chance.

Amber walked back to the table, determination in her step. It was late, the crowd was beginning to thin and there were now empty stools around the bar and more room on the dance floor.

Kyle and Derek were seated with a couple of other girls who Amber didn't know. Her drink was gone and so was her companion.

"Where's Jeff?" she asked Derek.

He glanced up at her and shrugged. "The last time I saw him, he was dancing with Gwen."

Derek turned his back on her, diving off into a long discourse full of suggestiveness that made the girl beside him giggle. If Kyle had been odd-man-out before, Amber clearly was now.

She wandered away and checked out the dancing for several minutes. Gwen and Jeff were nowhere to be found. They could have gone downstairs, she thought. Or they could have simply ducked out together. Amber suspected the latter.

She was tired. Her head ached and the music was making it worse. She wished she still had the dregs of her drink, but she was unwilling to spend her last eight bucks. Without even looking at her watch she knew she'd already missed the last bus. Getting home was going to be expensive or a very long walk.

A young, preppy-looking guy stumbled over in her direction.

"Hey, baby, you lost?" he asked.

"No," she answered.

"'Cause if you are," he continued, "I am considered quite a find."

Amber rolled her eyes.

"I'll bet you are," she replied.

The guy ignored her dismissive tone.

"You wanna dance?" he asked. "'Cause I can dance."

Did she want to start all over? It was nearly midnight. Could she meet a guy at midnight and have time to get to know him before closing?

Probably not. But at least she could get a free ride.

"Sure, let's dance," she told him. "That's why we're in this place."

4

After three days of leaving frantic midday messages, Ellen was desperate to talk to her lawyer in person.

His secretary was not about to let that happen.

"Mr. Marmer is not available at the moment," she said. "If you'd like to leave a message…"

"I've already left half a dozen messages," Ellen snapped. "I need to speak to him and I need to speak to him now."

"Mrs. Jameson, I'm sure he will get back to you at his earliest convenience," she said.

Obviously *convenience* was the operative word.

"I have a very, very urgent situation that I need to discuss with him," Ellen told her. "I've got to talk to him right away."

"I'll be sure to tell him," the secretary told her coolly. "And while I have you here on the phone, I'd like to remind you that there is a significant unpaid balance on your account."

"I am well aware of that," Ellen told her. "I am working now and I will be sending you a check at the first of the month, as soon as I get paid."

"So you'll be taking care of the remainder of the bill?"

"Well, no," Ellen hedged. "I won't be able to pay in full, but I do intend to pay something on it."

"How much will you be paying?"

"I...ah...I might be able to pay a hundred dollars."

The secretary actually laughed.

"Do you realize how much you owe on this account?"

"Of course I do," Ellen answered. "And I'm sure you realize, as does David Marmer, that I've just gone through bankruptcy. He got a lot more than most of my other creditors. And he knows me. He knows that I will pay what I owe, but it will be a while."

Ellen's money problems never ceased to humiliate her. But she'd already learned that people didn't actually die from embarrassment, they just wished they could.

"David was one of my late husband's oldest and dearest friends," she continued. "No matter what I owe him, I'm sure he would want to help me."

"And I'm sure he'll return your call when he has sufficient *free time* to do so," the secretary replied. Her opinion about the value of an old, dear friend was obvious, but her emphasis on the phrase *free time* was deliberate and even more telling.

With a click, the line went dead.

Ellen sat for a moment, the receiver still in her hand, staring into space. She didn't know what to do or to whom she could turn.

"Come on, God," she complained to the empty room. "If you were trying to teach me not to take a comfortable life for granted, I swear I've learned. This is enough already. I don't have my husband, our home, our business. If Wilma loses her place we'll be out on the street. You can't want that. I'm sure you can't."

She said the words, but without the certainty that

they meant to evoke. When Paul's cancer had been di-
agnosed she'd been anxious and worried, but she'd
felt a calm assurance that somehow everything
would be all right. That's the way life was. God was
good and life, for those who played by the rules—
people who were honest, hardworking, trustworthy—life worked out fine. It was a belief that she'd
held on to. It was her own personal brand of religious
faith.

Do right by other people and trust that God will do
right by you.

It was a simple understanding, not fraught with ob-
scure textuary or intricate ecclesiastical dogma. But it
had worked for Ellen for most of her life. Until Paul's
illness came along. Cancer was terrible. But it could
be beaten. People beat it every day. Ellen had been
determined that Paul would beat it. And when the
best therapeutic hopes were not covered on Paul's insurance, Ellen cashed in their savings to pay for them.
She got a second mortgage on the house. She borrowed against the business. She had never even considered not doing those things. Paul was her husband. He was Amber's father. They loved him.
Taking care of his health was expensive, but no
amount of money was worth more than his life. The
money was well-spent, an investment in Paul's
future.

They had to fight it. She could not let anything happen to Paul.

The thing about optimism is that once it is shat-
tered, there is nothing left to hang on to. People who
always expected the worst were never disappointed.
For Ellen, disappointment had come as a complete

surprise. And one that she had, as yet, been unable to rationalize.

"Please, God, get us out of this mess," she pleaded.

Mentally reciting the admonition that *God helps those who help themselves*, she reached for Paul's ancient Rolodex on the edge of her desk. She flipped through the yellowing cards, hoping for an answer. Or at least another lawyer. There were none to be found, nothing but tax attorneys.

Paul and David Marmer had been more than neighbors, they were friends. They had played chess together, gone on fly fishing trips and sat up late on summer nights speculating on life, money and business. Paul had kept his books and done his taxes. David handled whatever legal matters had come up. He'd written up their wills. Later he'd filed the bankruptcy and helped her sell the business.

David knew her situation. She didn't want to have to start all over with someone else.

Deliberately, Ellen steeled herself and swallowed her pride. She punched the numbers for his home phone. It rang twice.

"Hello."

"Peggy?" she said. "Hi, this is Ellen...Ellen Jameson."

There was a momentary pause that could have meant anything. "My God, Ellen," she answered. "How are you?"

"I'm all right," she lied. "I'm doing all right."

"How long has it been? I can't even remember when I saw you last," Peggy said.

"It...ah...I think it was at the funeral," Ellen said.

"Oh, yes, right." She sounded embarrassed. "And I meant to call, truly I did."

"I know," Ellen said. "I understand. We've all been so busy."

"That's so true," she said. "I've been taking ceramics at the Southwest School of Art. I'm actually getting quite good. I'm hoping to have a little showing at a gallery in the Blue Star. You'll just *have* to come."

"That sounds wonderful," Ellen said.

"And what have you been doing?" she asked.

Ellen had been dealing with grief, going through bankruptcy, losing her house, closing her business. None of those things seemed worth mentioning in comparison to the making of clay pots.

"I've got a new job," she said.

"Really? What sort?"

"Same old thing," Ellen answered. "You can take the girl out of accounting, but you can't take accounting out of the girl."

"Oh?" Peggy sounded puzzled. "David said that you'd given up the firm."

She had known. She'd known what her former close friend had been going through and she had been avoiding her. It hurt, but Ellen tried not to feel it.

"I'm working for somebody else," Ellen told her. "Another accounting service. Max Roper. Do you know him?"

"No...no, I don't think so."

Ellen was certain that she didn't.

"Anyway," Ellen plunged on, "I've got a really urgent legal matter that I need to discuss with David and I can't get past his harridan secretary."

"Oh, well...David has been very busy. I'm sure when he has time..."

"I don't have time," Ellen interrupted. "I need to talk to somebody about this now."

There was a moment of silence on the other end of the line. Guilt is a powerful force. As strong as love or hate, and with fewer defenses against it.

Finally Peggy spoke, "Okay, I'll have him call you."

It was barely ten minutes later when the phone rang.

"The girls and I are living with my mother," Ellen began after the pleasantries and excuses.

"That sounds like a good idea," David said. "Peggy says you have a job. It won't be long before you're back on your feet."

His tone was slightly condescending, but Ellen didn't have the luxury of being able to be insulted by it.

"My mother got a letter from Pressman, Yaffe and Escudero. Apparently her stepchildren want the house we're living in and these lawyers say that it is rightfully theirs. They've ordered us to get out immediately."

There was a moment of silence on the other end of the line.

"That doesn't sound good," David admitted. "What brought this on?"

"Nothing that I know about," Ellen answered. "I've met them a few times. My mother was only married to Wilbur about eighteen months. He was not in the best of health. I saw his children at their father's funeral. They apparently hadn't kept in close enough contact to even know that he and Wilma were married. They clearly weren't happy about it, but with their father already dead, there certainly wasn't much they could do about it."

"And that's all the contact she'd had with them?" David asked.

"I think there's been an ongoing battle," Ellen admitted. "His daughters wanted to get things out of the house. 'Their mother's things,' was how they described it. And the son came by a few times to suggest that he would give my mother some money if she would just go away. She didn't. So now they've got a lawyer."

"Pressman, Yaffe and Escudero aren't exactly shysters," David pointed out. "They must feel like they have some kind of case."

Ellen sighed heavily. "Well, my mother wasn't married to him for very long," she said. "And his will predated the death of his first wife. He left everything to her, because she was his wife at the time. It seems to me that since Wilma was his wife when he died, everything should go to her. Right?"

"I'm not sure," David admitted. "This isn't my area of expertise."

"Surely you have some idea," Ellen said.

David hesitated only a moment. "If the will was executed less than three years before he died and he left everything to his first wife by name," David told her, "then he intended that everything go to her. If she preceded him in death, which she did, then it's reasonable to assume that he would have intended that her heirs receive what was meant for her."

"That can't be right," Ellen said.

"Well, right or wrong," David replied. "It will be what Pressman, Yaffe and Escudero are arguing."

"Why would they want to do this?" Ellen asked. "The place isn't worth all that much."

David could only speculate. "Mahncke Park has

gotten pretty run-down over the last couple of decades," he said. "But with all this talk of the Broadway Revitalization, and the concept of making the whole area from downtown to Alamo Heights a big pedestrian mall, that old house begins to take on some new value."

"But that plan is years off and it may never happen," Ellen pointed out.

"And if it doesn't, then they haven't lost anything," David pointed out. "Right now the house is an asset, free and clear. They can borrow against it, rent it for income, or write it off as a loss. As long as it belongs to them. And they seem pretty sure it does."

"Can't we make some kind of deal with them?" Ellen asked. "We can come up with some kind of compromise. Surely there is something we can do?"

"My advice," David said. "Start looking for a place to live."

Ellen closed her eyes and took a deep breath. "I can't do that," she said, firmly. "We just moved in. I can't uproot us all over again."

"I don't think you have any other option," he said.

"Then you'll have to find another one," Ellen insisted.

There was a long pause before he replied.

"Ellen, you're going to have to find another lawyer," David said.

"David, you know I can't afford another lawyer," Ellen said.

He chuckled lightly. "You can't even afford me," he said. "You'll have to go to legal aid."

"I can't take something like this to the legal aid clinic," Ellen pointed out. "The kids there will be too intimidated by this law firm's letterhead to even try to help."

It was the truth, but it didn't make any difference.

"I'm a tax attorney," David said. "I'm not going to be able to win this one. I don't know anything about this kind of thing and I'm not taking on a prestigious firm like Pressman, Yaffe and Escudero. I'm sorry, Ellen, I simply won't do it."

"We're in one hell of a pickle," Wilma declared. "And for dang sure, you're mama is never going to be able to get us out of it."

Amber was seated with her out on the front porch. They were sharing a morning cigarette as Jet played with her doll on the steps. Jet was completely groomed and dressed, including shoes, socks and matching barrettes in her hair. By contrast the two women had yet to wash their faces or comb their hair and were lounging in dingy, threadbare bathrobes.

Amber was watching her daughter. She didn't look up as she answered.

"Yeah, I've been thinking a lot about that," she admitted. "I'm not sure what I should do."

"Well, somebody has got to start making some plans," Wilma said. "I've been thrown out before and believe me, once that kind of ball get's rolling, you might as well just pack your bags."

"You've been thrown out before?"

"Well, never like this," Wilma said. "I've never even imagined a situation like this. But I've been forced out plenty of times."

"When Mom lost the house, I thought it was a once-in-a-lifetime kind of disaster," Amber said.

"For a woman like your mom," Wilma told her, "it

probably is. I'm not a woman like your mom. I've had to pack up in the middle of the night a half-dozen times. Sometimes, I couldn't get along with the man or I couldn't keep up the mortgage. I swear when Bud and Ellen were little, seems like we had to move every time the rent came due."

"Really?" Amber was surprised. "I knew Mom had a couple of stepfathers, but I didn't think it was like that."

Wilma chuckled. "It was exactly like that," she said. "I was always skirting the rim of disaster. I floated checks on money I hoped to get, got my car towed for missed payments, had my furniture repossessed more than once. And I was on a first-name basis with the folks at the pawnshop."

Amber was frowning. "That must have been awful."

Wilma chuckled. "Actually, it was pretty exciting," she replied. "A housewife with a couple of little kids can be pretty boring. My life was many things, but it was never boring."

Amber laughed, fascinated. "Is that why you did it? To keep from being bored?"

Wilma shook her head. "No, I kept trying to make things turn out differently. But, somehow you get into a flow and it just keeps on going."

Amber nodded. "Except for Mom, who is always swimming against the tide."

Wilma eyed Amber critically. "You've got to give that gal some credit," she said. "She didn't have much to start with and she really made the best of it."

Amber shrugged. She was less than eager to give her mother any benefit of doubt.

"Anyway," Amber pointed out. "It's all gone now."

"Oh, the outside wrapping is all gone," Wilma said. "But inside Ellen's the same woman she always was. She believes just as strong. She fights just as hard. She just needs to find her a man, that's all."

"You're kidding, right?"

"Why would I be kidding?" Wilma answered. "A husband, specifically one that's got his own house, would solve all our problems. She'd just marry and we'd move in. Let Wilbur's dad-gummed brats have this shack. I never liked it that much anyway."

Amber laughed and shook her head. "Wilma, you are so totally non-p.c.," she said. "Women don't marry to get a house. That's not even fifteen minutes ago, it's a lifetime ago."

"My lifetime," Wilma said.

"Well…yeah," Amber answered.

"I may be old," Wilma said. "But unfortunately the world hasn't changed that much. The best chance for a woman to have a comfortable life and raise her kids with plenty to eat, warm clothes to wear and good schools to attend is for her to marry a good provider." Wilma eyed the young woman critically. "It might be something you should give some consideration to."

Amber rolled her eyes. "Oh, right. Like any guys I'd meet would be likely to provide anything more than cheap drinks, bags of dope and sperm samples."

Wilma didn't appear shocked as much as entertained. She gestured toward Jet. "Some of those sperm samples don't turn out too badly," she said. "Makes you wonder what kind of man he turned out to be."

"Oh, just the regular kind," Amber said. "One who says, 'I'll call you' and never did."

"Most women wouldn't let a phone call stand between them and a man they really wanted," Wilma pointed out.

"I didn't know him enough to know if he was a man I really wanted," Amber said. "And I think there was more standing between us."

"Like what?" Wilma asked her.

"Race, culture, our hopes, dreams, even our personalities," she said. It sounded lame even to her own ears.

"And then there was the matter of the wife and kids he already had," Amber added. She'd never admitted that part of it before.

She saw Wilma wince, but she didn't say a word. That's one thing she could count on. No matter how bad she screwed up, Wilma always listened, she never judged.

"Anyway," Amber continued. "Men today just don't get married if they can help it. And they can help it. With every kinky, pervy thing in the world available on any suburban street for free, guys just don't have to get married anymore."

"If you think marriage is about getting people in bed," Wilma told her, "then I'd say that you're the one who's non-p.c. and fifteen minutes ago."

"Oh, well, yeah, people still get married for *love*, I guess." Amber's emphasis on the word was disparaging.

"Yes," she agreed. "Love is one reason, but there's a whole boatload of others. And getting a roof over your head certainly qualifies in my book."

"Who would marry Mom?" Amber asked, almost incredulously.

"A lot of men would," Wilma answered. "Your daddy did and he thought he'd made a damn good bargain."

"Well, yeah Daddy," Amber agreed. "But that was a long time ago."

"Your mama is still a very attractive woman," Wilma pointed out. "She's good natured, even tempered and smart. There are a lot of men in the world who would find that combination irresistible."

Amber nodded, conceding the point. "But she doesn't go out. She never meets anyone. Unless you're going to get Sun Myung Moon to fix her up, who would she marry?"

"Well, I was thinking about that boss of hers," Wilma answered.

"Really? What do you know about the guy?"

Wilma shrugged. "Not that much," she admitted. "He owns his own business," she added hopefully.

"I thought Mom said he was old," Amber said.

"Age doesn't make that much difference," Wilma said. "No, I'm pretty sure your mother could just snap up that man. But she won't."

"Because she's still not over Daddy," Amber stated.

"It's not something you get over," Wilma said. "It's something that you live over."

"Yeah, but Mom's dragging it out too long," Amber said. "She's still stuck in place and it's going on five years now. It didn't take you that long to get over Wilbur."

"Wilbur?" the older woman looked at Amber and shook her head. "I was over Wilbur the day I met him. The man was tightfisted and selfish, just like his kids. He needed a cook, housekeeper and a nurse-maid. It was cheaper to marry me than to hire help. He'd already worked one wife to death. And he figured he'd get a lot less attached to me than he was to her."

"So that's why he married you," Amber said. "Why did you marry him?"

"I didn't figure the old coot was long for this world," Wilma said. "I thought a few years taking care of him was a reasonable price to pay for a little bit of security."

"You didn't care for him at all?"

"Oh, he was all right," Wilma said. "He had an interesting mind and occasional flashes of dry humor. But as I said, he was hardboiled and stingy. He had very few friends, even his children couldn't stand him. He wanted beans and potatoes for dinner every night—with everything. If I was fixing spaghetti, he wanted beans and potatoes with it."

Her remembered exasperation made Amber laugh.

"And he spent every waking minute working on crossword puzzles like they were the answer to the riddle of the Sphinx. The man nearly drove me to drink. But I did right by him. And I'm not sorry that I married him. I'm not sorry for anything I've done in my life. Sometimes I've been foolish, occasionally downright stupid. But it's all led me here, to what I'm doing today. I wouldn't have missed this."

With a nod she indicated the child on the front steps. Jet was playing grocery store. Lately it was her favorite game. Her Cabbage Patch doll, a red-haired African-American named Sheila Thompson, was getting thorough instructions on the purchase of lettuce.

Amber shook her head. She would never have thought that Wilma would be all that good at child care. She seemed more the kind of woman that other adults could appreciate. Jet had grown attached to her. Almost as attached as she was to Ellen.

"I don't think it will do any good," Amber said. "But if *you're* interested in Mom's boss, I think the best way to find out about him is to talk to that receptionist. She sounds like a meddling busybody to me. I bet she'd be absolutely prime for coming clean with everything she knows as well as everything she *thinks* she knows."

Wilma gave her a long look. "Amber Jameson," she said. "That sneaky, low-down conniving part of your personality, I want you to know, you get that from me."

Amber laughed. "Wilma," she said. "I know."

A Chevy Tahoe pulled up to the curb in front of the house. Both women tried to make out the identity of the driver, but the sunlight reflected against the windshield. It wasn't until he stood up beside the vehicle that Amber's puzzled expression turned to a frown.

"Look who's here, Amber," Wilma said, obviously delighted. "It's Brent."

Brent Velasco had been the boy next door when Amber was growing up in Elm Creek. They had been best friends, buds, since childhood. At one time they had shared every thought, every dream, every aspiration. As they got older, of course, things had begun to change. They had remained close friends until Amber had opted out of her Clark High School clique.

He came walking up the sidewalk, thinner, more muscular than Amber remembered. He seemed to have exchanged his chunky fat boy persona for a more confident frat boy role.

He stopped beside Jet and squatted down next to her, smiling.

"Hey there, Little Bit. Do you remember me?"

Jet shook her head.

"I'm Brent, a friend of your mommy's," he said.

He offered a handshake. Surprisingly, Jet ignored it and instead literally threw herself in the young man's arms.

He laughed and anchored the little girl against his hip as he rose to his feet.

"I think I've made a friend," he said.

"It looks like it," Wilma agreed.

"Jet's always been partial to strays."

Amber's comment was rather snottily made and Wilma gave her a questioning glance.

Brent chuckled.

"What are you doing here, Mr. Tall, Dark and Handsome?" Wilma asked as she rose to her feet to give him a hug. "I heard that you were up in Austin."

"I'm home for the summer," he told her. "I've got a job clerking in the Justice Center."

Wilma raised an approving eyebrow.

"I'm impressed," she said.

"Don't be," Brent told her. "Judge Flores is my dad's best golfing buddy. I don't think he necessarily hired me for my qualifications."

Wilma shook her head. "I'm sure he hired you based on the qualifications that you're going to have. Are you still planning on law school?"

Brent nodded. "This time next year I'll either be on my way or rethinking my life."

The comment was made so calmly, so casually,

Amber had to resist the infantile urge to kick him in the shins.

"I'm sure it will be more of the former than the latter," Wilma told him. "Do you still like coffee?"

"I don't like anybody's as much as yours," he lied.

"Sit here and catch up with Amber while I make a pot," she told him. He did as she bid him and made himself comfortable in the yellowing and frayed lawn chair. Jet seated herself on her mother's lap, still clutching Sheila Thompson. The little girl kept all her attention focused on the man in the chair beside them. As if he were some curious unknown creature from a fairy tale.

"You're looking good," he said to Amber.

She was already annoyed with him, her response was defensive and skeptical.

"Yeah, I guess most women look good to you wearing underwear and a bathrobe."

Brent nodded solemnly. "The bathrobe is the clincher for me," he admitted. "You can see all these near-naked hotties in the lingerie ads, but they never have on old terry-cloth bathrobes and fuzzy house shoes. It's a shame, really. You get no sense of what they are really like. I wish *Sports Illustrated* would put out an annual bathrobe issue."

Amber managed, with some difficulty, not to smile.

"I see that college hasn't improved upon your sense of humor," she said.

He raised his eyebrows à la Groucho Marx and faked a cigar. "You can't improve upon perfection."

Jet giggled and he repeated the elaborate gestures just for her.

"So what are you doing hanging around here in the slums?"

"Suburbia isn't necessarily my natural element," he answered. "So what have you been up to."

"I work," Amber answered. "You know work?"

He nodded. "I read about it in school," he answered. "It's what drives the economy, creates the tax base, makes America a strong democracy."

"Gives people something to get up for in the morning," she added.

"Or in your case, the afternoon."

Amber wanted to stick her tongue out at him, but managed to restrain herself.

"Everybody asks about you," Brent told her. "Lissa said she saw you in some pajama store in the mall. She said that you barely spoke to her."

"It's not a *pajama store*, it's a lingerie boutique," Amber answered. "And I was way too busy to chat about old times with Lissa. If she was offended then screw her. But then, you do, don't you."

Brent laughed. "Lissa and I haven't been an item since high school," he pointed out. "When I got into UT and she picked SMU we just shook hands and went our own way."

Amber shrugged. "Hey, you don't have to bare your heart to me," she said. "I couldn't care one way or another."

"Well, you should care," Brent said. "Lissa was your friend since third grade. She stuck with you long after you drifted away from the rest of us. She went racing to the hospital when Jet was born. She got us all together for that big baby shower. Now you can't even be bothered to talk to her."

"I guess she and I have gone our separate ways as well," Amber told him.

"Okay, but that doesn't mean you can't still be interested," he said.

"All right, all right. I can be interested," Amber said. "So how's she doing these days?"

Brent grinned as if he'd just won a big coup. "She's great. She's going to summer school this year, hoping to finish by December."

"Oh?"

"She's engaged to a really swell guy," he said. "They've set the date for March."

The bitterness that swept Amber was surprising, even to herself. Lissa was sweet and generous and fun. She'd never, by word or deed, ever been anything but good to Amber. Still, the prospect of her happiness evoked only jealousy and resentment.

"I wish her all the best," Amber insisted. "I just hope that when the whole world doesn't just fall down and worship her, she'll be able to cope."

Brent's brow furrowed. "Oh, I think she'll be fine," he said. "I'm just wondering if you will."

Before Amber could respond, Wilma was at the door and Brent jumped up to help her. She carried a tray with four cups of coffee, three were mismatched stoneware mugs, the forth a plastic rabbit with ears that folded into a handle.

"You brought coffee for Jet?"

"It's mostly milk," Wilma assured her. "I used to make it for you when you were little, remember?"

Amber nodded. "Mom didn't approve."

"I'm sure it's not something recommended in the baby books," Wilma admitted. "When I was growing up they said that if you drink coffee it will make you black. So people are probably going to accuse Jet of it anyway."

Brent laughed.

Amber did, too.

"I wish Mom could have heard you say that," she said. "That kind of talk drives Ellen crazy."

The explanation was directed toward Brent.

"Really?" he seemed surprised. "I always thought she had such a great attitude about life."

"Well, that was then," Amber said without clarification.

To Amber's taste, the coffee was nothing but ordinary. Brent talked as if it were the best he'd ever tasted. He *ummmed* and *ooooed* until Wilma was laughing.

"Reminds me of my mother's cooking," he told her.

"Your mother is the worst cook in this town," Amber pointed out.

"I know," he said. "And, Wilma, you are definitely a close second."

"I'm glad you came by, Brent," Wilma said. "I've got a legal problem that I may need your help with."

Brent shook his head and chuckled.

"I'm not a lawyer, Wilma," he told her. "I'm not even a law student. I just get the right sets of papers together. I don't begin to understand all that they mean."

Wilma gave him a little half smile.

"I'm not asking you to play Perry Mason," she assured him. "In fact, what I really need is Sam Spade. My stepchildren are trying to take my house away from me. You just nose around downtown and see what you can find out."

5

Ellen visited legal aid, played phone tag with her former friends and scoured the Yellow Pages to find a lawyer to take on her mother's case. As she predicted, the kids at legal aid were too intimidated by the prospect of Pressman, Yaffe and Escudero. And the more seasoned attorneys weren't interested in Ellen's virtual inability to pay.

Miraculously she was contacted by a lawyer whose office was just a few blocks from Roper's Accounting. He'd heard that she was looking for representation and agreed to accept a very modest fee.

Ellen was surprised but, after seeing his office, figured that he had fallen upon some very hard times.

His name was Marvin Dix. He was short, fast talking and with eyes that seemed to pick up everything. He had the hair-gel pompadour of an evangelist, but the gentle, concerned demeanor of a country parson. He assured Ellen, with utmost sincerity that his only interest was in trying to help her.

"Pressman, Yaffe and Escudero don't scare me," he boasted. "I've forgot more legal maneuvers than that whole law office ever knew."

"You have some idea of how you're going to contest this?" Ellen asked. "Can't we make some kind of deal with the family?" Ellen asked. "We could come up with some kind of compromise."

"Absolutely," Dix said. "I'm definitely going to appeal to their common decency and ask that they not throw your mother out on the street."

Ellen swallowed. "I don't know how far you'll get with that," she said. "Wilma has made no secret of her lack of regard for them. And she's made catty comments about their parents as well. I think they honestly believe that she not only married Wilbur Post to get control of his property, but that the marriage probably hastened his death."

"Is any of that true?" Dix asked.

"The last part is total nonsense," Ellen assured him. "The guy was on death's door when Wilma met him. Her care probably kept him alive longer."

Dix nodded with furrowed brow concern.

"The truth is often the first victim of the court system," he said. "The fact that Wilma was only married to Mr. Post for twenty-two months makes a very compelling case for validating the will."

"But marriage is marriage," Ellen pointed out. "Whether it's twenty-two months or twenty-two years."

"Yes," Dix agreed. "But even if it were twenty-two years, that's less than half of the forty-seven he shared with his first wife."

Ellen couldn't argue that. "They are sure to bring up Wilma's track record," she told Dix. "I don't think even *she* is sure how many marriages she's had."

Dix was thoughtful. "Yes," he said. "They'll try to make it look as if she preys upon lonely old men."

"That's simply not true," Ellen stated emphatically. "Wilma is a lot of things, but I'm convinced that she managed to be in love with every man she ever said 'I do' with.''

"I'm sure you're right," he said. "But being right doesn't change the way they will make things look."

"So what's next?" Ellen asked him. "Do you know what you're going to do?"

"Not yet," he admitted. "Not off the top of my head. But there are ways...there are always ways. And I'm the kind of fellow that can always come up with something."

Ellen didn't find his confidence particularly reassuring.

"We'll have to have more than just *something*," she told him. "We can't afford to be fighting this over and over. We need it settled and we need it settled for good."

He smiled at that. As if she'd finally said something that he could really work with.

From his desk drawer, he brought out an agreement for her to sign. Ellen glanced through it for a couple of moments. It must be some kind of a boilerplate, she thought. Most of it didn't apply to her particular circumstances, but, still, it made her somewhat uneasy. Purposely she shrugged it off. If you couldn't trust your own lawyer, who could you trust? She signed and she wrote him a check for fifty dollars up front and agreed to pay the rest of the modest fee upon resolution of the case.

It was almost too good to be true. Ellen left his sad little office with her head high. Martin Dix was the first good news she'd had since they'd received the letter.

As she walked back toward Roper's, she caught sight of Mrs. Stanhope hurrying down the street. Eyes straight ahead, a determined look on her face. The woman was off on some quest which might, or might not, be based on reality.

There was only an instant of hesitation before Ellen crossed the street to meet up with her.

Why isn't somebody taking care of this woman? What's the deal with her niece? She questioned heaven accusingly.

"Mrs. Stanhope," Ellen called out. "Mrs. Stanhope, wait."

The woman stopped and turned.

"Miriam?" Her tone was tentative.

"Violet," Ellen answered.

The woman's expression was incredulous. "The only Violet I know is Violet Mercer and she's been dead for twenty years at least."

"Actually, I'm Ellen," she corrected.

"Then why on earth did you say you were Violet?"

"Last time we met, you thought I was Violet," Ellen told her.

Mrs. Stanhope raised an eyebrow. "We've met?"

"Yes...ah...we had lunch together...at Helgalita's."

She looked vague, but then nodded tentatively. "Oh, yes, I think I remember," she said. "You walked me home."

"Yes, I did, that's right."

"It wasn't one of my better days," Mrs. Stanhope said. "I have good days and not so good days. I remember it, but it wasn't one of my better days."

"No," Ellen agreed. "It wasn't one of your better days."

There was a moment of uncomfortable silence between them.

"So where are you headed?"

The question seemed to surprise the woman. "Now?"

"Yes."

Mrs. Stanhope turned to look down the street. "I was…I was…" Her hesitation was accompanied by a look of dismay and a light self-conscious laugh. "Well, I was certainly headed somewhere," she said. "But where or why has completely gone out of my head."

The woman was obviously embarrassed and Ellen was embarrassed for her.

"Would you like me to walk you home?" Ellen asked.

"Oh, no," she answered. "I can get home." As if to prove it she pointed in the right direction. "Is there someplace around here where we can get a cup of coffee?"

The only place that was really close was Helgalita's. Ellen wasn't sure if she should take Mrs. Stanhope there—perhaps the place would set her off. Ellen knew nothing about old age, Alzheimer's, dementia. Perhaps the sight of her husband's former business drove her off the deep end. Ellen didn't know, but she didn't want to risk it.

"Come into my office," she said. "I was just about to get a cup of coffee myself."

Together they walked the rest of the way to Roper's.

"Oh…oh," the woman hesitated uncertainly. "Is this *your* office?"

"Well, I work here," Ellen told her. "Please come in. The coffee's not the greatest, but the price is right."

Ellen held the door as Mrs. Stanhope stepped inside, her curiosity overcoming her reticence.

Yolanda was standing at the counter, her eyes wide as a deer in the headlights.

"This is Yolanda, our office manager," Ellen said by way of introduction. "Do you know Mrs. Stanhope?"

"Uh…yeah, I mean, uh…hi."

Behind the woman's back Yolanda gave Ellen a sort of frantic, incredulous expression.

"Mrs. Stanhope came downtown for a cup of coffee," Ellen said. "I thought she could have one here with us."

"Yeah, sure," Yolanda said, still looking ill at ease. "Let me brew up a fresh pot."

"Don't go to any trouble," Mrs. Stanhope protested.

"It's no trouble, really. I was going to do it anyway."

Yolanda shot a glance into Max's office. Ellen was surprised that he was still in there. Rarely did anyone drop by the place that he didn't venture out to meet or greet, shake hands and pass the time of day.

"Come on in here," Ellen said. "This is my office. Have a seat."

Yolanda didn't voice the words, but Ellen could hear the question, *what are you doing?*

In all honesty, Ellen was asking herself the same thing. The last thing in the world she needed was another person to take care of. But the women obviously needed more attention than she was getting from her niece. And she had simply fallen into Ellen's lap. She hadn't volunteered, but she couldn't just ignore her.

Mrs. Stanhope sat in the client chair and Ellen

seated herself behind her desk. It looked like an ordinary consultation. But it felt entirely different.

The phone was ringing, but Yolanda ignored it, bringing them coffee instead.

"Cream and sugar?" she asked Mrs. Stanhope.

"Black," she answered. "Perfectly black."

Yolanda set the coffee down in front of her and handed Ellen her own.

"I'll just shut this door," she said. "Give you two ladies some privacy."

She mouthed the words "good luck" to Ellen as she shut them in the tiny, windowless space. Yolanda's attitude annoyed her. Mrs. Stanhope obviously suffered from Alzheimer's or senility or something equally distressing. It was unfair that she be treated as if she were contagious.

"I remember the man who used to work here," the woman said. "He did some work for my husband. Max Roper was his name."

Ellen was surprised. Mrs. Stanhope had seemed so out of it the other day, now she was just a regular, reasonable person.

"It still is his business," Ellen told her. "Max is right in the next office. Would you like to speak to him?"

"Speak to him?" the woman appeared clearly horrified. "Oh, no. I couldn't speak to him. I didn't know the man socially. He was a business associate of my husband."

"Of course."

"I never blamed him," Mrs. Stanhope said. "Some may have, but I never blamed him at all."

Ellen had no idea what to say about that.

The woman took a sip from her cup. "This is very good coffee," she said. "Very good."

"Yes, it's fine," Ellen agreed.

"And now you work here," Mrs. Stanhope said. "An accountant. I always thought that would be a man's job."

"Well, I'm not really an accountant," Ellen admitted. "I'm an accounting clerk. My husband was an accountant. I used to work for him."

Mrs. Stanhope's face took on almost a radiant look and she sighed. "Oh, how nice for you," she said. "When I was first married, Lyman allowed me to help out in the store. It was the nicest time I ever had. Just being with him all day."

Ellen smiled. She remembered that sense of camaraderie as well.

"Yes, I enjoyed it a lot myself," she said. "I quit when my daughter was born. If it hadn't been for her, I might have stayed on."

"Lyman and I never had children," she said, sadly.

"But you quit working anyway."

"Oh, I had to, dear," she said. "My parents didn't approve at all."

"They didn't want you working?"

"No indeed," she said. "My father was a professional man. No wife of his could even keep her own house, there were 'servants for that sort of thing,' he said." She chuckled lightly, looking somewhat mischievous. "When Papa heard that I was actually waiting upon people in the store, he was appalled. Lyman tried to reason with him. He worked the till himself, never soiling me with the handling of money. But it made no difference. Papa thought it was beneath his daughter. And faulted Lyman as a husband for that cause."

"I'm sorry."

"I am, too," she said. "I enjoyed it so much. And maybe if I'd stayed…maybe if I'd have been able to help…"

Her voice trailed off into nothingness, as if she had gone very, very far away.

Ellen waited, uncomfortable. She didn't know if it was better to let the woman ruminate or to call her back into the here and now. Finally she decided upon the latter course.

"I'm a widow, too," Ellen told her.

Mrs. Stanhope looked surprised and then concerned.

"Oh, my dear, I'm so sorry. How long has it been?"

"Five years," Ellen answered.

"Five years," Mrs. Stanhope repeated. "I'm sure it seems like yesterday."

Ellen nodded. In some ways it certainly did. But in others, it was as if it had been a lifetime.

"How did you meet him?" Mrs. Stanhope asked.

"We met in college," she told the woman. "We had a class together. After about the third day he moved to the desk beside mine. He said that it was the best seat in the house. He could copy off my answer sheets and admire my legs at the same time!"

It had been so long since Ellen had thought about that time. She laughed, unexpectedly, just recalling the memory.

Mrs. Stanhope laughed with her.

They spent the next few moments sharing courting stories. Mrs. Stanhope's included a debutante ball and an unworthy suitor. Ellen's was more nondescript with study dates and pizza parlors. It was wonderful reliving those times, when they were young and so much in love.

As the conversation lingered, the differences between those days and these drifted into her thoughts. The contrasts stung as sharply as if the pain were new.

Ellen changed the subject.

"The weather has been so mild the last few days," she said. "Have you been sitting out in your garden any?"

"My garden?"

"Yes," Ellen said. "You have a beautiful garden."

"Yes, I sit out there sometimes in the mornings," Mrs. Stanhope said. "Mornings are my best times."

"Mine, too," Ellen told her. "I'm really a morning person."

"The mornings are mostly like today," the older woman said. "In the mornings I can almost see myself. But then...you know...it fades and I'm...I'm lost."

She turned to look directly at Ellen. Her gaze was so intense and there was such a depth of sorrow that Ellen was momentarily taken aback.

"Mrs. Stanhope, are you all right?"

"I think I want to go home now," she said. "I've had my coffee and I think I want to go home. Can you call my niece, Irma?"

"I'll walk you," Ellen said.

"I hate to impose."

"It's no imposition," Ellen said. "And you know how Irma hates to be bothered while she's working."

"Yes...yes, that's right," she agreed.

Just as they stood up, there was a light tap on the door. Yolanda peeked inside.

"Mrs. Stanhope, your niece is here," she said.

Ellen's jaw dropped open in surprise. How on earth had the woman found her?

Mrs. Stanhope's reaction was decidedly more positive.

"Oh, how convenient!" she said, turning to smile at Ellen. She seemed immediately more lively and gave a lighthearted, almost girlish, giggle.

As they stepped out into the main office area, Irma gave Ellen a very disapproving, almost resentful look. As if somehow, it were her fault that Mrs. Stanhope had managed to get downtown on her own.

Ellen was equally cool in response, wanting to convey the notion that if Irma had been paying appropriate attention, Mrs. Stanhope wouldn't currently be standing in the office of the Cowboy of Taxes.

The older woman missed all these unpleasant, unspoken undercurrents completely. She was delightfully animated.

"Irma, I'm so glad you're here," she said. "I have so much to do today and I fear I've frittered away half the morning here gossiping. I'm prone to it, you know. Papa always said I was the most loquacious of all his girls. Do you know my friend?" she asked, indicating Ellen. "This is—" She stopped in midsentence. "Good Lord, I've forgotten your name."

"Ellen."

"Ellen? No, that's not it. I don't know anyone named Ellen."

"We need to get you home now," Irma interrupted. "It's time for your nap."

"All right," Mrs. Stanhope said. "But first we must

stop by the store. Lyman had already left for work when I got down to breakfast and I have to tell him about the dinner party at the Gleichmans. If I don't remind him, he'll work late and we'll not get seated until the middle of the entrée."

Mrs. Stanhope laughed at that statement as if it were a great joke. And amazingly, Irma joined her.

"Goodbye, dear," she said to Ellen. "The coffee was lovely and you really must come some Sunday afternoon for tea. Bring Sis and Willy and they can amuse themselves in the yard."

As they made their way out, Mrs. Stanhope questioned Irma. "Do you have any idea what has happened with all my coats?"

Ellen stared after them and shook her head. Mrs. Stanhope had been just fine. And then she wasn't.

"How did that woman find her here?" she asked, mostly to herself.

Yolanda answered. "Oh, I called her."

"What?"

"I knew you were in way over your head," she said. "And anytime we see her on the loose, we call for Irma to come pick her up."

"Is that necessary? She seemed to be doing fine before that woman showed up."

"She's a real loony," Yolanda said. "You never know what she'll be doing next."

Ellen was surprised at Yolanda's lack of empathy for the woman.

"It's not her fault, you know," Ellen told her. "Alzheimer's or senility or whatever it is, just happens to people."

Yolanda lowered her chin to eye Ellen over the top of her glasses.

"It does, but this lady's problem isn't old age," she replied. "She's been the local crazy lady since I was a little girl."

The car was in desperate need of an oil change. The man who did it so inexpensively for Ellen, was only available after six—when he got home from his real job. Ellen called Amber to ask her to go straight home, to relieve Wilma and see that Jet got supper and a bath.

Amber groused to her mother about it, but that was only by habit. In truth, she didn't mind spending an evening at home with Jet. The bar scene might be flashy and loud. But like any routine, a constant diet could get a little boring.

She was certainly needed. By the time she walked into the house, it looked as if Jet was taking care of Wilma, rather than the reverse. Her grandmother was lying on the living room couch, taking oxygen.

"Are you all right?" Amber asked her.

"Just trying to catch my breath," Wilma assured her and waved her off.

"Come on, Jet," Amber said. "Let's see what we can come up with for supper."

Her daughter trailed after her excitedly.

"Are you going to be here all evening, Mama?" Jet asked.

"Sure."

"Even after we have dinner?"

"Yes."

"Then are you going to give me a bath and read to me and put me to bed?"

"Yes, Jet," Amber answered, almost annoyed.

Her daughter was so clearly delighted to have

Mama all to herself, it made Amber feel strangely guilty for all the nights she spent away. Which was stupid, Amber assured herself. With Ellen and Wilma showering her with attention every minute, Jet didn't need anyone else.

In the kitchen, Amber opened the refrigerator and sighed heavily.

Checking out Wilma's fridge was no easy task. As always, it was crammed so full that the light could barely illuminate the contents, dozens of little plastic bags containing crooked neck squash, snow peas, endive and broccoli.

Amber dragged the trash can over to hold the door open and got down on her knees and began to weed out the oldest layer pushed far to the back. Most of it was still edible, though it was less than prime. She came across a bunch of bearded asparagus or some blackened cabbage slowly turning to soup. For a family near destitution, they certainly wasted a lot of good food.

Practically all of Wilma's social security check went to buy groceries. But since nobody really cooked, they probably didn't eat any better than those people who didn't know bib lettuce from kale. That was always the way it had been at Wilma's house. But it was getting worse.

"What are we going to cook, Mama?" Jet asked.

"We've certainly got plenty to choose from," Amber said. "How would you feel about a big salad?"

Jet frowned a little. "I kind of had a big salad for lunch," she said.

"Okay," Amber said. "What would you like?"

"I could eat the corn," Jet said. "And I like spinach."

"Corn and spinach it is then," Amber said.

"Remember sometimes, Mama, when you'd fix me macaroni and cheese from a box," Jet said.

"Sure, I remember," Amber answered.

"Gramma says it's no good, but I really like it," Jet said.

Amber grinned at her as if they were two wily schemers, plotting against a common enemy.

"If I can find a box, Jet Jameson, you can have it for supper," Amber told her.

It took a bit of doing and a number of pans, but a lovely meal of corn, spinach and boxed mac and cheese made it to the dining room table. By then Wilma felt well enough to join them.

Jet was in high spirits clearly enjoying herself. And they lingered long at the table before Jet's bath.

"You clean up the dishes, I'll clean up the baby," Wilma told her.

"Are you sure you're not too tired?"

Wilma shook her head. "She does most of it herself."

Jet nodded.

It didn't take long to get the kitchen in order. Amber was just hanging up the dish towel when the sound of happy running feet could be heard coming down the hallway. Jet came charging into the kitchen, bright eyed and full of natural energy and exuberance.

"I'm all clean and scrubbed," she announced proudly.

She was wearing her bunny pajamas and the plush, black on white Holstein-like bedroom slippers she referred to as her "cow-shoes."

"Great," Amber praised.

"Smell me," Jet said, offering her wrist.

Amber dutifully sniffed the fragrance on the child's arm.

"Oooo, very nice," Amber told her.

"It's strawberry," Jet said. "Wil-ma gave it to me, strawberry bubbles."

Amber smiled at her. She was such a good kid, so easy to please. And so grateful for any little gift, even the kind that most kids her age would have taken for granted. Maybe that was the upside of growing up on the edge. With all the people around her that were crazy about her, Jet had somehow never gotten spoiled.

"Where is Wil-ma?" Amber asked her.

"She went to sit on the porch," Jet answered. "She's having a nicker-teen fit."

The last, said with great solemnity, was undoubtedly a quote.

"Come on," Amber told her. "Let's get your hair done and get ready for bed."

"Okay," she said, scampering off. "Meet ya in the rocking chair."

By the time Amber made it there, Jet was already waiting for her, comb, brush and storybook in hand.

"What are we reading tonight?" Amber asked.

"*Gus and Button*," the child replied, indicating the brightly colored story about the adventures of a spunky little mushroom in a vegetable world. "It's my favorite."

"I thought *Goodnight Moon* was your favorite," Amber said.

"It's my going to sleep favorite," Jet explained. "*Gus and Button* is my getting braided favorite."

"Ahh," Amber responded, as if that cleared up everything. "So you like vegetables?"

Jet nodded eagerly.

Amber grinned at her. "You take after your Grandma Wilma," she told her.

"No," Jet insisted. "Wil-ma takes after me!"

Amber laughed as she seated herself in the bentwood rocker that had been a nursery gift. It now held a prominent place in the living room decor. Jet scrambled onto her lap.

"We'll take turns," Amber told her. "You read it first."

Jet, of course, could not read. But she knew the story pretty well and in an expressive and dramatic voice mimicked the tale as she turned the pages.

Amber had her hands full, sectioning Jet's dark hair and braiding it into a half-dozen little pigtails. Her experience with her own thin, stick-straight tresses had not prepared her for the thick, natural curls of her daughter. But she'd discovered, by trial and error, as well as questions at the beauty supply store, that a little moisturizer and braiding before bed kept it in control. Still it occasionally got napped up and tangled. Jet was brave and stoic, but Amber would do almost anything not to hurt her. Amber knew that she had already caused enough pain for everybody.

She'd started off in motherhood on the wrong foot. She had known all about birth control. She hadn't bothered to use it. Not that she deliberately tried to get pregnant. But she didn't try very hard not to.

Having a baby had been unplanned. Getting pregnant, however, had been something she used as a weapon.

Her dad had died and Amber had never felt so

alone. Yet, she found her mother's closeness stifling. Ellen wanted to hold her, comfort her, support her. Amber just wanted to get away, put it all behind her. She wanted to just forget about her parents—the living and the dead.

But a grieving soul couldn't live without connection. So one night in a dimly lit bar she'd connected up with Chris, a man as heartbroken as she herself. Chris's wife had been unfaithful. She was sorry, repentant, pleading for another chance. He wasn't sure if he could forgive her or even if he could live in the same house with her, or the same town with her.

Down from Dallas, as far in the depths as a man could go, he and Amber had shared their misery. Offered comfort to each other. Gave voice to the unutterable cry of pain with the honesty that one could offer to a stranger. It was a week of commiseration, soul sharing and sex. Then one morning Chris woke up and decided to go home.

"I still love her," he told Amber. "I still love her and I guess…I guess now she and I are even."

She hadn't asked for his phone number, not even for his last name. He was going back to his life and she needed to forget him and pick up the pieces of her own.

With a sharp intake of breath, the adventures of Gus and Button stopped abruptly as the comb caught in a snarl.

"Ooo, I'm sorry," Amber told her daughter as she clasped the hair above the tangle to try to ease it through without pulling.

Jet scrunched up her narrow little shoulders and held herself stiff, braced against the discomfort of hair care.

"I'm almost done," she promised.

"It's okay," Jet assured her, in her small, brave voice.

It took her a moment to smooth the mat out. As soon as she did, the little girl went back to her *reading*. Amber started plaiting the last pigtail.

Ellen was actually better at this than Amber. Ellen had taken on the task of raising Jet as if it were a new lease on life. Amber loved her child, but she just sort of stumbled through motherhood, leaving the big decisions to her own mother, and then resenting Ellen for making them. "All done," she announced and laid the comb on the nearby table.

"Yea!" Jet cheered.

She handed the book to Amber. "Now, it's your turn," she said.

Like warm butter, the child melted back onto her chest, finding just the perfect spot to rest her head and still see the pictures. The warmth, the touch, just the sweet smell of this little child made all the troubles of the world seem light. Amber may have screwed up her life, big time, but she had no regrets about having Jet.

She opened the book. "Waiting at the window for the whirling storm to stop," she began the story.

Jet was yawning before Belle, Pip and Cecil led Gus past the celery stalk temple.

6

Jet was singing to herself as Wilma cleared the bowl of mostly eaten cereal from the table in front of her.

"When's my birthday, Wil-ma?" she asked.

"In a few weeks," the older woman answered.

"Will I have cake and candles and presents?" The child's eyes were wide with the possibility.

"Absolutely," Wilma assured her. "It wouldn't be a real birthday without them."

Jet seemed reassured by that statement.

"Right now I need you to fend for yourself for a few minutes."

The little girl nodded solemnly. "Do you want your *ox-a-jim?*" Jet asked, worried. "I can roll it here for you."

"No honey," she assured the little girl. "I'm just going to use the phone. You stay kind of quiet and play with your pretties."

"Okay," she answered. "Sheila and me are gonna read the newspaper."

The child got down on the floor and propped the doll against the edge of the couch. She spread the *Express-News* out on the floor and carefully began to turn the large pages as she looked at the photographs and made up stories to tell about them.

Wilma smiled at her. Jet was such a happy, easygoing little girl. Obviously somebody had done something right. Wilma supposed that Ellen should get the credit.

Somehow Ellen had taken on Jet as if she were her own daughter, not Amber's. Stranger still, Amber seemed content to let her do it. Amber, who resented her mother inexplicably, and wouldn't have happily shared much of anything with her, had given over her only child almost completely. It didn't make sense to Wilma. But to be absolutely truthful, not very much that either of those two women did made much sense to her.

Ellen had always worked harder than any reasonable woman should ever aspire to. She'd lived a straitlaced, narrow, boring existence. Paul Jameson had been a nice man, but he couldn't have scared up any excitement in a Halloween costume. Poor Ellen had struggled through years of physical drudgery and emotional upheaval to take care of him. And now that her burden was finally lifted, was she out celebrating, having a good time? No, she missed the guy. She was pining after him.

And Amber, in her own way, was just as foolish. A bright, pretty girl with plenty of chances to go off to college, have fun and do all the wild, regrettable things that the young are famous for, had chosen instead to saddle herself with a child whose father she didn't seem to have any interest in. She had condemned herself to a dead-end job and a seemingly endless list of loser boyfriends. If she hadn't wanted college, Wilma could have understood. But she *had* wanted it very much. For most of her girlhood it had been all she'd talked about. And if she didn't believe in abortion, fine. Wilma would never have pushed her into having one. But what about all those loving, deserving, childless couples who would have been thrilled with such a pretty, sweet child as Jet. Amber had insisted on keeping the child. Yet, she treated her daughter more like a sister, and left all the real meat of motherhood to Ellen.

No, these women didn't make any sense to Wilma, even if they were her own flesh and blood.

By the time she got to the telephone, Wilma decided to take up Jet's suggestion and dragged her oxygen tank over beside her. She hated to admit it, but she was clearly getting worse.

It wasn't exactly a surprise. The best hope the doctor had offered was that if she quit smoking and took care of herself, she might halt the progression of the disease. Since she hadn't made much effort to give up the cigarettes, she could hardly expect anything else. She had always been accustomed to ignoring the advice of others.

Damn the torpedoes, full speed ahead wasn't just a familiar line from an old war movie, it had long ago become a kind of life motto for Wilma. When life and circumstance got in her way, she just pushed on through in her own indomitable style. When life gave her lemons, she didn't just make lemonade, she'd distilled it into lemon saki and drank to intoxication.

With that idea held firmly in mind she fitted the clear plastic tubes against her nose and turned on the valve on the tank before dialing the number of the accounting office. If Ellen answered, she'd pretend some errand or such. No need for any elaborate plan. Ellen never seemed to have a clue about deception.

She'd talked with Yolanda a couple of times. She knew the woman's modus operandi. Wilma was not above giving her a healthy dose of her own medicine. For a good cause, of course.

The phone rang only twice.

"Roper Accounting, we're the Cowboys of Taxes."

"Is this Yolanda? Yolanda Ruiz?"

"Yes, it is."

"Hi, Yolanda, I'm so glad I caught you. It's been such a day and I've had so much to do and I didn't know if I would get a chance to call but Mildred said I should and so I did, but I won't keep you if you're busy or going out or on another line or anything like that, because I know you're working and I've got a million things to do myself. Can you talk?"

"I...ah...yes...of course, I..."

"Oh, good, well Mildred didn't know much, but she assured me that you had the scoop, the whole scoop, and nothing but the scoop. And I just have to know. Not for myself, of course, but for my friend. You know her, but well, I'm not at liberty to say. And you know me, I'm not one for gossip. Can't tolerate it one bit. It's a plague on the earth, but when friends are involved, well you have to find out. You wouldn't be a friend if you didn't. And, well, you simply have to do what you have to do. It's what I have to do and I have to count on someone. Can I count on you for that, Yolanda?"

"Uh...uh..."

"Can you fill me in? Don't tell me anything that I shouldn't know. And believe me everything said to me is held in confidence, the strictest confidence, my lips are sealed, I'll never breathe a word. But you're his secretary and if he's, well, if he's not at all what he claims to be, then you owe it to her, who is your friend after all, not to keep her in the dark. Isn't that right?"

"Ah...yes, of course."

Wilma smiled. Every secret was about to be revealed.

With only minimal prodding and twenty minutes of her time, Wilma got the goods on Max Roper.

So, on the plus side he'd been divorced for a couple of decades with no young children or ex-wives to support. His business was healthy and his modest Alta Vista home was free and clear. He kept working by choice and by habit. He even owned an acreage near Uvalde where he ran a few goats and cattle.

But there were problems, real problems. In his younger days he'd had quite a reputation as a rounder. Apparently, he had never had any preference for a decent, hardworking woman when there had been brassy, fast living gals available. He was also sixty-seven—a quarter of a century older than Ellen.

But age didn't have to be an obstacle. Wilma knew her daughter was far too decent to judge a man by his years. And for a man of sixty-seven, Ellen would be a young beauty.

But in all honesty, it didn't sound as if the two had one dad-gummed thing in common. In fact, Wilma thought she seemed much more suited to the old fellow than her daughter.

That thought stopped her in her tracks.

It was too late for her, she reminded herself. She was old. She was tired. She was sick.

Did a woman really ever get that old, that tired, that sick?

Well, maybe some women did. But Wilma had

spent an entire lifetime not being anything like *some women*.

She made her way to the bathroom and checked herself out in the mirror. It was bad, plenty bad. She was definitely a sixty-something with no makeup and a desperate need for hair color.

Wilma knelt on the bathroom floor, unhooked the childproof latch and rummaged through the unpleasant items that she kept under the sink. There were ten-year-old sanitary napkins, an economy-sized Polident, and a box of medicinal douche packets, a huge jar of menthol suave, a container of drain declogger and bottles of every possible type of bathroom cleanser. Amongst this bounty, near the back, Wilma found one faded yellow box of Lady Clairol Ash Blonde.

Momentarily, she wondered how much the chemicals had deteriorated or altered after years on the shelf. Then she shrugged.

"If my hair falls out," she mumbled to herself, "then I'll stay home."

She dug out her reading glasses for a refresher on the directions.

"What you doing, Wil-ma?" Jet asked.

"I'm going to color my hair," she answered. "You want to help me?"

The little girl nodded eagerly. Between the two of them, the process would take up the rest of the morning.

All in all, it worked out pretty well. It had been a while since Wilma had really dressed up. She felt better, younger, stronger, just surveying the result. As a young woman, she'd resembled the actress Lauren Bacall. She'd probably never get Bogie to whistle today, but, still, she was humming "In The Mood" by the time she was ready to go.

"You look pretty, Wil-ma," Jet told her.

"Thanks, sweetie," she replied. "You're a great little confidence builder."

"Are we going to the grocery store?"

"Better," Wilma told her. They were seated in the living room, watching the street.

"Here's Brent," Wilma told her.

The Chevy Tahoe pulled into the driveway. Brent got out and walked around the hood. He'd come straight from his job and was dressed handsomely in a suit and tie.

"Hi!" Jet called out and waved, excited to see him.

He made a giggle face at the child. When he caught sight of Wilma, he gave a resounding "Wow!"

"You looking marvelous," he said in his best Billy Crystal imitation.

"We colored the gray in her hair," Jet explained. "Not with crayons—with goopy stuff."

"Well the goopy stuff looks great."

"Thank you," Wilma told him. "Thanks for coming on such short notice."

The young man shrugged. "When a guy's got two gorgeous ladies to escort to lunch, he'd better not be late."

"Lunch?" The child's eyes turned wide and expectant.

"Where are we going?" Brent asked.

"The Empire Bar," she answered.

Brent's brow furrowed, curious. "Kind of a strange place to take a three-year-old for lunch," he said.

"You're absolutely right," Wilma agreed. "Why don't you just let me off outside and you can take Jet somewhere, just the two of you. Give you both a chance to bond."

"Bond?"

Wilma didn't begin to explain and Brent was wise enough not to question further. He drove her downtown and let her off at the curb in front of the Empire Bar, an old, seedy but highly touted San Antonio tradition.

"Be back here in one hour," Wilma told him. "Just double-park and wait. Don't come inside looking for me."

"Yes, ma'am," Brent agreed. "Let me get the tank out for you."

"I'm leaving it here," Wilma insisted.

The young man's puzzled expression turned to worry.

"Wilma, you might need it," he said.

She waved away his concern. "I can live an hour without the damn thing," she assured him. "It cramps my style."

Brent didn't look happy, but he didn't argue.

"Okay, I get it," he said. "I know when I'm the third wheel. I'm leaving and I'm taking the little training wheel with me. We're going to McDonald's, so there. We'll be back at this spot at exactly one-twenty-eight."

As he drove off Wilma made her way to the front door. Chin high, shoulders back and a bright smile. This was how she'd won a hundred cowboy hearts.

The Empire had never been one of her hangouts, though she'd been inside many times. It looked much the same as it always had. Dark pine floors, beadboard ceiling with a half-dozen fans stirring a light breeze above the patrons seated at the long, heavy, brass and leather trimmed bar.

The last time Wilma had passed this way, it had been a place for serious, work-hardened drinking men to spend an honest dollar. Now a lighted salad bar stood where the shuffleboard table had been, and the tough experienced barmaids had been replaced by fresh-faced college kids in T-shirts and jeans.

Wilma seated herself at the very first bar stool. She fished a cigarette out of her purse as she surreptitiously checked out the other patrons.

"May I get you something to drink?"

Wilma looked up to find a pretty little blonde, probably no older than Amber.

"Give me a minute, honey," she told her. "I'm casing out the joint."

"I beg your pardon?"

"I'm trying to decide where I want to sit," Wilma explained.

The girl still didn't look like she understood, but she did walk away, giving Wilma a chance to check out the rest of the people in the place. There were thirtysomething bankers in conservative suits and exuberant tourists with maps and cameras. There was even a table full of secretaries having a birthday party. She didn't spot even one aging cowboy accountant with a turquoise bolo tie and boots.

She was beginning to think she'd made the effort for nothing, when a Stetson hanging on the hat rack above a very secluded back booth caught her attention. There was no way that she could assure herself of the identity of the person in that booth, without walking across the room. That hardly seemed to be worth the subterfuge. It was either him, or it wasn't. And he was definitely nowhere else.

Wilma got the waitress's attention.

"I'll take a Shiner Bock," she told her. "And I'll be seated in that back booth."

"Oh!" Now the young woman was very puzzled. "That table is already occupied."

"I know," Wilma said lowering her voice to a husky whisper and adding a bright smile. "Lucky fellow, I'm going to join him."

She made her way across the room, elegantly. Dredging up all the natural femme fatale that she'd kept in mothballs for so long.

I can do this, she assured herself silently. *I can do this.*

She kept at bay all thoughts of her age, her health and her track record. He was just a man, and if there was anything in the crazy world that she understood, it was men.

Wilma walked straight up to the booth, not stopping to observe its occupant until she was at the edge of the table.

This was Max Roper, she decided. This was definitely Max Roper. A big, long-limbed cowboy, thick white hair, fancy white dress shirt with snap flap pockets. Peering up at her through the top of bifocals was the most beautiful pair of true blue eyes that Wilma had ever seen in her life. It was easy to imagine that he'd been a rounder. What woman would have been able to resist him? She almost lost her nerve.

Then the moment was over. He suddenly seemed to realize where he was and that she was standing next to his table. The civilities of his upbringing came charging in upon him and he attempted to stand. A feat not easily accomplished in a narrow booth. He was momentarily awkward and clumsy.

Wilma relaxed.

"Keep your seat," she told him. "You don't mind if I join you."

She didn't frame her words as a question.

She seated herself opposite him. Withholding the smile that other women undoubtedly bestowed upon him so easily, she eyed him speculatively, as if she were taking his measure.

The waitress came.

"Here's your beer. Do you want some lunch?"

Wilma glanced at the man's plate. "What is he having?"

"He always orders the special," she replied.

Wilma raised a questioning eyebrow. "Really? A little boring, don't you think?" she asked him.

He shrugged. "I'm a boring guy," he answered.

She smiled at him—broadly.

"See, it's just like I told you," Wilma said to the waitress. "His lucky day."

Amber grabbed up her purse and hurried out to lunch before anyone had a chance to stop her. She'd asked for the time yesterday and mentioned it again this morning, but she didn't put it past Carly to come up with some excuse at the last minute to sabotage her plans. She was supposed to meet Gwen and Kayla at the Hole in the Wall for lunch and she could hardly wait.

She slipped out the mall's back doorway onto a brick-lined alley of little shops that catered to Alamo visitors. They sold papier-mâché armadillos, gaudy fake silver belt buckles and tiny ceramic replicas of the five Spanish Missions. Flags of Texas flew everywhere. They were a hot item. Amber always wondered what all those tourists from Wisconsin and Indiana did with their Texas flags when they got them home.

When Amber got to the street, she didn't wait for the light, but hurried across, dodging the slow moving downtown traffic. By the time she got to the café, her girlfriends had already snagged a table.

Amber waved at them, but stopped in the line in front of the order window.

"What's the soup?" she asked when it was her turn.

"Corn chowder."

Amber wrinkled her nose. "Then give me a turkey with avocado on seven grains, no mayonnaise or mustard."

"You want something to drink?" the guy asked as he wrote her request on a paper ticket.

"Water."

He rang it up on the register. "Two eighty-nine."

Amber had to count out the eighty-nine in change, using up her bus fare, but she wasn't going to worry about that now. She hurried over to her friends. They'd started lunch without her. Gwen was dawdling over a salad. Kayla was already finished, as evidenced by the abundance of empty plates stacked in front of her.

Amber seated herself, hanging her shoulder bag over the back of the chair.

"Hey, girlfriend," Gwen said. "You seem positively pumped to see us."

"I am," Amber told her. "It's a zoo at work. Must

be fiesta in Mexico or something, the place is swarming with Nationals."

Both her lunchmates made sympathetic noises.

Nationals, shopgirl slang for Mexican nationals, were the good news/bad news of San Antonio retail. Most visitors to the city from the contiguous forty-eight states were buying up Lone Star spoons, brightly colored tortilla warmers, or eclectic one of a kind craft articles. The middle class from south of the border wanted to shop in the mall. A Pennsylvanian could visit Gap or Victoria's Secret any time, but for the Mexican tourist these stores were unique, interesting and affordable. They kept mall retail healthy and growing. Unfortunately, they tended to arrive in mass on long weekends, holidays and school breaks, straining the workforce.

"You should call in sick tomorrow," Gwen suggested. "Let the other girls do it."

Amber shrugged off the suggestion. "Oh, I don't really mind," she said. "My commissions will be way up."

"I'm glad I don't get commissions," Kayla said. "Some days I feel so bummed I just sit at my desk faking it all day long."

"Let's not talk about work," Amber suggested. "How did it go with the flyboys?"

"Fine," Gwen answered. "But I'm sure you were right about that Jeff guy, real loser. And cheap, way too cheap. He didn't have a car and wasn't willing to spring for a motel. He tried to get me down on my knees behind some bush in the park. I've had enough of that kind of shit to last me a lifetime. That's why I like the guys I meet at my job. At least they all have a room!"

Gwen laughed delightedly at her own hotel humor. Kayla sighed heavily.

"Well, I really liked Brian," she admitted. "He was too sweet. And he really liked me, I'm sure of it."

"So are you going to see him again?" Amber asked her.

"I wish," she said. "He was only here for five weeks of special weapons training and we met them on their very last night in town."

"You are kidding?" Amber said.

"It was so totally awful," Kayla told them. "I was like fixing some breakfast for us, eggs and bacon even, and I go 'we are just great together' and he goes, 'yeah, but the timing is like all wrong for me and you know timing is everything.'"

"Timing *is* everything," Gwen agreed. "That's why he didn't say anything about how short-term he was until after you'd answered the booty call."

Kayla ignored that reality.

"He's already back in Biloxi," she continued. "And he expects to be deployed overseas in the next few months."

"Bummer," Amber commiserated.

"I'm so sick of having nothing work out," Kayla admitted.

"Oh, get over it!" Gwen complained. "Like men *ever* work out for anybody. It's a loser's game and if you let yourself get wrapped up in it, you're just a chump."

"I don't care about being a chump," Kayla said. "I'd just like…I'd just like a guy who was mine."

"Gag me!" Gwen exclaimed. "The next thing we know you'll be whining about a white dress and a veil. This is the new millennium, girlfriend. It just doesn't work out that way anymore."

Kayla looked so gloomy, that Amber felt sorry for her. Amber agreed with what Gwen was saying. She had yet to run into any guy who was looking for any happily-ever-after. But she also understood just exactly how Kayla felt. If she were being honest, she wanted the same thing for herself. A man who could love her and be devoted to her the way that her father had been devoted to her mom. That would be a pretty wonderful thing to have. But it wasn't realistic. Amber wanted to be realistic. But she wasn't sure that Kayla had to be.

The guy from the window called out her name and Amber hurried to get her food. When she returned to the table, she took the opportunity of the diversion to change the subject.

"I may be moving again," she said.

"You're kidding."

"Where?"

"I don't know yet," Amber told them. "My grandmother is being thrown out of her house by her stepchildren. If she goes, we go."

Amber took a bite of her sandwich.

"Can they just do that?" Kayla asked.

"If they've got money they can," Gwen replied for her. "If you've got money you can do anything. If you don't have money, anything can be done to you. It's a screw or be screwed world."

Amber hadn't reached her friend's stage of cynical.

"Ellen's got us a lawyer," she said. "She's trying to make the whole thing just not happen. She tells me not to worry, everything will work out, but Wilma, my grandmother, acts like it's a done deal. So, I don't know."

"I'd believe your mom," Kayla said. "I know she's like weird and all that, but she's really smart in a business sort of way. She knows how to do lots of stuff. It's probably just a matter of getting things straightened out. She can do that kind of thing. Your grandmother is like way old. What can she know?"

Amber shrugged. "Wilma's actually pretty cool. I suppose Ellen knows more about real estate and whatever, but she's…I don't know…she's just such a Goody Two-shoes. Her standard m.o. is the golden rule and she hasn't figured out yet that the rest of the world isn't up to the job."

"That's not a bad thing," Kayla said.

"It's not great," Amber told her. "Try to imagine being raised by Glenda, the Good Witch of the North! Believe me, growing up with that *always look on the bright side* crap can make you want to buy an automatic weapon and start taking hostages."

"Oh, she couldn't have been that bad," Kayla said.

"She was that bad," Amber assured her.

"How bad was she?" Gwen asked, like a comedian's response line.

"Okay, okay, let me think of something," Amber said, taking another bite of lunch and pondering her answer for a long moment.

"Okay, what do mom's tell you when you find a penny on the street?" Amber asked.

"That it's good luck," Kayla said.

"Only if it's head's up," Amber said. "Didn't your mother tell you that? Heads up."

Kayla and Gwen both nodded.

"Yeah, it's good luck if it's head's up," Gwen said.

"Is it bad luck if it's tails?" Amber asked.

The two girls looked at each other and shrugged.

"I don't think so," Gwen answered.

Amber nodded. "If it's tails up, it's just a penny. No luck attached at all and worth only one small cent in your pocket."

"So."

"So, from the time I was a little bitty girl, when I would find a penny and it was tails up, she wouldn't let me take it and put it in my pocket. Oh, no, she taught me to turn it over and make it lucky for some total stranger."

"You're kidding."

"Who would kid about weirdness like this?" Amber asked. "And there's more."

"No."

"Yes, to this day, if she drops change out of her purse she'll stoop down—not to pick it up, but to be sure that every coin is all heads up."

"That is like completely fried," Kayla said.

"Is there medication for something like that?" Gwen asked nastily.

"Maybe I should ask," Amber said. "Doctor? Is there a pill that will make my mother finally get it?"

"No such luck I'm sure," Kayla said.

"And for certain," Amber said. "Wilma's stepkids aren't going to look at that house as an ordinary penny to be turned over to bring luck to somebody else."

"It's too bad," Kayla said.

"No, wait," Gwen said. "I think this could be good. I think it could be really good."

Amber was incredulous. "Ah...right," she said, facetiously.

"No, I'm not kidding," Gwen went on. "This is what you need to get on with your life. You are so ready to get away from those women. I've been thinking about getting my own place. You know I'm sick to death of living with my loser family. I'm ready to get out, but I need a roommate to be able to afford it. And you need to get out and now this is a perfect opportunity...it's perfect."

Amber was immediately interested.

"Do you think we could afford an apartment together?" she asked.

"Of course we could," Gwen assured her. "I can almost afford one on my own. With your money too, we could practically live large."

Amber laughed. "I doubt that."

"Well," Gwen conceded. "We, for sure, could get us some kind of place. Between the two of us, we make more than Kayla, and she manages."

Amber nodded. "But we'd need a bigger place than hers."

"Yeah, well the two-bedroom apartments aren't that much more expensive."

"There's a two-bedroom for rent in my complex," Kayla told them excitedly. "It would be so cool if we all lived there near each other."

"My God, that would be even better," Gwen said. "We wouldn't have to take the bus, we could just come downtown with Kayla."

"I wouldn't even charge you for the gas," their friend assured them.

"What would it take for us to get into the place?" Gwen asked her.

Kayla was uncertain. "First and last month's rent, I guess, and probably a cleaning deposit."

"Damn, that's a wad of money," Gwen said and then glanced at Amber. "Do you have anything saved?"

"No, we've needed every dime I make just to get by," she answered.

"Well, I know a guy who might let me have it," Gwen said. "It's worth a try anyway. When can we look at the apartment? Can we go over there after work?"

"Sure," Kayla said.

Amber shook her head. "I'm going to be on the floor till eight."

"I might go look at it without you," Gwen said. "If I can get the money and the place looks good, why don't I go ahead and put down some cash on it."

Amber was startled. She felt like she was being rushed.

"I don't know, don't we need some time to think about it," she said. "We'll have to work out arrangements."

"What kind of arrangements?"

"For the kids," Amber said. "Who's going to take care of our kids?"

Gwen frowned at her. "The same people who are looking after them now," she said.

"But that means getting them up and dressed and to your mother's on the west side and wherever Ellen and Wilma are going to live."

"Amber, the kids aren't living with us."

"What?"

"We can't have the kids living with us," she repeated. "What would be the use of that? We'd be trapped in a couple of little rooms baby-sitting night and day. I'm moving out to get on with my life not to stop it in its tracks."

"I can't just leave Jet behind," Amber said.

"You're not leaving her behind," Gwen said. "She'll be with your mother. It's what's best for her. It's what's best for you. Don't let some guilt trip about motherhood cheat you out of your chance at having a life."

7

Ellen startled awake. She'd dreamed of Paul again. She'd dreamed of him sorting the laundry. It all seemed so ordinary, so unremarkable. He'd been talking to her, but she couldn't recall what he was saying. But she'd seen him, clearly, perfectly. She'd seen him as he'd been years ago, young, strong, healthy. She'd seen him separating the whites from the colors, turning his socks right side out. It was just Paul being Paul.

Except, of course, he was only a memory. Electrical impulses randomly flashing in her cerebral cortex. Through the dim gray light of early morning, she peered up at the urn that she'd left sitting on the chest of drawers like some decorator art piece. He wasn't Paul anymore.

Momentarily she closed her eyes and wished she was reduced to ashes in an urn. That finality, that peace, seemed infinitely preferable over the current state of her life.

With a deliberateness that was self-willed, Ellen tossed back the covers and rolled out of bed. She wasn't dead and she no longer even had the luxury to pretend to be.

She glanced at the clock at her bedside. 5:17 a.m. Not exactly wake up time, but she no longer wanted to sleep. She made her way to the toilet. At this hour of the morning at least there would be privacy. Four females sharing one bathroom didn't exactly promote family harmony.

"I know, I know," she whined a prayerful disclaimer toward heaven. "I should be glad we're not using a port-a-potty in the park."

She was glad. But not that much. The natural optimism, the exuberance for life, that had always been such a part of her personality now failed her. These days, she was faking it. She still talked as if the world was a fine and happy place. She still acted as if she believed that a benevolent God was in complete control. But there was a hollowness inside her that ached endlessly. That loss was more devastating than the house in Elm Creek or the business in the Bank One Tower. It was like Paul's death. Only it happened over and over again, day after day, an endless funeral of the soul.

Ellen brushed her teeth and washed her face. She stared at herself in the mirror. Looking…looking for evidence of change. She did look older. The years of splitting herself between being a full-time nurse and running a full-time business had taken their toll. She felt as if she'd struggled through a thousand years, but her eyes showed only the faintest trace of fortyish lines. Somehow it would seem more justified if her struggles and sorrows were immediately evident—if she could truly wear her grief like widow's weeds.

But people didn't do that anymore. In the new millennium red silk was proper graveside attire and friends sent sympathy cards with sentiment verging upon *Get Over It*. Just pick yourself up, dust yourself off, ad infinitum. Recovering from personal tragedy should be brief and out of public view—like taking the twelve steps at the Betty Ford Clinic.

Ellen was doing her best, but her heart wasn't in it.

It was Sunday, so she tiptoed into Amber and Jet's room and woke the child without her bothering her mother. It was nice, just the two of them, having breakfast, getting dressed in their best clothes, heading out to church.

She dropped Jet at her Sunday School class and went to her own Bible study group. They would reunite for the worship service in the sanctuary, eighth pew near the right side aisle.

Third Baptist was far from the largest in the city, but it was certainly big enough. There was seating for seven hundred and fifty, and on an average Sunday there were five hundred in attendance.

Third Baptist thought of itself as an inclusive church, a place of worship for all races and ethnic backgrounds. Its critics called it a "last chance home for Oreos and Éclairs." The congregation was made up, in large part, by refugees from other Baptist churches where they didn't quite fit in. There were blacks and Koreans and South American Protestants, mixes of people and marriages in every possible combination, lesbians and gays not low profile enough to go unnoticed in other congregations. And Baptist moderates, too left leaning for more mainline churches.

The pastor, Daniel Zambrano, a former Catholic priest, now a married minister with four children, was energetic, charismatic and ecumenical. Three-B Danny, he was irreverently nicknamed, but in the Christianity that he represented, everybody was welcome.

Ellen had made certain of that, for Jet's sake.

Perhaps most people sought spiritual enlightenment for their own betterment. Ellen's involvement with religion had been instigated mainly on behalf of someone else. When Amber was just a baby, Ellen had rationally concluded that regular church attendance should be included in the experience of the well brought up child. Her own background in that area was very sketchy. Twice a year, Christmas and Easter, Wilma had dressed her two kids in their holiday finery and trotted them off to the nearest house of worship. These biannual brushes with divine fire had been confusing and uncomfortable. Ellen didn't know the processions, procedures or the prayers. It was all strange and foreign. Added to that was the distinctly disconcerting feeling of being conspicuous. Not just because her family were virtual strangers, but also because Wilma, dressed to the nines, flirted outrageously with the ushers and sang all the songs in a deep throaty contralto that was more suited to the dancehall than the sanctuary.

For herself, Ellen would have allowed the earth to swallow her up before darkening the door on her own. But with the well-being of her daughter to consider, she'd gamely selected a congregation in her neighborhood and made sure that she and Paul were active participants. Over time, she'd simply been drawn in. She'd always believed in God rather tacitly, but as she became involved in the practice of worship, she'd somehow become a part of it. She couldn't point to a day or time and say, "that was the moment I became a person of faith." But it had happened and Ellen wasn't sorry.

Paul's death had tested her faith. But she still hung

on to it, whether by the strength of her conviction or simply force of habit, she couldn't say. She didn't know if God was leading her by the hand, but she was certain he was listening to her ceaseless complaints.

Ellen had just taken her seat when the organist began to play a rather jazzy version of *Savior Like A Shepherd Lead Us.* From the near side vestibule hall came a line of children dressed in paint-splattered white overalls. They all carried buckets and brushes.

Near the middle of the group came Jet, looking serious and determined. Her abundant black hair refusing the confinement of the painter's cap placed on her head. When she spied Ellen, her eyes lit up, but she didn't call out, wave, or even break ranks. A performance in front of the entire congregation was obviously a solemn undertaking.

The kids were lined up in two rows on the long steps below the chancel. Their teacher spaced them more evenly and whispered last minute advice as the music director took his place on the stage. He was a big, smiling, middle-aged black man with a resounding voice and a foot that was unceasingly tapping.

"We have a special treat this morning," he announced. "We'll open today's service with a song from our Three-and Four-Year-Olds Chorus under the direction of Miss Shawna Bagley. This is the youngest of our Children's Choirs and they've worked really hard on this. Let's give these little ones a Third Baptist welcome."

The congregation applauded wholeheartedly, though the three- and four-year-olds had yet to do anything but look adorable, which came naturally, of course. They were a postcard for ethnic diversity, a few pale blondes, a couple of Asians, black children, Hispanics and several, like Jet, who defied categorization.

Miss Bagley gave a few further instructions, quietly scolded the two boys on the end who were brandishing their paintbrushes as personal weapons. When she had their attention, she signaled the pianist.

God paints our world with the skies of blue
The green of earth
Yellow sunshine too
But God's favorite colors are me and you

Jet sang out strong and confident. She knew all the words as well as the movements and she effected them perfectly. Ellen felt a flush of pride. This wonderful child was as bright and endearing as her own little Amber had been.

It was amazing to her, how much the child had come to mean to her life. Of course, Ellen knew that grandmothering was a very special and highly valued gift. But Jet had become more than just a child to love totally and unconditionally. She'd become Ellen's avocation, her life's new work. It was the only part of her world that seemed to have reason and purpose, and certainly was the only part of her life that she could point to with joy and pride.

Jet had been a surprising gift. And one that Ellen never failed to thank God for. But she worried as well. And argued with Amber.

Her daughter flatly refused to acknowledge the exceptional challenges of rearing a biracial child. But Ellen blamed a lot of that on herself.

"Why didn't you tell me the baby was going to be

black?'' she'd asked her daughter in the hospital just hours after the child was born.

Amber shrugged.

"I didn't know for sure.''

"What do you mean by that?''

"Exactly what you think I mean,'' her daughter snapped back at her. Ellen had deliberately reined in her temper and attempted rational conversation.

"Well, now that you know, have you tried to contact the man? Is he going to take some responsibility for the child?''

"I can't contact him.''

"Why not?''

"'Cause I don't know his name, Mother,'' Amber answered with a sneer. "He was just some hot-looking black guy.''

"That's unbelievable.''

"I meet lots of guys,'' Amber said. "I don't remember them all.''

"He was black, didn't that catch your attention?''

"Not particularly,'' Amber answered. "Maybe if he'd had his name tattooed on his penis. You know all that talk about them being built bigger—it's a myth.''

"Amber!''

"Oh, sorry if I offended you, Mother,'' she said. "It's just…so easy.''

Ellen deliberately brought the discussion back to the subject at hand. "So the little girl is all ours,'' she said. "We'll have to do our best to make her comfortable in both cultures.''

Amber rolled her eyes. "Don't worry about that, everyone in the world is going to love Jet.''

"Jet? Is that what you've decided to call her?''

"Yeah," she answered. "That's her name."

"All right, then," Ellen said. "It's short, sweet. It's not a bad name. Both amber and jet are semiprecious stones. I guess that works."

"Maybe I didn't name her for a piece of jewelry," Amber said, nastily. "Maybe I named her after her dad."

"I thought you said you didn't remember anything about him?"

Amber's snide expression was full of hostile challenge. "I know he was jet-black."

Ellen had been stunned by her daughter's anger. And she'd understood, for the first time, that Amber's pregnancy was not really an accident. It was more like a cry of rage. And most of that was leveled squarely in Ellen's direction.

But Ellen was not particularly pleased with Amber either. She had wanted so much more for her only daughter. And it seemed as if Amber had settled for so much less.

The painting song ended and enthusiastic applause rang out. Miss Bagley turned and took a small bow and then directed the children safely down from the steps and into the congregation. They ran to their respective parents, eager, hopeful for that special, extraordinary praise that only a mommy or daddy was able to give.

Jet, of course, ran to Ellen.

"I did good," she announced as she reached her side.

Her grandmother agreed and gave the girl a big hug. "You were the very best," Ellen whispered. "Everyone was good, but you were the best."

Jet was deservedly delighted with herself as she seated herself in the pew.

She was well-behaved during the service, coloring the bulletin during the announcements and standing to sing during the hymns. She closed her eyes and held Ellen's hand during the prayers. Once the sermon began, she settled up next to her grandmother and took a nap. Ellen wrapped a protective arm around that warm little body and felt God's love with more certainty than she'd ever gotten from any bible verse or religious ritual.

Don't let anything bad happen to this child.

The prayer in her heart was more threat than entreaty. God hadn't healed Paul. He hadn't shielded Amber. If he didn't protect Jet…well, Ellen didn't know what she would do, but it wouldn't be good. She knew life held no guarantees, but she asked for them anyway.

It was a quarter to one before they arrived home.

Both Amber and Wilma were lounging around the living room. An old Cary Grant movie was being ignored on the television and somebody had been smoking inside the house. Ellen decided to ignore that. It was Sunday, after all, and she didn't want a fight. But the tightening in her own neck and shoulders told her one was brewing.

Jet went running to her mother, straightening her painter's cap on the way.

"I sang the painting song in big church," the little girl announced excitedly. "And everybody clapped and I didn't forget a thing and Gramma said I was the best one."

"It's nearly a quarter to one, you just now getting here?" Wilma asked.

Ellen didn't bother to answer.

"There's a hot dog and some chips in the kitchen," Amber told her daughter. "I knew you'd be hungry."

"Oh, boy!" the child said and hurried to find her lunch.

Ellen was critical. She knew she should keep her mouth shut. But she just couldn't seem to manage it.

"If you knew she'd be hungry, why didn't you fix her a decent meal instead of junk food? Do you know what they put into those hot dogs?"

Amber's response was equally faultfinding. "If you didn't find it necessary to go to that holy-roller, fire-and-brimstone church, you'd have gotten home in time to fix something for her yourself."

"We like the Baptist church," Ellen pointed out evenly.

"Catholics, Episcopals, even Methodists always manage to get out of church on time," Amber pointed out. "Those Baptists would keep you in the pew all day if they could."

"Jet loves this church," Ellen pointed out. "They have been very welcoming to her."

Amber snorted in disbelief.

"It's true," Ellen said. "Everybody smiles and waves at Jet. As one of the biracial children in the church she's a semicelebrity."

"And you think that's a good thing?" Amber asked.

Ellen wasn't honestly sure. Was it better to blend in and feel ordinary or to believe from the outset that you are unique?

"At least she's meeting other children," Ellen said.

"Yeah, and being accepted by them as a token," Amber replied. "All those nice little white children are going home and being patted on the head for their racial tolerance. How good they are to forgive her for the color of her skin. How nice they are to be friends with her, even if she's a child of color."

Ellen set her jaw tightly and tried to hold on to her temper. "Why do you persist in believing the worst of people?"

"Because it's most likely to be true," Amber answered with a sarcastic chuckle. "Baptist is a synonym for bigot, look it up in your thesaurus."

Ellen rolled her eyes before responding. "It's one of those weird inexplicably skewed perceptions that Baptists who happen to be African-American are considered fine, upstanding people, leaders in their communities. But white people with exactly the same beliefs are narrow-minded, ignorant, rednecks. What is that about?"

Amber didn't even attempt to justify her prejudice. "So you're going to raise Jet among the ignorant rednecks in the hope that she'll end up a leader in a black community."

"I'm just trying to give her a religious experience that isn't race based," Ellen said.

"Not race based?" Amber asked. "I'd say that race is pretty much all that congregation *is* based on."

"This is the best that I can figure out. What would you do?" Ellen challenged. "What's your plan to make a way for your daughter in this world?"

Amber's eyes narrowed. "I don't have a plan and Jet doesn't need a plan," she said. "Unlike you, I don't see field trips to the hood and instruction on homeboy culture as necessary. You're living in the past, Mother. By the time Jet grows up, half the country will be as multiracial as Tiger Woods."

"Well unless she turns out to be really good at golf, I doubt the other half will be all that accepting," Ellen said. "She's going to need to know who she is. She's going to need to know where she fits in."

"She fits in as my daughter," Amber insisted angrily. "She's not black. She's not white. She's not even biracial. I hate these stupid terms. She's just mine and that will be e-goddamned-nough!"

"It might be enough if you took any thought or interest whatsoever in her upbringing," Ellen said.

"Screw you."

"Don't you use that kind of talk in this house."

"It's not your house!"

"Stop it, both of you," Wilma intervened with a scolding whisper. "Do you think the child is deaf or that the kitchen is in the next building?"

Amber shrugged in that tough, *I don't care* manner that she effected so well. At least nothing more was said.

Ellen was genuinely contrite. She'd known when they'd walked in that Amber was itching for a fight. She should have avoided any kind of discussion at all. Certainly not one concerning Jet.

Wilma changed the subject.

"I hope while you were busy praying all morning you got around to asking God to find us a place to live."

"We don't need a place to live," Ellen said. "We're all settled in right here. I'm not letting anyone take this place away from you. I'll figure out a way to get around your stepchildren. This is Texas. People don't get thrown out on the street here."

Amber chuckled. "Yeah, they don't get thrown out, they just sort of ride off into the sunset."

Wilma thought that was pretty funny.

8

Amber was on the phone when, unexpectedly, Carly showed up at work. She considered pretending it was a business call, but decided she could never pull it off and why bother anyway.

"The place is dead this afternoon, but I've got to close so I won't be able to meet you until after eight."

"After eight is good," Gwen answered. "It's just going to be us."

"What's with Kayla?"

"You know she actually heard from Brian, that little shrimpy flyboy that she did a couple of weeks ago."

"No kidding?"

"Yeah," Gwen answered. "He like e-mailed her at work and now she hears from him every day."

"That's great," Amber said.

"Well, yeah, I guess," Gwen said. "But she is just totally into it and she doesn't want to do nothing. I go, 'hanging around your apartment waiting for him to come back this way, will get you nada and make you fat.' But she goes, 'I like him and he likes me. I just can't get psyched for going out.'"

"I get that," Amber said. "I mean I totally get it. Going out every night gets as boring as anything else."

"Yeah, well, her thing with this guy will just come to nothing," Gwen said. "Kayla will never see that loser again. He's just going to string her. And when she finally realizes that she's been played, you and I will have moved on and she'll have nobody to party with at all."

Amber hoped very much that Gwen was wrong.

She caught Carly's censoring glance from across the room and spoke more quietly into the telephone.

"The evil boss is giving me the eye," Amber whispered into the receiver.

"Oh, screw her," Gwen responded.

"She has no reason to get snippy with me," Amber said. "I'm completely caught up and, with Metsy and I both here, she doesn't even need to hang around."

"You should quit," Gwen told her. "Why waste your time selling panties. You hardly ever meet any guys there. And never any guys who are unattached. I'm sure I could get you a job here at the hotel. Wouldn't that be, like, so cool. We could work together."

Amber refrained from commenting. She didn't share her friend's enthusiasm. She liked retail and was not even slightly tempted by a hotel job. Deftly she changed the subject.

"What's happening with the apartment?" she asked Gwen.

"It's ready, and they are ready," her friend answered. "I can't keep stalling them forever. We've got to come up with the cleaning deposit. I think I can get that this weekend."

"Really?"

"Yeah, there's like a national dry cleaners convention at the hotel. Lots of old guys on the loose. I'll get somebody to party with and easily pick up a couple of hundred."

Amber hesitated momentarily. "You're joking, right?"

Gwen chuckled. "Oh, puh-leeze, Amber. Talk about your mother being an escapee from Goody-Two-shoes land. Get a grip, girl. When the weekend rolls around I'm going to end up having sex with some loser. It happens almost every weekend. I might as well know that up front. And if, once in a while, I bring home a few bucks instead of a broken heart, what-the-hell."

Amber had to admit, it sounded reasonable. But it was troubling, just the same.

"Have you told your mother about the apartment yet?" Gwen asked.

"No," Amber answered. "I was going to tell her yesterday, but she was late getting home from church and I was pissed off and started a fight. Stupid really, I don't know why I've got to fight over the same old things again and again."

"You just need to lose that woman. She's bringing you down," Gwen said, impatiently. "We've got to get going on this."

"I know," Amber agreed. "I just…I don't know…I hate to do it."

"Yeah, I know, there'll be a big blow up and lots of threats," Gwen said. "It was the same with my mother. She told me if I walked out now not to ever expect to get Dwight back."

"She said that."

"Yeah, but I just blew it off," Gwen said. "I told her she could have him. If I get to wanting a kid, I can always have another one."

"Oh, my God, you said that?"

"It's all bluff, Amber," Gwen said. "She doesn't want to be stuck with that flaky little brat any more than I do. She's just trying to control things. But I run my own life now. So she can just go screw herself."

Amber felt nauseated.

"I'm not sure I really want to give Jet up," she said.

"You're doing the best thing for her," Gwen insisted. "She'll have your mother and grandmother. She doesn't need you. And, for damn sure, you don't need her."

Carly walked by, her tone acerbic. "There are customers in the front, *if* you're not *too* busy."

Amber felt like making some rude comeback, but she didn't.

"I've got to go, Gwen," Amber said.

"Okay, see you at Durty Nellys a little after eight."

"Make it The Tunnel," Amber suggested. "If I'm going to be surrounded by tourists at least they won't be singing."

Gwen laughed and agreed.

Amber hung up the phone. She didn't so much as glance in Carly's direction, but she dutifully headed toward the front of the store. She heard the customers before she saw them. There was the tap of little feet and a delighted childish giggle.

Carly hated having kids in the store. They weren't really customers and they routinely made a mess of things.

Amber's perspective on it was a little different. The accompanying adult would not have darkened the door unless he/she was serious about buying something. And rather than dallying over the choice, a decision about what to purchase would be made before the child had time to become bored, restless or out of control. A quick no muss, no fuss sale. Amber liked it that way.

The man, facing away from her, was young but well dressed in a well-cut, expensive Italian suit. Probably could afford the best, she thought.

"May I help you?"

Before he had a chance to respond, her own little Jet came charging out from underneath a rack of lace teddies. She was wearing a see-through, sparkle-fringed thong upon her head.

"Hi, Mama!" she said, excitedly. "We came to see you at work."

"Jet? What are you doing here?" she asked the child as she removed the fancy panties from her head.

"I came with Mr. Brent," she said. "We're having lunch here and we come to 'vite you."

Amber glanced up, surprised. The young man she had failed to recognize from the back was her former friend from high school.

"I didn't recognize you without a ball cap and T-shirt," she said.

He shrugged. "Hey, I clean up pretty well."

She nodded. "So then why aren't you across town? No justice today at the Justice Center?"

"Lunch," he replied. "Jet and I are having lunch."

Amber looked incredulously at first one and then the other. "You and Brent are having lunch together?" she asked Jet.

The little girl nodded affirmatively. "We have lunch together every day," she said. "Just today, we come to 'vite you."

Brent was grinning at her. "Have you already eaten?"

"Ah, no," Amber answered. "But I usually don't take a lunch break until later."

"Oh, please, Mama, please come with us," Jet said.

Amber looked down in the little girl's eyes and her heart melted. She didn't want to deny this child anything. And the way things always worked out, it seemed like she denied her everything.

"I brought a sandwich with me," she told Jet. "And besides, I don't know if my boss will go for it."

The child's smile faded and she nodded accepting.

"Let's go ask her," Brent suggested, butting in.

Jet looked up at him, immediately hopeful.

"Will she say 'yes'?" she asked.

Brent shrugged. "I don't know, but it doesn't hurt to ask."

Sometimes, Amber thought, it did hurt to ask. And she was pretty sure this was going to be one of those times. Amber would have to lower herself to even make such a request. And Carly would take great delight in demonstrating her authority by forbidding it.

"No," Amber said. "I'm sure that I can't go. Maybe another time."

"Come on, Amber," Brent said. "At least ask."

"I'd rather not. We're not having a good day."

"It's as dead as Elvis in this mall today," Brent said. "She doesn't need you."

"It's not a case of need."

"Then what is it?"

"It's called a job, Brent. A real job," Amber said, snidely. "A preppy, college boy like you wouldn't understand."

He rolled his eyes.

"If you won't ask her, I will."

"No, you won't."

"Let me! Let me!" Jet called out and was racing toward the back before Amber could stop her.

"No wait," she called out. Amber managed to catch up with her, but not before they had attracted Carly's attention.

"Are you my mama's boss?" Jet asked.

Carly came walking across the room toward them. She was eyeing Jet critically. Amber felt almost as if she should step in front of the child to protect her.

"Who is your mama?" Carly asked, missing the obvious connection.

Jet clasped her mother's hand in her own.

"Amber Nicole Jameson," she answered.

Carly looked at the child, then at Amber. Her jaw actually dropped open.

"This is *your* little girl?"

"Yes, she is," Amber tried to keep her tone neutral, but there was a hint of the defensiveness in it.

"She is…" Carly hesitated. And then in a change so abrupt and drastic, Amber was almost at a loss, Carly's face brightened into a smile and she leaned down to get a closer look. "She is as cute as a button. Amber, you didn't tell us that she's as cute as a button."

Jet wrinkled her nose. "I'm not a button, I'm a girl," she explained.

Brent stepped up and offered his hand. "Hi, I'm Brent."

"Hi," Carly took his hand politely, glancing quickly at Amber and Jet as if trying to make some kind of connection.

"I'm Jet's lunch date," Brent explained. "But she's under age. Way under age, actually. And she thinks she needs a chaperon. We came to see if her mother might be available."

"I told them that I've got way too much to do," Amber said, wanting to decline before Carly had a chance to refuse her.

"Don't be silly," Carly said. "The store's at a standstill and you're going to be here until closing. Go ahead. Have a nice lunch with your daughter."

Jet squealed with delight and jumped up and down.

Amber shot a glance at Brent. His grin felt like a challenge. She could hardly insist that she *not* go.

"Let me get my purse," she said and headed toward the back.

She was annoyed. Not at Jet. She was glad to see Jet. But what on earth was her daughter doing with Brent Velasco.

By the time she returned Metsy had joined the little confab. She and Carly were chatting with Brent and Jet as if they were all old friends.

When the child saw Amber, however, she hurried over and grabbed her hand.

"I'll be back in an hour," Amber told Carly.

"Take your time," she said. "Metsy and I can surely handle anything that comes up on a slow day like this one."

"Are you sure we can't bring you ladies something?" Brent asked. "Tortellini? Manicotti? A liter of wine?"

The two laughed and waved them off. Amber was smiling, but she didn't feel like it.

They walked through the mall toward Freddie's Fast Italian. Jet was still holding Amber's hand and swinging her arm up and back. She was telling her mother about her adventures in the parking garage.

"And when you go around the corner," she explained. "You honk the horn so the other cars will know that you're there. 'Cause we don't want them running into us and smashing up Mr. Brent's car."

"No, we wouldn't want that," Amber agreed. She glanced over at Brent. "Mr. Brent?"

He shrugged. "It was her own idea. She told me that she's supposed to call grown-ups mister or missus."

Amber rolled her eyes.

"My mother's idea no doubt."

Brent nodded, agreeing. "I kind of like it," he said.

The restaurant, mirroring the mall itself, wasn't particularly crowded. They were seated right away in a corner overlooking the bend in the river, two flights below. The table's one inch square tiles of red and white mimicked the traditional Italian restaurant tablecloth. The food was also a quick and easy imitation of Neapolitan cuisine.

"I want spaghetti," Jet announced. "But no garly bread, just regular bread."

"Okay," Brent said. "Same for me, except I like garlic bread. It keeps vampires away."

"It does not," Jet challenged. "There aren't any vampires."

"My point exactly," he joked.

"Can Mr. Brent come to my birthday party?" Jet asked.

"What birthday party?"

"Wilma says I'm having a cake and candles and everything," Jet told her. "Can I 'vite Mr. Brent?"

Amber shrugged. "Hey, it's okay by me."

Since Brent was apparently buying lunch, Amber didn't scrimp on her order. She rarely had the luxury of a sit-down restaurant. And money she spent on food was cash she wouldn't have for partying. If Brent was paying, she was going to scarf down as much as she could manage.

"So what's this about you and Jet having lunch together every day?" Amber asked.

The two looked at each other.

Jet cupped her hands in front of her mouth as if whispering. "It's a secret," she said.

"A secret? I don't think you can have any secrets from me."

They seemed to consider that. Finally Brent spoke.

"We think that Wilma has a beau," he said.

"She doesn't have a bow," Jet corrected. "She's got a boyfriend."

"I don't believe it," Amber said.

"You'd better," Brent answered. "She meets some guy for lunch Monday through Friday at the Empire Bar."

"You're serious."

"Never more so."

"Who is he?"

"We don't know," Brent said. "Jet and I have never been invited to meet him. We just drop her off at the curb in front and pick her up there an hour later."

Jet was nodding in agreement.

"How long has this been going on?"

"A couple of weeks," Brent answered. "And she's looking better every day."

"Why is it a secret?"

Brent shrugged. "I don't think she wants Ellen to know."

"She'll never hear it from me," Amber assured him and the waiter arrived, loaded down with hot, hearty food.

Lunching with Max Roper was a surprisingly pleasant pastime. Wilma had, in all honesty, anticipated the kind of relationship she usually had with a man. A couple of chats, a couple of drinks and then a carefully veiled suggestion about his place or, if he was married, a cheap motel.

She might be in her sixties, but she wasn't beyond sex and in her experience, men might scrimp on blood pressure pills or heart medication, but they always had money to pay for their Viagra prescription.

Her time with Max didn't run in the usual direction. They didn't talk in suggestive innuendo, but rather as two thoughtful experienced adults.

"I love my work," Max told her. "It wasn't my first choice as a vocation, but I'm good at it. And it gives me a lot of personal satisfaction."

"That's a fine thing," Wilma told him. "Truthfully, I'm about half envious. I never did anything in my life that I'm particularly proud of."

Max chuckled. "Wilma, I can never tell if you're serious."

"I'm serious, all right," she said. "I never worked at a job I cared about and never cared about a job where I worked."

"What kind of work did you do?"

"Waitressing mostly," she answered. "I've worked in a five-and-dime, been a barmaid. I got on with the telephone company once, but ended up quitting to move to a new town. That's what I did, mostly. I never stayed anywhere very long."

"Following your husband?"

Wilma didn't want to reveal much of the truth. "More often chasing after him!" she joked.

Max laughed as she knew that he would.

"I guess you just never found a job that you were really cut out for," he said. "Not every woman wants a career. Managing a home, rearing some fine children, that's a more impressive accomplishment than building a Fortune 500 company."

Wilma had been deliberately vague about who she was and what kind of life she'd led. That was partly designed to add an aura of mystery to her presence. But she also didn't want him to find out that she was Ellen's mother. Not before the man was too smitten to just walk away. There was an old adage against mixing business with pleasure and men were usually pragmatic enough to follow it. At least when it was fairly convenient to do so.

So she related only the most generic of truths about herself.

"Honestly, Max, I wasn't interested in keeping house or raising kids."

He raised a surprised eyebrow.

"That's not saying I didn't do it," Wilma clarified. "I've got a boy and a girl. They turned out all right. But it was more *despite* their upbringing than because of it."

"I'm not sure I believe that," he said.

"You might as well," Wilma countered. "'Cause it is the truth. My son has a wife and three kids. They live in Luling because that's where I was when he graduated high school."

"It's not that far," Max said. "Luling's only an hour's drive or thereabouts."

"He might as well live in Australia," Wilma said. "They come to see me once a year. It's kind of like an annual dental checkup. They stay one hour and are pretty much openmouthed and uncomfortable the whole time."

Max chuckled.

"What about your daughter?"

"She's here in San Antonio," Wilma answered briefly, turning the question. "What about you? Do you have kids?"

"A boy," Max answered. "Of course, he's not a boy any longer. I'd say we're friends, we see each other frequently, but we're not really as close as a father and son might be."

"The young bulls and old bulls don't run together?"

"A little bit of that," Max admitted. "But more that we just don't know each other. His mother and I were never married. I was a young cowboy and she got pregnant or as I said in those days, she *got herself pregnant*. I didn't want to marry her, but I did my best to support her and the boy and I kept up with them. When he was four she married somebody else. She thought having me around would be more confusing than helpful. At the time I was glad to step out of the way."

"So you did."

"Mostly," Max answered. "She never tried to deceive him or anything. I always remembered his birthday. His mother got divorced when he was in high school. He had to pretty much make his own way working nights at the grocery store. I helped him pay for his college. He owns his own company now. He's done very well."

"That must make you really proud," Wilma said.

Max thought about that for a moment, then shook his head. "I'm impressed with all that he's accomplished. But I don't take any pride in it. I suppose I feel much like you do. His success is his own. My part in it was as much handicap as help."

Wilma smiled at him. "At least we won't get accused of living vicariously through our children," she said.

"Or at least we won't get accused by each other," he agreed. "But I'm not letting you get away that easy, Wilma. You're going to have to tell me what you do best. Everybody does something *best*, even if it's not any better than anyone else would do."

"Okay, well let me think for a minute," Wilma said. And then she laughed. "You know what I do best," she told him. "I pick out the best produce."

"Really?"

She nodded. "It's the only thing that I really know and understand. If they've got a stack of melons as high as a house and only three of them are ripe and sweet, I can find those three every time."

"How did you learn to do that?" he asked.

She shook her head. "I don't really know. My mama always had a big garden when I was a girl. But I always hated having to work in the dirt. And I've never so much as planted a petunia since I left home at seventeen."

"No green thumb, apparently," he said.

Wilma held up her hand as if verifying his statement. "Seems not. I always loved those roadside fruit stands. I was young and poor. And of course, the stands were usually cheaper and fresher than the store. Sometimes the farmer would show me how to tell if sweet corn was crisp or milky just by looking at the silks on the husk. Mostly I learned by trial and error. There's nothing that makes me madder than a pithy orange or a tomato that tastes like sawdust."

"I'm with you there," Max said.

"So anyway," Wilma said with a shrug, feeling strangely embarrassed as if she'd shown way too much of herself. "That's my best, my only best."

"I'd say that's an interesting skill to have," Max told her. "And very practical."

"Not as much as you'd think," she said. "When I see wonderful produce at its peak, I just can't resist buying it."

"And that's a problem?"

"It is if my refrigerator is already stuffed full of yesterday's perfect veggies," she said.

Max nodded, understanding. "You can't eat it up as fast as you buy it," he clarified.

"I don't really cook much at all," she said. "But I buy like I'm feeding an army. Can't seem to help it. Emelda Marcos has her shoes. I have asparagus and eggplants."

She'd made a joke of it and he laughed on cue, but it didn't deter him from the seriousness of his discussion.

"What you need to do, Wilma, is figure out a way to utilize your special skill in a way that's productive for you and helpful to others."

There was nothing that Wilma could think of, in her whole life, that was particularly productive or helpful for anyone. Nervously she fumbled for a cigarette in her purse. She tried not to smoke much in front of Max. They were of the same generation and much more tolerant of tobacco use than their offspring. Still, he didn't smoke and Wilma didn't want him to know how much she did. Or what kind of toll it was taking on her.

"Oh, I'm sure there's lots of ways I can utilize my talents," she said, sarcastically. "I could buy kumquats for shut-ins."

Max gave a low, deep-throated chuckle, but he wasn't distracted from the discussion.

"You can joke your way around this," he told her. "I'm willing to let you get away with that. But I'd speculate seriously on how you could use the skill you have in some fulfilling way."

Wilma didn't want to speculate on it. She didn't want to have to imagine what she had undoubtedly missed.

"Maybe I could have done something with it," she admitted. "I could have worked at a market or been a buyer or some such. But those are jobs for young people. Produce managers need to be able to do a lot of lift and carry. It's too late for that now."

"Too late?" Max sounded skeptical. "That's what people think when they're in their forties—that they've waited too late. But by the time you get to our age, and although you, my dear, are quite attractive, I believe that you're not all that much younger than me. By the time you're our age, you understand that it's only too late when you're dead."

Wilma laughed.

"Am I right?" Max asked.

"You're right," Wilma agreed.

"So let's think of some way you could use your talent."

She nodded and was thoughtful for a moment. "Of course, I could teach what I know. I take my little granddaughter to the store with me and we go through the produce and I show her how to pick things out."

"How old is your granddaughter?"

"She's almost four," Wilma answered. "Actually she's my great-granddaughter. I keep her while her mother works."

Max nodded as if filing the information away.

"Maybe I could do a show-and-tell at schools or storytime. Explain to the little ones about produce."

"That might be fun," Max agreed. "If you like children a lot. Do you enjoy them? Get along with them well?"

Wilma shrugged. "More so now than when I was younger," she admitted. "But I like my own better than other people's."

Max seemed to appreciate both her honesty and her lack of pretense.

"Kids aren't the only ones who might need to learn about this," Max said. "There are plenty of adults who don't know anything either."

"That's true," Wilma said. "I could teach classes. But produce isn't the kind of thing people would sign up for a course in. I'm not sure you could even drag it into a couple of hours. It's something you need to learn, one vegetable at a time over years."

Max agreed with her on that.

"Maybe you could have an information booth in the produce department," he suggested. "You could be there to answer people's questions. Perhaps have a fruit of the day that you're pushing. Teach the customers *one vegetable at a time*."

Wilma thought about that.

"I couldn't work a whole day though," she told him. "Who would take care of my granddaughter?"

"That's why they invented day care," he answered. "She's going to start school soon anyway."

"I don't have the stamina," she admitted.

"You look healthy to me," Max said.

"It's the cigarettes," Wilma admitted. "I can't breathe as well as I used to."

She wouldn't say any more. She would cut her tongue out before admitting that she needed oxygen to walk to the curb in front of her house.

"Quit," Max suggested.

Wilma rolled her eyes and gave him a dubious look.

"I've been smoking since I was fourteen," she told him. "I kept it up through two pregnancies and bought cigarettes when there was no money for food. I'm more likely to sprout wings and go flying across the room than to give up cigarettes now."

Max didn't look as if he quite accepted her answer, but he chose not to argue.

"Okay, you can just work a short while," he said. "You could do the after work rush when everybody's trying to find something for supper and get home with it."

"Would somebody hire me to do that?" Wilma asked. "I could work two or three hours a day. That would be great! Oh, I wish I could work at Dilly's. I love Dilly's, it's my favorite. Best produce in town."

Max was suddenly looking at her very strangely.

"What?" she asked him.

He hesitated. "Nothing, I was just thinking," he assured her. "It might not be cost effective to have you actually working in the produce department. They'd have to sell $150, maybe $180 more in produce per hour to justify having you there. And that doesn't even take into account the workman's comp, which considering your age might cost them a considerable amount."

"Oh." Wilma felt suddenly deflated.

"That doesn't mean that the right store chain in the right situation wouldn't have a way to utilize you," Max added quickly.

"Sure," Wilma agreed, not sure at all.

"We'll just have to think about it," Max said. "Talk about it."

Wilma nodded.

He glanced down at his watch. "I've got to get back to the office. Can I give you a lift somewhere?"

"Ah...no," she told him. "You go on."

Max took leave of her and caught the waitress to pay their tab. Wilma watched him curiously as he headed out. She'd made some kind of misstep and she didn't know exactly what it was.

What she did know was that she'd strayed way far from her agenda. Here she'd been talking for an hour about herself and what she wanted in the world, when even the stupidest, most naive females clearly understood that when you're courting, you always let the man do the talking, and the talking is most always about himself. The openness of Max's manner had gotten her off the track. She'd have to do a lot better tomorrow.

In the sliver of window between the neon beer signs, she saw Brent's Tahoe double-parked at the curb. She gathered up her purse and made her way out there.

The very well-mannered young man got out of the

car to help her, as always. Today it was very welcome. She was completely exhausted by the time she got into the car.

"Hand me my headdress, honey," she said to Jet, pointing toward the plastic hose draped upon the oxygen tank in the back seat. "I've got to get some air going."

Her little granddaughter helped her get the tubes in her nose and hooked over her ears before turning on the valve. By the time Brent got into the car, all that was left to do was supervise.

"How was your lunch?" he asked her.

Wilma had closed her eyes, lying back against the seat, relishing the relief of breathing.

"I don't know," she answered, honestly. "There's more going on than I can figure out."

Brent chuckled. "Sounds like you had the same lunch I did."

9

Cleo Payne's tax problems were every bit as complex and convoluted as Ellen had feared. It was really no problem writing an involved explanation to the IRS. Just stating the facts concisely took two single-spaced pages. And she was able to explain the circumstances and elaborate on the details for twenty more. She spent several paragraphs dwelling upon his age and confused mental state. As she was writing, her thoughts were more upon Mrs. Stanhope than Mr. Payne.

Yolanda's revelation that Mrs. Stanhope was, in her ineloquent words, *the local crazy lady*, had caught Ellen by surprise. That the woman might be mentally unstable, delusional, had never occurred to her. It was a little unsettling, although Ellen couldn't have said why. A mental health problem was a mental health problem. But somehow if the etiology happened to be old age, the victim seemed more sympathetic. It didn't make sense. Mrs. Stanhope was the same woman that she had been before Ellen knew about her past. But the very fact that she had a history of emotional problems suddenly made Ellen more wary and less willing to be involved.

There was a light tapping on the door and before she could answer, Yolanda peeked in.

"Marvin Dix called," she told Ellen. "He said he'd have to cancel this afternoon, but he'd get cracking on your case real soon. Get it, cracking your case?"

Yolanda apparently thought that was hilarious.

Ellen was not as amused. "He'd *better* get cracking on it soon," she told Yolanda. "We're really running out of time."

Yolanda's expression immediately turned to concern. "Next time I won't let him get by with just relaying a message," she said. "I'm sorry."

Ellen waved away her apology. "Believe me, it's not your fault," she assured the other woman. Deliberately she planted a brave smile across her face. Worrying wasn't any help at all. And causing other people to worry only made things worse.

"Things are going to work out fine," she said.

The last was a fair imitation of the woman that she used to be. Positive, upbeat, optimistic. She didn't feel it, but at least it felt better to say it.

"Have you got a minute to talk?" Ellen asked, deftly changing the subject.

"Sure," Yolanda answered enthusiastically. "Let me get us some coffee. We'll have a real klatch for a change." She took Ellen's cup and headed back out into the main office. Within a couple of minutes she returned with a tray bearing two coffees, a couple of packets of creamer and sweetener and a green box of Girl Scout cookies.

"Thin Mints, my favorites," she confided.

Yolanda made herself comfortable in Ellen's client chair and opened the cookies as Ellen stirred her coffee.

"I wanted to ask you some more about Mrs. Stanhope," Ellen said.

"The crazy lady?"

Yolanda asked the question with her mouth full. When Ellen nodded, she finished chewing before responding further.

"I don't know that much," she admitted.

"Well, tell me what you do know," Ellen said.

The woman gave it a moment's consideration.

"She's been crazy all my life," Yolanda said. "When I was just a little girl we'd be in the park and we'd see her walking down the street toward town and we'd all scream and run."

"Is she violent?"

"No…at least I'd never heard of it," Yolanda admitted and then added honestly. "If she was, you know I would have heard."

Ellen nodded.

"Truthfully, there's not all that much gossip about her anymore," Yolanda said. "Her niece lives with her full-time and keeps a pretty close watch on her."

Ellen had her own opinion about that, but didn't voice it.

"You must know something about her history," Ellen said. "Her background. Her family?"

"Oh, well, that," Yolanda began. "Most everybody knows that. She's one of the Grisham daughters, a very prominent family, part of the old three hundred."

Ellen had certainly heard of the Grishams. The old three hundred were the families of settlers who'd received land grants in Stephen Austin's colony. They might not necessarily be the wealthiest or most powerful people in the state, but they were among the most admired.

"And the old lady's rich as Croesus," Yolanda continued. "You know that huge complex on the west side, the South Texas Science and Technology Industries?"

Ellen nodded.

"She owned all that land," Yolanda said. "And developers paid a fortune back in the sixties to get it. Three million dollars, I heard. And that's when three million was really a lot of money."

To Ellen, and most people, it still was.

"The Grishams owned that?" Ellen was surprised.

"No, the Stanhopes," Yolanda said. "Or actually they're the Standerhaupts. I guess they Americanized their name. They owned all that acreage. It was a pasture for their dairy. Imagine getting that much for a section of grass and cow patties!"

Ellen shook her head, trying to picture it.

"You know I've seen Mrs. Stanhope's house in King William," Ellen said. "It's charming and well kept, but it's no fancy mansion."

Yolanda shrugged. "What can I tell you? The woman's nuts. I'm sure all the money is controlled by her nieces and nephews."

"Probably so," Ellen agreed.

"The old lady used to walk around town wearing these amazing fur coats," Yolanda said. "Winter and summer she was swathed in mink or fox or ermine."

"She told me something about her coats," Ellen said, trying to remember. "I think she told me that Irma took them."

Yolanda nodded. "Probably put them in storage for safekeeping. She wasn't wearing roadkill, those were expensive furs."

Ellen imagined, unkindly, that Irma was probably

protecting them from damage because they were undoubtedly part of her inheritance.

"What happened to her husband?" Ellen asked.

"He's dead," Yolanda replied. "She's been a widow all my life."

"She said he had a business relationship with Max."

Yolanda raised her eyebrows skeptically. "I can't imagine it," she said. "Mrs. Stanhope and her family—they aren't Max's kind of people. He's a great guy, but he never ran with the monied crowd. If he ever had ambition to hobnob with the lions of industry, he must have given it over years ago. Since I've known him, he's always been a man of the people. Kind of specializing in the difficult cases. He does high stress accounting for people who can only pay bargain basement prices."

"Except he really hates to give anyone the bad news," Ellen said, indicating the worst-case files that were now strictly her province.

"I tell him he takes it too personally," Yolanda said. "But Max says we're talking about people's lives and that's always personal."

The phone rang and Yolanda excused herself with the phrase, "Duty calls."

Ellen had just returned to her work, when she heard Max come through the front door. He hung his Stetson on the old-fashioned hat pegs in the waiting area and pulled a comb out of his back pocket to straighten his hair. She thought to waylay him as he passed her door and question his connection, tenuous though it might be, to Mrs. Stanhope.

She didn't get the chance as Yolanda called out to her.

"Do you know how long carrots stay good in the refrigerator?"

Ellen was so accustomed to responding negatively, that she almost said no before she realized that she might, in fact, have the answer.

"Are they stem on or stem off?" Ellen asked.

There was a hesitation while Yolanda relayed the question.

"Stem on," she replied.

"Only a couple of days, I think. The stem means they're fresh picked. Call my mother, she's home and she'll know exactly. She knows everything about produce."

Max who was just at that moment passing her door stopped in his tracks. He turned to stare at her, strangely.

"Your mother knows everything about produce?"

Ellen nodded. "Don't ask me how or why, but she knows everything about it," Ellen assured him. "I swear, edible plant life and getting married are the only two subjects in the world that she claims to have any level of expertise in."

It was a funny line. At least Ellen thought so. Max didn't even manage a flicker of amusement. With a puzzled look he retreated to his office.

When Amber showed up at The Tunnel in Sunset Station it was almost nine o'clock. The place was noisy and busy, but not too wild for a Friday night. The band played a funky jazz, which was great to listen to, but didn't do anything to crowd the dance floors.

Originally built in 1902, the former downtown train depot had been transformed into a youthful music

venue. The saloon area with its stained-glass windows and grand staircase was an aesthetic delight to
the eye. Amber hardly noticed as she scanned the
room for Gwen. She finally caught sight of her friend
and future roommate standing at the bar with two
men.

Amber hurried over in that direction, an apology
on her lips. She could have been here twenty minutes
earlier if a pair of teenage couples hadn't come into
the store just as she was about to close the doors. They
weren't intent on buying anything. The guys just
wanted their girlfriends to try on sexy lingerie and
model for them in the little alcove outside the fitting
rooms.

Discouraging this misuse of the merchandise was
store policy. Virtually every kid in America had come
up with this brilliant entertainment idea. Amber personally didn't care, as long as they didn't try to steal
anything. Which, unfortunately, they usually did.
This night, however, she had people waiting on her
and she'd been trying to close. Unable to keep a
watchful eye on the teens, she just wanted them out.
The two boys became angry and threatening. Amber
had to call security.

By the time the kids were hauled out and the paperwork was done, she was running very late. She
knew Gwen would be pissed.

As she approached, her friend was laughing loudly
and appeared to be more than a little drunk already.
The men at her side were an unlikely pair to be hanging with Gwen. One was a large, mustachioed fellow
obviously well over forty. The other guy in Dockers
and a plaid shirt was younger, but much shorter. He
had a round, ruddy face and a beer gut.

Gwen glanced up and spotted her.

"Here's Amber!" she said. "Girl, we were about to give you up."

"Sorry, I had trouble getting away."

Gwen ignored the apology, turning instead to the round-faced fellow. "So, Matt, what do you think? Was she worth the wait?"

The guy looked Amber up and down in a manner that was immediately both intrusive and demeaning.

The man nodded. "She sure looks like a hottie," he said to Gwen before reaching out a pudgy arm to wrap around Amber's waist. "What are you drinking, baby?"

She hated to be called baby. And she didn't like strange men putting their hands on her. Amber stiffened her spine and put as much distance as she could manage between her body and Matt's.

"I'll just have a beer," Amber said. "I'm going to make an early night of it."

Matt laughed as if that were a joke.

"Me, too, baby," he said. "I can hardly wait to get out of this tomb. It's dead in here."

As far as Amber was concerned, this was one of The Tunnel's better nights. She could enjoy the ambience and still hear herself think. But she didn't argue with the guy.

"This is Pete," Gwen said, introducing the older man beside her. "Matt and Pete are from Michigan. Their actuaries."

"Hi," Amber said, trying to smile politely, though the nearness of the man beside her was irritating.

Pete reached out to Amber as if to shake hands. She extended her own, but to her complete surprise, he bypassed it and squeezed her breast.

"What the hell!"

Amber jumped back startled, untangling herself from Matt's arm and slapping at Pete's hand.

"What do you think you're doing?"

"Just checking to see if they're real," Pete replied. With a chuckle he addressed his friend. "Looks like you got the best piece," he said. "I'm stuck here with the skinny titless wonder."

"Let's not be negative," Matt said. "I think the more correct phrasing would be titfully challenged."

Pete thought that was very funny.

Amber was angry. "You're drunk," she said, turning to walk away.

"What's the deal with her?" she heard Matt asking.

"Just a minute," she heard Gwen reply before coming after her. "Amber, wait."

She did, but not before she'd put a good bit of distance between her and the men from Michigan.

"Who are those dickheads?" she asked Gwen.

"Just a couple of guys I met at the hotel," she answered. "They're just here for a weekend conference and looking for a good time."

"Well, they can find it with somebody else."

"Come on, Amber," Gwen coaxed. "They're okay. We're just a little drunk, which we wouldn't have been if you'd got here on time."

"I had to close up," Amber pointed out. "I couldn't just walk away."

"I get that. It's not your fault," Gwen said. "It's not their fault either. Come on, come back. I'll get them to straighten up."

Amber wasn't keen on the idea, but she did it anyway.

"You guys be nice to Amber," Gwen cautioned as

they returned to the men at the bar. "When she's cold sober, she expects to be treated like a lady."

Pete laughed. "Let's get some alcohol in her then," he said.

Matt wrapped his arm around her once more. Amber remained wary, but he was nice, smiling.

"Are you sure you just want beer?" he asked her. "You look like a margarita girl to me."

"Vodka and tonic," she told him and he signaled the waiter.

Amber tried to catch up. She tried to be interesting and interested. Fortunately, Matt and Pete didn't require much input. They were having a great time, just the two of them. Joking with each other about their work, their lives. Gwen and Amber were mostly attractive afterthoughts. Pete groped Gwen every few minutes, and she cooed and giggled as if she enjoyed his attention. Having known Gwen for some time and being familiar both with the type of men she appreciated and her sharp-barbed, no-nonsense approach to relationships, her actions were, to Amber, completely mystifying.

Amber made a couple of ill-fated attempts to break up the party and go home. She was tired. She was bored. And strangely the pleasant lunch with Jet and Brent had somehow whet her appetite for more quiet places and less hip discussion.

A little after 10:30 a rock concert let out at the Alamodome and suddenly the place was full of people angling up to the bar for drinks, raising the noise level beyond any opportunity for conversation.

"Let's ditch this place," Pete suggested and a couple of minutes later they were down on the street.

Matt hailed a taxi. Amber got in the back seat next

to Gwen and Pete, who were taking the opportunity of relative privacy to commence an embarrassingly passionate embrace. Amber deliberately ignored them. Matt sat in the front seat next to the driver. She was going to suggest they go to the Bombay Bicycle Club or Stone Werks. They'd be able to carry on a conversation and she was hoping to grab a sandwich. She hadn't eaten since noon and the drinks she'd consumed had gone straight to her head, making her feel a little queasy.

To her surprise, Matt gave the cabby the name of his hotel. Of course, they had a club there, as well as a halfway decent grill. She still held out hope that she'd be able to get something to eat.

Gwen and Pete were really getting it on. Matt was shooting the breeze with the driver, quizzing the poor guy in broken Spanish. The guy, who looked to Amber to be East Indian or Pakistani, was too polite to correct the mistake and was answering only with smiles and shrugs and the meager Spanglish of his own.

Amber focused on the street outside her window. It was basic San Antonio nightlife. Reveling teenagers hollering to each other from passing cars. Groups of exuberant tourists consulting their maps. Horse-drawn carriages decorated with flowers. Mariachis and margarita vendors. She'd always loved the feel and flavor of it.

Tonight though, tonight she just wanted to be home.

She glanced down at her watch. Jet would be in bed already. She'd have her hair in little braids and be asleep in the middle of the bed, her thumb neatly tucked into her mouth. If she was there she'd gently pull it free and scoot her over to one side and lay down with her. Jet always woke, but just barely. Just enough to snuggle up next to Amber and lay her sleepy head against her mother's breast.

Amber smiled to herself. Jet was really something. She was like a living, breathing lump of pure sugar. Just having her around made the world sweeter.

It was going to be really hard to leave her behind.

That thought hit Amber like a splash of cold water. Gwen was undoubtedly right. She couldn't drag the little girl along with her. She was headed nowhere fast and that was not what she wanted for Jet. Ellen had more time for her. Ellen would take better care of her. No matter how bad things got, her mother always managed to make things work. Jet deserved better than Amber could ever give her.

The cab pulled up into the hotel's drive-through. A liveried valet opened her door. She got out and fumbled with the shoulder strap on her purse. Gwen slid out behind her. She was flushed and laughing.

"How's it going, Rob," she said to the valet who offered his hand.

"Didn't expect to see you returning to the job in a cab," he responded.

Gwen gave a throaty chuckle. "I got me a live one tonight."

They shared a laugh as if there were some private joke.

Pete got out and grabbed Gwen around the waist. They headed for the revolving glass door, leaving Amber standing alone on the sidewalk. Matt was paying the fare. She didn't know if she should wait for him or follow her friend.

She decided upon a little of both. Making her way

to the door, but then hesitating there. She kept Gwen in sight without completely blowing off Matt. He seemed to appreciate that. When he got out of the taxi he was smiling at her.

"I'm about ready for another drink, how about you?"

In truth, she was more hungry than thirsty, but she nodded.

They went into the hotel. He was better behaved now than he had been in the club. He was walking next to her, but didn't actually touch her in any way. Up ahead they could see Gwen and Pete. They had no such compunctions. They were hanging all over each other.

When they reached the hallway that led past the entrance to the club, Amber was surprised to see them head the other direction.

"Where are they going?" Amber asked. "The club's the other way."

"We've got drinks in the room," Matt answered.

Amber slowed her pace. She knew the score. She couldn't go upstairs with this guy and then pretend she didn't understand what was expected. Which would have been okay with her, if she wanted it, too. But she felt nothing for him. Nothing at all.

Changing her strategy, she began to hurry. They caught up with the other couple just as they were about to step on the elevator.

"Pete, I...ah...need a quick word with Gwen, okay?"

"What?" Gwen asked.

Amber motioned with her head to move away from the men. They were barely out of hearing distance when she spotted the rest room.

"Got to make a pit stop!" Amber assured the guys hurriedly and then dragged Gwen into the Ladies'.

Gwen looked at her as if she'd lost her mind. "Have you got a problem or something?" she asked.

"Are you too drunk to see that these jerks are making a booty call?" she asked.

"So what?"

"So I'm not answering."

Gwen sighed, exasperated. "Look, Virgin Princess, these guys are just looking for a good time. They're nice guys. Straight with it and happy to throw a few bucks in our direction."

"They have a name for that, Gwen," Amber said.

"*Brilliant*. I think that's what it's called," her friend replied. "We're going to need that money to get the apartment."

"This is not the way to get it," Amber said.

"Oh, oh, you're going to get like a bonus at the underwear store?" Gwen asked facetiously. "Or are you waiting for the Prize Patrol?"

Amber looked away.

"The Matt guy is even cute," Gwen continued. "It's not like you're having to go down on the decrepit, old scumbag. I gave you the better one."

Amber was shaking her head. "It's so...so... gross."

"Oh, puh-leeze," Gwen complained. "You can't tell me this is the first time you've had sex with some creep you didn't like."

She didn't respond to that.

"You got a condom?" Gwen asked.

Amber nodded.

"Then we're good to go," she said.

Amber followed Gwen back out to the lobby where

Pete was waiting for her with open arms. When they got within the privacy of the elevator, Matt wrapped his arm around her and pulled her close.

He was clean smelling with just a hint of some nice aftershave. Gwen was right. He wasn't really bad looking. And since he'd sobered up a bit, he wasn't even all that obnoxious. He wouldn't be the most disgusting man she'd ever slept with. Just the only one she did for money. Amber felt ill.

"I'm hungry," she said to him. "Couldn't we go to the bar and grab a sandwich or something?"

"We'll order room service," Matt told her.

The elevator stopped and the door opened. Feeling like a condemned prisoner, Amber stepped forward. Matt pulled her back.

"It's not my floor," he said.

Gwen and Pete hurried out. Pete was groping her butt, she was looking back at Amber, encouraging, warning, threatening.

The door closed and the elevator moved up. The space inside was small, but seemed enormously empty without the safe presence of her friend.

This was not what Amber had planned to do with her life.

"Did you go to college?" she asked suddenly.

Matt seemed surprised at the question. "Michigan State," he answered proudly. "You a football fan?"

"No."

The elevator stopped and the door opened.

"This is it," he said stepping forward.

Amber hesitated.

He was standing in the open door, eyeing her curiously.

"I...I don't think..." She looked up into his face,

not certain what to say. "I...I think I started my period."

His brow furrowed unpleasantly, then he shook his head.

"It doesn't bother me, if it doesn't bother you," he told her.

"It bothers me," Amber said.

"We'll work around it," he assured her. "I hate to brag on myself, but I've got a knack for innovation."

"I don't think—"

"We'll have a drink," he said. "We'll get you something to eat. We'll party."

"I don't want to do this. Just let me go."

"What?"

"I want to leave," she said.

He was shaking his head, disbelieving. "You spent all evening warming me up and now you want to walk?"

She hadn't encouraged him at all, she was sure of that. But she didn't feel as if she was in any position to argue.

"Just let me go," she repeated. "I'm sorry. I'm really sorry, but please just let me go."

He wrapped his arm around her and pulled her out of the elevator. "Come on, baby," he said. "You've already gone this far, the rest is just sliding downhill."

She was going through her gymnastic routine on the decking around the pool in the backyard. Twirling her ribbon stick and keeping the strip of two-inch-wide satin constantly moving in circles and swirls as she turned, pivoted, leapt and balanced.

The ribbon was her best event, though that wasn't saying much. She was too tall for a gymnast and had an awk-

wardness she just couldn't seem to get past. But practice makes perfect. If she wanted to do better, she'd just have to keep working at it.

She did an Arabesque with serpent spirals, her best movement, executing it perfectly. It was like dancing, but without all the frilly costumes. She was an athlete, not a ballerina. It suited her disposition better than her aptitude.

As she completed sequence after sequence coming toward the finale there was more cause for concern. The conclusion of the routine was a boomerang throw. She grasped the end of the ribbon. Tossed the stick and pulled it back toward her as she went up on toes and made a reverse pivot. Her timing was right-on. The stick was in perfect position and she made the catch. She stood flat-footed and arched, holding ribbon and stick above her head, for the final pose.

From the direction of the covered patio she heard a pair of hands clapping.

"Bravo! Bravo!"

With delight she glanced over to the man still applauding her. He was tall and strong and handsome. She had his eyes. Everybody said so. They were kind eyes.

Giggling, she ran over to him.

"Were you spying on me?" she asked. "You're supposed to be working. It's tax season, you know."

"Who can look at rows of numbers when there is a wood sprite frolicking in my very own backyard," he replied.

"We don't call it a frolic, Daddy. It's a workout."

He shrugged. "Well, whatever you call it, I call you talented, graceful and beautiful," he said. "But you've got to remember to smile."

"My teacher said not to," she explained. "He said the braces detract from the elegance and beauty. The expression needs to be a match of the musicality."

"The man's an idiot," he said. *"Nothing could detract from the elegance and beauty of Miss Amber Jameson."*

"Oh, Daddy, you're silly."

"I am silly. But you are smart and sweet and wonderful. Every time I look at you, I'm just in awe that an ordinary man like me could be a father to such an amazing creature as you."

He folded her into his arms. He was so warm, so safe.

"I love you, Daddy," she said. *"I want to make you proud."*

"I love you, too, little pumpkin," he answered. *"And I'm always proud of you. Always."*

His arms around her suddenly seemed too heavy and the scent of him was strange, it was wrong.

Amber opened her eyes to find herself twisted in the covers of a disheveled bed in a downtown hotel. The light from the desk lamp illuminated the room. The man in whose arms she lay was a stranger.

She pulled away from him.

The dreamy memory of her father's visage was so fresh and vivid that she felt it physically, like a painful kick to the stomach. Tears welled in her eyes. Tightly she squeezed them shut, pushing the old anguish away.

If her father hadn't died things would have been different. She would have finished high school. She would have gone to college. She would be headed for a bright future. But more than those things, if he hadn't died, he would still be here to love her.

Amber got up and began searching for her clothes.

"What are you doing?" The sleepy question came from the far side of the bed.

"I'm getting dressed," she answered.

He fumbled for his watch on the side table. "It's four o'clock in the morning," he complained.

"Go back to sleep," she told him. "I've got to get home."

She carried her things into the bathroom. She took a five-minute shower, scrubbing off the worst of her night. She had no urge to linger. She put on her clothes and brushed her hair, pulling it up into a scrunchy. Makeup free and ponytailed, in the mirror she looked like an entirely different woman than the one she felt inside.

Amber hung her purse on her shoulder and opened the bathroom door. Matt was standing there, leaning against the door frame. His hair was standing on end and he was wearing only his boxers.

"Here," he said, holding out a stack of bills.

"No, that's okay," Amber said, moving past him.

He pressed the money on her. "Cab fare," he said.

"How far do you think I'm taking a cab—Austin?"

His expression was stern. "You can't be walking around out there at this time of night," he said. "If you don't take a cab, I'll have to get dressed and come with you."

Amber sorted through the cash in his hand and took a ten-dollar bill. "This will get it," she said. "Thanks."

"Thank you, baby," Matt said.

"Don't call me baby, I hate that."

"Okay." He hesitated for a long minute. "I'm sorry. I don't actually remember your name," he admitted.

"Gwen," Amber told him. "Just remember me as Gwen."

10

<hr>

Saturday was cleaning day. At least it was for Ellen. Amber slept in, as per usual, and Wilma had never much believed in it.

"If God had wanted us to keep house, he wouldn't have invented maids," she would joke.

In Wilma's long, undisciplined and chaotic life, there had been very few maids. That didn't change her opinion about it one bit. Wilma had no need for order in her personal choices or her surroundings.

Ellen, on the other hand, felt much more in control of her world when all the rooms were spic-and-span and the dresser drawers were tidy.

She took on the Saturday morning ritual with only Jet's help. They put on aprons and tied bandannas around their hair. Jet did all the low dusting, chair legs and bottom shelves. Ellen took care of the higher areas.

The child was singing, in her sweet, angelic voice, one of the horrible songs that Wilma had taught her.

"When Puppy was little, just about so tall, he hiked up his leg and he wee-weed on the wall."

Ellen ignored the vocal entertainment and concentrated on the little girl's efforts. Jet was very careful and conscientious about her work. She took what she saw as an adult responsibility very seriously. Ellen wanted to nurture that, develop it.

She had taken it for granted with Amber. Her daughter had always been biddable and dependable. During Paul's illness when money had gotten tight, she'd never complained about the change in their lifestyle or the shortage of new clothes and spending money. Quite the opposite. She, on her own initiative, had gotten a job to help make ends meet. Those were some of their best times as a family. They were all pulling together for a common goal and hope was contagious.

That seemed far distant from the situation today. Amber still worked, but beyond that her level of responsibility was not in keeping with what Ellen would have expected of a single parent. She should be making a home for Jet, making a life for herself. Neither challenge seemed to rate high on Amber's to-do list.

Ellen hadn't seen it coming. Not her daughter's disillusion, self-destruction, unplanned pregnancy. Nor had she seen the inevitability of her husband's death.

Ellen wasn't sure who did realize it first. Paul, who quit talking about getting well? Or Amber who withdrew from family, friends, school? But it certainly was not Ellen.

She hadn't even allowed for the possibility. As long as there was a new treatment, an untried drug combination, an experimental protocol, she'd been confident that a cure was just around the corner. The doctors had been as upbeat as she was herself. Only the insurance company seemed to be throwing in the towel.

Paul had cautioned her against spending their retirement money. Ellen had had no qualms, not even hesitancy. It was an investment. They would spend their money to get Paul well and then the two of them together would build the business back. She'd envisioned Paul's health, his future, as if it were a blue-chip stock option. It turned out to be more like putting their financial future on a roulette table at 23 red. But she wouldn't have, couldn't have done anything differently. How much was a husband/father worth? How much should a wife be willing to pay? To Ellen's mind, the answer to both questions was *anything*.

She'd waved away his worries.

"I don't anticipate saving your life as a recurring expense," she teased.

"What if I don't recover?" he'd asked. "You'll have to start all over."

"If I have to start over, I will," she'd assured him.

But she hadn't. Not really. Beginning again was like swimming upstream. Exhausting, and more suited to younger and stronger people. Ellen was content these days to simply tread water.

"Look, Gramma! I found a penny," Jet called out to her excitedly.

Ellen glanced over to where the child was pointing. Sure enough, she could see a tiny metallic gleam just under the edge of the couch.

"Is it a lucky penny or just an ordinary penny?" Ellen asked her.

The little girl slid it out where she could get a better look and studied the coin.

"Is it the man that's lucky or the house?" she asked.

"The man," Ellen answered. "A very great man, Abraham Lincoln. He was a president and he made the law equal for people of every color."

Jet didn't seem interested in the history lesson. She sighed. "It's just an ordinary penny."

"Well," Ellen suggested. "You can put it in your pocket or you can turn it over and leave it someplace to make it lucky for somebody else."

The child was taking her options under serious consideration.

"If I give it to somebody else, will it be lucky for them?" she asked.

"Absolutely," Ellen told her. "I'm sure there are a lot of people who deserve some good luck today."

Jet nodded, thoughtfully.

Within the house they could hear the telltale shuffle of someone moving about and the closing of the bathroom door.

"Mama's up," Jet said delightedly.

She picked up her penny and deserted her dust rag.

Jet hurried into the kitchen and waited next to the coffeepot. She knew from experience that this was Amber's first stop on the journey of her day.

Ellen decided to take a break herself and make a fresh pot. She poured the last of the strong black elixir into the sink and rinsed the carafe. Behind her Jet was busy apparently adjusting her mother's chair. Ellen filled the machine with water and scooped the ground coffee into the filter. A small red light came on as she pressed Brew. Almost immediately a hot, steady stream of brown liquid began to flow.

But not soon enough.

"Don't tell me there's no coffee," were Amber's first words of the day.

"Five minutes," Ellen assured her.

"Good morning, Mama," Jet said.

"Good morning," Amber responded, before even glancing at the girl.

When she did look at Jet her brow furrowed and then she burst out laughing.

"My God, Mother, what's this *do rag* on Jet's head? You've got her dressed up like Aunt Jemima."

Ellen looked at her granddaughter, horrified.

"Amber, don't say such a thing," she scolded. "We were cleaning. I insist that in my own house, we avoid speaking in racial stereotypes."

"Just 'cause you don't speak them, doesn't make them not exist," Amber responded. "And remember, Mother, this is not your house."

"It might as well be," Ellen said. "I'm the only one who has any interest in keeping it habitable. Or are you thinking that I'm just the maid?"

"I help Gramma," Jet pointed out. "I'm a very good maid."

Amber looked at her mother, snidely. "If you're so sticky about stereotypes, I wouldn't think you'd train your granddaughter to be a domestic."

"Cleanliness in next to Godliness," Ellen declared, sounding like a priggish stuffed shirt even to her own ears.

It was, in its way, a victory for Amber, who looked momentarily pleased with herself.

"Who's Aunt Jemima?" Jet asked.

Ellen hesitated, not sure how much to explain.

"She's a lady who makes pancakes," Amber answered.

Jet accepted that explanation without question.

"Why don't we make some pancakes," Amber said. "You and me, you want to make some pancakes?"

Jet's eyes widened with delight. "Could we?"

"Jet had breakfast hours ago," Ellen said.

"I don't care," Amber told her.

It was a challenge. Ellen was tempted to take it up. Amber breezed in and out of her daughter's life with not nearly enough concern. She came and went as she pleased with apparently no thought to making something of her own life or bettering her daughter's. Ellen couldn't ignore her disapproval. But, she couldn't punish Jet for it either.

"Oh, please, can we, Gramma?" Jet pleaded. "Can Mama and me make pancakes, please."

The child's deference to Ellen didn't sit well with Amber.

"We can do anything we want," Amber told her daughter. "We don't need anyone's permission."

Jet looked at her mother as if she wanted to believe her. But she shot her grandmother a glance, just in case. Ellen wouldn't deny the child a special time with Amber.

"It's please *may* we make pancakes," Ellen told her. "And yes you may."

"Yea!" the little girl cried delightedly, clapping her hands.

"Just let me get some coffee down and I'll be ready," Amber told her.

Jet was clutching her hands together and grinning ear to ear.

"I can wait, Mama," she assured Amber. "I can wait very patiently."

Ellen poured the coffee for her daughter and directed Jet to get the milk from the refrigerator. It took the child a moment, digging through the fruits and frondescence of Wilma's most recent foray to the market.

Jet returned with the milk and, with Amber's help, poured a little into the coffee. She waited until her mother had taken a sip and had relaxed back into the kitchen chair before glancing at the floor and making a very dramatic gasp.

"Look, Mama!" Jet said pointing. "Look there, there's something under your chair. Look."

Amber followed the direction her daughter indicated.

"What is this?"

She obviously recognized what it was immediately, but still posed the question.

"It's a lucky penny, Mama," Jet told her.

Amber leaned down and picked it up, examining it thoughtfully.

"I think it's just a penny that got lost on the floor," she said. "I think it's just a plain old ordinary penny."

"Oh, no," Jet assured her. "It was ordinary, but I fixed it. I turned it lucky just for you, Mama."

"You think I need some luck?"

The question puzzled Jet. "Doesn't everybody?" she asked.

Amber didn't answer. She held the coin in her hand for a long moment before looking up at her daughter again.

"Thank you, sweetie," she said. "I'm lucky just to have a little girl like you."

Jet laughed. "That's not lucky at all, Mama. If I wasn't your little girl, whose would I be?"

Amber opened her arms and Jet flew into them to get a hug.

Over the child's head she eyed Ellen with both accusation and amusement.

Ellen shouldn't have felt any confusion. She wanted Jet to have time with her mother. And she wanted Amber to make wonderful memories of her daughter's childhood. She and Amber weren't in competition for Jet's love. The little girl had more than enough for both of them. Ellen knew that. But somehow, over time, her relationship with Amber had become so strained that every interaction had the potential for conflict.

"I suppose I'll leave you short-order cooks to your culinary creations," she said.

"Thanks," Amber said.

The batter had been a little runny, affording some very unusual-shaped pancakes more reminiscent of a Rorschach test than an all-American breakfast. They also varied in color from pale doughy beige to crisp black. But the experience had been entertaining. Jet's apron was dusted with flour and her hands were sticky with syrup.

"You get washed up and I'll fill the dishwasher," Amber told her daughter.

They had been let alone for their cooking experiment. The little house was not really big enough for three grown women and a child to get away from each other. The fact that both her mother and Wilma had managed to keep their distance must have been planned. That was good and bad. Amber wanted time alone with her daughter, but she certainly didn't want the company of her own thoughts. Not today.

Ellen was cleaning the bathroom as if she intended

to practice surgery there later. The reek of bleach overrode the more pleasant odors of cooking.

Wilma had come in, surveyed the activities in the kitchen and returned to the front porch.

Amber's time alone with Jet was precious. It wasn't as if she avoided the child, she was simply busy. She slept late and then had to hurry to work. Weekends were high commission days, so she almost always worked. And with two doting grandmothers at her constant beck and call, Jet never wanted for attention.

It would be different, of course, once she moved out. Then she'd have to schedule specific times to visit and they'd have planned activities. It could work out all right, she assured herself. It could actually work out better.

Jet hurried back into the kitchen. Her hands and face were clean and she was ready to help. Amber gave her a sponge and had her wipe down the counters. She expected to have to re-do them herself and was surprised at Jet's determination to do it right and to do it herself.

"Great job!" Amber's comment.

"I help Gramma and Wil-ma all the time," Jet said. "I'm a good helper."

"Of course, you are."

"But I like helping you best," Jet said. "'Cause you're Mama."

Amber was taking that in. All the love in the world was gleaming in her child's eyes and that gaze was directed squarely at her. It was truly awesome, in the fullest sense of that word.

A light tapping on the door frame interrupted.

Amber turned to see Brent standing there.

Jet squealed and went running toward him.

She flew into his arms and he lifted her up to the ceiling. She was giggling.

"Mama and me made pancakes," she told him. "They were scrunch-us."

"Scrumptious, huh. And I missed them."

"You missed 'em."

He glanced over at Amber. "I didn't even know your mother could cook," he said.

"Of course I can cook. Everybody can cook."

"I can't," he said.

"That's why he takes me out to lunch," Jet said. "Are we going to lunch today?"

"I thought you just had pancakes?"

"I did," she said. "But you didn't."

"I actually have a better idea," Brent said. "I wanted to take you and your mother on an outing."

"An outing!" Jet looked toward her mother, eyes wide in excitement. "He wants to take us on an outing." She turned back to Brent. "What's an outing?"

"It's just a little afternoon trip," Brent said. "A little, casual afternoon trip. No big deal, no big meaning to it."

The last was said for Amber's benefit. He needn't have bothered. Amber had no intention of going anywhere with him.

"I have to work this afternoon," she said.

"What time do you have to be at work?"

"Three o'clock."

"We have time to hang out, see some things," he assured her. "We can drop you off. It'll save you the time of the bus ride."

"I don't know…" Amber hesitated.

"Oh, please, Mama," Jet said. "We want you to go with us. Where are we going?"

"I thought we'd go to the McNay," Brent said.

That sounded great to Jet.

"We're going to the McNay!"

Amber was skeptical, uncertain. "You want to take a three-year-old to an art museum?"

"I'm three and a half," Jet pointed out. "And my birthday's coming up."

Brent shrugged, obviously not seeing a problem. "You're never too young for art. Isn't that the first thing people do with babies, show them pictures to look at."

Amber wasn't sure if it was quite the same thing.

"We won't be there long," he assured her. "As soon as you, or Jet, get tired of it, we'll leave."

"Please, Mama," Jet entreated. "Please go with us."

It almost seemed silly not to.

"I guess it wouldn't kill me," Amber said.

"Yeah!" Jet cheered and clapped.

In a few minutes, Amber found herself in the passenger seat of the Tahoe. Jet got herself into the fancy booster car seat in the back.

"You have a car seat?" Amber was astounded.

"I bought it for Jet, 'cause she's always hanging out with me these days," he answered. "And we want to keep her very safe."

The latter was directed to the little girl who nodded solemnly as she expertly buckled herself in.

"Besides," he added, grinning. "It's a real chick magnet."

"Yeah, I bet," Amber responded.

The drive up New Braunfels Avenue was short and virtually traffic free. Jet sang the entire way, alternating the theme from *Between the Lions* and something

Wilma had taught her about a fifth ace and a woman in scarlet.

Brent shared a secret smile with Amber, but she was immediately on-guard. She didn't want to share anything with him.

"Do you come here much these days?" he asked her.

Her eyes narrowed. "I think the last time was when I was in high school," she answered. "I'm poor, do you not get that yet? Poor people don't go to art museums." Her words were snide and defensive.

"They don't?" His tone was equally unpleasant. "I guess I always thought it was because they didn't know anything about art, including whether or not they liked it. You, at least as I remember you, love art. There's no reason why having your parents go bankrupt should change that."

"But it does," Amber told him.

"Well, don't let it," he said. "A free museum on the bus line. It sounds to me as if they want people to come. Money doesn't figure into it at all."

"When you're living hand to mouth your priorities are different," Amber said.

"Oh, sorry, I didn't understand," Brent said, facetiously. "Your priorities are different. My mistake. I thought you didn't have any priorities at all."

"Screw you!"

Jet had stopped singing.

"Screw you," she repeated.

"Jet!" they scolded in unison.

"Don't talk like that in front of her," Brent said.

"Don't interfere between me and my daughter," Amber shot back.

"Hey, haven't you heard, it takes a village to raise a child."

"Well it doesn't take the village idiot."

"It's the village idiot that's been spending more time with Jet this summer than her own mother," he pointed out.

"I didn't know a damn thing about that."

"And why didn't you know? You're her mother. You're supposed to be the one deciding where she goes and who she stays with," he said.

"When you have your own kids, then you can talk to me about it," she said. "I'm doing what *I* think is best for *my* child."

"You can't have it both ways, Amber. You can't pawn her off on your mother and grandmother and then claim that you're in charge."

"I didn't pawn her *off* on anybody," Amber claimed. "Unlike some people, I'm working at a *real* job."

"Why are you yelling at each other?" Jet asked from the back seat.

"We're not yelling!" they responded in unison.

"It sounds like yelling," Jet pointed out.

The two adults looked at each other for a long moment before sharing an embarrassed laugh.

"We were yelling," Amber admitted to her.

"Sorry," Brent said. "We won't do it anymore."

"Are you mad at each other?" she asked.

"No, we're just arguing," Brent said. "Don't you argue with your friends sometimes, when you're really not mad at them?"

Jet thought about that for a minute.

"I don't really have any friends but you and Wilma," the little girl pointed out.

"You have friends," Amber insisted, hoping that it was true. "What about…what about your little friends in Sunday School."

"Oh, yeah," Jet agreed, nodding. "I have friends on Sundays."

It was clear from the child's tone that she knew that there were a lot more days in the week.

"When you go to preschool, you'll have lots of friends," Brent assured her.

The child was excited about that. "When do I go to preschool, Mama?" she asked.

Amber shrugged. "I don't know," she said. "But I'm sure you'll go. I'll…I'll ask."

Ellen would undoubtedly know. She probably had Jet's entire educational future sketched out. It was embarrassing for Amber to admit that she hadn't even thought about it. Of course Jet would have to go to preschool. Did they do that at four? And then there was kindergarten. There was a public school in their neighborhood. She didn't even know the name of it, much less its curriculum or reputation.

The entrance to the McNay was a wide gate with impressive pillars. Much more imposing and grandiose than the Spanish-style stucco and tile mansion that housed the collection.

Mrs. McNay, a much married and perennially single woman, had been a contemporary of Georgia O'Keefe and knew many of the artists of the Taos School—some of whom had visited her here and painted at her home. But when she began collecting, she didn't limit herself to the genre of the southwest. Her private acquisitions included the works of Van Gogh, Degas, Renoir, as well as twelfth-century mosaics and modern sculptures. It added up to one of the finest smaller museum collections in the world. Upon her death, her art was put on display for the people of San Antonio and visitors to the city. There were no fees for entry to the museum or the grounds and no charge for parking.

Brent pulled into the lot and they got out and started up along the stone walkway through the gardens.

Jet was skipping ahead of them and laughing.

"Look, Mama, look. They've got a waterfall," she said.

"It's a fountain," her mother corrected.

"Can we go there? Can we go there?"

"We'll look at it later," Brent told her. "Let's go inside first and look at the pictures."

"Okay," the little girl agreed eagerly.

When they got to the door, Brent opened it for them and Amber cautioned her daughter. "This is a quiet place," she said. "We don't have to be silent, but we'll try not to disturb the other people."

Jet nodded. "Like the liberry," she said.

Amber's brow furrowed as Brent agreed.

"You've taken her to the library?" Amber asked, astonished.

"They've got books there," her daughter explained.

Inside the Spanish-style building with its stenciled beams and mosaic tiles, they walked from painting to painting. There was no grandiose discussion of the artist's style or the underlying theme represented. Jet would announce that the picture was a man or a house or a lake. Her highest compliment was "I know him" or "I've been there."

The interior courtyard with its lily pond and fantasy elements was Jet's favorite. Amber and Brent sat on a bench and watched her scamper through the foliage and carry on conversations with statues.

Amber was feeling surprisingly relaxed, happy almost. Though she would have hated to admit it, she was glad that Brent had wanted to do this. She was glad that he'd included her.

"Listen," she said, by way of apology. "I'm sorry that I went off on you in the car. I know that Wilma needs your help and I appreciate the time you spend with Jet."

Brent nodded, accepting, before offering his own mea culpa. "Jet's pretty cool," he said. "I've got no business telling you how to raise your kid, 'cause you are obviously doing something right."

"She is great, isn't she," Amber said. "I don't think I can take credit for it. It must be something innate in her. 'Cause no one in my whole family is any good at mothering. Wilma was distracted. Mom was smothering and I'm...I'm basically unavailable."

"I think you're too hard on yourself," Brent said. "And on Wilma and Ellen. Besides, dysfunctional parenting is kind of like the 'in' thing these days."

"Maybe so." Amber gave him a small smile and deftly turned the conversation. "So how's it going at the Justice Center?"

"It's interesting," he admitted. "More than I thought, really, when I accepted the job."

"What are you doing, I mean, besides working and baby-sitting Jet?"

He shrugged. "Seeing my old buds, doing some hiking, reading things that I like instead of things that are assigned."

Amber nodded.

"I've actually been hanging out with my folks quite a bit," he said. "My dad and I went to a movie together the other night. First time since I was about eleven, I think. I like them both better since they got a divorce."

"Your parents got a divorce?" Amber was flabbergasted.

"Yeah," Brent answered. "Almost two years ago now."

"I can't believe it."

He shrugged. "You're not the only one for whom life has gone on," he pointed out.

"I'm sorry, I didn't know," Amber said. "Are you okay with it?"

"Sometimes," he said. "Dad's got a girlfriend. I like her, but I think it probably hurts my mother. So I'm like conflicted or something. I'm just trying to live through it, let it be what it is."

"You should just get over that," Amber said. "Men are just guys. Though I guess I should have seen it coming. Your dad is like really good-looking. I could see him as a player. And your mom...I don't know...some people are so narrow, it's like they are walking sideways," she said.

Brent gave her a look.

"What?" she asked him.

"Nothing."

"It's something or you wouldn't be all puffed up like that."

"Okay," Brent answered. "I was just thinking how quick you are to sum up my parents. You're more complicated than that. I'm more complicated than that. I think we've got to assume there's more to them than the obvious."

"Well, yeah, I guess so."

"And I was wondering how you'd be if Ellen started bringing guys home," he said.

Amber gave an unladylike snort and shook her head. "She will never get over Dad. It just won't happen."

"That's the point of grieving," Brent said. "Not that you get over the person, but that you get on with your life."

Jet came flying over to them, arms waving gracefully, face angelic.

"Are you a bird?" Amber asked her.

"I'm not a bird, I'm a fairy," she said. "And this is my fairy garden."

"Pretty nice fairy garden," Brent said. "Are you ready to go upstairs with me? There's one more picture I wanted to show you."

She nodded. When Brent got to his feet she put her little hand in his.

"Are you coming, Mama?" she asked.

"Sure," Amber said, rising to her feet.

They took the outside stairway to the second level and walked along the balcony.

"Are we going to see the Embreys?" Amber asked.

Brent glanced back to look at her. "Do you like the Embreys?"

"They're my favorite," she admitted.

Brent grinned broadly. "Me, too, maybe we'll stop there, but that's not where we're going."

Inside the upper gallery, Brent directed them toward the very first piece of art that Mrs. McNay had ever bought.

The minute Jet caught sight of it, there was immediate recognition. "Look, Mama, it's Boo!"

Brent was grinning. "I knew she would like it," he said.

She obviously did.

"I don't get it," Amber whispered.

Brent looked at her puzzled. "It's a Diego Rivera," he said. "It's called *Portrait of Delfinia Flores*."

"I know that," Amber said. "Who's Boo?"

"You didn't see *Monsters, Inc.*?"

Amber shook her head.

Brent tutted disapprovingly. "We've really got to get you out more," he said.

11

⟶ ⟵

Ellen went to work early on Monday. It wasn't that she'd intended to, exactly. Another dream had awakened her at dawn. After she'd had all the coffee she wanted and was all dressed and ready to go, it seemed foolish just to sit around the house. So she had gone to work. The office was not yet open—she knew it wouldn't be. It was still early and Yolanda was always running a couple of minutes late.

There was nothing for Ellen to do but park and wait or drive around. It certainly made a lot more sense to park. But Ellen drove. She drove down into the King William district, past the house where Mrs. Stanhope lived.

What the woman had said had stuck in Ellen's mind. *In the mornings I can almost see myself.* Inexplicably, Ellen had an unwarranted desire to see Mrs. Stanhope herself.

"Okay, God, I don't know why I feel like I need to do this. But if you think I have some kind of comfort to offer this woman, I'm willing. Or at least I'm willing if she's out in the garden. If she isn't in the garden, I'm off to Helgalita's to get a cup of coffee," Ellen told anyone in heaven who might be listening.

She had never held any morbid fascination for mental illness. She didn't watch made for TV movies about multiple personality or schizophrenia. She changed the channel when PBS did a special on abnormal brain function. And she always considered novels that explained the motivations of people by virtue of their psychopathology as being easy cop-outs for lazy writers.

Nor was she fearful of it. She was knowledgeable enough to assume that while sociopaths and serial killers might be the darlings of books and films, the vast majority of people with mental illness were much more afraid of her than she should be of them.

Still, if Mrs. Stanhope wasn't in the garden, she would just drive by. If she didn't see her she wouldn't stop. It wasn't as if she really *needed* to get involved. The woman obviously had friends and family around her. And Ellen had plenty of problems of her own.

Ellen slowed the car in front of the charming little house. Sitting on a bench beneath an overhang of mountain laurel, Mrs. Stanhope was gazing into the eastern horizon.

Ellen wanted to roll her eyes at heaven. If she didn't have enough trouble in her life already, she was being given the formidable task of befriending the local crazy lady.

"Fine!" she said, to the supreme being on her prayer channel. "If you want me to talk to her, I'll talk to her."

She parked the car.

As she got out, she checked her watch. She'd only stay a few minutes. And she wouldn't stay at all if the woman didn't know her or seemed confused.

Ellen walked along the white picket fence to the little garden gate. It wasn't even latched. No wonder the woman managed to escape with such regularity.

Although, Ellen was sure she wouldn't want the woman locked in either.

There was a narrow edge of flowering liriope skirting the slate stone path. The garden was profuse with iris and cannas, rosebushes and trumpet vine. Ancient crepe myrtles of pink and white towered over the garden. The mountain laurel had already gone to seed. Lantana, with its multicolored blossoms, was at the height of its glory. Day lilies bent in the morning sunshine.

"Good morning," Ellen called out to the woman, stirring her from her reverie.

Mrs. Stanhope looked up, curious. Her sweet little face, looked somehow childlike even in advanced age. Ellen didn't see any indication of recognition, but the women did smile at her, welcoming.

"I'm Ellen," she said. "From the tax office."

She appeared puzzled. "Is there something wrong with my taxes? Oh, dear, you had better talk to Irma. She handles all those sorts of things."

"No, I'm not here about your taxes," Ellen assured her. "I came to see you. We had coffee together the other day."

She allowed the statement to simply hang out there for a long moment. Ellen was ready to do an about-face and march back to the car, when the older woman's face suddenly wreathed in smiles and she beamed at Ellen delightedly.

"Of course," Mrs. Stanhope said. "I remember you. You work in Max Roper's office. You're a widow like myself."

"Yes, yes I am."

"Sit down, sit down," Mrs. Stanhope insisted. "I am so pleased that you came to visit me."

The low wrought iron garden seat was not particularly comfortable, but it did afford a charming view. As she glanced around she discovered a wide covered porch not visible from the road. At a breakfast strewn table with coffee cups and newspaper sat Irma. She was speaking to someone on the phone. Her words muffled to obscurity over distance, but she was looking right at Ellen.

Not knowing what else to do, Ellen gave a slight nod of acknowledgement. Irma returned the wary greeting.

"It is so nice to have visitors in my garden," Mrs. Stanhope said. "I would love to offer you some tea or something, but I don't have live-in help anymore and the maids don't arrive until eight."

"I just had breakfast," Ellen assured her. "And I drink so much coffee at work, that I honestly try to avoid it everywhere else."

Mrs. Stanhope sighed, a little disheartened. "A proper hostess would serve tea, even if you had no interest in drinking it," she said. "It's been such a long time since I've been a proper hostess. I could ask Irma to brew up something, but…" Mrs. Stanhope lowered her voice to a whisper in confidence. "She's already working. When I disturb her at work, she gets very crabby sometimes."

"I don't need a thing," Ellen assured her.

"Irma is a very good person," Mrs. Stanhope said. "She doesn't have to stay with me, but she does. And she will listen to me talk about Lyman, sometimes for hours on end. She never even knew the man."

Ellen nodded. At least this morning the woman didn't think her husband was working at his store.

"Irma's been living here with me for years now,"

Mrs. Stanhope continued. "She never had any children and she's *divorced*."

The last word was said in a scandalized whisper.

"Oh, I'm sorry," Ellen said politely.

Mrs. Stanhope shook her head. "He's an obnoxious, selfish, mama's boy. Irma is well rid of him."

Ellen nodded.

"It was, however, the first divorce in the history of the family," Mrs. Stanhope pointed out. "If my father had still been alive, he never would have allowed it. But then, he wouldn't have allowed her to marry the man. He had very definite ideas about what family names his family could connect with. He was opposed to my marriage to Lyman. It was the only time in my life that I ever went against him. He never let me forget it. He said he would disinherit me and cast me out of the family."

"Parents often say things they don't mean," Ellen pointed out.

Mrs. Stanhope chuckled. "Oh, he meant it. And he did it. Wrote me completely out of his will," she said. "But of course, he couldn't seem to stay out of my life."

She was gazing thoughtfully in the direction of the porch.

"I often wonder what he would make of Irma," she said. "How could he help but be proud of who she is and all she's achieved? And how could she have accomplished anything if she'd not been allowed to pursue a career. He would never have let her work. He didn't let me help out at the store, even when I was a married woman and off on my own."

"It sounds like he was a very domineering father," Ellen said.

Mrs. Stanhope nodded. "He had very strong opinions about things," she said. "Even little things. My husband bought me a fox stole for our first anniversary present. Papa made me take it back. He said it was ostentatious—that a cloth coat was good enough for any woman."

Ellen remembered Yolanda's story about Mrs. Stanhope wearing furs year-round. Apparently she'd gotten over her father's opinion.

"I am just grateful that Irma has had a chance to live her own life and make her own mistakes," Mrs. Stanhope said.

The image of Amber flashed through Ellen's thoughts.

"Yes, I suppose it is best to make your own choices," Ellen said. "Even though, as a parent, it is hard to stand by and do nothing."

"I wouldn't know," Mrs. Stanhope said. "Lyman and I never had children."

Her voice sounded so sad.

"At least now you have Irma," Ellen said, with deliberate cheerfulness.

"Yes, Irma is truly good to me," Mrs. Stanhope said. "Living alone is not the best thing."

"I'm sure it's not," Ellen agreed.

"You and your husband must have been so proud when your child was born," Mrs. Stanhope said.

Ellen nodded. "Yes, we were thrilled."

"And was your husband a devoted father?" she asked.

"Oh, yes," Ellen told her. "Though I have to admit he was a bit scared when we started out."

"Really?"

Ellen related the story of her husband's reluctance

to take on fatherhood. He made it clear early in the pregnancy that he would be the breadwinner and the childrearing would fall to Ellen. When other daddies were fighting to get into the delivery room, he'd been content to wait outside. Once Amber was born he had been reluctant to hold her. He seemed afraid that he might drop her or break her. On the day they came home from the hospital, Ellen was holding Amber, but had to go to the bathroom. Paul was sitting in his chair reading. She had simply plopped the baby in his arms.

"I was sitting on the toilet and from the living room I heard this really high silly voice saying, 'Hello there, I'm your daddy.'"

Mrs. Stanhope laughed.

"Amber had him wrapped around her finger from that day forward," Ellen stated unequivocally.

"Oh, it must have been such a joy to be a mother," Mrs. Stanhope said.

"It certainly has its moments," Ellen said, smiling.

"And Amber still lives with you?"

Ellen nodded. "When I lost the house, my daughter and her little girl and I all moved in with my mother. And we've been there ever since."

"It sounds like a cozy arrangement," Mrs. Stanhope said with a rather wistful sigh.

Ellen chuckled lightly. "To tell you the truth, I don't often think of it as cozy. More like crowded and uncomfortable. I've never really gotten along with my mother all that well. And my daughter doesn't get along that well with me. Now we're all hemmed up together in a house with a three-year-old."

"Oh my goodness!"

"But you know how God is," Ellen said ruefully.

"Just when you start complaining, he makes you see how lucky you are, or maybe he lets you imagine how much worse off you can be."

Mrs. Stanhope's brow furrowed. "What do you mean?"

"My mother doesn't have clear ownership of the house we're in. She married the man who owned it a few months before he died. He never changed his will and his children want us out of there."

"Oh, dear, that is worrisome."

Ellen nodded.

"What are you planning to do?" Mrs. Stanhope asked.

"Fight them," Ellen answered. "What else is there?"

"Yes," the woman said with a sigh. "I suppose you must. They are family. But sometimes you must fight. Trying to appease them, trying to get along, that can make things so much worse."

Ellen's troubles seemed to worry Mrs. Stanhope almost as much as they worried Ellen. Her cheery face was sad now. She seemed to be troubled now and lost in thought.

Mrs. Stanhope gave a shudder of revulsion that was completely genuine. "I hate money," she said. "Sometimes I think it just exists to make people miserable."

Ellen was a little surprised at the vehemence of the statement. Especially considering Yolanda's assertion that Mrs. Stanhope was as rich as Croesus.

Why am I talking about my problems! Ellen scolded herself.

Ellen didn't want her to lose hold of the morning's lucidity. If Mrs. Stanhope could only see herself in the morning, then she should at least get the opportunity of seeing *herself*, not the worries and complaints of a woman she hardly knew. Ellen decided it was best to change the direction of the conversation, to talk about something more pleasant, something that Mrs. Stanhope enjoyed talking about.

"Tell me about your husband," Ellen asked, smiling brightly at her.

Mrs. Stanhope looked up at her, puzzled for a moment before she replied.

"He committed suicide," she answered calmly. "He hanged himself in the back room of the store. He had…" She hesitated on the words. "He had some business problems."

Ellen could hardly swallow the choking sound that shuddered in her throat. She was shocked almost beyond belief.

"I…I am so sorry," Ellen managed to stutter out. "I had no idea. I…"

"No apologies necessary, dear," the woman said. She was smiling brightly again, charming, animated. "I do wish we had some tea. If the maids don't arrive soon, Irma will just have to make us some."

Ellen glanced down at her watch.

"Oh, they will be here any minute," she said. "And I have to be at work."

"Oh, I'm sure your boss is a dreadful grouchy scowl," she said, almost giggling.

"No," Ellen said. "He's not like that, but I do like to be on time."

"Of course you do, dear," she said. "And he appreciates it so much."

"I thought you didn't talk to him?"

"Oh, now who is being silly," she said. "We have

our little spats now and again. But I've never stopped talking to him. Who would that punish more? Him or me?"

She giggled delightedly at her own little joke.

"You go on to the store then," Mrs. Stanhope said. "But you must bring Sis and Willy over to play one afternoon. I miss those little scamps tremendously."

Ellen rose to her feet. Mrs. Stanhope was smiling at her. She looked younger, happier. She was back in her dream world and she obviously liked it better.

"See you," Ellen said.

"Goodbye, dear."

As she walked down the stone path to the garden gate, she glanced up at Irma on the porch. She wasn't on the phone anymore, she simply had her eye on Ellen. Ellen offered a wave. Irma returned it in kind.

Poor Mrs. Stanhope. Her husband had killed himself and she'd gone crazy. Did that happen? Could one tragic event make a person crazy for life?

"What was that about?" she asked God as she climbed into her car. As usual, she received no direct answer.

Amber wasn't even fully awake yet. She had been sitting on the back step with Wilma. She was hoping to share a cigarette, but Wilma wasn't smoking yet today. Her morning hack, to clear her lungs, was unusually difficult. She'd put on her oxygen and kept it running. As she choked and coughed and spat into tissues, Amber tried not to take notice of the unmistakable sounds of her illness. It was difficult to ignore.

Finally, she'd gotten up to go for coffee. The pot was already half-empty. Though she was up much earlier than usual, her mother had already gone to work.

She was still in the kitchen when the phone rang.

"How much did Matt give you?" Gwen questioned eagerly. "Did you get your half of the deposit money?"

"Ten dollars for cab fare," Amber answered.

"You're kidding?" Gwen was taken aback. "Didn't you screw him?" she asked.

"Yeah, I screwed him," Amber answered, trying to wrap a shell of toughness around her vulnerability.

"That cheap bastard," Gwen complained. "The good-looking ones always turn out to be cheap. They think they're God's gift and that they're doing you some honor. I hope it falls off."

Amber didn't argue or concur. She thought the less said about what she was now thinking of euphemistically as *the Friday night incident*, the better. She had managed to avoid Gwen over the weekend, spending the day with Jet and Brent, working until closing Saturday night. She hadn't felt like clubbing and had simply caught the bus for home. But when she got to her stop, she worried that it might look suspicious, so she rode on up into Alamo Heights and sat in a quiet coffeehouse there. She was home by eleven and then slept the clock around and went straight into work on Sunday.

"I guess, we may have to just wait a little longer to get that apartment," Amber said.

Gwen gave a knowing chuckle. "Not nearly as long as you'd think," she said. "The old creep really came through for me on Friday and then I went out to *Dick's* with a couple of suits that I picked up at the hotel bar on Saturday. I've got this wad of bills. Enough to choke you."

"That's great."

"I'm calling the apartment manager this morning to tell her we're going to take it." Gwen was giggling with excitement. "It's really happening! I'm not sure I really believed that it ever would."

Amber tried to share her delight, but she couldn't quite manage it. She supposed that she hadn't really believed that it would happen either. Now that it was staring her in the face, she wasn't sure anymore that it was exactly what she wanted.

"I don't know if I'm ready for this," she admitted to her friend. "I mean, have we really looked at this logically. Shouldn't we have wheels first and…and better jobs or something."

"We are going to have wheels," Gwen told her. "And only one of us needs a better job."

"What do you mean?"

"This is *so* easy," Gwen told her. "There are guys here from out of town every day of the week. I'm thinking I can pick up an extra $500 a month without even trying. And you haven't heard the good news yet."

"What's the good news?"

"You know Kirsten, the mousy weasel that I work with. I've told you about her."

Amber had heard the name, but she couldn't associate it with any particular remark or story.

"Kirsten is leaving at the end of the month," Gwen continued. "And I told the boss I knew just the right girl to fill her position."

"Who?"

"You."

"Why would I want to change jobs?" Amber asked.

"Because you hate that damned underwear store," Gwen answered. "Carly's always spying on you. She's never going to let you get ahead. And if you can't get ahead there, there's not much chance elsewhere. You've been hanging around the mall since you were a kid. You're never going to be manager, and so you're never going to make any money."

"And I'll do better in a hotel job?" Amber was unconvinced. "It's the lowest pay scale in the city."

"It's the same as retail," Gwen assured her.

"But with no sales commissions," Amber pointed out.

"Depends upon what you mean by that," Gwen said, chuckling. "If I can pick up that extra cash, so can you. Between the two of us, we'll have furniture and a car and clothes. I tell you, Amber, this is our chance."

Amber didn't like the sound of that.

"You said it would just be once," she reminded Gwen. "We were just going to take the money to get the apartment. Now it's sounding like we should become regulars at this."

"Just until we get things rolling," Gwen assured her. "We get the apartment and get settled in, get us a car. Then we're back to doing what we want to. And who we want to."

Amber felt the queasy tightening in her stomach once again.

"I don't know, Gwen."

"You don't know about what?"

"It's hooking, Gwen," Amber said. "We can call it partying or picking up guys, but it's hooking."

"Get real," Gwen said. "It's not like we're going to

be drug addicts standing on a street corner in boots and a thong."

"That's just a stereotype," Amber said.

"We're not going to have a pimp, or do payoffs or even take calls," Gwen said. "We'll just meet guys at the hotel and agree to see them later. That's all it amounts to."

"People go to jail for that."

"Oh, puh-leeze," Gwen replied. "At least in jail we'd be living on our own."

"That's not true and it's not even funny," Amber said.

"Damn it, Amber," her friend said, angrily. "Do you think that you can just go on drifting forever?"

"Drifting? Gwen, if we look that up in the dictionary, we'll see *your* face, not mine."

"Hey, I'm the one putting a deposit on an apartment," Gwen told her. "You're just my potential roommate. And I'm not about to let you live off me like you live off your mother."

"I'm not doing that," she said. "I pay my way in this house."

"Oh, yeah, right," Gwen countered facetiously.

"Just because I don't want to be a prostitute doesn't mean I'm not willing to work," Amber said.

"Selling panties for eight bucks an hour," Gwen answered. "That's what you call work."

"I make commissions," Amber pointed out. "Retail is a tough job."

"You don't know from tough," her friend countered. "You've had it padded and easy all your life."

"What are you talking about?" Amber was incredulous. "I've been working since I was sixteen."

"Is that violins I hear? Gag me. You started working just to get out of the house, Amber."

"My dad was sick," she answered.

"Yeah, he was sick and so you couldn't be the center of the world anymore," Gwen said.

"You don't know what you're talking about!"

"I know about you. You were this blond suburban princess," Gwen continued. "Anything you wanted was just handed to you, like you deserved it. You still think you deserve it."

"That's not true," Amber insisted.

"It's true that you think you're better than me," Gwen said. "You think you're smarter, classier, *more worthy* than me."

"I just happen to have some self-respect," Amber countered. "I'm not some kind of slut."

"Oh, you're not some kind of slut?" Gwen feigned incredulity. "Aren't you the one who deliberately got herself pregnant just to get Mommy's attention?"

"That is untrue and unfair," Amber told her.

"You had to pick a black guy you hadn't seen before or since to really stick it to them," she went on.

"Shut up!" Amber said. "I was drunk and I liked the way the guy looked. Jet was completely an accident."

"Your baby was payback," Gwen insisted. "You expected to get a car for your sixteenth birthday and you've been in permanent whine mode ever since. You had your baby to piss off your mom."

"And you had yours to try to trap some loser into marriage," Amber shot back.

"Go to hell!"

"You first."

"At least I'll go in style with my own damned apartment."

Amber hesitated momentarily over that. And then burst out laughing. Gwen joined her.

"We do have our demons," Amber said, by way of apology.

"I just want mine to rest in a better crib," Gwen said.

"I need to think about all this, Gwen," Amber told her. "I just feel like it's rushing things. I need some time."

"How much time do you have?" Gwen asked. "I thought you were all going to be out on the street by the end of the month."

"Yeah, right," Amber replied. "I keep forgetting. Or I keep trying to forget, I'm not sure which."

"I'm ready to move," Gwen said. "If you're not moving in with me, I need to find somebody else."

Amber understood perfectly.

"I'll try to give you an answer this week," she promised. "I'll let you know about the apartment and the job and everything."

"Okay," Gwen said. "I just want you to remember, this may be your last chance. I'm sure it's mine. If I don't get out now, I maybe never will."

Amber hung up the phone with that thought still lingering in her brain. She might be trapped. It might be too late already.

She walked over to the coffee. She didn't want to think about Gwen. She didn't want to think about moving out, leaving Jet. She didn't want to think of any of those things. But she was going to have to. She was going to have to think about the future.

She had stopped doing that. When she realized that

her father had no future, her family had no future, she'd stopped thinking about a future for herself. Gwen was right. She was drifting. It was not an altogether unpleasant way to live.

She stirred her coffee and set the spoon on the counter. As she brought it to her lips, she turned and caught sight of someone in her peripheral vision. Momentarily startled, she turned to see Jet, quiet as a mouse, sitting at the kitchen table.

"I didn't know you were here," Amber said.

The little girl was still in her pajamas, but she looked wide awake.

"Can I have a pop-tart?" the child asked.

"I thought Gramma didn't let you eat those for breakfast," Amber said.

Jet shrugged. "You do."

It was irrefutable logic. Amber ignored it.

"Why don't I fix you some oatmeal," she said.

Jet didn't look too sure.

"I love oatmeal," Amber told her. "But it's only good when you fix a big pot. Why don't you go out on the step and see if Wilma wants some, too."

"Okay," the little girl said as she got up from her chair.

Amber began rooting through the pans under the cabinet.

"Mama?"

Jet was hesitating by the doorway, standing on one foot.

"What honey?"

"Why am I an accident?"

At first Amber didn't realize what the child was talking about. And then she recalled her conversation with Gwen. She wanted to slap herself. She never wanted Jet to imagine that she was anything but totally loved from the moment of conception. It was bad enough that she'd carelessly brought a child into the world who she couldn't afford to care for and who had no father. It was criminal to add to that any feeling of being unwanted.

Amber deserted the utensils and walked over to squat next to her daughter. She put her hands on the child's narrow shoulders and looked the little girl in the eye.

"Accident is not exactly the right word," she told her. "Sometimes we say things and we don't find exactly the right word."

Jet nodded, though she didn't appear convinced.

"You were not an accident," Amber assured her. "You were a surprise."

Jet thought about that only for an instant before breaking into a smile.

"A surprise? Like a birthday surprise?"

Amber grinned at her. "That's it, exactly," she said. "It was your birthday and you were our birthday surprise."

12

---◆---

Max laughed at something she said. Wilma loved to hear him laugh. He did it exceptionally well. It was a rousing bass that started deep down inside him and flowed through his whole body. It was as pleasant to watch as to hear. Wilma was keen on doing plenty of both.

After a little initial clumsiness that first day, Max had quickly gotten into the game. He was obviously enjoying himself.

The two were seated across from each other in the corner booth they both now considered their own. Wilma was munching on a hot pastrami sandwich and drinking a beer. Max always ordered the special. He was eating a less than healthy portion of chicken fried steak, smothered in gravy.

He had waited to order until she arrived. They had made no prior arrangement to meet. None was even suggested. But after only a few days, he'd begun to expect her.

A really good game player, Wilma knew, would have pulled the rug out from under him and not shown for a day or two, just to make him wonder.

Wilma wasn't all that keen on playing. She liked being with him. And she was old enough to realize what a gift that was. She didn't want to waste any opportunity to be with him by evoking any tired scheme. Besides, Max seemed impervious to scheming. Like her, he'd pretty much seen it all.

Unlike her, he didn't seem to be able to ferret out any information about who she was. Or he wasn't trying. That worried her a bit. They had shared few details of their personal lives beyond names. At first Wilma encouraged it to be that way. For good reason.

Wilma needed to be deliberately vague about who she was and how she lived. If he found out she was Ellen's mother, Ellen was certain to find it out as well. And though Max might suspect she had ulterior motives, Ellen would be absolutely certain of it. And being the forthright, honest, principled woman she was, she would spill the beans immediately.

So she had hedged, eschewed and dissembled. Perhaps he'd taken his cue from her, but he never asked anything about her past or revealed much about his own. That was unusual. It was Wilma's experience that most men talked about themselves, their possessions and their work. In that order.

Max rarely spoke of any of those things. And Wilma found it very refreshing to discuss subjects that were significantly less mundane.

"I think there has to be some kind of divine plan," Max said as he picked up his iced tea. "Or at least I hope there is."

His glass had made a wet ring atop the table. He carelessly wiped it away with a paper napkin.

Wilma shrugged. She wasn't in complete disagreement, but she was a good deal more skeptical.

"There might be or there might not. What difference does it make?" she asked him.

"Oh, I guess it makes me feel safer," he replied,

thoughtfully. "The direction of a life can be turned one hundred and eighty degrees on a dime. I guess it feels better to me to believe that there is some purpose in all of it."

He was certainly right about that.

"I've never given it all that much thought," Wilma admitted. "But I'd venture to say my daughter is in perfect agreement with you."

"Really? Tell me about her," he said.

Wilma had never really talked about Ellen before, but it seemed safe enough to do so in a general way.

"My daughter was never like me," she said. "I have never been quite able to get my ducks in a row. She's had her whole life set up just so neat and tidy."

"Do you envy that?"

Wilma shook her head. "No, I can't say that I ever did," she answered honestly. "And in the last few years, things for her have just gone to hell."

Max tutted sympathetically. "Too bad," he said. "But, sooner or later, it happens to all of us."

"All of us?" Wilma wasn't so sure.

"Don't tell me that hasn't happened to you," he said.

Wilma shrugged. "Yeah, but I always figured that I deserved it."

Max chuckled lightly. "*You* probably did!"

Wilma accepted the good humored jibe before taking another swig of her beer.

"I've certainly made a wrong turn or two in my time," she told him.

Max turned more serious.

"The truth is, Wilma," he said. "I don't hardly think that *any* turn in life is particularly a wrong turn."

Wilma eyed him skeptically. "Everything is beautiful, in its own way." Her tone was deliberately sarcastic.

He laughed out loud at that. "Wouldn't go that far," he admitted. "But I do think that if life's a road map, far too many people are trying to get on the expressway."

Wilma smiled at him. She liked his eyes. She liked his voice. She liked his long lean frame in his Western cut suit.

"You would, I suppose, suggest a road less traveled," she said. "I don't think that's original with you."

"You're likely right," he said. "Not much in this world is original with me."

She chuckled politely at his self-deprecating humor.

"I'm not saying that people should necessarily avoid the main roads," he explained. "They just have to be aware that the expressway is still under construction, so to speak. You're going to find detour after detour, and you may just end up running out of gas somewhere."

Wilma considered the analogy, nodding. "Honestly, that sounds more like me than my daughter," she said.

"Really?"

She nodded. "But I've always likened my life more to a game of musical chairs," Wilma said. "I've been going around in circles, landing somewhere just because the music stopped and there was an open seat."

Max looked at her thoughtfully.

"It's a fun game," she told him.

"I suppose so," he seemed to agree. "But just when

you're getting comfortable," he said. "The music starts up again."

Wilma smiled, then nodded with resignation.

"That's true," she said. "It's very true. I have to give my daughter credit. She's always wanted security and stability. She went after it whole hog. And she still keeps that goal firmly in mind. Even if it's further away now than ever."

"Maybe she just needs to redefine the meanings of those words," Max said. "I've had to do that a time or two."

Wilma shook her head, disbelieving. "You impress me as a man who knows exactly what he wants and goes after it."

Her words were true, but they were also the kind of statement designed to make most men puff up with pride and bluster into false modesty. Max was clearly not most men.

"There's a truth to that these days," he admitted. "But I swear I was forty years in the wilderness getting to this place."

"Now that's hard to believe," Wilma said.

Max gave a little shrug. He appeared to be paying a lot of attention to the use of his steak knife. Wilma knew it was a diversion.

"So are you going to tell me?" she asked. "Or leave me to imagine that you crawled through mosquito-ridden, snake-infested jungles on your hands and knees just to get to this bar?"

He laughed again, just as she knew he would. "Are you saying this bar *isn't* a mosquito-ridden, snake-infested jungle?"

"This is San Antonio," she reminded him. "Mosquito-ridden, snake-infested are attributes more commonly associated with Houston.''

He rewarded her caustic wit with a chuckle.

"Come on, now. Confess," she coaxed. "How did you get to be the gravy-sopping cowboy you are today?"

Max looked down into his glass and shook the ice in his tea, but didn't hesitate to answer.

"You've mistaken me, ma'am," he said in a low intimate drawl. "I'm not a cowboy. I'm a certified public accountant."

Wilma feigned surprise. "I take it that was one of those sudden turn-on-a-dime experiences that you hoped was a divine plan."

He nodded and then took a swallow as if girding himself to tell the tale.

"I wanted to be a cowboy, all right," he told her. "It was my ambition from the time I was big enough to straddle a fence rail and pretend to be on horseback."

Wilma smiled at him.

"I came by that quite honestly," he said. "My dad was a cowboy and his dad was a cowboy and back as far as anybody could remember the men of the family had always been cowboys."

"A fine tradition," she pointed out.

Max raised an eyebrow. "A cowboy's life is rough, poor and unmercifully short," he said.

Wilma nodded. "I've seen all those old John Wayne movies, too," she said.

"And it was even more complicated than the Duke ever let on," Max said. "The days when they kept full-time ranch hands on a place was a thing of the past when I was still a child. These days a big spread might keep a manager, but the working hands are part-timers, college kids or dirt cheap day labor."

"You couldn't be content with that," Wilma said.

Max didn't argue. "Any fellow with any grit or ambition gets his own ranch and runs his own cattle," he said. "That's the only way to ever make it pay."

"So why didn't you do that?" she asked.

"I flat-footed couldn't afford it," Max said. "Most of the big cattle ranches came into being when land was cheap. I found out mighty quick that if I wanted my own place, I'd better be well-heeled enough to lay down a fortune for it."

"Weren't there loans?" Wilma asked. "Ranching is like a small business, isn't it? You can borrow money to get started."

"It's a really risky small business," Max answered. "The profit margin on ranching is so small you can barely keep up with the interest. And if beef prices go down for a couple of years…well, you're busted."

Wilma nodded. She'd heard enough stories and met enough fellows down on their luck to believe it.

"If you want to cowboy and you don't inherit a place," he said, "then you're either a rich man playing at cattle ranching or you're working a second job to support yourself."

Wilma nodded. "We may have all been created equal," she said. "But that's the last time the field is level."

Max swirled the last piece of his chicken fried steak into the thick white gravy.

"That was a real hard lesson for a young man," he told her. "When you've dreamed and hoped and planned something for as long as you can remember

and then suddenly see it completely out of reach…"
His voiced trailed off and he shook his head.

"You must have been very disappointed," Wilma
said.

"Disappointed?" Max peered at her over the top of
his glasses. "I wasn't *disappointed*. I was mad as hell!"

His tone was inarguable. He shook his head as he
recalled that time.

"I was in a fury," he said. "All I wanted to do was
curse and scream and smash my fists through things.
It was my first real face-to-face encounter with the reality that life is unfair. I knew there was injustice in
the world and I'd seen plenty of cause for grievance.
But it had never, in my short life, directly affected me
or been so irrefutable and without remedy."

"What did you do?" Wilma asked.

"I did what angry young men always do," he replied. "I drank too much, drove too fast and lived too
wild. I was at the honky-tonks night after night,
sleeping most of my days. Working only when I had
to and trying not to think further ahead than my next
glass of Jack."

Wilma took a swig of her beer, noticing for the first
time, that he always drank iced tea. She'd assumed it
was because he was headed back to work. And that
might be true. Or it could be more.

"My friends, my family," Max continued. "They
didn't know what to make of it. I'd always been responsible, dependable. They didn't understand it. I
didn't understand it either. I wanted to be the person
that I'd always been. But I could no longer see any
reason to be that way. My future was going to be less
than I wanted it to be. So, as far as I was concerned, it
might as well be no future at all."

"Kids do that," Wilma said. "They don't know where they're going, so they just go crazy. It's almost a stage of life."

"It's a stage that lots of folks never live long enough to get past. And those that do, have often wasted so much of their life that they're playing catch up from then on."

"Are you playing catch up?" she asked.

Max shook his head. "I was lucky, damn lucky," he answered. "One morning my head just suddenly cleared and I saw that while owning a ranch was the thing I wanted most, it wasn't the only thing I could do."

"So what happened."

"I decided I'd go into the army," Max said.

Wilma nodded. "Lots of young men do that," she said.

Max agreed. "Fighting was something I thought I could sink my teeth into. But as it turned out, I didn't go."

"Why not?"

"While I was waiting at the recruiter's office I heard that if I went to A&M and got into the corps of cadets, they'd let me enlist as an officer. That sounded like a better idea than being a grunt."

"You went to Texas A&M?"

"I'm an Aggie," he admitted. "Just don't start with the jokes. I've heard them all."

"Wouldn't dream of it," Wilma assured him.

"I liked College Station," Max said. "And I learned two things there."

"Only two things?"

"Two that made the difference," he answered.

"Tell me."

"One. I don't ever want anything to do with any kind of military life of any kind."

He was so adamant it made Wilma laugh.

"And the second thing you learned?"

"That I'm pretty good with numbers, especially the ones with dollar signs attached," he said. "So after graduation, I worked around in some big companies for a couple of years and saved enough to open my own CPA firm. I've been doing business in a little place a few blocks south of here ever since."

Wilma felt a surge of pride and admiration. Her heart was fluttering in the fond adulation more often found among the seriously naive. She almost wanted to applaud. She liked Max. She really liked him. He was warm and genuine, honest and honorable. Max hadn't frittered his life away on bad luck and disappointment. He'd wrestled it to the ground and made it something of which he had much cause to be proud.

"And now, you have your place in Uvalde, your own ranch, your own cattle," she pointed out. "Everything that you hoped for, you made happen."

For a second, she didn't realize that something was wrong. Even when she did sense that the atmosphere had changed, it was only that the man across from her had suddenly become less relaxed. He hadn't moved a muscle, yet he was on full alert, wary. It wasn't until he spoke, so softly and calmly, that she realized how absolutely up to her eyeballs she had stepped in a pile of it.

"Wilma," he said, quietly. "I never said a word to you about my land out in Uvalde."

13

The deadline for vacating the house was approaching at breakneck speed and Marvin Dix had yet to give Ellen any hope at all.

"We're going to try mediation," the lawyer told her when she finally tracked him down. "You could never afford to fight them in court, so we're going to try to make some kind of deal."

"Just so it's a deal where we don't have to move," Ellen told him.

"I dunno," Dix told her, less than hopefully. "They've filed every kind of brief and motion I've ever heard of. You wouldn't believe the pile of papers that have landed on my desk. And this is just for the hearing!"

She'd left a dozen voice messages for the man on both his office phone and his cell. It was only when Yolanda showed up with his home number that she'd even got to talk to him.

"This is the part of the job I hate," Dix told her. "I really don't like the paperwork."

Ellen was knocked for a loop by that statement. Despite what could be viewed weekly on TV dramas, it was Ellen's observation that the practice of law was basically *all* paperwork.

"Have you found the chink in their armor yet?" she

asked him. "Do you know how we're going to fight this?"

"I just haven't been able to get all of it read yet," Marvin admitted.

Ellen heard the lawyer's words and glanced heavenward.

What's going on up there? she mentally demanded. *I pray for someone to represent me and you send a graduate of the Lameness Online School of Lawyering.*

To Marvin Dix himself she said, "We are really counting on you. If you don't think you're up to the job, you have to tell me so that I have time to find someone else."

Dix immediately went into sales mode.

"Now, don't you worry about a thing," he said. "I'm on the job and I can do the worrying for both of us."

Even two worriers might not be enough. They might be out on the street.

"Don't let it come to that!"

She knew it sounded more like a threat than a prayer, but she figured that God knew exactly how she felt.

Ellen flipped through the file of the Chinese restaurant on Durango Street, but she couldn't keep her mind focused. She'd already lost one house and a business and a lifestyle and a husband. She couldn't just let this go. If they lost this house, she feared her family would fall apart. Where would they go? How would they live?

If Paul were still here, none of this would be happening.

The thought came to her unexpectedly, and it was inappropriate. Paul had nothing to do with Wilma's in-laws or Mr. Post's will. Thinking he had wasn't all that unusual. Ellen had gotten in the habit of thinking that every bad thing in the world could somehow be traced back to Paul's death. It was not true. She knew that. But it seemed that way.

Looking back on those days before he was sick, before cancer became a permanent resident of their home, the world, in memory, had been imbued with a rosy glow. Somehow they had always been safe, life had been good when Paul was still with her.

Ellen wanted to cry. She wanted to roll on the ground and howl with grief and misery. She was sure it would make her feel so much better. But it was no longer possible. She would always be sad about losing Paul. She would always miss him and wish he was still walking around. But the grief, the mind-numbing, all enclosing grief was gone. It was, in itself, a kind of refuge, but now it too was gone. It was time to face up to the world now. But Ellen didn't want to face up to the world, she wanted to retreat from it.

"Tired of living, scared of dying," she quoted. But in all honesty, living was more scary than dying. Dying seemed so easy. That's why Paul had done it. She knew that. He was so worn out, so spent, so exhausted from the fight, he just let himself die.

Ellen wanted to do the same. But she couldn't. Unlike Paul, who knew that Ellen would take care of everyone he loved, she had no one to take care of those around her. Wilma could hardly manage on her own. Amber was throwing her life in the Dumpster with both hands. And Jet...Jet needed her so much. Ellen was the one reasonable, functioning adult in the child's life.

That was a scary thought. Ellen's life was barely firing on half its cylinders. If she was the functioning one, Wilma and Amber were really looking bad.

Inexplicably her thoughts turned to Mrs. Stanhope. She was a woman clinging to the past with a death grip.

Ellen had been by her house several mornings since the revelation of the facts of her husband's death. Mrs. Stanhope was sometimes perfectly calm and rational for the entire visit. But more often than not she drifted into the strange dream in which she lived. Though their conversations were mundane in the extreme, they were all so very pleasant. They talked about the garden and the weather. Mostly they talked about their husbands.

Ellen had relayed story after story of her life with Paul. Their struggles with the business. Their joys with Amber. Vacations and Christmases. Lazy summer days by the pool. Hectic Aprils doing taxes in shifts.

Mrs. Stanhope reciprocated with tales of society life in the San Antonio of the 1950s. Her stories were witty and often barbed with humor—mocking conventions.

Ellen was delighted to listen, but she also talked because Mrs. Stanhope seemed to enjoy it. It was a strange friendship—one Ellen would never have sought out. But she valued it. There was no one else that allowed Ellen to dwell so pleasantly in the past for so long.

Yolanda came tapping on her door.

"Mrs. Stanhope is causing trouble down at Helgalita's. They want you to get there as quick as you can."

"Me?" Ellen asked, looking up from the file. "Why haven't they called Irma?"

Yolanda shrugged. "I don't know, I guess Helgalita thought you were closer."

Ellen was on her feet immediately and out the door. "Call Irma," she said. "Tell her we're on our way." Yolanda nodded and picked up the phone.

"I'm sorry," Ellen said to Max as she hurried past.

He waved her off. "Take as much time as you need."

His gracious offer wasn't all that welcome. Ellen didn't want to deal with Mrs. Stanhope's delusions. She was okay when she was just another lonely old woman. But when she was acting crazy, Ellen was truly at a loss as to what to do.

Come on, God. Give the woman a little relief from this. And Helgalita and I could use a break as well.

Half a block from the restaurant, Ellen could see the little circle of customers cowering on the sidewalk at the doorway.

Ellen excused herself and walked right through them. She could hear Mrs. Stanhope before she saw her.

"There is absolutely no excuse for this," the woman was saying angrily. "How are we expected to sell merchandise when you've crowded the store with these tables, allowing these people to eat here. Don't they have homes to go to? If they are not customers of the store they needn't be on the property."

"Lady, it's not your property!"

Helgalita's voice had already risen to an irrational shriek. She was holding a dish towel as if she intended any moment to utilize it as a weapon. Ellen was fairly certain that while Helgalita's reactions might be justified, they exacerbated Mrs. Stanhope's problem.

"You need to be more mindful of our current situation, Madam," Mrs. Stanhope scolded. "If my husband cannot sell these goods then he can't meet his payroll. That isn't just untenable for us. Your family and those of all our employees will suffer as well."

"Having some crazy woman stalking my business is more suffering than I deserve in a lifetime!" Helgalita complained loudly, throwing her hands up in the air.

"What are you doing just sitting there?" Mrs. Stanhope asked of a man drinking coffee in the corner. "This is not an icehouse, sir. Please do your loitering elsewhere."

"Leave my customers alone!" Helgalita screeched.

"Excuse me! Excuse me!" Ellen interrupted as she stepped between them.

Both women turned to look at her.

Helgalita spoke first. "She's in my place again, scaring away my business and—"

Ellen held up her hand to silence the woman.

"Mrs. Stanhope," she said with very deliberate calm. "I can take care of this for you. Are you ready to go home now?"

The woman looked at Helgalita and then at Ellen. She heaved a great sigh of relief.

"Thank goodness you're here," she said. "Yes, please take me home. There is so much to do. We have a dinner party this evening with the Geyers. I came to remind Lyman."

"I'll let him know," Ellen told her as she gently took the woman's arm and eased her toward the door.

"You keep that crazy old lady out of my place or I'm calling the cops on her!" Helgalita called out as the final shot.

Ellen didn't even bother to respond.

Out on the sidewalk, they made their way through the curious crowd of onlookers. Mrs. Stanhope's head was held high. Ellen was defensive. They walked arm in arm down the street, the scent of summer flowers in the air.

"It's certainly hot enough today," Mrs. Stanhope said.

"Yes," Ellen agreed. "Yes it is."

"Who is that woman?" Mrs. Stanhope asked. "I don't remember Lyman hiring her. Yet she's at the store every time I visit these days."

"Her name is Helgalita," Ellen told her simply. "She owns a little Mexican restaurant."

"Well, she certainly is a peevish sort, isn't she?"

Mrs. Stanhope had squeezed up her face as if just biting into a green persimmon.

Ellen chuckled. Then the image of the furious little fat woman ready to attack Mrs. Stanhope with a dish towel was suddenly the funniest thing she'd ever seen. Once she started laughing she couldn't seem to stop. And as contagious as humor is, Mrs. Stanhope was shortly laughing with her, and that was even funnier.

The two of them were weaving like two drunks on the sidewalk gasping for breath as they shook, practically cackling with humor. Ellen thought her sides might burst open.

But when she glanced up she saw Irma coming toward them, her face set in stern lines, she managed to get hold of herself immediately.

Mrs. Stanhope was far less easily curtailed.

"Irma dear, hello," she called out. Apparently delighted to see her niece. She wanted her to join in on the fun.

"This is the best laugh I've had in...oh, heavens, I don't even know when," she said.

Irma managed to crack a tight smile.

"I'm glad you are out having a nice time, Aunt Edith," she said. "You told me you were going to take a nap in your room."

"Oh, did I?" Mrs. Stanhope asked. "Well, perhaps I still will. My heavens what a card Violet is. We've always had such fun together." The woman stopped abruptly and turned to look at Ellen, her expression curious.

"I called you Violet," she said. "But you are not Violet."

"I'm Ellen."

"Ellen," Mrs. Stanhope said the name as if it were totally new to her. "Ah...have you met Irma."

"Yes."

The two nodded to each other politely.

"Since Irma is here, I'll leave you with her," Ellen said.

"You're not staying for tea?"

"No, I must get back to work."

Mrs. Stanhope's brow wrinkled, puzzled.

"Do you work for my husband?" she asked.

"I work for Max Roper," Ellen answered. "Do you remember? You had coffee with me in my office."

"Max Roper? Yes, of course, Max Roper," Mrs. Stanhope said. "He is working on a business deal with my husband. He's looking for a buyer for the dairy farm Lyman's parents left him." Mrs. Stanhope laughed as if she'd said something funny.

"I told Lyman, if we can't sell it, we can always run it. I married him when he was a dairyman, I wouldn't mind being a dairyman's wife."

She grinned at Irma and chuckled lightly.

"You know Lyman," she said. "He wouldn't hear a word of it. He said he'd rather die first."

Ellen could see immediately when the words from Mrs. Stanhope's own mouth reached her ears. The words tore at her heart and darkened her visage. Her brow furrowed with sad confusion.

Ellen and Irma shared a quick glance at each other. And then focused their concern completely on the woman between them.

"Irma, I believe I'd like to go home now," Mrs. Stanhope said. "It must be my anemia again. I am just so tired."

"Lean on me," Irma said, putting her arm around the woman's shoulders.

"I'm not sure that I can make it home," Mrs. Stanhope told her.

"Let's try," Irma said. "If we can't make it, I've got my cell phone, we'll call a cab."

"A cab?" Mrs. Stanhope found that thought amusing. "It's only three blocks away."

"We can call a cab to take us thirty feet if we want to," Irma said.

"Yes," Mrs. Stanhope said, nodding. "We've got the money now. We can do whatever however we want." The woman hesitated a moment. "If we can make it home, I think I just want to lie down."

She didn't tell Ellen goodbye. Mrs. Stanhope

seemed to have forgotten her existence completely. Irma did leave her with a nod of thanks.

Ellen watched them walk down the sidewalk of the wide, tree-lined street, before turning back to retrace her steps to her own very real and ordinary world.

Max didn't come for lunch at the Empire Bar the day after Wilma had admitted knowing about his ranch. His open, easy friendliness had immediately disappeared and he'd excused himself.

"I have to go back to work," he said. "But I'm sure you know that."

Wilma didn't have any idea as to what to say or how to explain. Not unless she confessed all and she certainly wasn't ready to do that.

After a mostly sleepless night, smoking cigarettes between bouts of oxygen use, Wilma decided that the only thing she could do was tell the truth. Maybe not the whole truth, but at least enough of it to make her confession credible.

She was fully prepared to do that. But it seemed as if she wasn't going to get the opportunity. The first day he didn't show she wrote it off as a fit of pique. The second day, she was surprised that he could hold a grudge. By the fifth day, sitting alone nursing her beer and chain-smoking in their booth, she knew she'd made some kind of irrevocable mistake.

Wilma felt queasy. She wanted to go into the ladies' room and throw up. But she knew her stomach was too tied up in knots. She was getting a cold or something. She hadn't felt quite right for a couple of days. She was tired and she should have just stayed home.

But she'd come anyway. She knew in her heart that

he wouldn't be here again today, but she'd come anyway, just hoping.

She'd lost men before, she told herself. Somehow that was no comfort. Max was special. He was funny and interesting and he was a man whom she felt was her equal.

That was a curious thing she thought had always separated her from other women of her generation. They were always trying to be equal with the men they married. Wilma had never been married to even one whom she'd considered smarter, emotionally stronger or more determined. In her whole life, she'd never met a man whom she honestly felt could do her justice. Finally, she'd met her match. And he'd left her at this table like so much loose change.

Wilma tried to sort out where she'd gone wrong. How could it have worked out right? She went over and over their entire time together. She tried to remember everything that had been said. Every look that passed between them, every joke they shared. She second-guessed herself on every move she made.

Maybe being Ellen's mother wouldn't have caused a problem. He was not the kind of man to be bothered by such. And if Ellen had caused trouble, surely she could have handled her. Wilma could have been honest with him from the beginning. Let him know who she was and where she was coming from. But then what could she have given as an excuse for seeking him out? That she was trying to rope in a new husband. Not many men would have found that to be particularly titillating.

Wilma's head began to pound. And not at her temples, like a typical headache, but on the crown of her head, like something had hit her. She didn't feel like herself. The queasy feeling was now accompanied with dizziness. She took a couple of deep breaths. They didn't seem to help. She needed her oxygen.

She glanced down at her watch to see how close it was to pickup time. Her vision was blurry. She squinted and got two images of the watch dial, neither of which she could actually read.

Wilma leaned back in the booth. The room spun as if she were drunk. She looked at the half-empty glass of beer still sitting on the table. Alcohol was not the cause of this.

She motioned to the waitress.

"I'm not feeling very well," she said. "A young man is supposed to pick me up. Could you look and see if he's waiting outside. He drives a gray Tahoe."

"Sure," the young woman said. "You want to settle up now?"

She gave Wilma the check, but Wilma had to ask her to read it. Painstakingly she counted out the money. It was like her brain wasn't working. She couldn't seem to think, she couldn't seem to count.

"He's not there," the waitress said, when she came to pick up the cash.

"Can you keep an eye out for him?"

"Sure," the girl said. She glanced through the money on the table. "You want change from this?"

Wilma had no idea if she was leaving a great tip or none at all.

"Please, just keep an eye out for that gray Tahoe."

By the time she was informed that Brent was out at the curb, she knew something was very wrong. It wasn't just that she felt old, tired, and disappointed. Though all those things were true. Wilma was not at all herself. She was gasping. Taking in huge volumes of air, but somehow it wasn't working. It wasn't helping. All it seemed to accomplish was to stir up huge volumes of phlegm. Walking outside to get in the car was not a possibility.

"Tell him he has to come in here and get me," she said.

Within a few minutes, Jet came running up to the booth, bubbling and excited.

"Wil-ma, we had a picnic!" Jet announced. "We went to the park and ate sam-witches. I fed the ducks in the water and…"

Her little voice trailed off.

"What's wrong Wil-ma? You look kinda funny."

Brent was beside her then and he was looking at her as well.

"Let's get Wil-ma some oxygen," he said.

Wilma didn't argue, she was gasping for breath. It was as if there was no air around her. It was so strange. Everyone else in the world was breathing fine. But she was suffocating. With no water in sight, it still felt like drowning. She just felt so strange. And she was just so tired. It was as if everybody was talking from a long way off. All she wanted to do was go to sleep. She thought she could just fall asleep, right there in the Empire Bar.

She woke up and Brent was holding her in his arms.

"What happened?"

"You fainted," he said.

"The last time I fainted, I was pregnant," she told him.

"Look, I'm going to carry you to the car, okay."

"If I can just lean on you," Wilma suggested.

"Just put your arms around my neck," he said. "Jet, you pull the oxygen bottle behind us."

"This is not necessary, I can walk," she told him.

Fortunately, he ignored her. Wilma felt like a limp dishrag and she couldn't seem to snap out of it. She'd had plenty of tough days when she was short of breath and feeling exhausted, but the oxygen always fixed that. Just connecting up would perk her up immediately. But she was breathing it in now and it wasn't helping much at all.

She was drawing it into her lungs in huge gasps and then choking and coughing.

"Did you carry me out here?" Wilma asked.

"Yeah," Brent answered. "But I promise not to make any jokes about you putting on weight." His joking was deliberately lighthearted, but nonetheless, he sounded a little strange.

"Where are we going?" Wilma asked.

They were not on their usual route home, but near the bus station on Soledad Street.

"I'm taking you to a hospital," Brent said.

"No, no, there's no need for that. I'm fine," Wilma assured him.

He wasn't buying it. "We're going to a hospital, Wilma," he said. "And we're getting you checked out."

"Brent, it's nothing," she repeated.

"If it's nothing, then they'll let you go home," he told her.

She adjusted the ear curves on her breathing tubes. "But not before they nag me crazy about the cigarettes. I just had a moment of weakness, in there. I'm fine now."

"You were absolutely gray," Brent said. "I've never seen anybody that color who was still alive."

"Don't kid yourself, kid," Wilma told him. "I'm going to outlive you."

She tried to add a chuckle to the boast, but it deteriorated into a cough. And a minute later she was close to exhaustion again.

"I'm just getting a little cold," she told him. "Nothing to worry about."

In her peripheral vision she caught sight of Jet, her dark eyes as wide as saucers.

"I just have a cold," she repeated to the child. "Sometimes you get a cold, don't you?"

Jet nodded. "Do you have a temperature, Wil-ma?"

"No, I'm fine," she assured her. Even to her own ears the words sounded false. She was tired. And she'd been smoking too much. She'd cut back for a few days and she'd feel better.

She began gasping again. Wilma knew how it must sound to the two young people in the car with her. It was as if she were fighting for her life and they were helpless, watching the whole thing.

She fainted again and when she awakened the Tahoe was parked in a strange parking lot. Brent was talking on his cell phone.

"We're at the emergency room at Christus Santa Rosa," he told someone on the other end of the conversation. "Jet's with me. She's fine. I don't have your mother's number, you'll have to call her."

He glanced over in Wilma's direction.

"She's waking up," he said.

"Don't talk about me in third person," Wilma said.

"I'm the third person," Jet chimed in.

"We're going in now," Brent told the caller.

It sounded like a tired line from an old Hollywood war film.

"I'll let you know," he finished, and snapped the lid closed on his phone.

"Over and out," Wilma told him. "You should have said over and out. It sounds much more official. I don't want to go to the hospital."

Brent ignored that. "Okay," he told her. "So here's the deal, I'm coming *over* there and you're getting *out*."

He turned to Jet. "Stay here with Wilma for a second while I get a wheelchair," he told the child.

"I'll take care of her," Jet promised.

"I don't need any wheelchair," Wilma protested. "I can walk."

"You just want to test out whether or not I can carry you across this parking lot," Brent told her. "Believe, I can do it. But I'm not about to risk my position on the lacrosse team."

His teasing made her feel a little better, but Wilma was very aware that she was being taken to the emergency room. That couldn't be a good thing.

She glanced back at the child still secured in her car seat. Jet looked scared. She wanted to soothe the little girl's fear.

"So, have you decided what you want for your birthday?" Wilma asked.

Jet shook her head.

"Well, whatever you want, you just tell Wil-ma. I'll move heaven and earth to see that you get it."

Jet nodded. "Can you breathe, Wil-ma?" she asked. "Brent told me it was hard for you to breathe."

"I'm better now," she assured the child, but it was a lie. She was gasping again, finding it harder to talk.

It was by sheer strength of will that she tried to hold on until Brent was back with the wheelchair.

He was within sight when she allowed herself to ease into the blackness.

Wilma floated in an out of consciousness with only quick glimpses of the world around her. A circle of strangers moved her from the wheelchair to a gurney. A light was shining in her eyes. People asked stupid questions.

"Do you know where you are?"

"Can you tell us your name?"

But mostly no one talked to her, they simply talked to each other.

"We've got a blue bloater here. As soon as we get her stable we want to move her to MICU."

"Sats are seventy-eight percent."

"Have we got an ABG on her yet?"

"Her lung reserve is still good, we're getting a lot of wasted ventilation."

Wilma slipped in and out of consciousness. Sometimes she wondered if she was even there. Or if she was there, did anyone know it?

"I'm cold," she said once.

Almost immediately a warm fluffy blanket was tucked in around her. At least I'm not dead, she thought as she drifted down to the bottom of the gray again. If she was dead, they wouldn't wrap her in anything warm.

"Mrs. Post! Mrs. Post!" A loud voice caught her attention.

She opened her eyes to a familiar face.

"Mrs. Post, I'm Dr. Reberdi, do you remember me?"

"I'd like to forget," she told him.

He ignored the sarcasm and gave her no credit for humor.

"You've got bronchitis," he said. "We're going to admit you and keep you here until you're feeling better."

"Bronchitis?" Wilma said. "Can't you just give me some pills and send me home?"

"No, I don't think so," he said. "Do you have any family here with you?"

"I...ah...yeah, I think so."

"Her daughter's out in the waiting room," a nurse informed him.

She was glad the doctor was leaving. She was too tired to carry on a conversation.

The next time she opened her eyes she was in a dimly lit room. It was night. How did it get to be night? A good-looking young man in green scrubs and latex gloves was trying to read numbers on a huge green plastic bottle attached to the wall.

"We're going to give you an inhalant," he told her. "It's going to help your lungs do a better job and get more oxygen into your body."

Wilma put a hand to her face and encountered a big mold of plastic. "Where's my oxygen lines?" Wilma asked.

"We can get more to you with the mask," he told her. "Don't worry, you're going to be fine."

"I wasn't worried," she assured him. "I feel fine."

He laughed a little at that. Wilma wasn't sure why. She did feel fine, she wasn't in a lot of pain, she wasn't even gasping for air. The only problem she seemed to have was holding on to consciousness. It was like a dream that wasn't a dream. She couldn't really go to sleep. But she couldn't seem to wake up either.

14

The waiting room was noisy and crowded. Jet, who had been so good, was getting bored, tearing pages out of magazines and scattering them over the floor. Amber probably should have scolded her and made her sit. But she didn't. As long as the child's temper tantrum remained fairly mild, Amber was going to let her get away with it. If she could, Amber would have cheerfully begun ripping and throwing stuff herself.

She hated hospitals. She'd spent way too much time in them. And her family's batting average had not been good.

It felt strange to be sitting here, not working, just waiting. She'd expected Carly to give her a hard time about getting off.

"My grandmother's in the hospital" was one of those excuses so lame it was like a running gag.

To her surprise, Carly was extremely gracious. Volunteering to work her hours and suggesting that she stay with her family as long as she was needed.

"Thank you, Carly," Amber said, more than a little embarrassed by her supervisor's deliberate kindness. "I won't stay any longer than necessary."

"Hey, I know that," Carly said. "This place would fall down around my ears if I didn't have you to pull up the slack."

She said it like a joke, but with enough sincerity to catch Amber by surprise.

"I appreciate how hard you work for me," Carly told her. "I'm glad to get a chance to return the favor."

Amber didn't know quite what to make of that. She'd always thought Carly to be the bogeyman in her working life. Having her act like a concerned friend sort of put the world on a tilt.

She'd met up with her mother at the crosswalk on Commerce Street in front of the mall. Ellen's expression was one Amber always described as "white zone." Her mother always claimed that she was praying. Whatever her excuse, Ellen was obviously operating on automatic pilot, actual thought processes were engaged elsewhere. But they managed to find the emergency room as well as Jet and Brent.

"We don't know anything," he told them. "She was just really gray looking and she kept gasping and choking."

"I'm just so glad you were there," Ellen said. "Normally she and Jet are at home alone. I can't imagine what might have happened if you hadn't come by."

Brent shot Amber a look that was pure question. Should they enlighten Ellen as to where Wilma had been and what exactly was going on? Amber would have voted "no" but she didn't make her feelings known fast enough. Brent was already explaining.

"She wasn't at home," he said. "And I was baby-sitting Jet."

Ellen's brow furrowed, bewildered.

"What are you talking about?"

"Wilma has been meeting some guy for lunch for

the past several weeks," he said. "I've been watching Jet for her."

"Wilma has been meeting some guy?" Ellen's incredulity faded quickly and she shook her head in resignation. "I should have suspected something like this. Wilma always thinks *men* are the answer to everything."

Ellen glanced over at Amber accusingly. "Did you know about this?"

"Only what Brent has told me," she assured her mother. "Wilma didn't say anything to me. I don't know why she felt like she had to keep it such a secret."

"Who knows how Wilma thinks? If she actually does think. When it comes to men I wouldn't be surprised to find out that my mother marries them first and thinks about it later!" Ellen replied. "I should have known she'd be up to something like this. It's her m.o. The last thing we need is for her to get involved with another sick old coot who happens to have a house we could live in."

"Maybe it's not like that," Amber said. "He might be some really nice guy and they have tons of things in common."

Ellen was skeptical. "Wilma doesn't work like that," she said. "To her, husbands have never been helpmates, they've been meal tickets." She turned back to Brent. "Who is this guy? Did you see him?"

Brent shook his head. "We always just met her at the curb. Today the waitress came out and said she was sick and needed help. Nobody was with her and I never got a look at the guy previously."

"But she's met him several times," Ellen said.

"For weeks, every day, Monday through Friday, high noon at the Empire Bar," he replied.

"The Empire Bar?" There was recognition in her voice.

"Yeah, does that mean something?"

"Maybe," she answered. "It could be just a coincidence."

"What?"

"I think I know who she's been meeting," Ellen said. "And why she kept quiet about it."

The discussion of Wilma's love life ceased abruptly as the receptionist called Ellen over to the desk to fill out forms and provide insurance numbers.

Amber took a seat. Brent sat beside her.

"I'm sorry you got dragged into this," Amber told him.

"I didn't get dragged into it," he said.

Brent shrugged. "Wilma gives me an excuse to hang around you and your family."

"Oh, yeah, I'm sure dysfunctional is very entertaining," she said.

"Your family seems to be functioning just fine to me," he said.

Amber rolled her eyes. "Yeah, we're doing great," she told him facetiously. "We're completely broke, practically homeless and I'm considering changing jobs so it will be easier for me to pursue a part-time vocation as a whore."

She made the revelation exclusively for shock value. It didn't have quite the effect she wanted.

Brent chuckled.

"You think I'm joking?"

He shook his head. "I think that no matter what

you choose to do, even that, you'll always be productive and successful."

"Productive and successful." She repeated the words with incredulity. "You're being an ass, aren't you?"

Brent shrugged. "Not any more than usual," he answered. "I don't think you get it, Amber, how much all of your friends admire you."

"Yeah, right," she said. "They all want to work at the mall."

"They all see that you've taken this really crappy situation of losing your dad and your family going broke and you've just rolled with it, never missing a beat. Even managed to have a kid in the process."

Amber didn't buy it. "Yeah, well I guess my old friends just admire me from a distance," she said.

"Hey, none of us dumped you," Brent pointed out. "You walked away from us."

"I don't have anything in common with you anymore," Amber said.

"Nothing except friendship."

"Look, you're all in college and doing that whole scene," she said. "I hang with people who are more like me."

"More like you in what way?"

"They work, they party, they have kids," she answered. "I hang with people who aren't kids themselves."

Brent chuckled but laid his hand upon his chest. "One direct knife to the heart," he said.

"I would never stab you in the back," she assured him, glibly.

"I can't decide if you don't respect us, or just resent

us," Brent said. Amber didn't get a chance to respond. Jet came trotting up to them, book in hand.

"Read me this," she demanded of Brent.

The worn dirty copy of *Curious George Goes To The Hospital* was missing its cover, but thankfully it seemed to have most of its pages.

"I'll read it to you," Amber said.

Jet's brow furrowed stubbornly. "I want Brent to read it," she said.

"He's had to hang with you all day," Amber said. "I'm here now, I'll read."

"I want Brent to read it!" The little girl raised her voice angrily.

"I don't mind doing it," Brent told Amber.

"Fine," she said. "Jet probably thinks you read better because you go to college."

"I'll read to you, Jet," Brent said, lifting the child to his lap. "But I think you should say 'sorry' to your mama for snapping at her."

"Don't tell *my kid* what to do!" Amber shot back. "You are nothing to her."

"I'm her friend," Brent said. "And friends tell each other when they are way off base. You're out there, Amber."

She knew he was right, but his being right was not exactly something she could welcome.

Jet apologized to Amber. But Amber didn't apologize to Brent. She simply ignored him and pretended to read *People* magazine.

Curious George had just eaten the puzzle pieces when Ellen walked over from the counter. She was carrying Wilma's purse.

"They don't really know anything yet," Ellen said.

"They've called her doctor. Once he's evaluated her, someone will come out and talk to us."

Amber nodded. Brent went back to reading. Just the sound of his voice, low and calm, was somehow reassuring, soothing.

Amber didn't want to be soothed.

"Hand me Wilma's purse."

When Ellen did, Amber opened it up and pulled out a pack of cigarettes and a lighter.

"I'm going outside to have a smoke," Amber announced.

Ellen immediately set her jaw in anger and frustration. "Those things are killing your grandmother," she pointed out.

Amber shrugged. "Life's not so great that I'd want to do it for that long anyway," she answered.

It was a great exit line. Amber walked across the waiting room and through the automatic doors to the heat of a summer afternoon. She found an ashtray inconveniently located some distance from the nearest bench or shady overhang.

Amber stood in the sun and lit up. She was annoyed with herself and everybody else.

It's not fair! She wanted to whine.

But who would she whine to? Her mother who'd lost so much and still kept working, hoping, praying every day? Her grandmother who was fighting for every breath? Her former friend who just wanted to help? Or to Jet who had the supreme bad luck to be born to such a mother as her?

Brent was right about Amber. She had pushed away the people who cared about her. She continued to do it. But she couldn't seem to stop. Memories of her past, her family's life together were all rosy tinged, dreamlike, unreal. And her future looked to be unending tedium and disappointment. She couldn't even look forward to the excitement of going truly bad. She was not destined for prison or about to get herself hooked on drugs and alcohol. She was not brave or foolhardy enough to give in to the dark side of her nature. Even the partying life was more habit than pleasure.

Amber knew she would continue the very boring day by day struggle to get by. Nothing to anticipate and very little to regret.

Brent came up beside her, squinting without his sunglasses.

"Why are you standing in this heat?"

Amber pointed to the large metal receptacle full of sand and discarded butts.

"I believe this is the smoking section," she said.

Brent nodded. "Yeah, that's the thing about cigarettes," he said. "You have to walk through the world dragging an ashtray behind you like a ball and chain."

"Do you express these sentiments to Wilma?"

"She knows that I worry about her," he said. "But I try to keep the nagging to a minimum."

"Can I get the same deal?"

He shrugged. "If that's the deal you want."

Amber didn't know how to answer. She ground out the rest of her smoke and moved to a shady spot near the doorway. Brent followed her.

"Is my mother watching Jet?" she asked, trying to see through the darkened windows of the waiting room.

"Yeah, another kid showed up," he said. "The two of them are trying to demolish the building, I think."

Amber gave him a wry grin. "Well, as long as they are playing nicely together."

He chuckled with her.

It was a cozy, almost intimate moment of sharing. The kind that they used to have together, back when they were *really* friends.

"I'm sorry about what I said to you in there," she told him. "I do appreciate the kindness you've shown Jet."

"I like her," Brent said. "She's a really neat kid. You've done a great job."

Amber rolled her eyes. "That's just it," she said. "That's why I got so pissed off. I'm not doing a good job. I'm not doing any job at all. I let Wilma and Ellen take responsibility for Jet, but then I resent the hell out of them for it."

"I guess that means that you're like, really human, huh," Brent said.

"I'm human all right," Amber said. "Not unique or accomplished or special in any way. When you look up *ordinary* in the dictionary, you see my picture."

He laughed out loud at that. "You seem pretty exceptional to me," he said. "And I think Jet would agree."

Amber was thoughtful for a moment.

"I do love Jet," she said.

"Oh, is that like a big secret?" Brent asked. "It's written all over your face every time that you look at her."

"I want the best for her," Amber said. "She didn't ask to be born. I chose to give birth to her and I chose to keep her with me. I really want her to have the best."

"A mother who loves her is a good start at that," Brent said.

Amber shrugged that off. "Wilma spends more time with her than I do. I love that old lady, but I wouldn't describe her as a great role model. And she smokes around Jet, I know she does. Then when Wilma's not there, it's my mother. And that's really scary."

"You can't fault your mother as a role model," he said.

"No, although she's too upbeat, and way too quick to see good in everything."

"And that's a fault?"

"It can certainly lead to a lot of disappointment," Amber said. "And I see Jet being a lot like Ellen. They both have that happy, optimistic thing. What's going to happen when Jet goes to school thinking the world is full of friendly people and she gets hit smack in the face by racism?"

"Maybe she'll duck."

"Oh, puh-leeze, I'm being serious here."

"So am I," Brent said. "Jet's a smart, happy, self-confident little girl."

"You think that will keep trouble from showing up at her door?"

"No, but it will give her something to fight back with when it does," he answered. "Bad things happen in every life. In our own time, we all face our own share. The people who love us can only protect us so much. And then they have to just trust that we can take care of ourselves."

"But the world can be so cruel and Jet is so little. What if she *can't* take care of herself?" Amber asked.

Brent grinned at her. "You think Jet's like your

mother. But I think she's a lot like you. And you've already proven that you're up and ready to handle about anything life throws your way."

A candystriper from the reception desk came through the doors.

"The doctor is coming out to talk to Mrs. Post's family," she said.

They hurried inside.

Ellen had white coat syndrome. That's what medical people called it. An irrational fear of people wearing white coats. The sight of one could inexplicably raise the blood pressure, cause dizziness and heart palpitations.

Ellen was suffering all three as Dr. Reberdi came to give them the word on Wilma's condition. She didn't particularly consider her own reactions all that irrational. People in white coats had disappointed her more times than she wanted to remember.

It's a raw deal. We've had enough. No more death for my family. Not for a while.

It was not a particularly rational prayer, but it was a very sincere one.

Jet, who had been happily building a magazine fort with a little boy, deserted the child to come stand next to Ellen. Her little hand clutched Ellen's own, as if she recognized that her grandmother might need her.

Amber and Brent came inside. Both looking young and anxious.

"I'm Wilma's daughter," she told the doctor. "How is she?"

"She's doing pretty well for a person who's inflicted as much damage on herself as she has," he answered.

Ellen felt her whole body relax.

"Thank God," she whispered.

"She hasn't quit smoking has she?" Dr. Reberdi asked.

"No," Ellen answered.

"I think she's cutting back," Amber lied, as if tweaking the truth might help.

The doctor gave her an over-the-top-of-the-glasses look of disbelief, but didn't dispute her statement. "She's going to have to do better than she's done," he said. "I keep telling her that there are just so many little airways down there and only a finite amount of tissue, once she's destroyed it all, there just isn't any more."

"She seemed to be getting along pretty well," Ellen said. "The last few weeks she hasn't been sleeping that well. She's been under a lot of stress. But normally she seems fine."

"She's not fine," the doctor said firmly. "She has emphysema. It's a debilitating, often deadly disease."

"I realize that," Ellen told him. "But my mother is a very strong woman. And she has really good genes. Her mother lived to age ninety. She eats a balanced diet. And she's getting around, getting a lot of exercise. As long as she uses her oxygen, she's okay."

"That's the way this disease works," Dr. Reberdi said quietly. "It's insidious. You keep on doing the things that you do. Your lungs just keep working harder, making up for the damage. You wheeze a lot, get tired going upstairs, but you think you're doing all right. You use more oxygen and then a little more, but you think that's okay. Then one day, you get a little infection, a touch of bronchitis and you just don't have any reserves. You've got no lung tissue left to take anything in. And you're dead. That's what's going to happen to your mother. If she doesn't stop smoking, completely and soon, she's just not going to have anything left to breathe with. And then, well the end is inevitable."

His tone was matter-of-fact, almost annoyed. Any compassionate bedside manner he might possess, had obviously been saved for the bedside.

Ellen swallowed hard. "I don't think my mother can quit smoking, Doctor," she said. "She's smoked all her life. Or all her adult life anyway."

"She told me she started when she was fourteen," Amber piped in.

"Fourteen!" Even Ellen, who knew her best, was surprised at that. "That's forty-seven years. You can't quit something you've been doing for forty-seven years."

The doctor didn't seem impressed. "Everybody can quit," he said. "They just have to want to bad enough. Maybe Mrs. Post isn't that interested in having a future. If she's not, then there is not anything that you or I or anyone else can do about it."

The relief that Ellen had felt earlier had been very negatively tempered by the doctor's pessimistic sense of doom.

"But this is a very slow, long-term disease," Ellen said. "Emphysema can kill you, but it takes years and years."

"What happened to her today, is a late stage of the disease process," he said. "She's not getting enough oxygen to the brain. She's taking it into her lungs, but she doesn't have enough alveolar wall to process it and get it into her blood."

"How much does she have? How much does she need?"

"How much you need depends on the person," he said. "Five percent, ten percent, she still might be able to have some quality of life. How much she actually has we don't know yet. We don't want to run a lung volume test until we get her in a little better shape."

"So she is going to get better," Ellen said.

"We're giving her antibiotics to fight the infection and a bronchodilator which will help her absorb more of the oxygen she takes in. It should get her back on her feet fairly soon. But this is no cure. She is going to continue to decline as long as she continues to smoke."

Ellen looked over at Amber. Her daughter met her gaze. They were going to lose Wilma and they both knew it. This was the beginning of the end. Just like with Paul, except then, Ellen had refused to accept it. Then she had insisted that Paul fight. She had no hope of getting Wilma to do the same.

"Mrs. Post is at a point here where she is not going to get any better," Dr. Reberdi said. "And without some significant changes in her behavior, she will get worse, much worse."

"Worser than a nicker-teen fit?" Jet asked. "Wil-ma hates to have a nicker-teen fit."

The doctor ignored the little girl and Ellen hushed her as she patted her head, hoping that the child had not understood a thing that had been said. She'd forgotten Jet was there. This was no lesson that a child should be forced to comprehend.

"Is she awake? When can we see her?" Ellen asked, deliberately changing the subject.

"They are moving her upstairs, we're putting her

in an intensive care unit for the next several hours. They have a schedule, you can see her every hour for about fifteen minutes. If she doesn't get worse, she'll probably be moved to a regular bed early in the morning."

Ellen nodded.

"I've told her and I'll tell you," the doctor said. "Quitting smoking these days is not like it used to be. We've got medications, patches, programs. It won't be easy, but we can do a lot to make it more comfortable."

Ellen nodded again, but she didn't feel any sense of optimism. Wilma had never given even the slightest consideration to quitting. Ellen saw no reason for her mother to do so now. She was stubborn. She'd lied to get the oxygen. She'd probably lie to get some medication. But as soon as she was steady on her feet, she'd be lighting up in the hospital stairwell.

"Thank you," Ellen responded. "I will certainly talk to her about it as forcefully as I can."

"That's all we can do," Dr. Reberdi said, his expression for the first time showing signs of sympathy.

He urged them to contact him if they had questions then he, and his white coat, disappeared back through the doorway of the inner sanctum of the emergency room.

The three adults stood there and stared at each other for a long moment, not saying anything.

"Wil-ma can't come home?" Jet's question was full of concern.

"She'll come home in a day or two," Ellen assured the child with the warmest, most hopeful smile that she could manage.

"Is she going to miss my birthday?" Jet asked. "My

birthday is coming up and I don't want Wil-ma to miss it."

"We'll see," Ellen said.

The answer didn't suffice for Jet. She turned to Amber.

"Mama, we can't let Wil-ma miss my birthday," she said.

"She won't," Amber assured the little girl. "Some-how we'll make sure that she won't."

Ellen was disappointed in her daughter's response. But she thought it best not to go into it in front of Jet.

"You're going to have to take Jet home," Ellen said. "She's hungry and she's going to be tired. And a hos-pital emergency room is the best place in town to pick up a nasty cold or flu."

"What about you?" Amber said. "I'm the one who's used to evening work and late nights. You've been up since daybreak. You must be exhausted."

"I'm okay," Ellen assured her. "I'll stay here until Wilma's in her room. I just need to see her, reassure myself that she's all right. You go on and take Jet and I'll call you to come get me later."

Amber didn't look like she wanted to agree. And it turned out that she didn't have to.

"I'll take Jet home," Brent said. "I can get her some-thing to eat and get her to bed. You two can both stay here. Then you can come home in the car together whenever you're ready, and nobody will have to pick anybody up."

Neither woman had an opportunity to respond to that before Jet burst in with her approval.

"Brent can take me to McDonald's," she an-nounced. "And then when we get home he can read me *Gus and Button*. That's my favorite. It's Wil-ma's favorite, too."

So it was settled. Jet kissed them both and waved goodbye as she walked out the door, hand-in-hand with Brent.

Ellen and Amber were barely seated when Ellen thought of something and jumped up.

"We need to give him the car seat," she said.

"He has his own," Amber told her.

"What?"

"Brent bought a car seat so Jet could ride with him," Amber said.

Ellen raised an amused eyebrow. "That guy never gives up," she said.

"What do you mean?"

"Oh, just that he used to try to impress you with books he'd read and music he was into," Ellen said. "Now he's trying to show what a great father he'd be."

"That's your fantasy, Mother," Amber said. "He's not even remotely interested in me."

Ellen shook her head. "Yeah, like a twenty-one-year-old single guy has nothing better to do this summer but hang out with us."

The automatic doors opened and a young couple, he looking wide-eyed and afraid and she so pregnant she resembled a shoplifter smuggling an armchair out under her shirt, made their way inside. The woman was immediately seated in a wheelchair and after only a couple of questions, she was whisked away.

"You are like way off about Brent and me," Amber told her. "There is just no they're, there. The guy and

I used to be friends. Now we have nothing in common and no interest whatsoever in each other."

"He was crazy about you for a very long time," Ellen pointed out.

Amber waved that suggestion away. "That was years ago," she said. "We were both in the honor society and we both had braces. By the time I left school we'd already gone our separate ways. He was totally hooked up with Lissa."

"And you were pregnant with another man's baby," Ellen reminded her. "Most guys would take that as a signal that you weren't particularly interested in them."

The receptionist called for the family of the little boy that Jet had been playing with. They were being sent home with a prescription for antibiotics and some saline nose drops.

"I wasn't interested in Brent then and I'm not interested in him now," Amber told her, emphatically.

"You could do a lot worse," Ellen said. "He's a nice, smart, good-looking guy with drive and ambition."

Amber rolled her eyes. "And guys like that don't get involved with girls like me. Try to get this part, Mom," Amber said, snidely. "I'm a basic beer-party kind of girl. Not little wifey material."

"You are whoever you want to be, Amber," Ellen told her. "Don't place these ridiculous limitations on yourself."

"You're as bad as Wilma," she said. "Thinking that men can solve everything."

"I don't think that men can necessarily solve *any-thing*, but I do know from experience that it's easier to raise a child with one than without one."

"You think I need more help to raise Jet?" she asked. "I can't imagine why. I've already got you butting into it every minute of the day and night."

"Butting in?" Ellen was incensed by her suggestion. "I'm not butting in, I'm trying to help."

"Because you think I can't do it myself," Amber said.

"I just think you don't always think things through," Ellen said. "You're young and still finding your way. It's absolutely normal to get things wrong."

"What am I getting wrong?" Amber asked, her tone defensive.

"Nothing irreversible," Ellen said. "Not even anything big. Just little things."

"Such as?"

Ellen thought for a moment. "Well, what you said to Jet just a few minutes ago."

"What?"

"She asked you if Wilma would be at her birthday party," Ellen pointed out. "And you said that she would. I know that's what you want. I know that's what we all want. But it's not good to promise things to children that you have no control over being able to deliver."

Amber just stared at her for a long moment before she responded.

"That's rich," she said, facetiously. "Absolutely rich. How many times, hundreds of times, thousands of times, did you reassure me that Daddy was going to get well, that Daddy was going to be fine, that everything was going to be just exactly as it always had been?"

Ellen felt as if she had been slapped. She let the sting of the equivalent blow sink through her.

A man walked through the doorway and over to the reception desk. He was carrying a motorcycle helmet. His jeans were torn and he was bleeding from his elbows.

"I'm sorry," Ellen told Amber. "I suppose I have a lot to answer for as a mother. Maybe I just want to help you so that you'll not make the same mistakes that I did."

Amber shrugged with unrealistic bravado. "Hey, you want to do better with Jet than you have with me, go for it," Amber said. "She's probably got more potential as a daughter than I ever did."

"I don't want to take over parenting your daughter," Ellen said. "I'm only picking up slack. If you would knuckle down and take responsibility for your own child, nobody else would have to."

"Then you wouldn't have a damn thing to live for," Amber said. "You could just crawl up in the bed with Wilma and then you could both go to meet your late lamented husbands over on that golden shore."

"That is a very cruel thing to say."

"Yeah, well the truth hurts," Amber told her.

"That's not the truth."

"Isn't it? You've been sleepwalking ever since Daddy died," she said. "And by the way, hello! You weren't the only person that happened to. I was just a kid. I lost my father and I felt like I'd lost my mother, too. If I hadn't given birth, I doubt you would have noticed I was still around."

"Is that why you had Jet, so that I'd notice you were still around?"

"I had Jet because I was stupid enough to get pregnant and then excited by the prospect of bringing another life into the world. My father's grandchild. Someone to belong to *me*."

"No one ever truly belongs to anyone else," Ellen told her. "And in a mother/daughter relationship, it's always the child who has the most claim on ownership."

"So I screwed up," Amber said. "That's no big news. I've been screwing up routinely now for years. It's okay. I've got a plan to fix things once and for all."

"How's that?"

"I'm moving out," Amber said. "Gwen and I are getting an apartment together."

Ellen was momentarily stunned into silence.

"Can you afford that?" she asked finally.

"We think we can," Amber said. "We both work full-time and she's found a very reasonably priced apartment in the same complex as our friend Kayla. Kayla has her own car, so we'll be able to hitch a ride with her when we need one. We've almost got enough money together to move in."

"So you've been planning this for quite a while," she said.

Amber shrugged rather than answered.

"What brought this on?"

"Well, with the problems with Wilma's house, I thought that maybe now was the time to get out on my own," Amber said.

"Your grandmother is not losing that house," Ellen told her. "If I have to walk up and down outside with a placard, she's not losing that house."

"I hope not," Amber told her. "But whether she does or doesn't, it's really not going to affect my decision."

Inside Ellen was a jumble of emotions, deliberately she tried to remain calm.

"I know that every young person wants to be out on their own," she said. "It's completely natural for you to want that. All the chicks leave the nest eventually. It's what I want for you, too."

"Thanks, Mom."

Ellen folded her hands prayerfully and propped her chin upon them, looking at her daughter.

"But you haven't lived on your own yet," she told Amber. "I'm not sure you realize how difficult it can be."

"As long as we can pay the rent and buy food, I don't see that it's much different than what we've got going now," she said. "Instead of having you and Wilma as roommates, I'll have Gwen. We get along really well."

Ellen listened to what she said and she did nod, but only slowly.

"Wilma and I are more than just roommates, I think," she said.

"Oh, well, sure," Amber agreed. "You are my family. But most everybody agrees that it's harder to live with family than with friends your own age. It's just easier for Gwen and I to understand each other."

"I'm sure that there are ways in which friends are easier than family members," Ellen agreed. "Because you are not as intimately involved. But they can also be less tolerant. What if she doesn't like you leaving dishes in the sink or your laundry strewn everywhere?"

"I can be neater," Amber assured her.

"What if she spends all her money on clothes or music and expects to eat the food that you bought."

"We'll work that out."

"What if Jet's little singsong stuff gets on her nerves," Ellen said. "Not everybody likes kids."

"Gwen has a little boy of her own," Amber said.

"Really?"

"Yeah."

"And how old is he?"

"Eight."

"Oh my goodness," Ellen said. "Then he's in school already."

"Yeah."

"So what if he and Jet don't get along?" she asked.

"He's not going to be living with us," Amber said. "He's living with Gwen's mother."

"Oh," Ellen said.

Amber took a deep breath. Now was the time. She had to tell her mother and now was exactly the moment to do it.

Unfortunately, the words got stuck in her throat.

"You have to think very carefully about this," Ellen said. "There are lots of details to be taken into consideration. I won't try to stop you or hold you back in any way. You are a grown-up, adult woman with your own life. I'm really proud of you for wanting to take charge of your own little family. But it won't be easy. And I'm sure you know that I won't be able to help you."

Amber nodded.

"I always thought that you would go to college," Ellen said with an almost wistful sigh. "Even after Jet was born and you had all the parenting considerations, I hoped that you would find something that interested you and really pursue it."

"Mom, the whole college thing was shot the minute Dad died," Amber said.

Ellen's expression was puzzled.

"It was never your father's death that kept you from college," she said. "It was having a baby. Jet is, quite rightly, your first priority. Truthfully, with Wilma ill, I hate for you to tear Jet away from things that are familiar."

"I'm not tearing Jet from anything," Amber said. "I'm leaving her with you."

15

It wasn't that late when they arrived home from the hospital, only a little after ten o'clock. As Ellen had predicted, their visit with Wilma had been very brief. She didn't look great, but she'd been looking so spiffed up the last few weeks that seeing her faded and old was a bit of a shock. Amber decided that fixing her hair and doing her makeup would mean immediate improvement.

Weakness, however, was not cosmetic, and her grandmother could hardly hold her head up to take a sip of water through a bent straw.

"Don't look so worried," Wilma told Ellen. "It's just a touch of bronchitis. I'll be back home in a couple of days."

The nurses came to shoo them out. Ellen made sure that Wilma could reach her call button and kissed her goodbye.

When it was Amber's turn, Wilma didn't let her go that easy.

"Do you have my purse?" she asked in a whisper.

Amber glanced back toward her mother. Ellen obligingly stepped out into the hallway.

"Mom's got it," Amber said.

"Damn! Do you have any cigarettes on you?"

Amber had Wilma's pack in her shoulderbag, but she dodged the question.

"I don't think you can light up in here," Amber told her. "The whole building is smoke-free and with this oxygen going and a big red sign on the ICU door, I don't think tobacco is going to be a possibility, unless you're chewing."

"I could make them haul me out on the roof or something," Wilma said. "I hate to be cornered somewhere without my cigarettes."

Amber nodded sympathetically, but didn't volunteer to help her. She'd plainly heard what the doctor had said. Cigarettes were going to kill Wilma, and soon, if she didn't stop smoking. Like Ellen, Amber didn't think it was very likely that Wilma would quit. But it wasn't within her capabilities to aid and abet her continuing.

"Maybe the doctor will give you a patch or something to get you through the next day or so," Amber said. She kissed Wilma on the forehead. "Get better, we need you at home."

Amber caught up with her mother outside the doorway.

"Did she ask you for cigarettes?"

Amber nodded.

Ellen didn't question her about whether or not she handed them over. Amber didn't know if that meant her mother assumed she had or not.

They walked together, mostly in silence to the car. The discussion about Amber leaving Jet had been effectively tabled. But the fact that it was now out in the open made it seem, at last, as if it were likely to happen. It was, at the same time, both exciting and painful. She loved Jet. She wanted to be a part of her life. Could she be satisfied with such a small part?

Thinking about it made her head hurt, so she made a determined effort to think about something else. Ellen let her drive. That helped a lot. Although she had been at the very top of her driver's ed class and had earned her license on the first try, her opportunities to drive were still rare enough to be pleasurable.

The Tahoe was parked on the street when she pulled into the driveway. The lights were on in the living room. Brent was sitting in Wilma's chair in front of the TV, asleep. Amber bypassed him to check on Jet.

She was sound asleep as well. Her hair wasn't braided and the buttons on her pajamas were mismatched, as if she'd done them up herself, but she looked like a little angel. Amber bent down and placed a feather-light kiss on her forehead.

When she came out of the room her mother was in the kitchen.

"Should I call Bud tonight and tell him about Wilma or wait until the morning?"

Amber gave her an exaggerated frown. "Do we have to tell them at all?" she asked. "They'll just show up at the hospital, all smug and superior. I'd hate for Wilma to have to take them on when she's not in top fighting condition."

Ellen was trying to look disapproving, but she was amused.

"My brother's wife is a bit of a snit, isn't she?"

"That's understating it, Mom," Amber said. "She's the ultimate snit-meister, the snit-o-rama, the snit-isimo."

"Okay, maybe I'll ask Wilma before I call them."

"Good thinking."

"You'd better wake the baby-sitter and send him home," Ellen said with a nod toward Brent in the other room.

Amber nodded. "I think I'm going to wake him up and make him take me out for a drink," she said. "I'm wide-awake."

If her mother disapproved, she managed not to show it.

Amber went into the bathroom and repaired her hair and makeup, before returning to the living room to nudge Brent awake. For a second he looked confused.

"Is it past your bedtime, sleepyhead?" she asked him.

Brent grinned and rubbed his hand over his face.

"How's Wilma?" he asked.

Amber shrugged. "She's pretty weak, but I think she's okay. She asked me for cigarettes."

"And that was a surprise?"

She shook her head. "No, I guess not.

"Did you have any trouble with Jet?"

"That kid? She's a little sugar," he said. "She practically tucked me in."

Amber smiled.

"Well, I guess I'd better be going," Brent said.

"I was hoping you'd take me out for a drink," Amber said.

He glanced down at his watch. "Sure," he said. "Where would you like to go?"

"The strip, I guess," she answered, referring to the two miles of rowdy bars and hip dance clubs along North St. Mary's frequented by college kids and the younger set.

Brent screwed up his face in distaste.

"Couldn't we go someplace a little more mellow," he suggested. "All those drunks and dopers are just too much for me on a Wednesday night."

Amber thought for a moment. "Okay," she said. "It doesn't have to be too noisy. It might be nice to just relax and chill."

"And maybe we can get some pie!" he said.

"Pie?"

He put a finger to his lips and gave her a secretive look. "I'm taking you to my favorite late night hangout," he said. "And they serve pie."

They got into the Tahoe and he drove them to Earl Abel's, a San Antonio landmark on Broadway and Hildebrand, that was not much changed since its heyday in the 1960s. It had the same decor, the same menu and for the most part, the same waitresses. Twenty-four hours a day they served drinks and burgers and chicken fried steak and pie.

Amber ordered vodka tonic.

Brent ordered coconut cream.

"This is a kind of celebration for me," Amber said.

"Yeah?"

"Tonight I finally told my mother what I'm going to do," she said. "I've been putting it off for weeks and tonight I just told her."

"What did you tell her?"

"That I'm moving in with my friend, Gwen," she answered. "We're getting an apartment together and we're not taking our kids."

Brent's fork stopped in midair. He looked over at her, puzzled.

"What do you mean 'we're not taking our kids'?"

"We're going to go out on our own," Amber said.

"She has a boy. I have Jet. We're going to leave them with our moms."

He continued to look at her.

"What?" she asked finally.

"That's what I'd like to know," he said. "Just hours ago you were complaining about how you get sick of everyone interfering between the two of you."

"So?"

"So now you're response to that is to throw up your hands and say, 'Jet is yours, I'm out of here.'"

"That's not what I'm doing," Amber said.

"Then explain to me, please," he said.

She hesitated. "It's nothing you would understand."

"Why don't you think so?" he asked.

"Because…you've never had to make hard choices," she said.

His fork hit the pie plate with such force it could have broken it.

"That's bullshit," he declared adamantly. "Yeah, it's true, both my parents are living. I haven't brought any children into the world. I don't even have to support myself. But, come down from the cross, Amber. You are warm and safe and your little girl is healthy and happy and never goes hungry. There are a lot of people out there who would trade places with you in a skinny minute."

"Yeah, I know, there are starving children in Africa," she responded sarcastically.

"Yes, there are," he said. "And there are starving children in San Antonio as well."

"I'm sorry about those people," Amber said. "But you don't understand. I'm fighting for my life here. If

I don't get out on my own, now, I probably never will."

"Why would you even think that?"

"Because it's true," Amber said. "You don't understand, because you've got a future."

His brow furrowed. "We've all got a future," he said.

Amber shook her head. "No, we all don't," she said. "I don't. I've got what I've got right now. Tomorrow looks a lot like it. And the next day looks the same. Nothing is going to change for me. I'm going to work at a job that pays next to nothing. I'm going to live hand-to-mouth, never getting ahead, until I start getting behind. Then it's all downhill from there. You have the hope, no more than that, you have the *expectation* that life is going to get better for you. I don't have that."

"If you don't have that," he said, "then get it."

"I can't," Amber said. "I missed my chance."

"Your chance at what?"

"At what you've got," she said. "You and all my used-to-be-friends from Clark High. You're all going to college, figuring out what you want to do in life, dreaming dreams and making plans. I'm selling underwear."

Brent looked at her intently. "That's what this is all about—college?" he asked. "Do you think you can't have a great life or good future because you didn't go to college?"

She didn't answer.

He rolled his eyes. "I wish you could meet some of the losers that I know at college," he said. "Believe me, these flake-o-dudes have nothing on you."

"They have a chance," Amber insisted. "Sure, maybe they'll piss it away, but they've got it."

He couldn't argue that.

"So somehow deserting Jet is going to be a substitute for college," he said.

"I'm not *deserting* Jet," Amber said. "She is going to live with my mom and Wilma. You make it sound like I'm leaving her in a locked car in a parking lot. Jet will be better off if I leave her at home."

The phrase "at home" momentarily caught Amber up short. Jet's home would never be with her.

"Your mother has a ton of problems and the way the doctor told it tonight, Wilma won't be around that long," Brent said. "Do you think they deserve to have that kind of responsibility dumped on them?"

"I *deserve* to have a life," Amber told him, very annoyed. "I deserve to have a young life, a fun life. As for my mother, she'll finally get to raise Jet however she likes. And she's one of those women who thrive on responsibility. I'm not and I don't want to be."

"Wow, this all sounds really lucky for you," Brent said, facetiously. "You just walk in and out of the kid's life and other people clean up the mess."

Amber didn't like the sound of it, but she had no idea how to dispute his words.

"What is this going off on your own suppose to get you?" he asked.

"It'll be easier to get ahead if I don't have Jet," Amber told him.

"Get ahead of what?" he asked. "Are you going to try to go back to school?"

"I told you, I missed my chance."

"College isn't just one chance," he said.

Amber rolled her eyes and ground the words out

between clenched teeth. "Where would I get the money to go?" she asked him. "It costs thousands of dollars a semester."

"There's financial aid," Brent said. "And you don't have to go to an expensive state university, there's community college and you can go part-time."

"Community college? Oh, yeah, like that counts," she said. "It's just high school on steroids. None of the kids from our group at Clark ever considered community college."

"We're not at Clark anymore," Brent said, his jaw firm. "At community college they have real teachers who give real classes where you learn real things. If you think it's too easy, then dig deeper. The profs will be glad to let you."

"It would take years for me to get a degree going part-time," Amber said. "I'd be thirty at least!"

"I hate to be the one to point this out," Brent said. "But you're probably going to get to be thirty anyway. You're the one who thinks that college is so important."

He made it sound possible. Amber wanted it to be possible.

"It's such a long shot," she said. "Maybe I couldn't hang in there. I mean, maybe I could do it, but what if I couldn't? As you said, Mom has her own problems and Wilma's not well. We're about to get thrown out on the street. I might start school, but it would be really hard to keep it up. If we move into another place, there will be rent to pay. And if Wilma couldn't keep Jet, then I'd have to pay for child care. But if I leave Jet and move in with Gwen, at least I'll have my own place. Maybe after a while, get a car."

It sounded insufficient even to her own ears.

"Is that what you're going to tell Jet when she gets to be our age?" Brent asked. "I gave up being your mother so I could get an apartment and a car."

"Go to hell!" Amber said, scooting out of the booth and leaving in a dramatic huff. It was an excellent exit line, but as she walked home, she couldn't quite get past the truth that had provoked it.

Ellen hadn't slept well, so she'd gotten out of bed early and headed downtown with the excuse that she had to get a head start on the job. She and Amber had decided that Amber would keep Jet this morning and then bring her down to the tax office when she went to work at three.

The fact that she packed a thermos of Earl Grey and some shortbread cookies might have called into question her destination had anyone been awake to take notice. Fortunately, nobody was.

Ellen drove the Chrysler down Broadway, through the business district and on to King William.

Give me a light heart, she asked sincerely. It was a much needed prayer. Things were weighing very heavy. Wilma. Amber. Jet. It was all just too much.

She was eager to see Mrs. Stanhope. The woman would be sitting in her lovely garden this morning, thinking happy thoughts about a life that once had been. Ellen was sure of that. And she wanted to be there with her. She wanted to talk about Paul. Remember old times. Just be content to live in the more pleasant past.

She parked at the curb near the garden gate and gathered up her basket of goodies.

Mrs. Stanhope was seated at her usual location. As always her attention seemed to be focused on the eastern sky. The slate stone path was damp and slippery from predawn-timed water sprinklers.

From the back porch she could hear Irma, as usual, talking on the phone. Ellen offered a polite wave in her direction. He response was equally tepid.

"Good morning, Mrs. Stanhope," she said as she approached the little garden nook.

The woman looked up. Her expression was momentarily reticent. Then as she recognized her visitor, her eyes lit up.

"Ellen," she said. "It's Ellen, isn't it."

"Yes, ma'am, good morning."

"Good morning to you," the woman responded. "Please sit down. I can't offer you any tea—"

"I brought some to offer you," Ellen said.

"Oh, my."

"I remembered that the maids don't arrive until eight and I thought we could share some tea before I have to go to work."

"What a lovely idea," Mrs. Stanhope said. "Should I invite Irma?"

That was the last thing that Ellen wanted.

She smiled brightly at the older woman. "Perhaps we shouldn't bother her," she said. "Irma seems to be very busy already."

Mrs. Stanhope sighed. "Yes, she is very busy. She works much too hard, but she enjoys it so much."

"I'm sure she does."

"I worked in my husband's store for a short time," Mrs. Stanhope said. "Of course, Papa put a stop to that. 'Young women of good family do not engage in commerce,' he said. And whatever Papa said, well we had to go along with it."

Ellen could almost see the joy of the morning fading with that thought. Ellen didn't want to see it go.

"You must tell me about the parties you used to give at this house," she said. "You must have given some very lovely parties."

Mrs. Stanhope immediately brightened. "Oh, yes, indeed," she said. "I was a very eager young hostess and Lyman was extremely proud of me."

Ellen pulled the table between them and set up their little breakfast tea as Mrs. Stanhope reminisced lovingly upon the gala occasions she'd orchestrated and witnessed decades earlier. Ellen thoroughly enjoyed the sentimental journey among the local ladies of leisure, in their dresses by Chanel or Dior, their pillbox hats with netted veiling and their ever-present and pristine white gloves.

She told a delightful story of one season's pinnacle social event that was attended by the former governor's daughter, Miss Ima Hogg. During the planning of the event, one wickedly spiteful young matron kept referring to the renowned Miss Hogg as Madam Pig. It was all very humorous until during the evening after being presented to the lady, the silly matron had slipped up and called her that to her face.

Ellen laughed.

Mrs. Stanhope tutted reprovingly. "Miss Hogg very generously ignored it, but it was a dark day for San Antonio society," she said, before her stern visage turned to a smile and she giggled as well.

"Enough about me and my fond memories," Mrs. Stanhope said. "Tell me, how is your lovely family."

Momentarily, Ellen was at a loss for words. The last thing she wanted to do was delve into it all: Wilma's smoking herself to death. Amber's moving out, and herself suddenly conscripted into parenthood of a little girl not yet four. It was foolish in the extreme to burden Mrs. Stanhope with her problems. For all her eagerness to listen, she had her own issues that obviously had never been resolved.

"Everyone is doing well enough," Ellen answered. "My mother's health is not the best. There are things that come up day to day, but we are fine." It sounded like the truth, even to her own ears. "My granddaughter turns four this week."

"Oh my goodness, four years old," Mrs. Stanhope said. "She must be charming."

"We think so."

"So what has happened with your house?" the woman asked. "I recall that you were in the middle of some unpleasant family conflict and that your mother's house might be taken away."

Ellen hadn't remembered telling her that. It was surprising to her that she'd done so. Even more surprising that Mrs. Stanhope had remembered it.

"Nothing is settled yet," Ellen told her.

Mrs. Stanhope nodded. "Well, please don't give it another thought," the woman said. "I told Irma about it and she said they would never be able to do it. This is Texas and we have laws to protect people from being pushed out into the street."

"Yes, thank you, Mrs. Stanhope," Ellen said. "I'm sure everything will be fine." Ellen changed the subject. She could not bear to discuss the prospect of her emphysemic mother attempting to recover her health in a homeless shelter. "Everything will be fine," she repeated. "How could it not be on such a lovely day. I can't remember when this springlike weather has lingered so long into summer."

They finished their tea and cookies.

Ellen talked about her fifteenth anniversary. She and Paul went to Round Top for the symphony and stayed in a charming little inn.

Mrs. Stanhope drifted in and out of the present. When she announced that Lyman was putting stockings on sale for half price and that she should stop by the store and pick up a pair, Ellen knew she should be leaving.

"He says all the ladies want seamless now," Mrs. Stanhope explained. "But for half price, I doubt many ladies of my acquaintance would complain about a nice, well-sewn seam along the back of the calf."

"I really have to go," Ellen said, gathering up her impromptu picnic. "Thank you, Mrs. Stanhope, for a lovely morning."

Leaving, Ellen felt Irma's eyes upon her. She acknowledged her presence with a nod. It wasn't particularly pleasant having the woman watching her as if she were about to steal the silverware, but Ellen dutifully gave the niece credit for attempting to protect a very sweet and charming lady who must be very vulnerable to conniving strangers.

Ellen put the picnic things into her car and headed toward the office. She was actually a few minutes late. Not a particularly great idea after leaving early yesterday and planning to have her granddaughter in the office in the afternoon.

No one appeared to notice as she came in. Max was already in his office and Yolanda was on the phone. She held the receiver against her chest and whispered a quick, "How's your mother?"

Ellen answered, "Better." And Yolanda went back to her conversation.

It was not possible, however, to ignore Max. Ellen needed his cooperation.

Ellen poured herself a cup of coffee and went to face the lion in his den.

"Max? May I have a word with you?"

"Sure, sure," he said, looking up from a pile of papers he'd been perusing. He had on his reading glasses, half frames on the bridge of his nose. They gave him a more scholarly air than his normal cowboy appearance.

"My mother is in the hospital," she said.

He nodded. "Yolanda told me when I got back yesterday," he said.

"She has bronchitis, complicated by emphysema," Ellen said. "She's doing better than she was yesterday, but she's going to be in the hospital for a couple of days."

"We all have these family emergencies," he said. "You can be as flexible with your work schedule as you need to be."

Ellen was surprised that he didn't show more interest in Wilma. She had been certain that Max was the man her mother had been seeing at the Empire Bar. But perhaps she was wrong. He certainly didn't behave as if he knew Wilma at all.

"My mother normally keeps our granddaughter," Ellen told him. "Jet is not quite four. Her mother, Amber, works evenings at the mall. I told her to bring Jet here when she goes to work."

The man's eyebrows went up at that.

"I think Jet is well behaved enough not to be too much of a distraction," Ellen said. "If not, then, I'll take her and my work home with me."

"Well, whatever you have to do," Max said. "It's a pretty confined space for a small child."

"Yes, well, it's only until my mother is better," Ellen said. "Assuming that she does get better. The doctor is very clear that if she doesn't quit smoking, it's going to kill her and very soon."

Max shook his head. "It's hard to quit," he said. "It was easier for me to get off the liquor than fags."

Ellen was startled at his words.

"I didn't know you'd had a drinking problem," she said.

Max chuckled. "My *drinking problem* was that I was a stupid, blind drunk," he said. "That was probably before you were even born. But a man doesn't forget his past. Nor does a woman, I suppose."

He and Wilma probably had more in common than she'd thought.

"Anyway, Jet will be here around three o'clock."

Max nodded.

Ellen started to leave. She stopped abruptly in the doorway and took a sip of coffee and waited.

He looked up again.

"Max, what can you tell me about Edith Stanhope?"

"You should probably ask Yolanda," he said. "I'm sure she's more up on the local gossip than I am."

Ellen shook her head. "All she knows is how Mrs. Stanhope is these days. Confused and delusional. What did she used to be like?"

"She's one of the Grisham daughters," Max said. "She was the 'pretty one' people said."

"Mrs. Stanhope told me that you were in business with her husband," Ellen said.

"I kept his books," Max told her. "He was one of

my very first customers. We were both starting out, new in business, new to business."

"Mrs. Stanhope talks about him all the time," she said. "He was the love of her life. I just wondered what kind of man he was."

Max thought about that for a moment.

"What kind of man he was?" Max repeated. "Well, I'd say...I'd say mostly, he was nervous."

"Nervous?"

Max nodded. "He was real edgy, couldn't stand still for long. I think that's why he hated the dairy business so much."

"The dairy business?"

"Yes, his parents had run a dairy business," Max said. "They left it to him when they died, but he was just a little bit too high-strung to work around cows, I suppose."

Ellen shook her head. "It's funny, I would never have got that impression from Mrs. Stanhope."

"Probably because he wasn't nervous around her," Max said. "I remember seeing them together several times. He just lit up like a firefly when she was around. And she just gazed at him like he was the King of the Mountain."

"So they were very much in love," Ellen said.

"Yes, I think so," he said. "And also very well suited. She was, I believe, mentally frail from childhood. Back then they thought any weakness of the mind ran in families and the Grishams already had a very eccentric aunt who eventually had to be sent away to a sanitarium."

"Really?"

"I think a lot of people suspected that there were things that were not quite right with Edith early on,"

Max told her. "But she seemed to get along well enough. She was smart and happy and cheerful."

"She still is," Ellen said.

Max nodded. "But there was something curious about her and when she met up with Stanhope, well they just seemed to fill in all the chinks in each other's armor."

"So they were a perfect match," Ellen said.

"Most people thought so, except of course, Edith's father," he said. "The old man never liked Stanhope. Maybe he was so set against a marriage between she and Lyman because he worried about their tendencies getting passed on to another generation. Whatever it was, he treated Stanhope terrible. If being around Edith made the guy less nervous, being around her father made him more so."

"Her father doesn't sound like a very pleasant guy."

"He wasn't," Max said. "And he just wouldn't leave them alone. Nothing that Stanhope did was good enough, poor bastard."

"Mrs. Stanhope told me that he killed himself."

Max sighed heavily. "Yeah, one evening he closed up the store, just as usual, and then walked into the back room and hanged himself."

"Because of his father-in-law or because he was nervous?" Ellen asked.

"Because his business had failed," Max answered. "If you had been here then, I'd have put a Post-it note on his file and Yolanda would have made you call him. He was selling dry goods. There were big department stores opening uptown. Everybody wanted to shop there. It wasn't his fault. It was a change in consumer demand. It happens. Businesses fail. People go bankrupt. It's a fact of life. Some people have a hard time facing it."

That was true, Ellen thought. And some people never faced it at all.

16

If a person is ill and in need of rest, the last place they'd ever want to be is a hospital. At least that was Wilma's take on it. It seemed as if someone was in waking her up every few minutes. At approximately 3:00 a.m., they decided to move her from MICU into a semiprivate room. It was hours before they got her completely settled in. And when they finally did and Wilma had just fallen back to sleep, the inhalation therapist showed up for a predawn treatment, followed by morning vital signs before it was light, and ultimately breakfast a few moments before seven. Wilma was not sure what the day shift did all day, but the night workers were busy little bees.

Through everything, there was the pervasive and unanswerable desire for a cigarette. They were giving her a tranquilizer to take the edge off the cold turkey aspect of being cooped up in a nonsmoking room and she had a nicotine patch stuck to the back of her arm. Neither was a panacea for the edgy, nauseating, groggy-headed discomfort she was feeling.

She could breathe better. That was quite true. And she wasn't experiencing as much hacking and mucus as she was accustomed to, but that did not in any way counter the abject misery of not having tobacco. Overall, she was weak as a kitten, but the need for nicotine seemed to give her strength. She had to get strong enough to get in a wheelchair. Once there, she would wheel herself out of Texas if that's what it took to get a smoke.

But it was going to be a while before she could get there.

The day dragged on in minute by minute boredom. Her roommate, who had perked up considerably in the hours since her arrival, was a woman with a planned life. She planned to watch the TV tabloids until her soaps came on. Apparently, she was also a little hard of hearing, so the baby-sitter's confession of having seduced grandpa's gay boyfriend reverberated around the room at high decibels.

When the telephone rang at 10:00 a.m., she felt as if she'd already been in the hospital a week. It was Ellen.

"I didn't want to wake you," she said.

"No danger of that," Wilma told her. "This place is busier than a one-legged man at a butt kicking."

"Is the doctor there? Who's that talking?"

"It's the television," Wilma replied. "I hope if my doctor has decided after forty years that he's really bisexual, at least he won't tell me about it."

Ellen laughed. "I'm sure he won't," she said. "He seems like a stodgy, conservative family man."

"Those are the kind you have to watch out for," Wilma assured her.

"I'm going to try to get over there after work," Ellen said. "I have Jet and they won't let her upstairs, so I don't know exactly how I'll manage. But I will."

"I have no doubt of that," Wilma said. "You've done everything you ever set out to do and more."

Lunch arrived before 11:30, simultaneously with

another inhalation treatment. She dutifully took the medicine into her lungs before settling down to cold baked chicken and half-congealed gravy.

The afternoon was equally leisurely. She managed to nap through most of two hours of soap operas. But she was wide-awake when the roommate switched to a *telenovella* on a Spanish language channel. Wilma had lived in Texas long enough to have picked up a spattering of the language—enough to get the gist of what was going on, without having to be bothered with any of the esoteric detail.

She was just getting interested in the action when Dr. Reberdi showed up. He appeared to be in a bit of a hurry, but he was a man with an agenda.

"You have to quit, Wilma," he said. "Your lungs can't take any more of it. You have to give up cigarettes and you have to give them up for good."

"I'm thinking about it," she lied.

He didn't believe her. "There's no wiggle room here," he said. "No need for game playing. You either quit or you die, that's the truth and it's all I can tell you."

He listened to her heart and lungs. He and the nurse helped her sit on the side of the bed, ostensibly to see if she was going to faint. She didn't. Wilma dangled her legs as she attempted to maintain as much modesty as a backless hospital gown allowed.

"How soon can I get out of here?" she asked him.

"Tomorrow maybe," he said.

"My great-granddaughter is coming to see me this afternoon," Wilma told him. "She's three and they won't let her upstairs. Do you think these gals could get me in one of those wheelchairs and get me out to the patio or something so I can see her."

The doctor raised an eyebrow. He obviously had not been born yesterday.

"You can get up in a wheelchair and they can wheel you to a window where you can wave to her," he said. "You're wearing that nicotine patch, it ought to take care of any physical withdrawal symptoms that you're having. I want you to be smoke free while we're medicating you and trying to get you back on your feet."

Wilma felt like the girl in *The Exorcist*. She wanted to roll her head backward and spew vomit on him. Unfortunately, she couldn't.

After he left she clung steadfastly to her resentment.

When she was out of his control, she would do exactly what she wanted, she reminded herself. If she wanted to smoke a hundred cigarettes a day, it was none of his damned business. It was her life and she'd live it exactly as she pleased. No starchy, cob-up-his-butt M.D. would be telling her how she could or could not live her life.

Interspersed with the tirade was the sure and certain knowledge that the doctor wasn't lying to her. Smoking was going to equal death. Initially she reacted with bravado. She would look death straight in the face and spit in his eye! But, of course, death was far too illusive to come at her straight on like that.

Calmly she rationalized that she'd lived a fun life if not a long one. She'd lived to see her children take up their own lives and even long enough to see her granddaughter become a mother herself. That was far longer than many people were allowed. She ought to be quite willing to die. She wasn't.

Ellen and Amber needed her. Jet needed her. But it

was more than just being needed. She had things she still wanted to do. Wilma thought about her conversations with Max. What had he told her? She needed to figure out a way to use her knowledge. And she said that it was too late.

"That's what people think when they're in their forties," he'd told her. "By the time you're our age, you understand that it's only too late when you're dead."

Truly, she didn't want to die yet. She wanted to live and do more things, new things. She wanted to have a long road of life still in front of her.

But she couldn't envision a life without smoking. It was so much a part of who she was, how she lived, her expressions, her mannerisms. It was captured in thousands of fading photographs always with a cigarette in hand. It was tied forever in memories of a million ashtrays. Smoking had been the introduction to every morning's cup of coffee and the finale of every act of sex she'd ever enjoyed.

There was no way she could give that up. It would be worse than dying, it would have been as if she had never lived.

With the help of one of the nurses, she got out of bed and took a few steps around the room. It nearly exhausted Wilma completely, but she knew she had to build up her stamina before they'd let her go home.

As the afternoon moved on from Rosie to Oprah to the local news, Wilma tried hard to recover her strength. She took another inhalation treatment. She sat up on the side of the bed and willed herself not to faint.

She'd already picked at her somewhat bland and

boring supper when Ellen arrived, rushing in as if she'd run all the way from the south side office.

"I'm sorry it took me so long to get here," she said. "I've had Jet with me at the office since three and everything just took longer to get done. How are you? You look better."

Wilma nodded. "I think the greatest danger in this place is death by boredom."

Ellen smiled. "That means you're improving," she said. "If you're really sick, you hardly notice the place."

Wilma couldn't argue with that.

"Where is Jet now?" she asked.

"She's in a little hallway reception area around the corner," Ellen answered. "I couldn't leave her downstairs in the waiting room. There are just too many people coming in and out."

Wilma agreed.

Ellen pulled up a chair and seated herself next to her mother's bedside. At first she was merely chatty and entertaining. Telling Wilma about her day at work, especially about the novelty of having her granddaughter at the office. Especially delightful was a story about Max being a little grouchy about having a child underfoot then discovering the two of them at his desk. He was teaching her how to make stick people from *0*'s, *L*'s and directional slashes on his old Underwood typewriter.

Ellen was watching her carefully as she told this story, so Wilma was certain that she was suspicious, but she deliberately kept her expression bland enough to reveal nothing.

Ellen questioned her about the doctor's visit.

Wilma's answers skirted the lecture she'd received and dealt only with her imminent release.

"So if you can't get off from work to come get me," Wilma said. "Maybe you could call Brent, I'm sure he'll do it."

Ellen nodded. "We may have to call him," she agreed. "Though I think we're currently trying to avoid taking his help."

That surprised Wilma. "Why?" she asked.

Ellen shook her head. "I'm not sure. Amber didn't go into detail, but apparently the two of them had some kind of argument."

Wilma snorted and shook her head. "Those two are in a spat all the time," she said. "Nothing new about that."

Ellen looked thoughtful. "Maybe there is," she said. "I wouldn't be surprised to hear that he's blasted her for her latest plan."

"What plan?"

"Well, she told me that she was moving out," Ellen said. "She and some girlfriend she parties with want to get an apartment. I figured that nothing would come of it. It's just too hard to raise a child on your own. She's got a much better deal with us to help her."

Wilma nodded.

"Last night she told me that she's still planning to move out," Ellen said. "And she's leaving Jet with us."

"What?"

"Her friend has a child, too. They are just going to go on with their lives and leave the kids to the grandmas. It must be the latest in cool mom chic."

Wilma looked closely at Ellen. Her daughter appeared to be saddened by this turn of events, but resigned to it. Had Ellen become so inured to things going wrong that she no longer knew how to rail against them?

Wilma had not.

"That is not good," she said firmly. "Don't let it happen."

"I'm not *letting* it happen," Ellen said. "It's happening whether I like it or not."

"No, it won't happen unless you allow it to," Wilma said.

"You must think I have a lot more control than I do," Ellen said.

"When it comes to this, you're in complete control."

Ellen shook her head. "Amber's not a little girl anymore," she told her mother. "I can't tell her what to do. She comes, she goes, she does what she wants. She hasn't listened to anything I've said for years."

"Because you haven't had that much to say."

"I haven't got anything to say about this either," Ellen told her. "It breaks my heart that she could do this. But if she is willing to walk away from her daughter, all I can do is try to pick up the pieces."

"They are not your pieces," Wilma said.

"There are grandparents all over this country raising their kids because the parents can't or won't," Ellen said.

"True," she agreed. "And if Amber were emotionally unstable, in a dangerous relationship or addicted to drugs, I wouldn't wait for her to give us the baby—I'd help you take her away. But Amber has none of those problems."

"She certainly has something wrong with her thinking if she's willing to do this."

"She's just young," Wilma said. "She's young and shortsighted, the way we all are at that age. And she's not doing her duty by her daughter because you've made it far too easy for her not to bother."

"Me? Oh, this is my fault now."

Wilma sat up in bed a little too fast and felt faint. She managed to get past it. She had something important to say.

"I never tell you how to handle your daughter," she said. "Not just because I know you wouldn't like it. But because I know that you are a better mother to Amber than I ever was to you."

Ellen didn't even try to disagree with her.

"I never was all that good at parenting," Wilma continued. "But, I can see this one thing clearly. If Amber doesn't take responsibility for her own child, she will never be able to take responsibility for her own life."

"How can I make her do that?"

"You're going to have to tell her 'no'," Wilma said. "You're going to have to remind her that she chose to bring Jet into the world. That's a life-changing experience. It's too late to go back."

"I'm not sure she can even understand that," Ellen said.

Wilma had more confidence. "I had you when I was her age and I was easily as silly and selfish as she is. The difference was that I didn't have anyone I could hand you off to. For better or worse, you were mine all the time. Maybe I didn't do the best job, but you and your brother grew up all right. And despite all, I think you know that I love you. Amber wants to be the driving force in Jet's life, but it's just a lot easier to let you do the driving. If you refuse to do it, she'll be forced to manage on her own."

"What if she doesn't? What if she neglects Jet or...or puts her in foster care?"

Wilma waved that away without concern. "I don't think that's about to happen. I don't understand you, Ellen. You've always been the undampenable optimist. The one who could always feel the sunshine, even through the clouds. Why can't you do that now? Amber loves Jet, she wants to be her mother. That's why she's always fighting for her. She won't let anything happen to that child. You know that as well as I do."

Ellen's brow was furrowed. "But what if I'm wrong," she said. "I can be wrong."

Wilma hesitated. The statement was out there. She knew what it meant. She didn't want to turn the knife, but sometimes, it had to be turned.

"Because you were wrong about Paul?" Wilma said.

Ellen didn't answer.

"You wanted your husband to live. That's no great failing," Wilma said. "You wanted him to live, you prayed that he would live, you believed that he would live. You believed it long, long after everyone else, including Paul, knew that he would not."

Ellen's eyes welled with tears. "I knew he would get well," she said, quietly, sorrowfully. "I wouldn't even consider anything else."

"You wanted it to be true," Wilma said. "That's not a terrible thing."

"I think it was terrible for Paul," she admitted. "He wanted to talk about dying, he wanted to unburden himself. He wanted to be sure that we were going to be okay. I didn't let any of that happen."

Wilma's heart was breaking for her daughter, but she didn't interrupt her.

"Poor Paul," she said, through choking tears. "I think his last thoughts must have been that he was letting me down. It was bad enough that he was having to die, to be sick and miserable and in pain. All that was bad enough without the added guilt of failing to live up to my optimistic expectations."

"Is that why you haven't been able to just let him go?"

Ellen began to cry in earnest. Wilma let her. It had been a long time since she had done it. Early in her grief, she had cried every day. But Wilma knew that it had been years now that Ellen had been stoically writhing in emotional pain.

"Paul tried to talk straight with me," she admitted. "He said to me, 'Ellen, I'm dying' and I scolded him. I told him, 'Don't ever say that. Don't ever say that to me.' How terrible it must have been to be dying and the one person you were closest to, the one person who was supposed to be there for you, the one who was sharing your life, didn't want to hear about it."

"Ellen, honey, we all have regrets," Wilma said. "That's what death is like for those who are left behind. It's chances missed and moments lost. 'I could have done this' or 'I should have said that.' Everybody feels that way. The closer you are, the stronger you feel it. You know how much Paul loved you. He knew how much you loved him. You were both trying to protect each other. It was just something that was beyond the reach of either of you."

"I don't want you to die, too," Ellen said.

Wilma should have expected the words. She understood the sentiment. And she dreaded her response.

"Oh, honey, I am so sorry, truly I am," she answered.

Amber knew she should probably go straight home. Wilma was still in the hospital and her mother had been taking care of Jet since that afternoon before three. She'd have to be up early in the morning. Her mother left for work at dawn and it just wasn't possible for Jet to sleep in. She always had so much energy in the morning.

Amber had every intention of going straight home, but just as she was totaling up, Gwen called on her cell phone.

"We're at Zinc's," she yelled over the din around her. "You gotta come over here, we're having a great time."

"You sound very drunk," Amber told her.

"Yeah, I'm about half shit-faced," she admitted. "I got two really hot babe-magnets here buying me drinks. With you not here, I have to drink twice as fast."

Gwen thought that was very funny and began to giggle.

"I need you to come on over and help me handle these guys," she said.

"I was going to just go home," Amber told her. "I'm really tired."

"Don't go home," Gwen said. "Come over here and meet us. We're having a great time. You're really going to like these dudes I've dug up."

Gwen thought that line was funny, too.

"I've got some great news," Amber said. "I've confronted my mother and it's a hundred percent go for the apartment."

"All right!" Gwen shouted for joy. A response not typically acceptable at Zinc's but if two guys were buying the booze, it was certainly understandable.

"Come on over here and let's celebrate, girlfriend," Gwen said.

"I don't know," Amber hedged. "I'm really tired."

"You can't be that tired."

"My grandmother is sick."

"You're old grandma is sound asleep by now, get over here."

Gwen was right. Her mother was undoubtedly home from the hospital and she and Jet were snoozing away by now. There was no need for Amber to hurry home to watch them.

Besides, her mother was going to have to get used to not having Amber around. In just a few weeks, she'd be out on her own, living as large as she pleased, partying every night if she wanted to. Ellen would just have to learn to cope.

Amber locked up, waved good-night to the security guard and made her way out of the building. There were lots of lights on the street, lots of action still going on downtown. She didn't mind walking the half-dozen blocks to the bar.

It was hot. The west wind coming in off the desert was no cool breeze, it blew as hot as a hair dryer. The heat zapped a lot of her energy. When she finally arrived at Zinc's, she was hoping for a comfortable place to sit down and a cool splashy drink.

Gwen was having none of that.

"Amber! Amber! Come here, meet my friends."

She was standing on a chair to catch Amber's attention through the crowd. Gwen had on a really short tight skirt and makeup that was so heavy it was positively Goth. The combination made her friend appear downright skanky.

Pasting a smile upon her face, Amber moved through the crowd of well-dressed up-and-comers and their hanger-on friends who frequented the new, hip bar. The place was noisy and crowded and hot, even with the air-conditioning on full blast.

When she finally reached Gwen and the guys, her heart sank. The pre-advertised babe-magnets were actually just balding fortysomething suits. Everything about them said *married men*.

Where does Gwen get these guys? Amber thought to herself. But she knew, they were conventioneers from the hotel, who thought of Gwen as a hooker.

"Amber, this is J.J. He's kind of with me." The taller, thinner one of the two twirled his fingers in lieu of a wave. "And this is Craig," Gwen continued the introductions. "This is my friend, Amber, that I told you about."

"You're like a lingerie model or something, right?" Craig said to her.

Amber shook her head. "No, I don't model it, I just sell it."

"Babe, if you model it, I'll buy it."

Craig thought that was really funny. J.J. thought it was funny. Gwen thought it was funny.

Amber met her glance.

"What you need is a drink," Gwen said. "Craig, buy this girl a drink."

Amber didn't really want a drink. She wanted to go

home. She wanted to get in her pajamas. She wanted to crawl in bed with Jet and go to sleep.

But, of course, she couldn't do that. Gwen quickly made it clear that they had been waiting on her all evening. Now the party was supposed to begin in earnest. Amber couldn't just slink off home and be boring. Even if that was exactly what she wanted to do.

"Vodka tonic," she told the waiter when he arrived.

"Make that a double," Gwen told him. "She's trying to catch up."

There were no extra chairs. It was decided, without much input from Amber, that rather than Craig giving up his chair to her and having to stand, Amber would just sit on his lap.

There were a couple of jokes about lap dancing versus lap drinking, but Amber managed to be a good sport about it. He played a little bit of grab-ass, but nothing that was particularly abhorrent.

Amber distanced herself with politeness, listened to the conversation, swirled the ice in her glass, and sipped her drink for what seemed like hours.

The guys were not terrible. Craig actually seemed kind of sweet.

"What kind of work do you do?" she asked him.

"Oh, I'm an insurance adjuster," he said. "We're all here in town for the national conference."

Amber smiled. "Of course you are," she said.

Somehow there were never any other guys except those just passing through.

"We're just here for a couple of nights," he said. "We want to party a little bit, have a little fun, you know."

Amber knew exactly.

She'd barely finished her drink when the talk turned to moving on. The place had lost all its shimmer. It was on to some new bar with some new crowd and some more drinks.

Gwen wanted to go dancing. It made Amber's head hurt to think about it, but nobody really consulted her. She excused herself and made her way to the ladies' room. She used the john and washed her hands. She was standing in front of the mirror, reapplying lipstick when a familiar face walked up behind her.

"Kayla?"

"Amber!"

They embraced and put their cheeks together, kissing the air.

"It's so cool to see you, it's been forever," Amber said.

"I know," Kayla admitted with a nod. "It's my fault. I just haven't been out at all. I've missed you. How have you been? How's Gwen?"

"She's great. She's outside, actually," Amber said. "She's locked on to a couple of guys, as per usual. I guess we're going dancing."

"Gwen is always crazy for dancing," Kayla said.

"And I'm crazy for always going with her," Amber said. "Have you heard our big news?"

"No, what?"

"We're really moving into an apartment," Amber said. "The one we looked at in your complex."

"That's totally cool."

"Yeah, I'm really excited. We should be there in just a couple more weeks. I just finally had to get it straight with my mom and all, yek, I hate that."

"Yeah, well, for sure," Kayla agreed.

"So now maybe we'll see you more often."

"I don't know how we could miss each other," she said. "The complex isn't that big."

"And we'll need to ride with you downtown," Amber said.

"Oh, yeah, right," Kayla agreed. "I said I'd give you a lift downtown."

"You know, if you still want to," Amber said, giving her friend an out.

"Oh sure, yeah, that's great," Kayla assured her. "I come downtown every day anyway, and the rest of the car is empty. Of course, I gotta be down here at eight. I know that's not really good for you."

"No," Amber said. "But hey, I might start working with Gwen. I don't know, something will work out."

"Sure," Kayla said. "Something will work out."

"So…ah…you're not hanging out here by yourself?" Amber asked.

"Oh, no," Kayla assured her, laughing. "I'm here with Brian."

"Brian?"

"Yeah, he came to see me," she said.

Amber was frantically searching her brain.

"Who's Brian?" she asked finally.

"You remember, the flyboys, the ones who left for Mississippi?"

Amber did remember the short, geeky guy who just sort of naturally made his way to Kayla—the least attractive of the three of them.

"He came back?"

Kayla nodded. "He's on leave for four days, and he came to see me."

"That's terrific."

"Oh, you don't know the half," she said. "He's like leaving to go overseas and like his folks wanted him to come home and he told them like, 'no, I've got this girl in San Antonio and I want to spend my last nights in the States with her.'"

"Oh, wow, that is so romantic," Amber said. "And after only meeting you that one time."

"I gave him my e-mail address and we've been writing back and forth at least every day, sometimes twice a day, sometimes six times a day!"

She giggled delightedly and Amber couldn't help but join in with her. "Oh, Amber," she whispered. "I think this is it. I think that after all this time, this is really like the real thing."

"Shut up! Are you sure?" Amber asked.

Kayla nodded enthusiastically.

"Have you…have you used the *L* word?"

"Not in person," Kayla admitted. "But we say it in e-mail constantly."

"Who said it first?"

"He did."

"Oh, my God!" Amber hugged her. "I'm so excited and so happy for you."

"I'm happy for me, too."

They hugged each other. Amber teared up.

"Look at me, I'm going to cry here," she said.

"I could cry, too," Kayla said. "Just from, like, the joy of it. Come out and say 'hi' to him, okay."

"Absolutely," Amber said.

They wound their way through the crowd. Amber recognized him on sight. He was still as geeky looking as before, but he had a more confident bearing now, an amazing change for just a few short weeks.

"You remember my friend Amber," Kayla said.

He offered his hand. "Of course," he said. "It's great to see you."

"I ran into her in the bathroom," Kayla said.

"That's good," Brian answered before confiding to Amber. "I was beginning to worry that Kayla'd slipped out the back and dumped me."

"Oh, like I would!" Kayla responded, laughing.

He laughed with her. Amber watched him. When he looked at Kayla there was a smile in his eyes that was lit from the inside. He really was feeling the *L* word. Amber did want to cry.

"I'd better get back to Gwen and the guys or she'll be thinking that I slipped out the back as well," Amber said.

"Tell her I said 'hi,'" Kayla said. "And congratulations on your new place."

"Thanks," Amber said. "Great to see you again, Brian. You're a smart guy coming back here for Kayla."

Amber waved goodbye and made her way back to the table. Gwen and her conventioneers had already vacated it and were waiting at the front door.

"Where in the hell have you been?" Gwen asked, annoyed.

"I saw Kayla," she answered. "She's here with her flyboy. He came back to see her. They look totally dopey together. I think it must be the real thing."

Gwen's eyes widened. "B.F.D.," she responded nastily. "I hope you didn't ask them to come with us."

"I didn't even think of it," Amber replied honestly.

"Good," Gwen said. "That Kayla is such a loser."

17

Saturday morning was Jet's birthday and it was cloudless and hot. And the news was very good. Amber's promise was going to be kept. Wilma would be home in plenty of time for the four-year-old's party. Ellen got up early and made a cake. She used to make very fancy ones for Amber, decorated in her daughter's big interest of the year. Ellen had done every favorite from Big Bird to Barbie.

The one she was making for Jet was not exactly complex. One round cake pan and four little cupcakes. With the right placement and the appropriate color of icing, they'd make a recognizable *Blue's Clues* footprint.

Jet was so excited about her birthday that she was practically jumping off the walls. Amber had come home very late the night before and was still in bed even with the cake out of the oven, the whole house smelling of it and her daughter stuck in repeated verses of *Happy Birthday to me-ee!* at the top of her lungs.

Ellen had given a great deal of thought to what Wilma had told her. Maybe she was some kind of bad-mother enabler. But could she just throw Jet at the mercy of Amber's better impulses?

A few years ago, she would have said unequivocally "yes." Her daughter had been a tower of strength. A teammate Ellen could depend upon. Amber made good grades, brought home a paycheck and could be called upon day or night to take vital signs, flush out an IV drip or just sit and talk to her father and make him laugh.

Ellen had counted on Amber a lot. She'd expected so much and Amber had never let her down. Was that why she expected so little now? Since the day she found out Amber was pregnant, she had allowed her daughter to feign incompetency and opt out of any responsibility in that which she had no interest.

Amber had been so lucky! She had a bright, beautiful, healthy child. A biracial child with no father in the picture and only two old white women to care for her. Amber didn't seem to worry about Jet's care, her education, her future. So Ellen had done that.

Maybe Wilma was right. It was time that she stopped.

"Jet," she said. "I have to go to the hospital now and pick up Wilma. Wake your mother and tell her she's got to get up and watch you."

The little girl's brow furrowed. "I could go with you," she said.

"No, you wake your mother," Ellen told her. "Wilma and I will be back here in an hour or so."

The time element turned out to be quite a bit more than she'd bargained for. The doctor had been delayed on rounds and the two of them had to simply sit there, bags packed with Wilma in a wheelchair until he got around to seeing her one more time and signing the discharge order.

In great detail, the nurse went over the medication schedule. She talked to Wilma loudly and using small words, as if she thought the woman was both hard of hearing and not very bright. Wilma tolerated it, Ellen thought, because she was just too desperate to get out of the place.

Finally Dr. Reberdi showed up. He listened to Wilma's heart and lungs both seated and standing.

"I can really help you if you're willing to quit smoking," he told her. "We put you on a cessation medication two weeks before you stop. You pick a date to go smoke free and you commit to taking the medication for six months. Since you don't have any allergies or other health problems, you really are a very good candidate for this, Mrs. Post."

"I'll think about it," Wilma answered quickly. Quickly enough to sound completely dismissive.

Dr. Reberdi nodded, resigned.

He shook Wilma's hand and then Ellen's.

Hurrying ahead to get the car from the parking lot, Ellen pulled into the covered loading zone to meet Wilma and the nurse's aide. She was only a couple of minutes ahead of them. But as soon as Ellen turned into the drive she saw Wilma in the wheelchair, her oxygen turned off and a cigarette in her hand.

Angrily, she got out and walked around the car.

"Did you give these to her?" she asked the nurse's aide accusingly.

"No, ma'am," the woman responded, offended. "She was carrying them in her pocket. I would never *allow* anyone to smoke this close to an oxygen tank, even if it *is* turned off."

Ellen looked at her mother. "Who gave you that pack?" she asked.

Wilma shrugged. "A hospital is just like prison," she said. "Cigarettes are a tradable commodity."

It wasn't a real answer, but Ellen let it go. There was not much else she could do. She and the nurse helped Wilma into the passenger seat. Ellen rolled down the window. Normally, she didn't allow smoking in her car. But she knew if she said that now, she'd just be stuck waiting here at the curb while Wilma finished her cigarette.

After her mother was buckled in with her oxygen at the ready, Ellen thanked the nurse and walked around to open the driver's door, sliding behind the wheel.

Ellen didn't say another word about it. Wilma would do what she had always done. Ellen was hardly in charge of her own destiny, so she wasn't likely to be able to take over her mother's.

They drove through town, Wilma watching the sights go by with such obvious pleasure it was as if she, indeed, had been in prison.

When she finished her cigarette she crushed the butt in the ashtray. Wilma leaned back in the seat and sighed, pleasurably.

"I tell you, Ellen, it's better than sex," she said.

"What?"

"That first cigarette," Wilma answered. "It's better than sex."

She ignored that comment.

When they arrived home, Brent's Tahoe was parked in front of the house. If he and Amber were having some kind of disagreement, it was impossible to tell by the young man's manner.

He was right there by Wilma's door by the time the car stopped, and appeared perfectly willing to carry her into the house if need be. Fortunately, she made the trip on her own two feet, leaning heavily against him.

When she got inside and settled in her chair, Jet, who hadn't seen her since they'd taken her to the hospital climbed eagerly into her lap and wrapped her little arms around the older woman's waist.

"I'm so glad you're home, Wil-ma," she said. "I haven't been to the grocery story in a really long time."

Wilma laughed and hugged the little girl tightly.

"I had to come home," she told Jet. "I wanted to be here for your birthday party."

Ellen insisted that the occasion be postponed until after lunch. She cooked pork chops, spinach, macaroni with cheese and applesauce. Jet's favorite menu.

She took charge of the cooking and allowed Jet to entertain her birthday guests, and vice versa. The kitchen was as hot as Hades. With the price of electricity, Ellen couldn't bear to turn the air-conditioning to a more livable level. Instead she got Brent to help her move the kitchen table out under a tree in the backyard. They ran a long orange extension cord out to the area and set up the fan. It wouldn't be perfect, but they could live with it. A picnic atmosphere was far more party friendly than a hot kitchen.

At Ellen's direction, Brent set up a folding table a few feet away. She covered it with a bright pink sheet and a crocheted tablecloth. And they put the cake and the birthday gifts upon it. Along with the wrapped and tied packages that she and Amber had bought was a larger gift wrapped in the Sunday comics. It had yellow twine for a ribbon and a big red sticker that read To Jet From Mr. Brent.

The contributor of that gift was currently employed

blowing up colorful balloons and tying them to the limbs of the trees.

"Those look great," Ellen told him. "It really makes it seem like a party."

Brent stepped back to observe his work and nodded in agreement.

"Anything else I can do?" he asked.

"No, I think I've got it," Ellen told him. "But I did want to tell you how glad I am that you came to her party."

"I wouldn't have missed it," Brent assured her. "And I wanted to see Wilma, too. She's looking so much better than the day I took her to the hospital."

Ellen was philosophical. "The doctor says that it's just a temporary respite. If she doesn't quit smoking, she won't get better."

Brent sighed heavily. "Any evidence that she might give it a try?" he asked.

Ellen shook her head.

"Dang, I'm sorry," he said.

"Me, too," she answered.

She went back into the kitchen. The pork chops were simmering in a light sauce. The macaroni was bubbling nicely. There was a sink full of spinach to be washed and she got busy at it.

To her surprise, Brent came to stand beside her. Ellen had thought that they'd finished their conversation. Obviously he had something more to say.

"I...I wanted to tell you..." he hesitated.

Ellen had known the young man for years. He had been one of Amber's friends since childhood. There was not a shy or hesitant bone in the fellow's body, but something was obviously troubling him.

"What is it?" she asked him.

"Well, Wilma asked me to check up on her house eviction. She wanted me to look up the papers, ask a few questions, stuff like that," he said.

Ellen was surprised, both that Wilma would ask him and that he would take his time to do it.

"Oh, Brent," she said, rubbing his back in a comforting, motherly fashion. "That is so sweet of you. You didn't have to do that."

He shrugged off her praise.

"I talked with this guy who's the paralegal for the lawyer representing Mr. Post's family. I told him how sick Wilma was," he said. "I asked if there was a way to get them to back off, give an extension or something."

"What did he say?" Ellen asked.

Brent shook his head. "He said if Wilma's sick then it's even more imperative to get the matter settled. If she were…if she were to die, it would make everything even more complicated. The lawyers are pushing to clear it up as quickly as possible."

Ellen let those words sink in thoroughly. With everything that had happened: Wilma's illness, Amber's decision to move out and leave Jet, the crisis of losing the house had somehow found its way to the back burner of Ellen's worries. She hadn't heard from Marvin Dix in several days. Hopefully it was because he was coming up with some tremendous winning strategy that couldn't miss.

"With the mediation hearing already on the schedule," he continued. "The paralegal seems to think that the whole thing will be completely resolved and you will be moved within the next two weeks."

"Two weeks?" A knot tightened in Ellen's stomach. "I hope he's wrong about that," she said.

"One more thing I think I ought to tell you," Brent said, again showing some reticence.

"What's that?"

"This guy told me something, maybe he didn't intend for you to know, but he didn't ask me to keep it in confidence."

"If you think you shouldn't tell me, then don't," Ellen said.

"I think I have to tell you," Brent said.

His expression was very concerned.

"What is it?"

"He said something about your lawyer, Dix," Brent told her. "He told me that the man was a real lowlife and not much better than a crook."

Ellen shrugged off his words. "In a legal battle it's rather typical to vilify the representation of the opposition," she said.

Brent nodded. "I'm sure that's true," he said. "But that wasn't what this guy was talking about. Apparently Dix is pushing hard for a financial settlement. He's made it clear that Wilma is willing to let go of the house—she's just waiting for the price to get high enough."

Ellen was stunned.

"That's not true," she said.

"I told the guy I was pretty sure that money was not what you wanted," Brent said. "I told him you just want to live in the house."

"That's right." Ellen was genuinely puzzled. "Dix knows that, too," she said. "Why would he be trying to negotiate us out of it?"

"Well, according to this paralegal, Dix can have some pretty nasty fine print in his contractual agreements. He gets his fee that you agreed to, plus forty percent of any money he collects for you in a settle-ment. If you get the house, he gets nothing but his fee. But if he makes the cash deal he's pushing—in which Wilma vacates the house and they pay her thirty thousand dollars—you're out on the street with only three years' worth of rent and he's $12,000 richer."

Ellen was appalled. "You don't think the paralegal could be making this up?" she asked.

Brent shrugged. "I don't think so," he said. "Why would he? Who recommended this Dix guy to you?"

She groaned aloud. "Nobody recommended him," she said. "No one else was willing to take my case," Ellen said. "I thought he would be better than nothing."

"You could have been wrong about that," he said. "What do you know about what he's doing for you? Have you seen any of the papers he's filed?"

"No, I don't know a thing. The man ducks my calls constantly."

"Well, it may not be true," Brent said. "But I wanted you to be aware that it's a possibility."

"Thanks, Brent," she said. "I appreciate your help and I really will check into it."

He poured the cold applesauce in a bowl and helped Ellen put the hot food on the table.

Ellen felt as if the walls were closing in on her. The knot in her stomach continued to worsen. She needed to go off somewhere and think everything through. But for Jet's sake she pasted a smile on her face and walked into the living room.

The little girl and Wilma were playing grocery store. Amber was their slightly preoccupied check-out person.

"Come to birthday dinner," she called out to them.

"We're going to have to eat it so that we can have cake."

"I want to eat it," Jet assured her, jumping to her feet.

"Go on outside and Brent will show you the place of honor," Ellen said.

The little pair of four-year-old feet went running through the house and out the back door. Amber and Wilma came a little more slowly. Wilma looked great and was able to ambulate the distance under her own steam. Ellen followed her out.

They all found a place at the table. With their mismatched schedules, it was rare for them to eat together as a family. It was even more unusual to have a guest. There weren't enough chairs and Ellen ended up sitting on the vanity stool from her mother's bedroom.

Wilma folded a paperboy's cap for Jet from a brightly colored newspaper insert. She wore it proudly, calling it her party hat. She gazed around her, excited and pleased, as if a cake, a few balloons and a late lunch out under a tree were a magical experience.

Amber picked up the pork chops, put one on her plate and was passing the platter to Wilma when Ellen asked Jet to say grace. The food stopped abruptly, but her daughter looked more annoyed than guilty.

The little girl dutifully bowed her head and recited a prayer that Ellen had taught her.

Who will teach Jet to pray if I don't? Ellen asked God. *If you want Amber to be her mother, then I'm going to have to trust you to make her worthy of the job.*

"Amen," Jet finished proudly. Immediately she

was lauded with glowing compliments on her excellent abilities.

And the pork chops began their circuit once more.

The meal was filled with laughter and exuberance. Amber and Brent were pretty much ignoring each other, but there was plenty of conversation elsewhere to take up the slack.

When it was time for dessert, Ellen brought out the *Blue's Clues* cake. She lit the four candles, their glow barely visible in the afternoon shadows.

"Happy Birthday to you…" Ellen began and everybody joined in.

Jet blew out the candles and got every one in the first try. She applauded herself.

The cake was doled out in huge slices with much laughing, especially when it was discovered that the icing made everyone's lips and tongue blue.

Finally it was time for presents. Ellen cleared the table while Amber laid the bounty before the young princess. Jet picked up the first one and started to tear into it.

Ellen tutted. "You must read the card first," she told her. "And then thank whoever gave it to you, before you open it."

Amber made a whiny, disapproving sound. "I never understood why you have to say 'thank you' before you even open the box," she complained.

"To show that you are grateful to get a gift, no matter what it is," Ellen told her.

"I'm grapefull," the four-year-old insisted.

Nobody doubted her.

Jet opened the card. It had a little girl and a big pink four. She had Amber read it to her. The verse was a sappy childhood sentiment, but Ellen liked it.

"It's signed Gramma," Amber said finally.

Jet looked up at Ellen. "Thank you, Gramma," she said politely. "Can I open it now?"

Ellen nodded.

Jet tore at the paper revealing a container with doll figures.

"What does it say? What does it say?" she asked her mother eagerly.

Amber read the box. "Harriet Tubman Playset—An innovative approach to teaching the richness of the African-American heritage. Includes five-inch articulated Harriet, Runaway Slave Girl and Baby, Donkey Cart, Bloodhound, Miniature Freedom Quilt and Campfire."

Amber rolled her eyes and gave her mother a long-suffering look.

"Oh, brother," she said.

Jet had no such negative reaction.

"I want to play," she said. "Can we play it now?"

Ellen was gratified by the child's response, but urged Jet to set Harriet aside for the moment and open the rest of the presents.

The next card was from Amber and featured a little round bear in a ballet suit. Jet thanked her and opened the gift. It was a cool, little-girls fashion doll called Groovy Girl. She was dressed in a soccer uniform, but she also had a lavender party dress with a tiny fake fur stole.

"At least she's not a blonde," Ellen said.

Amber shrugged. "I tried to get a blond one, but they were all out."

"I like this one," Jet said, wrapping the fur around the doll's soccer uniform.

Brent's gift had no card, so Amber just read the to and from names on the sticker.

Jet thanked him and opened it up. On the top was a *Blue's Clues* CD.

"We don't have a CD player," Amber said snidely. "We'll have to take it back and get a tape."

"It's not music," Brent told her. "Open the rest of it, Jet."

"It's heavy," she said.

He got up to help her.

They tore away the paper. A black laptop computer was revealed.

"You got her a computer?" Ellen was stunned.

"It's not new," Brent explained quickly. "It's my old one. It's outdated for my schoolwork, but I think it will work well for Jet to do games and stuff."

"Wow," Ellen said.

"Isn't that something!" Wilma agreed.

"Jet doesn't know anything about computers," Amber said. "She's only four, she won't be able to work that thing."

"Jet knows a lot about computers," Brent argued. He turned to Jet. "This CD works just like those ones we got with your kiddie meals," he said.

"Ohhhhhhhh," she said nodding. "I can do that." Her words were spoken with complete confidence.

"She's been playing on my computer, so I thought I'd get her one of her own," he said. "There's lots of great stuff out there. You can even get educational games at the library. You don't have to buy anything."

The last was said without any hint of condescension.

"I think it might really help her if she's familiar by the time she gets to kindergarten," Brent concluded.

Ellen was very pleased. It was a very sweet, thoughtful gift. And because it was a castoff, it didn't even feel inappropriate or too expensive.

"I guess you're right," she said. "Jet is growing up in a digital age. I hadn't even thought of her needing a computer."

"Me neither," Wilma chimed in. "I suppose I thought she'd be able to parlay her knowledge of ribald beer tunes and vegetable buying into a useful elementary school education."

That comment brought laughter from Brent and Ellen.

Amber didn't appear to share their delight.

"What a stupid thing to buy a four-year-old," she said.

"She can operate it. I've seen her," Brent said.

"You've been helping her," Amber pointed out. "She'll never be able to do it by herself."

"She'll do just fine," Brent said. "She's a natural. And she feels comfortable with computers."

"Somebody will have to help her," Amber said. "And neither Ellen nor Wilma know anything about them."

"I think I can manage," Ellen contradicted. "The world of accounting has been digital for a couple of decades now."

Brent agreed. "You're the one who doesn't know anything about them, Amber," he said. "I guess you're waiting until they turn Howl at the Moon into a cybercafé."

His words angered Amber so much, it was almost possible to see steam coming out from her ears. Amber glanced toward Jet as if to make certain the child was not looking in her direction, then to Brent she mouthed the words "fuck you."

Brent smiled, not particularly nicely and replied, "No, thanks."

Hastily Ellen changed the subject. "Well, Jet, you got some really nice presents. Do you think this was a very good birthday?"

The little girl agreed enthusiastically.

"And you're not done yet," Wilma said. "I still owe you a gift, don't I?"

Jet smiled at the older woman.

"I'm sorry I haven't been able to get out and get you a present yet. But you remember I promised you that I'd give you whatever you want."

Jet nodded. "I remember you promised, Wil-ma," she said.

"So you have even more birthday wishes that may come true," she said.

"This is the best day ever!" Jet declared enthusiastically. "Don't you think so, Mama?"

Amber looked up. "Of course it is," she said. Her smile was brittle, but she maintained it.

18

After the birthday party, Amber decided to stay home for the evening. It wasn't some monumental decision. She went downtown every day. It was stupid to have the night off and go downtown anyway. She'd actually spent a pleasant evening. Jet seemed so delighted to have her home.

They dressed and undressed her Groovy Girl a dozen times, winning both the champion soccer game and the beauty pageant. Amber even played Harriet Tubman, pulling the donkey cart with the girl and her baby in it. Jet named the bloodhound Poochie and Amber didn't have the heart to tell her he was supposed to be the villain of the story.

Jet was irrevocably drawn to the computer. She wanted to play her *Blue's Clues* game and she insisted that Amber help her. She was, of course, not nearly as ignorant of the digital universe as Brent Velasco might believe. The work schedules, sales reports and inventory at the store were all on electronic spreadsheets. And Amber had brought with her from high school a rudimentary understanding of operating systems. She could see immediately that in five years things had gotten a lot fancier, but it all seemed easier as well.

Brent was right about Jet. She had absolutely no

hesitation about the equipment. She set her CD into the drive and was ready to go. He'd set up shortcuts on her desktop that even a four-year-old could follow. Amber watched and listened as her daughter went through the clues and hollered out the answers to the questions.

Amber thought she shouldn't have been so sharp with Brent about it. It was a nice gift and it was nice of him to give it to her. She hadn't been able to stop herself from being snippy with him. He was sure to believe that it was the result of their argument the other night.

Amber was honest enough with herself to admit that was only a part of it. The real issue was a lot less straightforward. It was a kind of jealousy. That was the only way to describe it. It annoyed her that somebody else got to give her things that Amber didn't think about giving her. She hated the feeling that when it came to Jet, everyone knew better than she did. But wasn't that the reason she was giving Jet up? That was the excuse, but Amber didn't like to think it was the reason. She was torn. She wanted it both ways. Part of her needed to be the main person in Jet's life, to have the final say, and be the ultimate authority. But there was that overwhelming temptation that lured her out to have fun and live the life she might have had if things had somehow worked out differently.

Jet abandoned the computer to set up a tea party for Harriet and Groovy Girl. Amber watched for a few moments and then began clicking through the computer herself. She was looking for Spider Solitaire when she realized that Brent's Internet service was still set up, including his stored password.

"So he thinks I know nothing about computers," she muttered to herself before plugging the phone line into the back of the unit and logging on to his account.

She checked his e-mail, hoping to find some incriminating love note or a vital message that she could delete. There was nothing but spammy junk. Even after checking his site visits history, there was nothing funny, embarrassing or defaming that she could really enjoy eavesdropping upon.

With a sigh of defeat, Amber pulled down a search engine and just began to surf a few sites. She called up her company's Web page and looked at some of the merchandise. It was mostly older than what they were carrying in the store. She saw they were posting career opportunities and she clicked on that, just to see what kind of hype they were putting on their job classifications.

As she read through the assistant manager position she noticed an Educational Opportunities button on the navigation bar. Curious she clicked on it.

According to the Web site, full-time employees with positions of assistant manager or above were eligible for loans, grants and scholarships to attend college. It was the stated policy of the company to encourage higher education, and work schedules could be adjusted to meet classroom needs.

Amber raised an eyebrow at that. It had never occurred to her that she might be able to get tuition money from her job. But, she reminded herself hastily, she was probably going to change her job. She was going to work at the hotel with Gwen, so they could get a car and furniture and nice things for their apartment.

As she supervised Jet's tooth brushing and hair braiding bedtime ritual, she convinced herself once again that leaving Jet was going to be best for her and best for Jet. Her heart melted at the little girl's obvious delight at having Mama home to put her to bed.

She crawled in eagerly, obediently, but with her eyes still bright with birthday excitement.

"What do you want me to read you tonight?" Amber asked.

Jet immediately scrambled off the bed to search through her stack of books on the shelf above her toy box.

"Here it is," she said after a couple of moments of diligent searching. "This is the one *you* read to me."

Jet climbed back on the bed. She snuggled up against her mother and handed her the book.

Smiling, Amber recognized *Goodnight Moon*, the story of a not-so-sleepy little bunny.

"I know this one," she told her daughter.

Jet nodded. "This is the one you read to me, Mama," she said and putting a small hand beside her mouth, she lowered her voice to a whisper. "I don't let Gramma read this one anymore. It's between you and me."

Both the words and the sentiment were unexpected. Amber hugged her daughter close for a moment and then read her the story. As they said goodnight to each and every thing, she felt her daughter's body relax beside her. When they reached the end, she was yawning. The little girl scooted down in the bed and Amber covered her with the sheet and tucked it around her the way she liked.

"Good night, Jet," Amber said, leaning down to plant a kiss on her daughter's nose.

"Good night, Mama," she said.

Amber snapped off the bedside lamp, but she didn't leave immediately, she sat in the darkness gently stroking her daughter's forehead until her breathing deepened in sleep.

She let herself out of the room, quietly closing the door behind her. Ellen was seated alone in the living room.

"Is Wilma outside for a smoke?" Amber asked.

"I suppose so," Ellen answered.

Amber started in that direction.

"Don't go," Ellen said.

Amber hesitated. "Mom, I'm not going out there to have a smoke with her," she said.

"I know you're not," Ellen assured her.

"Wilma and I are kind of buds. She and I, you know, we've got a lot in common," Amber said. "I've always been more like her than I am like you. But I'd never sabotage her health."

"I know you wouldn't."

"In fact, I've decided to quit," Amber said. "I can't really afford it anyway and I never liked it that much."

"I'm glad," Ellen said. "I'd hate for you to end up as sick as your grandmother. But that's not what I want to talk to you about."

"What is it?"

"Could we sit down here for a minute," Ellen said. "I'm sure this will go a lot better if we're both more relaxed and comfortable."

"Okay, sure," Amber said. She seated herself in the rocker and crossed her legs casually. Her mother looked weird. She had that strange, heartsick but determined expression that she used to have when she'd given Amber updates on her father's condition. She said it wasn't about Wilma. So it must be that she had finally become resigned to losing the house.

"So have you heard anything on the eviction?" she asked.

"Not anything helpful," Ellen answered.

"Is that what you want to talk to me about?" Amber asked.

"No," her mother answered. "I want to talk to you about your plan to move out," Ellen said.

Amber nodded. "I have to talk to Gwen," she said. "She's paid the deposit and the rent is due on the first. We have to decide on when we're going to move in and what exactly we're going to need. We haven't worked out all the details."

Her mother's elbows were on the arms of the chair, her hands steepled together thoughtfully.

"One of the details you have to work out is Jet," she told Amber quietly. "You can't leave her with us."

"What?"

"You can't leave her with us," Ellen repeated. "I'm afraid we're not really in a position to take her now. It's best that you keep her with you."

Amber's first reaction was that her mother was joking.

"What do you mean?" she asked.

"Wilma and I have discussed it," Ellen said. "And we are in agreement that Jet should go with you."

"You're throwing me out?"

"No, of course not. You're welcome to stay, or you're free to go," Ellen explained. "But either way, Jet is your daughter. She will be with you."

"Because of Wilma's illness?" Amber asked. "She seems to be getting back on her feet pretty fast. But I can help out around here with Jet until she's a hundred percent."

"It's not about Wilma's illness," Ellen said.

"Then what is it about?"

"It's about a child being with her mother," Ellen said. "It's a very simple concept."

"Mom, you're not serious about this?"

"I have never been more serious in all my life," Ellen said.

Amber was momentarily speechless. She'd expected an argument, she'd expected threats, scolding and recrimination. But if she had thought anything, she'd have thought that her mother would fight to keep Jet. Not come up with an ultimatum to send her away.

"Jet can't come with me," Amber said. "This place is not right for her. It's a singles apartment."

"Then I suppose you'll have to find something different. You and Jet are a family. If families aren't welcome, you're not welcome."

"This won't work," Amber said. "You can't turn me into a family for Jet."

"I didn't turn you into a family," Ellen said. "You did that yourself when you gave birth to her."

"You're still holding that against me?"

"Not at all," Ellen said. "I am so glad you had that little girl. I can't imagine a world without her. But she's your child and you have to take responsibility for her."

"I can't take care of Jet, you know that," she said.

Ellen shook her head. "I think that you can," she said. "And I believe that you will."

"Of course you do, Mom, you're a total optimist," Amber said. "You're always just disgusting with hope, assured somehow that everything will work out. My life is not going to work out, Mom. I live wild. I party all the time. Gwen, my other friends—we're not ever going to be the ladies from the bridge club. Gwen's a slut. And I'm…well I'm not the kind of person who needs to be an innocent kid's mom. I can't offer her any kind of decent, stable life."

"Maybe a decent, stable life isn't what Jet needs," Ellen said. "You're always saying I shouldn't fill her head full of sugarplum fairies. Maybe a dose of harsh reality will be good for her."

"That's not what I want for my child."

"Well, that's for you to decide, isn't it," Ellen said. "She is your child."

"I have to work nights," Amber said. "Who would she stay with?"

Ellen shrugged. "Maybe you can't work nights," she said. "Maybe you have to work when she's in day care. Or maybe you have to go on welfare. Those are things you have to figure out."

"Those are insolvable problems!"

"Other women solve them," Ellen said. "I'm confident you can, too."

"I can't believe this."

"I think you have to."

"Mom, you promised when Jet was born that you would help me," Amber reminded her.

"And I have," Ellen said. "I have been pulling up the slack for you for four years. I don't regret it. I loved it. I have a bond with my granddaughter that lots of women would envy. I'm grateful for that."

"But not anymore."

"Amber, I'm always willing to be there to support you and back you up," Ellen said. "But letting you walk away is not the same as helping you. It's the worst thing I could do."

"How do you think you are going to stop me?" Amber asked. "I can leave this minute and there isn't a thing you can do about it."

"Careful, Amber," she said. "You're reminding me of when you used to stamp your foot and say, 'make me!'"

"Well you can't make me," Amber said.

"There are laws against abandoning children."

"You're threatening to call the police?"

"Maybe the Department of Social Services," Ellen said.

Amber shook her head. "You wouldn't do that," she said.

"If I had to, I would," Ellen said.

"Mom?" Amber was incredulous.

"Don't count on my continuing to treat you like a crazy, mixed-up kid," Ellen said. "You're a grown-up woman now, just like me. And you've got to find your own way in the world, just like I do. Sure you're going to make some mistakes, have some regrets. You wouldn't be human if you didn't. But you'll manage to muddle through just like the rest of us."

"This is not happening," Amber told herself unconvincingly. "I understand that you're really pissed off that I'm moving out. But there is no way you can convince me that you're willing to risk Jet's happiness this way. You love her and you want what's best for her."

"I do love her," Ellen agreed. "But Jet is your daughter. You are the one who has to do what is best for her. I have my own daughter. I have to do what is best for her."

* * *

The inside of the Empire Bar was dark, cool and familiar. Each of the waitresses took the opportunity to welcome Wilma back and inquire about her health.

"Nothing quite like passing out in a place to make people remember you," she remarked wryly to one young man.

She was dragging her oxygen tank with her today. It was the only way that Brent would agree to allowing her to go alone. And she simply had to be here. This was Max's place. She was hoping that he would show up. But even if he didn't, she wouldn't want to be anywhere else.

At least she was feeling better. The medicine had helped her breathing. The laying off cigarettes for a couple of days might have been good for her lungs as well. But the rest of her body certainly didn't like it. She had been, in turns, both jittery and lethargic. Nothing tasted right and she'd been constipated. Now that she was back smoking, the rest of her life had returned to normal.

Or as normal as a woman can get when she knows that she is killing herself, one pack at a time.

"You don't see any evidence of cancer," she pointed out proudly to that stuffed shirt Reberdi.

"None whatsoever," he assured her. "And I don't think you'll develop any—you're probably not going to live long enough. You don't have to get cancer to die of smoking."

So she was on her way out. Wilma could accept that. Nobody lived forever. Everybody knew that. Wilma just couldn't quite get past the fact that she was needed here. Ellen, Amber, Jet, they all depended upon her. And with Max she'd thought, she'd hoped, that she still had a life ahead of her.

What would that life cost?

If she gave up smoking, it would be forgoing the most constant and steadfast pleasure of her sixty-one years of life. But, she might live to see Jet's next birthday. She'd have nothing to do with her hands and no way to really kick back and relax, but she might be more of a help to her daughter and granddaughter. She might have to admit that all those years she'd smoked, she'd been wrong. But then, she had been.

"Wilma?"

She was startled from her thoughts and glanced up hopefully, expecting to see Max.

She did see him, sort of.

The man standing beside the booth had Max's lean cowboy frame, penetrating blue eyes and thick hair. But the hair was dark, not white, the eyes were not wearing glasses and the lean cowboy frame was covered with a very chic and expensive Italian suit. He was carrying a sharp leather briefcase that gave him the look of a prosperous lawyer or investment banker. But somehow the moves were not right. He was much too relaxed with himself. Still it was possible and it was best to be on her guard.

"Are you a lawyer?"

"Me? No."

"Are you here about my house?"

"Your house?" He looked puzzled. "No, I don't know anything about a house. Are you Wilma?" he asked again. "Wilma Post."

"Yes," she answered. "I'm Wilma Post."

He nodded. "Max told me that I'd find you here," he said.

"Max?"

"Max Roper, he's my dad. Do you mind if I sit down?"

She shrugged and he eased himself into the booth across from her. He was a nice-looking man in his late forties. He moved confidently as if he was easy with himself. He looked prosperous, even more than that, he was rather distinguished with just a touch of gray at the temples. He appeared to be a man who was accustomed to having things his way.

"Is Max all right? Why didn't he come himself?"

"I guess he thought if we met alone, we'd get to know each other better and faster," he said.

Wilma couldn't imagine why, but she didn't say so.

"I've been coming every day for a week now," he told her. "I was beginning to think you were a figment of Max's imagination."

Wilma raised an eyebrow. "I don't believe that Max Roper has figments of the imagination," she said.

The man chuckled. "Sounds like you know him," he said.

"Yes," she answered. "Is Max...how is Max? I haven't heard from him in a couple of weeks. I've been sick myself. That's why I haven't been here."

He glanced at the breathing hose attached to her face. "I trust that you're feeling better now."

"Oh, yeah," Wilma told him. "I'm almost ready to take on a ten round bout for *Wrestle World*. I'm just waiting on a ruling about whether dragging an oxygen tank into the ring is covered by the Americans with Disabilities Act."

He chucked. "Max said you had a wry sense of humor."

"Oh, really?" Wilma responded. "And what else did he tell you?"

"That you know more about fruits and vegetables than any green grocer in the universe. And that you can talk about it in a very engaging and entertaining manner."

Wilma snorted. "Well, the truth is, if your favorite topic of conversation is produce, you'd better talk in an engaging and entertaining manner or you'll be talking to yourself most of the time."

He laughed out loud at that.

Wilma liked the sound of it. It wasn't the deep bass that his father had, but it was a nice, genuine, straight from the heart, kind of laugh. She decided that she liked the younger Mr. Roper. He was a chip off a very fine block, and he was okay on his own as well.

The waitress came by and brought Wilma her mixed greens salad.

The man passed on lunch, but ordered an iced tea.

Wilma tossed the vegetables a little to distribute the vinaigrette dressing more evenly.

"What kind of lettuce is that?" he asked her.

"Sangria."

"What are those purple things?"

"That's radicchio."

"Do you ever see things in your salad and you don't know what they are?" he asked.

She chuckled. "Sometimes," she said. "But I always try to find out. It's amazing what people will tell you if you ask."

He smiled.

"I've got a question for you," he said.

"Okay."

He set his briefcase on the table and opened it.

From the inside, amidst the neat organization of papers, he pulled out an almost heart-shaped plant product with a pitted, leafy-looking skin about the color of artichoke. He set it on the table before her.

Wilma eyed him curiously as she speared lettuce onto her fork.

"So?" she asked.

"Do you know what this is?"

"It's called sherbet fruit," she answered. "Some people call it custard apple. The real name is cherimoya."

The fellow was visibly surprised, but pleased.

"What can you tell me about it?" he asked.

"What do you want to know?"

"Whatever you know," he answered.

Wilma chewed her lettuce for a moment while she thought about it.

"It's called sherbet fruit because it has the texture of sherbet when it's chilled."

"Is that the way you eat it?"

"You can," she agreed. "But more often it's either cubed up to be combined into a fruit salad or it's pureed for a dessert topping."

"Can I just wash it off and stick it in my kid's lunch box?"

"Not if you like your kid," Wilma warned. "The skin and the seeds are not very digestible. His teacher would have to give him a bathroom pass that would last all afternoon. But if you cut it up and put it in a container, he'd probably love it. And it's high in fiber and vitamin C."

"If I was going to buy one of these, how would I know which one to pick?" he asked.

Wilma continued to eat her lunch, but she reached over to examine the piece of fruit on the table.

"You want to avoid the brown, discolored skin," she said, indicating a small patch with her finger. "But this time of year, there is going to be some. Just stay away from any moldy stems." She turned it up and examined it. "I think this one will be fine."

He nodded. "May I borrow your knife?"

Wilma handed it to him. He set the knife to the skin as if he were about to peel it. She stopped him.

"Cut it in half," she said. "Then scoop it out and eat it with a spoon."

He did as she suggested. "Tastes pretty good," he told her.

She nodded in agreement.

"Supposedly they were highly favored by the ancient gods of the Andes," Wilma said.

"Really?"

"It's the oldest known fruit of the western hemisphere," she explained. "It gets its name, cherimoya, from Quechuan, the language of the Incas."

"The language of the Incas," he repeated thoughtfully as he savored the fruit's flavor.

"There are still native speakers of it in Peru, Bolivia, Ecuador, high in the mountains."

"So that's where this came from," he said. "South America."

"Sherbet fruit is grown mostly in Chile," Wilma said. "But this particular one actually came from Spain."

The man's expression was incredulous.

"That's right, that's what the produce manager told me," he said. "But how can you know that?"

Wilma shrugged and smiled, evasively.

"Are they different colors? Different sizes?"

She shook her head.

"You didn't taste it," he said. "How could you possibly know?"

She chuckled.

"You're going to hate yourself when I tell you," she said.

"Tell me anyway."

"Because the growing season is in the summer. It's winter in South America now."

He hesitated only an instant and then groaned.

"You're right, I do hate myself," he said.

"I hope it doesn't last long," she said.

He smiled. "No, with a find like you, I'm sure I'll recover quickly."

"That's what all the guys tell me," Wilma scoffed sarcastically.

"You've passed the test with flying colors," he said.

Wilma gave him a long look. "I didn't realize I was taking a test," she said.

"Max said you were a whiz," the man told her. "But I wasn't going to take his word for it."

"So you brought your cherimoya down here to play Stump the Old Lady?" Wilma asked.

"I just wanted to make sure that Max knew what he was talking about," he said. "He was right, I really can use somebody like you."

Wilma was completely baffled.

"Use somebody like me? Besides being Max's son, who in the hell are you?" Wilma asked.

"You don't know?"

"Would I be asking if I did?"

"I'm Homer Dilly," he answered. "Max told me

that you were a big fan of my stores, especially my produce department."

"Max Roper is your father?" Wilma was stunned.

"Yes," he said. "It's…ah…a long story."

Wilma remembered it. The girlfriend he got pregnant and never married. The son whose life he stepped out of when he was four and stepped back into when his stepfather got a divorce. The son who had "done well." Dilly's wasn't the biggest grocery chain in town, but it was locally owned and run, and a well-known supporter of scholarship programs and health-care research.

"I'll tell you the truth," Homer said. "If you were fifty instead of sixty, I'd hire you today."

"Hire me for what?" Wilma asked. "What in the devil are you talking about?"

"I'm talking about a job," he said. "Max told me that you were looking for a job. And I'd like to give you one."

Wilma was astounded. Max was mad at her. But he'd asked his son to give her a job.

"Let me get this straight. You'd like to give me a job," she said. "But I'm too old."

He nodded. "I know it's not p.c. to say this, but I honestly think you're too old to work full-time in a busy produce section," he told her.

"It's not just un-p.c. to say it," Wilma pointed out. "It's against the law. Haven't you heard of age discrimination?"

"I have and I'm against it," the man said. "Anyone who can work and wants to work should be judged by their abilities, not by their birthdays. But unless you're hiding a body builder's physique under that slim silhouette, I think it would be very hard on you trying to load, stack and cull a full-service produce department. Especially while rolling that tank behind you."

He was right about that, of course. Wilma could hardly keep up with a cooperative four-year-old for a few hours a day. There was no way she could work on her feet for forty hours a week.

"Even if you were in better heath, the physical requirements alone would probably do you in. And a woman your age working under those conditions is just a workman's comp claim waiting to happen."

"Well, thank you very much," Wilma said. "I didn't ask you for any job. I'm not even sure I'd want one if you offered, but it's nice to know that you'd be able to turn me down with a clear conscience."

He chuckled.

"You're feisty," he said. "I should have expected that. Max always likes the feisty ones."

Wilma didn't comment on that.

"Besides," Homer said, "I'm not turning you down. I think it would be a waste of your talents to have you doing grunt work in a store. I have a better idea I want you to think about."

"What better idea?" she asked.

He spooned himself out another bit of the sherbet fruit. "I need a new promotion vehicle for my stores," he told her. "I know that my edge on the competition in this town is the produce."

"Absolutely," Wilma agreed. "You have the best by far."

"Thank you," Homer said, smiling at her. "So how do I highlight that? How do I make that difference so important that people will drive past another store intentionally to go to mine?"

"You have to let them know," Wilma said.

He shook his head. "The people who care do know," he pointed out. "We've been touting it in commercials for years now. Everybody who cares about produce knows about our produce."

"I see."

"So what our challenge is," Homer said, "is to make more people care about their produce."

"And you have a plan?"

Homer nodded. "For most people an apple is an apple. If it doesn't have a worm in it, then it's fine. You only know the difference if you *know* the difference. What we, at Dilly's Fine Foods, need to do is educate the consumer. Learning is a good thing, we all believe that. Nobody can be opposed to it."

"So you want to have classes about fruits and vegetables?" Wilma asked.

"I thought about that," he said. "I thought about it, but who would come? The same people who shop in our stores. No, we need new people. People who aren't volunteering to learn anything. Where do you get people like that?"

"I haven't the vaguest idea," Wilma admitted.

"You get them on television," Homer said. "I want to buy a minute a day spot, five days a week during the local news. Not to show our stores or announce our bargains. I want them to feature the Dilly's Produce Lady."

"The Dilly's Produce Lady?"

He nodded. "Yes, Wilma, that's you."

19

————◆———

"Just tell your mother to go fuck herself," Gwen insisted when Amber filled her in on the ultimatum. "You can't let her run your life. She's a snarly, controlling bitch and you've got to set her straight."

"This is not about my mother," Amber said. "It's about my daughter."

"She's a kid," Gwen pointed out. "Kids do fine. Somebody always takes care of them. If not your mother, somebody else."

"I don't want somebody else taking care of Jet," Amber said.

"Well, you sure as hell can't do it," Gwen said. "Maybe you can stash her somewhere during the day, but are you going to drag her around to the bars with you at night?"

"No, of course not," Amber said.

"So you're just giving up on your own life?" Gwen asked.

"I'm not giving up my life, I'm just giving up an apartment," Amber said. "It's not that big a deal."

"It is!" Gwen told her. "This is probably your very last chance to get out and be on your own. You're never going to get enough money together to have your own place, not if you take that kid with you.

And it's not like the kid should even be your problem."

"What do you mean by that?"

"If your mom hadn't spent all the money, lost your house and screwed things up so badly, then you wouldn't have got knocked up in the first place," Gwen said. "It's her fault and she's the one who ought to suffer with the kid."

"No one is going to suffer with Jet," Amber said defensively. "She's a great kid and we're lucky to have her."

"Yeah, right," Gwen scoffed. "So lucky to have a ball and chain dragging you down forever."

"You're full of it," Amber insisted. "My life is better because of Jet."

"Your life is *over* because of Jet," Gwen yelled at her. "And what am I supposed to do? I've put down money for this apartment and now you're just stiffing me for your share."

"I'm sorry, Gwen," Amber said. "I'm truly sorry about that. Maybe you can find another roommate or…"

"Just don't call me anymore," Gwen said. "I don't need losers like you. You think you're better than me. You always have. You think I'm wrong about everything. But I'm going to be the one with my own place and lots of parties and friends and all of it. You're going totally nowhere, just so you can take your kid with you."

"She's my kid," Amber said. "I don't have any choice."

"Oh, gag me," Gwen replied. "You know, you're always bad-mouthing your mother, but you're just like her, trying to do the *right* thing, like there is some right thing. I get screwed in the process. You make me sick."

Gwen slammed down the phone.

Amber hung up her receiver more thoughtfully. She could hardly blame Gwen for her anger, but surprisingly she felt no regret. If she allowed herself the truth, she wanted to be with Jet. She wanted to be her mother. Amber just wasn't convinced that she was up to the job.

"Troubles?" Carly asked.

Amber startled. "I didn't realize you were here," she said, glancing down at her watch. Carly had shown up early. Amber had thought she and Metsy were in the place alone.

"Is your grandmother all right?"

"Oh, yeah," Amber answered. "She's back to her usual self and taking care of Jet already."

"Oh, that's good," Carly said. "I heard her name mentioned and if there was a problem with like babysitting, I was going to offer help."

"You were going to offer to baby-sit?"

Carly made a comic face feigning terror. "No, not that," she admitted. "But I can be flexible."

Amber gave her a look and shook her head.

"Carly," she said. "I honestly don't get you."

"What do you mean?"

"You are always on my case about something," Amber said. "But lately you're suddenly into trying to help me out. What's the deal?"

Carly looked at her eye to eye. "The deal is, you're a good employee," she said. "I don't mind filling in when you've got someone sick in the family or issues with your child's day care. But I hate like hell covering for you coming in late 'cause you've been out drinking all night. We don't need that kiddie-crap at this store. We need people who want to sell product and make money."

Amber shrugged. "I can sell the product," she said. "But I'm sure not making much money."

"You're making the highest commissions in this store," Carly pointed out.

"But it's not enough for me to live in my own house and support myself and my kid," she said.

"People do it all the time," she said. "It's a struggle, but they get by. They just keep working at it and they get by."

"I want more than that," Amber said. "I want more for myself. I want more for Jet."

"What exactly do you want?"

"I want the kind of life I had," Amber said.

The words were out of her mouth before she'd even had the time to think about them.

"What do you mean?" Carly asked.

Amber hesitated only for an instant. "I mean the life my parents had, before my dad got sick," she answered. "I want my own business and a nice house in a good neighborhood, my own car and a saving account to send Jet to college. My parents had all that."

Carly nodded. "Where did they get it?"

"Where did they get it?" Amber repeated. "What do you mean?"

"Did they inherit a bunch of money? Did they win the lottery?"

"No, of course not," Amber said.

"Then where did all that come from?"

"Well, my mom worked to send Dad to college," she said. "When he got out, they saved money until he could open his own CPA firm and then they worked and saved and invested and made a lot of money."

"Okay," Carly said. "So you know how they did it. You've just got to figure out a way to do the same."

Amber chuckled humorously. "I don't think there is much chance that my mom could send me to college. But I was thinking that maybe I could send myself."

Carly raised a surprised eyebrow. "To college?"

"Community college." Amber explained. "I saw on the company Web site that they have money to help employees with that. It would take me years and I don't know for sure that I could make it, but I'd like to try."

She could tell from Carly's expression that she was worried.

"So are you thinking to go on part-time?" she asked.

Amber shook her head. "I couldn't afford to do that. I was thinking that our busiest days around here are the weekends," she said. "If I worked nine to nine on Saturday and Sunday and a couple of nights during the week, I'd still be full-time and still have days free for classes. I could continue to do the buying, the accounts, the schedule, the payroll. That's really where you need me most anyway."

Carly's brow was furrowing thoughtfully.

"Don't answer right now," Amber cautioned. "Think about it."

Her boss nodded.

Through the rest of the morning, Amber went over and over the conversation in her head. She still didn't understand herself or what she wanted. But one thing had become clear. If she wanted her own life, then she had to be responsible for making it what she wanted.

She got caught up in a trousseau sale that went on interminably as the mother and daughter argued furiously about what was traditional versus what "all her sorority sisters" got. Amber managed to keep her smile but wanted to shake them both and say, stop this silly bickering! This should be a wonderful experience to remember together, not another thoughtless face-off!

When she finally managed to ring up the sale, which included some of the most beautiful and reasonably priced pieces in the store, neither woman was completely happy.

These two had everything that she and her mother had lost.

But there was something she and Ellen had that these women had missed out on somehow. Amber supposed she wouldn't have realized that if they'd been able to keep the wonderful life that they'd had.

"Hey, girlfriend," Metsy said, as she walked by. "Your hunky boyfriend/baby-sitter is up front with the kid."

Amber glanced in that direction, a smile immediately crossing her face. "Great! Thanks." Then after a moment's pause, she added as an afterthought. "He's not my boyfriend."

Metsy gave her a look. "Girl, I'd get that one pinned down before somebody else beats you to it," she said.

Amber ignored her and headed to the front of the store to find her daughter.

Jet was wearing a see-through lace nightgown over her *Bob the Builder* overalls.

"What are you up to?" Amber asked laughing.

The little girl came running. "We're taking you to lunch again," Jet answered. "Miss Carly said we could."

"Oh, she did, did she." Amber looked over at her.

"Sure, go on," her boss said. "This pair would probably kidnap you if I didn't let you go."

Amber retrieved her purse and Jet put the nightgown back on the rack and the three of them headed out for some soup and salad at the Food Court.

"I take it Wilma's back at the Empire Bar," Amber said.

Brent nodded. "I hope she's not overdoing it," he said. "But she absolutely insisted and I just couldn't turn her down."

"I hope this guy is worth it," Amber said.

Brent nodded.

"Listen," he said, a little chagrined. "I want to apologize for my behavior at Earl Abels."

Amber shrugged it off.

"And the way I was at your house when Wilma came home," he added.

"Forget it," Amber told him.

He glanced down at Jet. "At least you know that I only talk to my friends that way. I would never be so pushy with strangers."

"Only because strangers wouldn't put up with you," she pointed out.

He shrugged.

"But you weren't so far off the mark," Amber told him. "In fact, I've decided not to get the apartment. And I'm thinking about going to community college."

"Really?"

"Yeah, I talked with Carly about it this morning," she said. "The company has some college assistance in their benefits package."

"That's great!" he said.

"Of course, it's still community college," she said. "And I'm still a single mother, living with my family."

Brent shook his head. "Everybody has to start someplace," he told her.

They went through the serving line and got their food. For a moment, Jet balked, demanding a hot dog. But Amber convinced her that vegetable soup was a better choice.

"But it's hot outside, Mama," Jet pointed out.

"And when it's hot, a bowl of soup will cool you off."

Jet nodded reluctantly and accepted it.

Brent was obviously not convinced, he whispered to Amber behind Jet's back. "What kind of nonsense is that?"

She shrugged. "It's something my mother always told me."

Ellen had missed her mornings with Mrs. Stanhope. She missed the eastern sunshine, the pleasant conversation and the escape. They sat together in their little garden retreat. Ellen poured the tea and Mrs. Stanhope reflected upon the past. She told a funny story about her and her favorite sister, Irma's mother, tampering with the elastic on their elder sister's petticoat. It had broken on perfect cue as the young lady waltzed through the ballroom and caused such a shock to the sister and an amusement to her siblings, that a half century later, Mrs. Stanhope still laughed nearly to tears recounting the incident.

"I am quite myself this morning," she told Ellen. "I feel quite myself."

"That's wonderful," Ellen said.

Mrs. Stanhope smiled. "I don't believe *wonderful* is the most apt description, but I won't argue."

The two were thoughtful together for several moments.

"Have I told you about my husband's death?" Mrs. Stanhope asked.

"Yes," Ellen said. "You told me that he died."

"But did I tell you how he died?" she asked, with a certain tone that indicated she was aware that she had not. "Lyman committed suicide. He hanged himself in the back room of his store."

"I...I had heard that," Ellen said.

"Ah..." Mrs. Stanhope nodded. "I'm sure there was a great deal of talk about it. At the time and over the years. Fortunately, I've been rather oblivious to that."

Ellen nodded, not knowing what to say.

"Do you remember the day your husband died?" Mrs. Stanhope asked.

The question, so direct, took Ellen momentarily aback.

"Yes," she responded, after a moment. "I remember it vividly."

Mrs. Stanhope just looked at her, so she continued.

"He'd been unconscious most of the day," Ellen told her. "When he was awake, he'd be suffering in such pain. They'd give him more medicine and he'd be out again."

Ellen hadn't thought of that day in so long. Now

the image rolled out before her, so clearly, so complete in all its nuances.

"At one point, he was trying to stay awake, trying to be with me," she said. "He wanted me to stroke his forehead, the way his mother had when he was sick as a child. I did it for what seemed like hours. I thought my arm might fall off, but it gave him so much comfort, I didn't have the heart to stop. His voice was so croaky and so weak. He asked me to sing to him. I couldn't think of a song. I must know a million, hymns and Beatles songs and Broadway melodies, but right then, I couldn't think of anything. 'What would your mother sing?' I asked him. He told me, 'Jesus Loves Me.' So I sang 'Jesus Loves Me.' I sang it and I sang it and I sang it. Even after I realized he was gone. I kept singing it, hoping that wherever he was, he could still hear me."

Tears pouring down her face, Ellen had closed her eyes. She was not seeing anyone, but the gray, gaunt face of the man she had loved.

She opened her eyes when Mrs. Stanhope clasped her hand.

"Lyman was late coming home," she said. "I thought he'd forgotten the Gleichmans party. I was completely dressed and ready to go and still he hadn't shown. Finally, I walked up to the store to get him. I was so annoyed. The whole way I was going over in my mind how very tedious it was to always be home waiting for him. The door was locked and he didn't answer. I hadn't passed him on the street, so I knew he must be in the back. I used my key and went inside. I never liked the store when it was dark, so I hurried through toward the light switch in the back room. As soon as I turned it on, I saw him. I didn't

scream right away. It was almost as if I didn't immediately believe it. But of course, it was true."

"Yes," Ellen answered, knowing exactly that feeling. "It's as if your heart just won't allow you to believe that it has happened."

"Sometimes, I still don't," Mrs. Stanhope said.

They sat together, silently for long minutes. The tea
grew cold. Mrs. Stanhope was gazing into the morning sunshine.

"I can't bear to let him go," she said. "It was all
such a waste."

"Yes," Ellen agreed. "It was such a terrible waste.
Sometimes I think I can't go on living without him."

"I don't," Mrs. Stanhope replied simply.

Ellen understood more than she ever had.

"It was over money," Mrs. Stanhope said. "Did
you know that? That he killed himself over money?"

Ellen nodded.

"He was losing the business. He owed everyone in
town. He'd even humbled himself to ask my father
for help," she said. "Papa turned him down."

Ellen could hear the enduring censure in her voice.

"Papa asked him for collateral and all he had was
the acreage that had been his parent's dairy farm,"
she said. "He would have sold it if he could have, but
he didn't have a buyer or the time to wait for one.
Papa laughed at him. He told Lyman he had no use
for a cow pasture. He was Lyman's last hope. I told
him that we would be all right. That no matter what,
at least we'd be together. It wasn't enough. He took
his life three weeks later."

"I'm so sorry."

"Did he think it would be easier for me to face it all
on my own?" she asked. "Probably, he wasn't think-

ing at all. I just wish he could have stayed. He couldn't see what was around the corner. Within a few short years, we were rich.

"I sold the cow pasture that my father didn't want," she said. "It made me rich. If Lyman could have waited we would have been fine."

That thought seemed to disturb her and she gazed into the eastern horizon once more as if mesmerized by it.

"Papa tried to take over my money," she said abruptly. "Did I tell you that? Papa said I wasn't competent to manage it."

Mrs. Stanhope chuckled, but there was more anger in it than humor.

"I bought myself fur coats," she said. "I bought a dozen at least. Papa had said I couldn't wear fur, but a rich woman can wear whatever she wants. At the hearing, he talked about my coats, he said the inappropriateness of a woman buying herself fur coats was proof that I wasn't fit to handle my own affairs. I reminded Judge Witmeyer that I had seen both his wife and his mother at social events in my own home wearing furs." She laughed. "Papa had never been kind to the judge or his family. I kept control of my money. And I wore those coats every day. If Papa were to see me on the street, I wanted him to see me in one of those coats. Irma says I don't have to wear them anymore. Papa's dead now, but sometimes I forget."

The silence settled in between them once more.

"Do you forget?" Mrs. Stanhope asked Ellen.

Ellen shrugged. "Sometimes I forget the little things," she said.

Mrs. Stanhope nodded. "Maybe you should try to

forget the big things," she said. "It's not all that difficult really and it makes life a good deal less painful.
You could forget your husband's death."

The suggestion surprised Ellen. "I wouldn't want
to forget that," she said, honestly.

"But I can see that it hurts you so much," Mrs. Stanhope said.

Ellen nodded. "But for he and I..." she hesitated,
not sure how to explain. "It hurts so much, but it was
the closest we ever were together. It was the actual
moment when our relationship was stripped of every
kind of pretense and posture. I believed to the very
end that he would live. And he let me believe it, up
until that moment. When it was just the two of us, not
talking about it, not trying to prepare each other or
sustain each other, just two people who were one, going to the brink together."

"And only one of you came back."

Ellen nodded. "I had to come back."

"So now you've got to keep going," Mrs. Stanhope
said.

"Yes," Ellen said.

They sat in silence together for a long time as the
sun rose higher on the eastern horizon. Finally Mrs.
Stanhope smiled at her and took her hand once more.
"I won't keep you," she said, brightly. "But do tell
Willy and Sis that I have licorice in my kitchen that I
am saving just for them."

Ellen was startled. Mrs. Stanhope had said she was
herself this morning. And she still seemed very much
in the here and now.

"I'm not Violet," she told her.

Mrs. Stanhope nodded. "But you could be," she
said. "You remind me of her."

Ellen smiled and gathered up her things. As she walked toward the garden gate, she felt strangely cheerful. It didn't make sense, but tears were often cleansing and she genuinely felt better.

She took in a great gulp of air. She had to go on. Even Mrs. Stanhope knew that. It was one foot in front of another until she could see her way through again, but she had to keep going.

"Ellen!"

As she stepped through the gate she was hailed from the porch. Irma stood there. Dressed mannishly in navy blue slacks and an oxford shirt with the sleeves rolled up, she came down the steps and motioned Ellen over. She was so controlled and forceful that even such a benign gesture seemed like a command. Ellen didn't even consider ignoring it.

"Good morning," Ellen said.

Irma returned the greeting.

"I saw you in the garden with Edith," she said. "You were crying, I was just wondering if there is anything I could do to help."

"Oh, no," Ellen answered too quickly, almost embarrassed. "Mrs. Stanhope was...she was *herself* today and we were talking about our husbands' deaths."

"Oh," Irma said. "All right then, I didn't mean to intrude."

"No, it's fine," Ellen said. "Thank you for your concern."

"Edith told me that you were having some legal troubles with your house," Irma said. "I thought something might have gone wrong with that."

A very inappropriate burst of humor bubbled to the top and Ellen actually giggled.

"Sorry," she apologized. "It's simply that everything has gone wrong with that. I think I'm finally going to have to face the fact that we are going to have to move."

Irma's brow furrowed. "That can't be true," she said.

"I'm afraid it is," Ellen told her. "We have a mediation hearing scheduled for tomorrow where it's to be decided. I found out my lawyer wasn't dealing straight with me and I fired him. So now I'm going to have to represent my mother myself. I haven't the faintest idea how I'm going to manage that."

"A mediation hearing?" Irma repeated.

"Yes," Ellen said. "Our family and our lawyer is in one room and their family and their lawyer is in another room and a mediation lawyer goes between the two trying to work out a deal."

"I know what a mediation hearing is," Irma told her, very gently. "I'm a law professor at St. Mary's University."

Ellen bit her lower lip to keep her jaw from falling open. "I had no idea," she said.

"But you don't need a mediation hearing," Irma said. "I can't imagine why one was even set up."

"My lawyer thought it was the best way to handle it," Ellen said.

"Who was your lawyer?"

"Marvin Dix."

Irma tutted and shook her head. "Second-class ambulance chaser," she said.

Ellen couldn't argue. "I couldn't find anybody else," she said. "I just went through a bankruptcy. I don't have any money to pay anybody and the kids at legal aid were afraid of the plaintiff's lawyers."

"Who are they?"

"Pressman, Yaffe and Escudero."

Irma raised an eyebrow.

"Pretty formidable, I guess," Ellen said.

Irma shrugged. "You can be the Chief Justice and if you haven't got the law on your side you don't have any better chance of winning than Marvin Dix," she said. "Come on inside."

Ellen followed her into the house as Irma continued to ask questions about the specifics.

"So Wilma was legally married to Mr. Post, but he died without making a new will," Irma stated.

"They were only married about twenty-two months," Ellen said.

"That doesn't matter," Irma said.

"My mother has been married a number of times. I don't even know how many," Ellen admitted. "I think the Post family's intent is to suggest that my mother married their father just to inherit from him."

"Your mother was married to him," Irma said. "There wasn't any fraud or deception perpetrated there."

"No," Ellen said. "She married him. I don't know if she loved him, but she married him."

Irma smiled at her. "Not loving him has no standing in the law," she said.

Her office, on the side of the house that overlooked the garden, was woody and masculine, but softened with vases of fresh-cut flowers and crocheted doilies. She offered Ellen a chair and seated herself behind the huge mahogany desk. She retrieved a phone number from her palm pilot and picked up the telephone and dialed.

They waited only a moment before someone answered.

"William Pressman, please," she said into the receiver. "This is Irma Landingham."

"Landingham?" Ellen repeated in a hushed whisper.

Irma looked up at her. "I'm the governor's first wife," she explained. "I don't accept alimony, but I trade on the name occasionally if it suits me."

Ellen barely had a moment to let that soak in when William Pressman took Irma's call.

"Uncle Willy," she said. "How are you doing? How are Celia and the grandkids."

There was a pause as Irma listened to his answer.

"We haven't seen you in so long," she said. "Aunt Sis was by to see Edith a couple of months ago. But we haven't seen you since Christmas."

From one side of the conversation, it was apparent that he had an excuse. He also had a question.

"She's about the same," Irma answered. "She still talks about you nearly every day."

Ellen's jaw dropped open as she made the connection.

"That would be wonderful," she said. "We'll be looking forward to it. Actually, I have another purpose in calling."

She laughed good-naturedly.

"No, I don't always," she said, obviously feigning an insult. "I had to find out what on earth your firm is thinking about, persecuting Mrs. Wilma Post."

Irma was writing something on a notepad as she spoke.

"Yes, I said *persecuting*. I understand that there is a mediation hearing scheduled for tomorrow, but I'm filing a summary judgment this afternoon. If you want to have any say in this at all you need to call me here at home before twelve."

That statement led to a rather lengthy response from the other end of the line, to which Ellen was not privy.

"Yes," Irma said, finally. "Her name is Post, *P-O-S-T*, Wilma."

She was tapping her pencil impatiently.

"Thank you, I'll be waiting on your call."

Irma hung up the phone and looked over at Ellen.

"I don't think it will take until noon," she said. "I expect that the attorney actually handling the case will call me back in twenty minutes or less. It will take a half hour tops to get it settled."

Ellen shook her head. "I don't understand this," she said. For weeks this problem had hung over her head like an ax about to fall. Suddenly, out of nowhere, it was not an ax but an annoying feather pillow. "Is it because you're the governor's ex-wife?" Ellen asked her. "Or a law professor? Or because William Pressman is your uncle?"

Irma shook her head. "No, it's black letter law," she said. "If your mother was legally married to Mr. Post, she gets to stay in the house until she dies or vacates of her own free will."

"If that's the law, wouldn't the lawyers at Pressman, Yaffe and Escudero know that?"

"Of course they would," she said. "And they do. The suit was filed just to nudge your mother. To make her think it might be too much trouble to stay put."

"It would have worked," Ellen told her. "She was ready to go. I was the one who insisted that we had to stay there. She didn't think we could win."

Irma nodded. "It happens to people all the time," she said. "Filing a suit is not the same thing as defending a suit. Attorneys file them all the time, knowing that if they get to court they get thrown out. You just have to know your rights and stand your ground."

"But Wilbur Post's will left the house to his late wife," Ellen pointed out.

"And upon *her* death to *her* heirs," Irma agreed. "That's exactly what happens. Except that Article 16, section 52 of the Texas Constitution guarantees that your mother gets what's called a Life Estate. She can't sell the property or give it away and you can't inherit it from her. But she can live there as long as she likes."

"That's all we've ever asked," Ellen told her.

20

A well-lit corner of the produce department at Dilly's Fine Foods had been rearranged to function as a location set. There was a long cutting board counter set against a backdrop of a refrigerated rack of lettuce in a vivid and varied palate of green. There was a camera set up on a tripod and numerous lights and reflectors. Beneath it all ran a web of lines and cables that Wilma found difficult to maneuver the oxygen tank through.

The director hollered at one of the young grips to help her.

"I can take this thing off," she told the director.

He shook his head. "I think you should go with it," he said. "It's not unsightly and it's defining. We don't want you to be confused with a half million other old ladies in this town."

Wilma would have scolded the young man for such a statement, but he'd already turned to something else. And she supposed that she wasn't all that different from the half million other *old ladies* in the community. Besides, the director, Kenny, was twenty-eight going on fourteen and undoubtedly a summa cum laude graduate of the Joan Rivers School of Tact.

Homer had been as good as his word. When he got

an idea, he went forward with it at breakneck speed. Wilma had hardly had time to even roll the idea over in her mind before he had her shooting a studio test.

Kenny had initially been skeptical, but it seemed that Wilma had one of those faces that worked on camera.

"Did anyone ever tell you, you look like Lauren Bacall," Kenny had said. "I mean how she looks now, not back when she looked good."

The guy was not astute enough to pick up on either the icy smile or the thickly layered sarcasm in her "thank you, Kenny." But he was good at his job. He made her attractive on screen and made her produce beautiful.

Today they would shoot all five of the week's one minute segments. It was only five minutes of air time, but even with good luck it would take them most of the day to do it. There was no writer, no specific dialog assigned. A board in large, easy to read letters hung beneath the camera. It said: Stop by the produce department of your Dilly's Fine Foods today. It was the only line that she was definitely supposed to get in.

In the first spot she would be comparing four kinds of lettuce. The next would show how to peel and seed a cantaloupe. Then she'd demonstrate the best way to thoroughly wash spinach. Next she would compare and contrast different varieties of peaches. And finally, for the Friday spot, she'd present the spotlight produce of the week. This was an opportunity to present some unusual fruits and vegetables. Today's choice was gobo root.

Surprisingly, Wilma wasn't nervous at all. She was feeling well and she knew she looked good. They'd worked out a schedule where Amber could stay home with Jet the day that Wilma had to work. Jet liked that a lot. And it also made Amber available to help Wilma with her hair and makeup. Homer sent a limo to pick her up. That undoubtedly perked up the neighbors in Mahncke Park.

The grip, who was about Wilma's height, stood in her place behind the counter for much of the set up. But when it was time to light the set, it had to be Wilma standing there, her hair, her clothes, her oxygen tubes. Finally it was time. She did her part without a hitch. Then it was back to waiting.

To avoid having the same clothes every day in a week, Wilma started out in a gray suit with a scarf. For the second segment she would lose the scarf. In the third she would have the scarf and not the jacket. The Thursday and Friday spots, she had a pale blue blazer and a neckerchief.

It was a long day for a woman of her age and health, but Wilma stood it well. She spent most of it just sitting around. And she used that time to peruse the produce department and make notes about future spots she might do.

It was afternoon during the taping of the Thursday spot that her attention was inexplicably drawn away from the camera, and she saw Max Roper on the edge of the crowd watching her.

She flubbed slightly, although she recovered quickly enough that Kenny didn't insist they shoot again. But she wanted to. On the second take, she came through perfectly.

As the team reworked the set, moving out the peach baskets for the collection of exotic vegetables, Wilma motioned Max to come to her.

"I'm going to take a minute," she told Kenny.

He acquiesced, distracted.

Wilma was trying to negotiate the wheels of the oxygen tank over the cables on the floor.

"Let me help you with that," Max said, picking it up for her and carrying it.

"I love the way you men always want to take charge," she teased. "Whether it gives you a hernia or not."

"Not," he assured her.

"This thing is pretty handy," she told him, indicating the tank. "But it's not something that fits neatly in my hip pocket."

He nodded agreement.

They made their way to the little coffee bar between the produce section and the front entry hall. Max found her a stool at the end of the counter and then dragged one from between two customers farther down.

Wilma watched him. She had missed the sight of him, the tempo of his movements and the road map of lines upon his face. She'd never seen him outside of the Empire Bar, where dark shadows could disguise age and wear. But even in the clearly lit fluorescence of the supermarket, he still looked good to her.

He smiled as he pulled his stool up beside her and took a seat.

"You're looking well," he told her.

She laughed, lightly, but her tone was wry. "Yes, I'm one of those glamorous TV personalities," she said.

He never missed her sarcasm and raised a sardonic eyebrow in response.

They ordered coffees. Wilma got a straw with hers.

It was pretty hot to drink that way, but it kept her from messing her lipstick.

"Homer told me that you'd been sick," he admitted more seriously. "I hope I wasn't the cause of that."

"I have emphysema," she told him. "It may have some links with heart disease, but not, I don't think, of the broken variety."

"Did I break your heart?" he asked.

Wilma shrugged. "A lady would never tell," she said. "And a smart women wouldn't either. I leave it to you to decide which grouping I fall into."

"Truthfully, Wilma," he said. "It doesn't matter. I'm a sucker for either designation."

They laughed together.

"It seems I owe you an apology," he said. "Homer told me that you didn't know he was my son."

Wilma nodded. "I had no idea," she told him.

"I'm very proud of him, but that's between he and I. I don't go around boasting that he's my kid," Max said.

"You're not really the boastful type," Wilma pointed out.

Max shrugged. "That's not the reason," he said. "As you can obviously see, he's very wealthy and successful. A lot of people have come my way trying to use me to get to him with a plea or a deal or a scam."

"I'm sure," Wilma agreed.

"So I am cautious about mentioning him unless there is some reason to do so," he said.

"Some people would be delighted to use their child's name to feather their own nest," she said.

"Maybe so," Max said. "But my nest has feathers enough for me. Homer takes care of his mother, a slew of younger half brothers and sisters and a family of his own. I'm not a big fish, like he is, but I've made a place for myself in this pond."

Wilma wouldn't have admired him more if he'd told her he'd won the Nobel Prize.

"So anyway," Max continued. "As soon as you told me about your produce obsession, I knew that Homer would find some really good use for you."

He hooked one boot heel on the stool railing and crossed a long, lean limb over his knee.

"When you went on and on about how much you admire the stores," he continued, "I knew you and Homer were a perfect match. He tries to surround his business with very smart, very unique and interesting people. It's the secret of his success. I knew he'd be crazy about you. But I worried."

"Because you weren't sure that you could trust me," Wilma said.

Max nodded. "From the beginning you were mysterious," he pointed out. "You just showed up out of nowhere. You were short on purpose and details. And long on those melt-a-cowboy smiles. I knew that you were up to something. You had to be. It all fit so well that it made me suspicious."

He hesitated, eyeing her speculatively.

"When it was obvious that you'd checked up on me, that you knew a lot more about me than I'd told you or that you'd revealed about yourself, I immediately thought that I was being set up," he said.

Wilma nodded slowly and made no comment.

"There are men, I suppose, who could just leave it at that," he told her. "They could just admit that they jumped to the wrong conclusion and move on. But it seems that we still don't have the whole story straight here. And until we do, I don't think I can just let it go."

"All right," Wilma said. "I'll tell you the whole story."

Max folded his arms across his chest as if ready to patiently hear her out.

She took a deep breath.

"Well, it's true that I didn't know that dear Homer, whom I adore, by the way, was your son," she said. "I'm sure that you are very proud and rightfully so."

Max nodded.

"I was somewhat mysterious and evasive with you," she said. "And that was not accident. I did it because I didn't want you to find out about my daughter."

Max looked puzzled. "You told me that you had a daughter," he pointed out. "You had some rather nice things to say about her. And made it clear that you don't think she's much like you."

"She isn't like me," Wilma said. "And yes, I did tell you about her. But I didn't say that she worked in your office."

Max's eyes widened.

"Ellen Jameson is my child."

"Well, that's certainly a surprise," he said. "But, you know, I thought there was something strangely coincidental about her and you."

"I'm glad you never caught on," Wilma said. "I think that maybe she has, but I haven't revealed a word to her."

"So Ellen told you about me?" Max asked.

"She talked about you from time to time. Just enough to make me interested," Wilma said. "And she'd also mentioned what a fount of information your receptionist, Yolanda, can be. I got the complete lowdown scoop on you from Yolanda, including the detail about your ranch in Uvalde. She didn't mention Homer Dilly."

"Because she's been specifically told not to," Max said. "Yolanda's a talker, there's no getting away from that. But when you work among people's financial records and their personal papers, you have to be able to keep a confidentiality. When something is not to be told, you couldn't pry it out of that girl with torture."

Wilma nodded. "An interesting twist to her character," she said.

"I could never have kept her at my office," Max said, "if she wasn't one hundred percent trustworthy and discreet about the things that matter."

That certainly was true.

"So Ellen is your daughter," Max said. "What I don't understand is why that had to be a secret?"

"Well, you might not want to get involved with someone connected to your office," Wilma said.

Max raised an eyebrow at that. The answer wasn't particularly convincing.

"More than just you finding out about Ellen," Wilma admitted. "I didn't want Ellen finding out about you."

"Why not?"

She took another sip of the hot coffee through the straw as she formed her answer.

"I told you that my life had been a lot like a game of musical chairs," she reminded him. "What I probably didn't make clear was that at every pause in the music there was a new man in my life. I'm sort of the Mommie Dearest version of the Old Woman in the

Shoe. I've had so many husbands my children didn't know what to do."

Max shrugged. "At our age, a lot of folks can have a checkered history."

"For me, I think, it was more than that," Wilma answered, honestly. "As I told you, I never really had any kind of career or goal or even any real dreams for myself. I had my kids by accident and raised them basically on automatic pilot. I just kept moving from man to man. That was all I knew to do with myself, with my life. Whenever things got bad, I'd find me a new fellow, figuring that would make things better."

Max was listening intently.

"When my last husband passed away," she said. "I had a little house and my social security. I just figured that I'd sort of retired from the love-em-and-leave-em lifestyle."

Wilma hesitated.

"I guess you know some of the trouble my daughter has been having lately," she said. "She's a really fine woman. She's a much better daughter than I have ever deserved. Her husband's death and the bankruptcy and most recently the threat of losing my little house, is a lot to put on a woman who's been through so much in the past few years. I wanted to fix things for her. I wanted to help."

Wilma gestured toward the set in the produce section. "It never occurred to me that I might be able to bring home a paycheck to put in the kitty. The only way I knew how to get money was to marry some."

She sighed heavily.

"So the long and short of it, Max Roper, is that I wasn't being sneaky, conniving and underhanded because I was trying to get hooked up with a job from your son. I was being sneaky, conniving and under-handed so that I could get you to fall for me."

Max slowly shook his head and chuckled. Disbelief evident in the sound of his voice.

"Wilma, Wilma, Wilma," he said. "You are really something else."

"I guess," she admitted. "Seduction isn't quite as straightforward as it used to be."

"Oh, I wouldn't say that," Max told her. "It worked, didn't it?"

The lovely old iron bridge had been built in the 1890s with elaborate cresting and finials to span the San Antonio River at St. Mary's Street. It served that purpose for more than forty years, when it was abruptly removed from that busy crossing and relocated in Brackenridge Park to allow picnickers to drive their cars on either bank of the river.

Ellen parked the Chrysler Concorde on the far side. She and Wilma, Amber and Jet got out and began unloading their celebration repast. They had brought charcoal to make a fire, hot dogs to roast, a watermelon to cut, homemade piccalilli relish and macaroni salad.

Once the food was unloaded, they hesitated.

"You want to do it before or after we eat," Wilma asked Ellen.

Ellen looked at Amber, as if for guidance. "I think we should eat first," she said. "It's late and I'm sure Jet is hungry."

Amber nodded agreement.

Within minutes they got the charcoal going though, of course, it wasn't really ready for cooking for another half hour.

Jet and her mother spent the time getting a Rugrats kite into the air.

Wilma sat on the picnic bench watching them and smoking. Ellen was watching them, too.

"They are like two kids instead of mother and daughter," she said. "Amber is having as much fun as Jet."

"It's time she had some fun," Wilma said. "You can't get too much of it in one lifetime."

Ellen could not argue with that.

The afternoon was glorious. Officially it was autumn, but in south Texas summer was just beginning to wind down. School was back in session. The absence of other children and the usual crowds made noon on a Thursday the ideal time to visit the park.

Amber was on her new schedule. The previous week she'd taken classes for the first time in five years.

Wilma's produce spots were running regularly on television. She wasn't exactly a celebrity, but people recognized her when she and Jet made their visits to the grocery store.

Ellen continued to keep moving forward. One foot in front of the other. She didn't know where she was going, but she was determined to get there.

Hey up there! Thanks for the sunshine and the cool breeze, she prayed. *It's a great day for moving on.*

"I think it's time to be roasting some dogs!" she called out to the two healthy, laughing children scampering in the grass.

"Let's roast some dog!" Amber hollered back.

Jet giggled and came running. "I wanna roast a dog," she said. "Lemme roast a dog."

Wilma had cut some hickory limbs from their backyard tree for "weinie roasters." Ellen slid the hot dogs on the end of the sticks and allowed Jet to hold hers over the little fire. The four-year-old thought it was great fun. It would have undoubtedly been quicker just to grill them, but what fun was cooking hot dogs if no sticks were involved.

And fun was what Jet Jameson was after today. She was into knock-knock and didn't let up once during the meal.

"Knock knock."

"Who's there?"

"Yaw."

"Yaw who?"

"You don't have to get so excited about it!"

Jet squirted more mustard on her buns than any of the women had ever consumed at one sitting in their lives. And she declared adamantly that the only food in the world better than her grandmother's piccalilli was her mother's macaroni salad.

For dessert there was watermelon. And once the seed spitting contest commenced, even Ellen was roped into participation.

The meal was one long pleasant memory.

Wilma was hugging Jet.

"You are the sweetest baby girl in the world," she told her.

"I'm not a baby girl, Wil-ma," Jet protested. "You forget. I'm four now."

"That's right," Wilma said. "I still owe you a birthday gift, don't I?"

Jet nodded. "I remember you promised me anything I wanted," she said.

"That's exactly right," Wilma said. "Have you thought about what you want?"

"Uh huh," the child said. "I've been thinking about asking you."

"Well, ask me," she encouraged.

Before Jet had time to do that, Ellen interceded. "I hope it doesn't cost too much money," she said gently. "'Cause Wilma doesn't have a lot of money."

"Just let the child say what she wants," Wilma scolded. "We'll worry about what it costs when we go out to buy it."

"I don't know if it costs anything," Jet said. "I don't think it costs anything."

"It doesn't matter," Wilma said. "What is it that you want?"

"I want you to mind the doctor, Wil-ma, so you won't die," Jet said in her sweet, little girl voice. "I want you to quit smoking your cigarettes."

The silence in the park was nearly deafening.

Ellen wanted to pipe in, to say something, to assure Wilma that they hadn't put the child up to it, to explain to Jet that some things you ask for, people just aren't able to give to you. She did none of that. She watched Wilma gaze down into the bright, brown eyes of her little granddaughter for a very long moment. She laid her aged, wrinkled hand over the little girl's tiny one.

"I...I'll try," Wilma said. "I will try."

Amber set her hand upon Wilma's. "That's all any of us can do," she said. "We just try."

Ellen topped their hands with her own. "Somehow I just know that we'll succeed," she said. "But then, you know what an optimist I am."

They all laughed.

Wilma pulled the pack of cigarettes out of her

pocket and threw them on the charcoal fire. Within seconds they were a brightly glowing flame.

"I think it's time now," Ellen said.

From a secured box in the trunk of the car, wrapped in a blanket, Amber pulled out the urn and handed it to her mother.

"You're sure?" Amber asked. "You're ready?"

Ellen nodded.

Jet clasped her mother's hand and held Groovy Girl in the other. Wilma pulled her tank. They walked back to the bridge, stopping in the middle of the span.

"There's no place that's more the heart of San Antonio than the river," Ellen said. "I can't imagine anyplace else that Paul would rather be."

She opened the top of the urn. Before she'd even tilted it, the breeze had reached down inside and grabbed the light gray ash and whisked it away. Ellen turned it sideways and in an instant the ashes were a fine cloud floating above the water. And then they were the water.

"Goodbye, Grandpa," Jet said, clapping, delighted.

Ellen followed her lead. "Goodbye, Paul," she whispered. "I'm moving on."

The women stood there on the bridge together for long moments, just watching the water hurrying its way downstream.

"What are you going to do with this?" Amber asked, indicating the urn.

Ellen shrugged. "I'll keep it as a remembrance, I guess."

"Paul was in there five years," Wilma pointed out. "I've hardly stayed anywhere that long in my life."

Her words broke the solemnity of the moment. Ellen hugged her.

"Look! Come look!" Jet called out, motioning to them excitedly.

"What is it?"

"Hurry, come look," the little girl insisted.

All three women did.

Resting on the pavement next to the curved metal bridge brace were four pennies. Each one face up.

The Thrill of Victory

A classic love story by
New York Times bestselling author

SANDRA BROWN

Stevie Corbett is in jeopardy of losing everything she's sacrificed and worked so hard for—her career, her reputation, her future. *Her life.* Now she has just two weeks to make a monumental decision, but her fate rides on keeping the truth a secret.

Judd Mackie's job is to uncover secrets. He's spent the last few years trailing Stevie, determined to expose her as the spoiled glamour girl he believes her to be. Then a chance meeting with Stevie offers him the story he's been dreaming of.

He's waited years for an opportunity like this to fall into his lap. Now he has the chance to scoop the story of the year and let the whole world know the truth about Stevie. All he needs to do is betray her trust....

Available the first week of March 2003 wherever hardcovers are sold!

MIRA®

Visit us at www.mirabooks.com

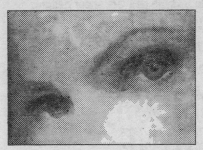

Grace Notes

New York Times Bestselling Author

CHARLOTTE VALE ALLEN

Grace Loring is a successful author with many devoted fans who find comfort in her honest writing. Accustomed to abused women contacting her via her Web site to ask for advice, Grace is sympathetic when a troubled young woman e-mails her. In the course of their correspondence, Stephanie Baine reveals details of a nightmarish life: her terrifying abduction as a teenager; the complete lack of support from her parents; the abuse at the hands of her husband. But after several weeks of an intensive exchange, the e-mails abruptly stop and Grace begins to fear the worst. Then the e-mails resume. What Grace comes to learn casts doubt on everything she believed about the person she thought she knew. Who is Stephanie Baine? Has *anything* she's told Grace been true? Is she really a woman in danger, or is something else—something sinister, even deadly—going on?

"A moving portrayal of the power of love to heal."
—*Publishers Weekly* on *Parting Gifts*

Available the first week of March 2003
wherever paperbacks are sold!